BUILT

BY JAY CROWNOVER

The Saints of Denver Series
Built

The Welcome to the Point Series
Better When He's Brave
Better When He's Bold
Better When He's Bad

The Marked Men Series
Asa
Rowdy
Nash
Rome
Jet
Rule

BUILT

A Saints of Denver Novel

JAY CROWNOVER

wm

WILLIAM MORROW
An Imprint of HarperCollins*Publishers*

BUILT. Copyright © 2016 by Jennifer M. Voorhees. All rights reserved. Printed in the United States of America. No part of this book may be used or reproduced in any manner whatsoever without written permission except in the case of brief quotations embodied in critical articles and reviews. For information address HarperCollins Publishers, 195 Broadway, New York, NY 10007.

HarperCollins books may be purchased for educational, business, or sales promotional use. For information please e-mail the Special Markets Department at SPsales@harpercollins.com.

FIRST EDITION

Designed by Diahann Sturge

Library of Congress Cataloging-in-Publication Data has been applied for.

ISBN 978-0-06-238594-9

16 17 18 19 20   OV/RRD   10 9 8 7 6 5 4 3 2 1

Dedicated to the best dad any gal could ask for. My dad has always had a way about him . . . a rock-solid reliability that has made him forever my hero and number one badass. Because life is never easy we haven't always seen eye to eye, but at the end of the day I have always known whatever needs to be done, my dad will be there to take care of it. He's the real deal and few people I have encountered have managed to live up to his legend.

This one is for you, DadVo.

INTRODUCTION

Are you guys ready for this? I am so ready!

A new adventure. A new cast of characters. Something so different yet still familiar and comfy like a favorite pair of well-worn jeans.

I have to tell you that it only took one second, a single moment when these two met, for me to know they had to have a story and that it had to be epic. It had to be special, and larger than life, because frankly Zeb Fuller is both of those things. I needed to do my bearded wonder justice. Without Sayer and Zeb and their undeniable spark there would be no Saints of Denver. (I actually posted about the fact that they needed a book the second they met on Facebook when I was in the middle of writing *Rowdy*.) Their chemistry in that tiny little moment was so bright, so electric, so addicting, that it exploded in my head and I just knew they would be a perfect mess and that trying to get these two together was going to be a challenge I couldn't resist.

I adored writing this book. I loved getting to go back to places that feel like home, but seeing them and describing them in a whole new way. I know it will make my readers happy to see some familiar faces (it's always nice to check up on old friends here and there) but I sure hope the new ones steal your heart along the way. I'm pretty sure they will. ☺

If you are a new reader just being introduced to all my crazy, welcome, I'm so glad you are here with me. Strap in for a sweet, sexy, often unpredictable ride.

If you are a longtime reader who is familiar with the series that started this whole journey, I'm sure you're curious how the time line in the new series relates to the Marked Men series. While it might not be an exact match, in my head the start of the series takes place in the six months between the end of *Asa* and the epilogue in the final book. So that fall/winter before Rome and Cora's wedding is when all the madness and sexiness begins.

As always, thank you, kickass readers, so much for being here. Thank you forever for letting me be here. There will never be a better place to be.

The fact that I get to keep doing this, that this is my actual, real-life job, never ceases to amaze and humble me. You've let me tell so many stories, let me bring so many interesting, valuable, important people to life with my words . . . it's a dream come true and I couldn't do it or have any of these opportunities and escapades without you.

You are EVERYTHING!!!

I have not failed. I've just found ten thousand ways that won't work.

—Thomas A. Edison

PROLOGUE

I met her at a bar.

She had a beer bottle in her hand even though she looked like she should be sipping champagne out of an expensive flute, and that inexplicably turned me on. She was pretty and looked completely out of place in the no-name bar sitting across from one of my oldest friends who also happened to be her long-lost brother. He was the reason she was here. In that split second that I laid my eyes on her I wanted to be the reason she stayed.

I knew it was rude and that the two of them needed some time together, some time to figure out what they were to each other now that she had blasted into his life unannounced. If I was a better friend I would have left them alone. As it was, I made my way over to the tiny table and sat down. I was covered in saw-dust and had drywall mud caked in the hair on my head and on my face, but she didn't flinch or bat an eyelash when I purposely broke up their party of two and placed myself as close to her as I could without actually touching her.

My buddy Rowdy St. James lifted his eyebrows at me as I stared at her while he introduced us. Sayer Cole. Even her name was elegant and sophisticated sounding. She was an enigma, this lovely woman who seemed like she should be in any place but this bar with the two of us. She'd showed up out of the blue a couple of months ago claiming to be Rowdy's half sister, claiming that they shared a father, claiming that all she wanted was to be in his life and have some kind of family of her own. She looked too delicate to be that brave. Came across as way too proper to have said "fuck it all" and picked up her life to move it someplace unknown without being sure of her welcome. She looked like silk, but if my guess was right about her, it was silk wrapped around steel.

Luckily Rowdy was a good guy. After the shock of discovering he wasn't alone in the world, and once he realized he had someone tied to him by blood forever and ever, he had warmed up to the idea of having a sister and appreciated that the sister was Sayer.

I liked Rowdy a lot. He was a stand-up guy and a good friend, but I had a feeling I was going to like his newly found big sister even more. In my usual tactless way I asked him without looking directly at the knockout blonde, "So you have a sister? A hot, classy sister?" A sister that was also a lawyer, so beautiful and smart.

I expected a giggle from her or an eye roll at the outlandish compliment, but what I got was a wide-eyed stare of disbelief as eyes bluer than anything I had ever seen on earth danced between me and her brother like she wasn't sure what to do with herself or with my overt interest in her.

I thought that I had gone too far, pushed the beautiful stranger too far out of her comfort zone. I was a big guy and knew I looked far wilder and rougher than I actually was. I figured it might be too much for a woman already obviously out of her element and depth to take.

Instead, Sayer surprised me and I could see by the way he stiffened that she surprised Rowdy, too. While she wasn't exactly overflowing with welcome and warmth, she did ask me about the current project I was working on after Rowdy explained I was a general contractor and had rebuilt the new tattoo shop he worked in. She seemed genuinely interested, and when I told her that my specialty was rehabbing old houses and giving them new life, her eyes practically glowed at me. I wanted to feel her to see if she felt as smooth and polished as she looked. I wanted to leave streaks of dirt on her perfect face to mark the fact that I had touched her, that she had let me touch her. It was a primal and visceral reaction that I couldn't explain and I liked the way it felt. Liked the weight and heft of it in my blood even if I knew the feeling wasn't likely to be returned.

She told me all about a fantastic but crumbling Victorian she had purchased that was falling down around her. She asked me for a business card and I saw Rowdy stiffen across the table. I sighed and rubbed a hand over my already messy hair. I watched her eyes follow the light cloud of dust that escaped the strands. I was great at my job, loved what I did, but I couldn't do anything with her or for her without laying everything on the line. Especially not with Rowdy giving me the death glare from just a few feet away.

I dug the card out of my wallet, and when I handed it over our fingers touched. I saw her eyes widen and her lips part, just barely. She looked a little dazed when I grinned at her.

"You take that card, but understand that the man giving it to you has a past."

She blinked at me and cleared her throat. "What kind of past?"

It wasn't something I liked to tell a beautiful woman when I first met her. It was something I liked to work up to, liked to prove was behind me, but with this one it seemed like I wouldn't get that chance.

"I tell everyone that I do any kind of work for or that considers hiring me on for a project that I have a criminal history. I spent time locked up for a few years, and while I'm not proud of it I can't deny it happened. I was a hotheaded kid and it got me in trouble, but I'm the best at what I do, so I hope that doesn't discourage you from giving me a call." Hopefully for more than some construction.

Usually I got a concerned frown followed by a hundred questions about what had led me to serving time. I got none of that from the stunning blonde. She tilted her head to the side and considered me silently for a long moment before reaching down and slipping my card in her purse. If anything, I could have sworn she was wearing a look of sympathy when she told me softly, "I see it every day from the inside. Sometimes the system simply gets it wrong." A slight grin turned her mouth up at the corners, and I wanted to lean over and kiss it. "People make mistakes. Hopefully they learn from them."

I don't know that "wrong" was accurate in my case so much as misguided, but the complete lack of judgment or censure coming from her made me want to pull her into my arms and hold on to her even more. I had made a mistake, a huge one, one that I was forever going to have to carry around with me, but I had learned from it, was still learning from it. That kind of understanding from a total stranger was so rare, especially coming from someone in the legal field. I wasn't accustomed to someone looking at me and seeing me, just me, not an ex-con loser after I explained where I had been. It was wildly refreshing and attractive. I couldn't quite get a handle on what made the woman tick, but I would welcome any opportunity she gave me to figure it out. I found her outwardly flawless and pristine demeanor tempting to taint with my dirty hands and ways, and there was something about the way she watched me, the way she turned toward me like she was drawn to me, that made me think maybe I wasn't alone in the inexplicable pull department.

Rowdy left and she stayed.

We had a couple more beers and talked some more about her house and what she wanted done with it. She already hired one contractor but felt like the guy was ripping her off. It happened a lot in the industry, so I wouldn't be surprised if the guy was taking her for a ride. Spending time with her was easy. She was fun to talk to and really fun to look at. I really wanted to get my hands on her house and of course on her, and I felt like she was maybe, kind of, slightly leaning in the same direction when I made the mistake of asking her about her past.

I asked about where she had been before she found out about Rowdy and decided to move to Denver so that she could get to know him. I was curious what kind of life she had where she could leave everything behind and not be missed. Really I wanted to know if she had a boyfriend or husband stashed somewhere, but the simple inquiry must have touched a nerve. The next thing I knew she had paid out the tab for both of us and disappeared into the night. She went from glowing and bright to frigid and untouchable in the span of a heartbeat.

I figured I blew my shot by being too blunt, as always. I assumed she probably did have someone else in the picture and had been friendly and polite only because I was good friends with her brother. I thought I would never hear from her again and was baffled why the thought of that made my chest ache and my heart feel like it weighed two tons.

Imagine my surprise when she called me and hired me to renovate her house a week later without a bid, without a contract, without even knowing if I was half as good as I claimed to be.

Of course I accepted, but I knew once I was inside I would need to knock down and rearrange more than just the walls of the house, in order to get at something beautiful and lasting.

Love is friendship that has caught fire. It is quiet understanding, mutual confidence, sharing and forgiving. It is loyalty through good and bad times. It settles for less than perfection and makes allowances for human weaknesses.

—Ann Landers

CHAPTER 1

Sayer

Six months later

Can't sleep?"

The soft question sent the glass of white wine I'd been chugging like it was cheap beer falling from my fingers and clattering noisily to the beautifully refinished hardwood floors under my bare feet.

The glass shattered and wine splashed everywhere as I put a hand to my chest and looked over my shoulder at the pale ghost of the young woman I was currently sharing my newly renovated living space with. Her light brown eyes were huge in her face, and, like always, she looked like a delicate fawn ready to bolt at any noise or quick movement I might make.

I took a deep breath to calm myself down and gingerly picked myself out of the broken glass minefield so I could get a towel and the broom to clean up the mess. "Why aren't you asleep, Poppy?"

I knew the answer. The old Victorian I bought just a few

weeks after relocating to Denver was huge, had three separate levels, was made of sturdy wood, and had heavy, solid doors on each room. None of that was enough to keep the sounds of this young woman's screams of terror as she had nightmare after nightmare from reaching me. They weren't as frequent as when she'd first moved into my home. In fact they hardly ever pulled me from my own troubled dreams anymore, but every now and then I would hear her voice through the walls, hear heartbreaking sobs echoing across the rafters, and my brittle heart wanted to snap in two for her.

She pushed some of her long, caramel-colored hair behind her ears and lifted an eyebrow at me. "Bad dream. How about you, Sayer? Why are you still up?"

I cleared my throat as I bent down to sweep up the glass.

It was late.

I was really tired.

I had a full day at work tomorrow and I needed to be up early enough so I could swing by the gym before I went into my office.

I had also agreed to have drinks with a fellow attorney after my final court appearance of the day. It was a semidate I had already rescheduled twice, so I couldn't reasonably back out again without looking like a complete jerk. Doing any of that on a few hours of sleep was less than ideal, but I was getting used to running on fumes lately. I, too, was having dreams that woke me up in the middle of the night, that left me shaken, heated, and too wound up to stay in bed.

Only my dreams weren't terror inducing—they were good. Oh, so fucking good. They were better than good. They were the best dreams I had ever had. Hell, the dreams were better than any kind of actual sexual experience I had ever had while wide-awake. They were the kind of dreams that had me jerk-ing up from a dead sleep while I panted and sweated. I woke up twisting in my sheets and touching myself because the man that starred in each and every single one of them was nowhere around.

Control was everything to me, and Zeb Fuller made me want to lose it even when he was sound asleep in his own bed all the way across Denver.

I'd paid him a fortune to turn this broken-down, sagging, sorry excuse for a house into a stately, soaring, and magnificent home, and so Zeb had his hands all over my real-life dreams, not just my naughty midnight ones. He had finished the last of the remodel a couple of weeks ago, and ever since I found myself missing the sounds of hammering, drilling, and the rumble of his deep voice. All the dirty, sexy things I secretly wanted him to do to me were chasing me into dreamland, making for rough mornings and some serious dark circles under my eyes. I was pale anyway, so there was no hiding the evidence of Zebulon Fuller's effect on me.

It was stupidly simple. I had a crush that I couldn't shake, and it terrified me.

It made me feel off balance, unsure, and so damn sexually frustrated I wanted to pull out all of my long, blond hair by the roots just for a distraction.

I swore softly as a piece of glass slid across my fingertip when I bent down to usher the mess into the dustpan. I stuck the bleed-ing digit into my mouth and grunted in annoyance at myself. I had learned before I could walk that showing any kind of emo-tion was a weakness, a fatal flaw that would end with you in tears as the victor stood over your broken, weeping form with a look of pity and disgust on his face. I shouldn't have jumped when Poppy startled me. I was supposed to be made of more glacial stuff than that. I didn't react to anything—ever. Poppy was still staring at me with wide-eyed curiosity, so I pulled my finger out of my mouth and wiped it on the yoga pants I had worn to bed.

"I was having weird dreams, too. I thought a glass of wine would help put me back to sleep." My tone was frostier than I meant it to be, but old habits were hard to break. My coolness was habit and it was armor.

She shifted her weight a little and again I was reminded of a timid woodland creature always ready to flee from danger. She was so pretty, so delicate, and no one should have had to endure the things this young woman had been through in her short lifetime. Poppy Cruz was only a few years younger than my own twenty-eight, but when her amber eyes assessed me with a knowing that felt ancient, it seemed like she was aeons ahead of me in both life and experience. Even though I had been raised by a father who was a tyrant, and had had to put my mother, who loved him and tried to please him right up until her last breath, in the ground before I was old enough to drive. My formative years had been spent trying to live up to standards I could never reach and mourning the loss of a woman I loved and loathed equally.

"You've had a lot of sleepless nights since Zeb finished all the work on the house. You seem . . . unsettled."

I wanted to roll my eyes in exasperation with myself but held it back. I shouldn't seem any way to anyone. My cracks were starting to show and that unnerved me to no end.

Was "unsettled" another word for horny enough to climb the walls? Because if so, then yes, I was most definitely unsettled.

And I felt ridiculous for it. I'd never had the mere thought of a man distract me or cost me much-needed shut-eye before. I was supposed to have more restraint than that.

I dumped the broken glass into a plastic shopping bag and tossed it all into the trash. It took a few more minutes to wipe up the wine that was on the floor and that had splattered on the cabinets and bottom of the fridge.

"I guess I got used to living in the chaos of construction. Everything seems so neat and tidy now. So new. I'm sure I'll get used to it. This is my dream home, what I always wanted. I think maybe the fact that I finally have it is still settling in. That's all." I had grown up in a home where what I wanted or needed wasn't permitted, so the fact that I had something that was mine, that was tangible, solid, and real, something that was untouched from the taint of the past, still took my breath away when I thought about it.

I made sure everything was back to being spotless and snatched a bottle of water out of the fridge before turning back to Poppy when she quietly said:

"I thought maybe you were missing having Zeb around. He's kind of hard to ignore."

He most assuredly was hard to ignore.

Tall, tattooed, and built like a guy who hauled heavy stuff around and swung a hammer like Thor should be, Zeb was impressive, to say the least. But it went beyond the work-hardened muscles, low-slung tool belt, and the flirty charm he liked to throw around so effortlessly. There was something rock steady and so certain that shined out of his dark green eyes when he looked at the world around him and the people in it. There was an inherent confidence and assuredness that poured off of him when he looked at a person, like he knew without a doubt whatever he was bringing to the table was a thousand times better than what anyone else in the room had to offer. God, I could hardly handle how hot it was when he smiled and rubbed his hand over his neatly trimmed beard. Especially when that smile and knowing smirk was directed right at me.

I had never been into beards, and I always thought I preferred a well-groomed, well-dressed man. A man who looked great in a suit and tie and knew all about expensive cologne and hair product in the proper amounts.

As it turned out, what really flipped the switch on my usually inactive libido was a guy who looked like he could cut down a tree with one swipe and had unruly dark brown hair that looked like it rarely saw a comb or brush, let alone any type of product. It was a guy who made a sweaty T-shirt and torn jeans look like high fashion who kept me awake all night long while I fantasized what those work-toughened hands would feel like sliding across my naked skin.

I didn't know what Zeb Fuller had done to me or to my common sense. All I knew was that he was keeping me up at night and making me resent every single time I turned icy and cold when he flirted with me. I hated that I couldn't act normal around him because all I wanted to do was rip his clothes off and climb all over him. I wasn't familiar with any of those emotions, so as a defense I locked them all down.

My awkwardness and ineptitude in the face of Zeb's overt masculinity meant that I could never find any words beyond polite pleasantries, clichés, and platitudes, which I had no doubt gave him the impression that I was nothing more than a stuck-up bitch. I never intended to treat him like the hired help, but somehow that's exactly what I had done, and now the job was finished, Zeb was long gone, and I was having phantom orgasms simply thinking about having his hands and mouth on me while I tossed and turned in my very empty and very lonely bed.

So yeah, I missed having him around. I missed watching him, hearing him, and even smelling that unique scent that all men who worked hard for their money seemed to have. Sweat and accomplishment mixed in with something that just screamed hard work and sex appeal.

I pushed my long hair back over my shoulder and raised my eyebrows at Poppy in a questioning expression similar to her own.

"You didn't seem to mind him roaming around the house while he was here," I said casually.

Poppy had had a horrible experience with her abusive ex-husband, and in the aftermath the beautiful young woman had shied away from all physical contact with the opposite sex, including my brother, with whom she had grown up. It was crippling, and when I started work on the house I worried how Poppy was going to handle having so many strange men in and out of the place that had been her sanctuary since she started to recover from her abduction.

Initially she handled Zeb and his crew banging around the Victorian by never leaving her room. She spent all day locked in there with a dresser in front of the door until one night when I was supposed to get home early to look at paint samples with Zeb but was running late. When I finally got there, I was stunned to find the bearded giant and the fragile flower with their heads bent together while they looked at paint samples in my torn-apart kitchen. I was so stunned that when Zeb mentioned that

Poppy really liked an unusual shade of reddish orange for the walls, I blindly agreed to the choice, even though neutral and serene was much more my personal style.

After the shocking splash of color made it onto the walls I was surprised at how much I loved it. It took me a few days beyond that to realize it was the same shade as a field of poppies, and then I loved it even more. When Zeb left, I tenderly prodded Poppy about how the big man had coaxed her out of her fortress.

It was simple really. He told her he needed a woman's opinion. He wanted to make sure he was in the right wheelhouse and gave her the choice and the control. If I hadn't already wanted to kiss him, his simple understanding of how Poppy needed to take back the reins of her life would have made me want to jump him on the spot.

Zeb Fuller was a nice guy. Ugh . . . a nice guy I couldn't stop thinking about or picturing very naked. He had tattoos on either side of his neck and ones that peeked out of the collar of his shirt. He had ink that decorated the back of each hand and wild swirls and designs that covered every inch of both of his arms. I wanted to see what else marked his skin and then I wanted to drag my tongue across every single inch of it.

Poppy cleared her throat and walked over to get her own bottle of water out of the fridge. She leaned next to me on the island with its fancy marble top and sighed softly. Even the noises she made sounded like a fragile flower fighting to stay upright in the wind.

"I like Zeb. I was surprised that I did, but I really do. He reminds me of Rowdy and he didn't look at me like I was broken. Not once. Eventually I'm going to have to leave this house, go back to work, and I know that means I have to stop thinking every man out there is going to hurt me. Zeb is huge; I mean, he's just so BIG, but nothing about him is threatening or scary once you get to know him. I think he was good practice for me, and I love how the kitchen turned out. I would've died if it ended up looking terrible considering it was the first decision I've made on my own in a really long time."

Rowdy was my younger brother, who I didn't know existed until a year ago when my father died leaving his secrets printed in black and white in his will. Rowdy had grown up in entirely different circumstances than my own, with Poppy and her older sister, Salem. After some time and some tragedy, Rowdy and Salem had figured out they were always meant to be together, which meant he cared even more for Poppy and her current state of mind than he normally would. She was family and now that I'd found Rowdy, had dropped every part of my old life, and moved halfway across the country to get to know him, so was I. My father's final stab in the back, his last cruel act of manipulation, had actually been the best and only gift he had ever given me.

I reached out an arm and wrapped it around her thin shoulders so I could give her a squeeze. Unlike her older sister, Poppy was missing any kind of curve or thickness on her frame. She was a waif and sometimes I thought she was going to disappear right before my eyes. I also wasn't terribly surprised when she wiggled out of my grip. She wasn't the biggest fan of touching even if it came from a safe place.

"I can call him back to . . . I don't know, I'll ask him to build a deck or a fence or something, if you want more practice." I was only half kidding. I would love an excuse to have him back within ogling distance.

Poppy laughed and it was such a rare and precious sound it made my heart squeeze tight. I'd never had a roommate before, never shared my space with anyone so closely, or had anyone else to give my time to aside from my clients. I cherished the time I had with this young woman so much that I often wondered if Poppy was healing more than just herself on her journey to take her life back. I refused to acknowledge the scars and wounds etched deep in my psyche and that festered all over my soul from growing up in the care of my father. But occasionally Poppy would say something, or reach out and touch me, or my little brother would call just to check up on me, and old injuries I purposely ignored would tingle as they fought to knit themselves together despite my persistent denial that they existed.

"No, but thank you for the offer. Rowdy calls me every Thursday night when Salem goes out with her girlfriends and asks me to have dinner with him. I always say no because I panic at the thought of being alone with him and going out in public around all those other people, but I think next time he asks I know can say yes. I can do this."

I nodded and tried not to seem overly excited. I didn't want to pressure her in any way. "That will make him very happy and I think it'll be good for both of you." I nudged her with my elbow. "And if you need me to get off work early or want me to come because it's overwhelming you, just say the word and I'll make it happen." Rowdy would understand if she needed me as a buffer. He always understood.

She gave me a tiny grin that looked like a baby bird trying to figure out how to fly for the first time in its hesitancy.

"Thank you. That means a lot." She walked around the giant island and headed toward the room that was hers at the very back of the house and as far away from my master suite in the converted attic as it could get. She knew her screams of terror carried and had made it clear she wanted to be as unobtrusive as possible while she recuperated in my home. "Good night, Sayer. Sweet dreams."

There was a note of humor in her voice that made me think that maybe I hadn't been as coy about what—or rather who— was keeping me up at night as I thought. I sighed and made my way up to my own room.

Zeb had transformed the abandoned and decrepit attic space in the house into a retreat that anyone would love. It was modern but still had the vintage charm that came with an old house. The colors were all pale grays and soft blues. It was a place where I could shut out the rest of the world after a rough day in court or when I had a client and a case I couldn't let go of. He made me a paradise in my own home, and the only thing that would be even better was if he would strip and climb into the massive, four-poster, king-size bed with me.

I called myself every kind of fool I could think of as I took in the tangled sheets and the pillows tossed in every direction. My imaginary Zeb got more of a reaction out of me and out of my body than my very real ex-fiancé ever had. I had been involved with Nathan for years and not once had he made my entire body quake, bow up, or tremble from head to toe on the verge of an explosion that had every kind of sweet heat imaginable in it. That was why I had stayed in the relationship for as long as I did. There was no passion, no overwhelming rush of lust and desire that I wasn't equipped to deal with. Nathan was safe, easy, and I didn't have to pretend not to feel anything because I legitimately didn't feel anything other than the bland security that being with him offered.

There was nothing wrong with Nathan. He was kind. He had a good job. He looked good in a suit and liked all the same things I did . . . well, all the things I had been convincing myself I liked up until my father died and my life turned upside down. And I truly believed that Nathan loved me even though I wasn't very emotionally responsive and worked way too much. He cared about me a lot even though we both knew I was never going to rock his world in the bedroom and that he was never going to be my top priority. It had taken the passing of my father and the discovery of my brother for me to realize that no matter how much effort Nathan put in and how accepting of my frosty personality he claimed to be, ours was ultimately a relationship I didn't choose for myself. It was a relationship I chose in order to make my father happy and to keep him off of my back. I picked Nathan because it was what was expected of me.

I knew Nathan deserved better than someone who was only putting forth the bare minimum in order to keep the relationship alive, so despite his protests and his assurances that I was all he wanted, no matter what that looked like, I ended the engagement and packed up and moved to Colorado in search of a new life and a new family. I got both in spades and also a startling wake-up call when a filthy, unapologetic, and ruggedly handsome Zeb Fuller had sat down across from me at a tiny bar table while I was talking to Rowdy.

The way Zeb affected me was one of the main reasons I wasn't going to back out of the semidate I had arranged with Quaid Jackson tomorrow. Quaid was the kind of guy who seemed to like reserved blondes who were more comfortable in front of a judge than they were between the sheets, and it didn't hurt a thing that he was also disgustingly handsome and over-the-top suave. The term "lady-killer" had been invented for guys like Quaid, and the way I felt around him, pleasant, warm, but generally unaffected was a reaction I was familiar with. Quaid didn't make me panic or want to strip naked and throw myself at him. Quaid was safe.

He was a criminal defense attorney who had a legendary reputation in Denver. We had gotten to know each other when my firm handled his very messy and very public divorce not too long ago, so I was really hoping all he had in mind was a friendly get-together because there was no way the man could be ready to jump into anything serious after the kind of train wreck he'd just endured. I was hoping time and attention with the handsome blond attorney would force my hormones to get their shit together and stop screaming Zeb's name. After tonight, I wasn't so sure it would work, but for the love of God, I needed to get some sleep and I was desperate.

I straightened out the bed, put the pillows back where they belonged, and hit the lights. I stared up at the ceiling and prayed that the rest of the night would be Zeb free. Of course, as soon as my eyelids got heavy and sleep began to beckon, I began to wonder what it was like to kiss a mouth that was hidden in a beard, and this, of course, led to thoughts about what that facial hair would feel like as it rubbed against other parts of my body. My eyes popped open wide, so I groaned and gave up. It was either a cold shower or battery-operated-boyfriend time. Neither sounded as pleasurable as the thoughts that were keeping me up in the first place, but a girl had to do what she had to do, and sadly I had been taking care of my own needs far too much lately.

Stupid, illogical crush. This was torture and the only solace I had was that in the past, I had always been too cold, too distant from my emotions to ever feel anything like this. It was my first crush in my entire life and it felt like it might kill me.

CHAPTER 2

Zeb

I turned my head when one of the guys from my crew called my name, and immediately regretted the lapse in concentration. Behind the filtered mask I had on to protect my lungs from all the deadly things that came out of the walls in these old houses, I dropped a litany of filthy words as the hammer I was in the middle of swinging came down and smashed mercilessly onto my thumb. It happened in my line of work, but lately stupid, preventable accidents were becoming more and more frequent because my head was up my ass and rooted firmly on my last job—or rather the stunning blonde that had hired me to do it.

One of my younger crew guys, Julio, gulped when he noticed the murderous look on my face and the way I was shaking out my hand. He held up his own hands in a gesture of surrender before I even said a word. My temper had been on a shorter fuse than usual lately and the guys that made up my crew had obviously taken notice. It made me feel like a dick, but there was nothing I could do about it. My head was all wrapped up in Sayer

Cole and her endless legs and chilly demeanor, and nothing I seemed to do could pull it away from her.

"What?" I pulled the safety mask off my face and forced myself to ask the question in a level tone instead of barking it out like I wanted to. I flicked my throbbing digit with my index finger and swore as it burned like it was on fire. I nailed the sucker good. It was going to be a lovely shade of black and blue when I took my work gloves off and I would be lucky if the fingernail didn't fall off.

"There's a lady out front looking for you." Julio's heavily accented words took me a second to process. I lifted my eyebrow and put my hammer in the slot that was made for it on the leather tool belt that hung low on my waist.

"Looking for me for what? Is she with the city? Or one of the neighbors?"

Permit people were always dropping by to make sure everything was in order when I started tearing apart historic homes in order to return them to their original glory. I was also pretty good at turning them into something completely new and fantastic, but I still had to have the right licenses and permits in place in order to do so.

Julio scratched the back of his neck and flushed a little. "I didn't ask. She's real cute, though." The kid was young, not even out of his teens yet, but he was a hell of a hard worker and really good with his hands, so even if he wasn't always the brightest member of the team, I knew he had plenty of time to learn and grow. He just needed a shot and someone not to give up on him.

I shoved my hands through my hair and snorted when a cloud of centuries-old plaster dust floated up from the motion. I was covered in all kinds of construction debris . . . I always was.

"Inspectors can be both female and attractive, Julio."

The kid shuffled his feet and looked down at the bare flooring we had spent all day yesterday putting into the vernacular 1870s cottage-style home that was my latest renovation project.

"I know. She just asked if Zebulon Fuller was on-site and I told her you were. She started for the front door without a hard hat or a mask or anything, so I told her the house wasn't safe. I don't think she's a pro or anything. She seems a little . . ." He twirled his finger next to his temple indicating he thought the woman might be a little bit off.

I sighed. If she wasn't a pro she was probably an angry neighbor wanting to complain about the construction noise or the mess. It happened all the time, but over the years I had gotten pretty good at keeping the peace as my business grew and expanded, taking my reputation and name along with it.

"All right, I'll handle it. Can you finish stripping the wall and pulling the plaster off so we can get drywall up tomorrow? Wear a mask. That old paint is no good and dangerous."

I dealt with lead paint removal so much in these old homes that I'd had to get certified in order to be a lead-removal-certified contractor. What I did was never easy and there were always lots of hoops to jump through, but I lived for the sense of accomplishment I got by saving rotten and falling-apart buildings from ending up condemned or bulldozed. I loved to give something no one else wanted or believed in a second chance.

I shook the rest of the dust out of my hair and ran my hands over my beard to shake whatever was stuck there loose, too. I'm sure I looked like I had been rolling around in baby powder but there wasn't much that could be done about it. I was in the middle of a workday, and didn't have time for uninvited guests—in person or the one that wouldn't leave my mind. I already had enough of a distraction hounding me in the form of a lovely lady lawyer. My still-aching thumb was proof of that.

I stepped out of the hole in the front of the house where the original door had long since been kicked in and rendered useless by squatters or trespassers, and immediately caught sight of a young brunette woman who was indeed very easy on the eyes and who was pacing back and forth on the dead lawn. Her arms were crossed over her chest and she was moving in such an obviously agitated way that I knew whatever she was here to talk to me about wasn't going to be any fun. I cast a baleful look at the sign that was in the yard that had FULLER CONSTRUCTION on it along with my name and number. It wouldn't have been too hard for her to figure out who was in charge of the project. I told myself that I needed to rein in my sour mood and forced what I hoped passed for a pleasant and professional smile on my face as I approached the woman.

"I heard you might be looking for me. I'm Zeb Fuller, how can I help you today?"

The woman paused in her tense pacing and I watched her eyes go wide when they landed on me. I got that reaction a lot from both men and woman, so it didn't surprise me. I was a big dude—really big—and the fact I had ink scrolling up both sides of my neck and across the backs of both of my hands often gave people the impression that I was a much bigger and much badder threat than I really was. The beard and the fact that I looked like I could level the house behind me with my bare hands obviously unnerved her.

She uncrossed her arms and lifted a shaky hand to her mouth. It was my eyes' turn to widen as the woman suddenly started to cry. Not silent trickling tears either, but big, full-bodied sobs that shook her tiny frame from head to toe. I took an instinctive step forward, which caused her to immediately take a step back. I held my hands up in front of me to show I meant her no harm and also took a step back, giving her some space.

"Hey, you were looking for me. You're on my jobsite. I just came to see what I could do for you." I hated to see a woman cry. It killed me. Growing up, it had been me and my older sister and my mom. My dad took off when I was too young to remember what he looked like, so that meant I was always the man of the house. I didn't let anyone make the woman I loved cry, so when this one went all weepy on me it immediately sent me into protector mode. "I'm really sorry if I scared you."

She bent over and put her hands on her knees while sucking in audible breaths. Her curly hair fell forward to cover her face, and I could see her shoulders were still shaking. I was getting really concerned when she held up a hand and choked out:

"Just give me a minute. You look just like him and it threw me for a second." She was still breathing heavily and making no sense. It was my turn to cross my arms over my chest as I watched her physically pull herself together. It took a long time.

"I'm not following. I look just like who?"

She pulled herself back upright and shoved her hands through her wildly curly hair. Her gaze raked over me from the top of my head to the tips of my worn work boots, and when she was done she was shaking her head. Not typically the reaction I got when a woman checked me out but I would take it if it meant the tears stopped.

"I know I'm coming across like a lunatic, but I swear I'm not. It took me a couple of days to track you down since I didn't have a name or anything to go off of. You took me by surprise. I'm sorry for losing it on you like that. It wasn't the first impression I was hoping to make."

I was already grouchy and impatient. I didn't have the time or the patience to deal with the maze of words this woman was winding around me.

"Lady, I don't know what you're talking about and I have to get back to work sometime in the near future. This house isn't going to renovate itself. I need you to tell me what I can help you with or I'm walking away."

She cleared her throat and took a step closer to me. I could see her choosing the words she wanted to use very carefully as she told me, "My name is Echo Hemsley. My best friend in the entire world was a woman named Halloran Bishop." She paused like either of those names or the women attached to them should mean anything to me. When I didn't reply she kept going and I could see her lip quiver and her hands shake as she did so.

"Halloran had a rough life. She made a lot of bad choices, had terrible taste in men, and used a lot of really awful things to help her deal with her issues." The woman took a deep breath and I could see the tears well up. "She was also the kindest, gentlest person I had ever met and I never gave up hope that one day she would be able to get control of her life."

I frowned. "Okay, but I still don't know why any of that has you on my jobsite. I don't know you or your friend."

I mean I knew a lot of woman . . . A LOT . . . but all of them I could remember and I never went to bed with anyone without knowing their first name. I enjoyed being single and the freedom to play around, but I wasn't a douche bag about it. In all honesty, my bed had been very empty and my nights very uneventful

ever since a certain leggy lawyer had become the center of every
fantasy and daydream I had. I wanted *her*. Only *her,* and no one
else would do. It sucked because so far no matter how much I
showed my interest, she wasn't having it. She seemed absolutely
oblivious to all of it.

Either that or she was keeping our relationship professional
and casual because she knew that she was so far out of my league.
My business was doing great considering how new it was and I
made good money, but even with all I had accomplished in such
a short amount of time, the fact was that I was always going to
be an ex-con and blue collar instead of blue blood.

I was admittedly impressed and slightly captivated that my
past never once seemed to be an issue—at least I didn't think
it was an issue until I started trying to express my interest in
her. I was irrationally disappointed when she froze me out after
how calmly she seemed to accept my revelation when I first told
her about my past. I thought she was different, understanding,
nonjudgmental, but when it came down to it, Sayer was just like
everyone else that couldn't see past the bars once they knew
they were there. She pretended like she didn't notice the way
I watched her every move, and that she didn't feel the way the
air got thick and heavy between us whenever we were together.
She brushed off every compliment I tossed her way and ignored
every sexual innuendo that I threw at her. Eventually I got the
hint that she was okay with me working for her but dating her
and getting her into bed was never going to happen. She wasn't
into me the way I was into her, and no matter how much game I
leveled at her she wasn't budging. Hence the crappy mood I was
perpetually living in these last few weeks.

"You're right. You don't know me, and it's very possible you don't remember Halloran because you only spent one night with her. Do you remember a bar called Jack and Jill's?" When I just stared at the woman blankly she pulled on her lower lip and puckered her eyebrows in a little frown. "Maybe if you think about the day you got out of prison, that will help jog your memory."

I jerked my head back at those words and narrowed my eyes. Five years ago I had been released from prison after serving two and a half years on an aggravated-assault charge. I refused to let my mom or my sister, Beryl, meet me on the day I got out; in fact I hadn't even told my family what my release day was.

At the time I was angry, bitter, and had so much resentment and hostility still pent up over the reasons behind my arrest and the subsequent changes in my life, that I knew I needed to blow off some steam and get my head on straight before I saw anyone that loved me. I needed a few days to get back to the man they knew and not the one prison and life on the inside had turned me into.

I might not remember the name of the bar, but I did recall that I had walked aimlessly for a few blocks once the bus dropped me off at the first stop in Denver. The state prison was miles and miles away in Canon City and I swore to this day that the bus ride back home took days instead of a few hours.

"I might recall finding a bar that day but still don't know anyone named Halloran."

I had a bad feeling about where this conversation was headed. I didn't hide my past but it wasn't exactly my favorite topic of conversation either. It was unnerving that this stranger seemed to know so much about me.

That day was far from one of my finest.

Sure, I was free and it felt good to be out, but the girl I was in love with when I got locked up had moved on, left me not even six months after I went away. Meanwhile the bastard that I had nearly killed with my bare hands was still free and unchecked, allowed to do whatever he pleased even if that included using his fists on unsuspecting women. The injustice of it all festered inside me, making me a ticking time bomb ready to go off again. My fuse was always primed and just looking for an igniter. To tame the explosive fury that was still churning inside of me and to kill the craving that two years of no booze and no women had left burning in my guts, I figured the best place to scrounge up both would be the first seedy bar I could stumble into. I would get my fix of whiskey and a willing woman and then face both Beryl and my mom feeling somewhat like my old self.

"She was about this tall." The woman held her hand up a few inches over her own head. "She was blond, blue-eyed, really pretty, and, like I said, supersweet."

I didn't miss her past-tense use of the word "was." It was the second time she had referred to her friend that way. "Was?"

The tears started up again and the woman wrapped her arms around herself like she was giving herself a hug.

"Like I said, Halloran had terrible habits and terrible taste in men. Both of those things caught up with her last weekend. She was shot and killed over a drug deal gone wrong on East Colfax. Her new boyfriend was a drug dealer and thought it was perfectly safe to take her along on a pickup. Halloran should've known better, but she never thought things like that through. They were attacked by a rival dealer and his crew. Halloran was shot eleven times, the boyfriend was hit more than twenty."

The woman could barely get the words out, and I couldn't stand idly by any longer while she sobbed all over my jobsite. I walked over to her and pulled her into a tight hug even though

she was a stranger and not making any sense. She needed someone to comfort her and I was the only one around to do it.

"I'm sorry about your friend."

She didn't hug me back, but she did nod her head where it was
pressed against my chest. She took another steadying breath and
moved away from me while wiping her cheeks off with the back
of her hand.

"You might not remember her, she did tell me the night she
met you that you were very drunk, very angry, and also kind
of sad. She was in the bar because her boyfriend at the time had
just kicked her out after knocking her around and she didn't
have anywhere else to go. She said the two of you started trad-
ing horror stories; you told her all about the guy that hit your
sister and how you went to jail because you stopped him. She
was smitten. You were brave, stood up for someone that couldn't
stand up for themselves, and well . . . look at you." She waved a
hand in my general direction as bits and pieces of that day started
to pepper my brain with memories.

I'd always had a thing for blondes. Add some tragedy and whiskey to the mix and there was a very good chance I had gone all
in on the booze and sex and just couldn't remember any of it. I
vaguely recalled sitting at the bar while someone that smelled
sweet and gazed up at me with sad blue eyes took up the stool
next to mine. I remembered heavy words and solemn kisses. I
remembered gentle touches and liquor-fueled decisions. I even
remembered the itchy comforter from the no-tell motel that I
had woken up in, facedown and hungover like a motherfucker.
I couldn't remember the girl, her name, what she looked like, but
I remembered that she made me feel better for just a moment
and that I wanted to hurt the person who had made her so sad.

"Are you trying to tell me I hooked up with your friend?" I wouldn't deny that it was a strong possibility and any reason this woman had for tracking me down now after all this time was making me break out in a cold sweat. I could clearly follow the trail she was leading me down without bread crumbs. The destination simply didn't seem possible.

"Yeah. You guys hooked up, but like always, Halloran made the wrong choice and went back to the guy that was beating on her. She told me she skipped out on you the next morning without even giving you her name." The woman who said I should call her Echo tucked some of her curly hair behind her ears and looked at me with tired hazel eyes. "She saw you on the news when they did that story about the tattoo shop you were renovating in LoDo. I don't think she meant to tell me but it slipped out . . . she saw you on the TV and said, 'That's Hyde's daddy.'"

I knew it was coming, had felt it as soon as she told me I had hooked up with her friend. Fury, whiskey, and a pretty, sad girl led to really bad decisions on my part. I had been having sex since I was fifteen, and I could count the number of times I had done it without protection on one hand with most of my fingers left over. Unfortunately one of those times was the night I got out of jail.

"You're telling me I fathered a child with your dead friend?" It sounded harsh but my head was reeling and I was suddenly having a hard time breathing. The ground under my boots felt less solid than it had a minute ago and everything inside of me wanted to call her a liar and throw her off of my site.

She nodded. "Yeah. I mean, at the time I didn't really think anything of it. Halloran has had a lot of boyfriends and Hyde has had a lot of 'special' uncles throughout the years. I wouldn't bother you, would never have tried to find you if it wasn't an emergency. Because of how she died and her history of drug use, the state took Hyde. He's with Social Services now on his way to a foster home. If you don't do something they're going to put him in foster care and then try and adopt him out. He's going to get lost in the system."

I balked and fell back a step. "If I don't do something? Seriously, lady, I don't even know if what you're telling me is true."

She nodded and dug around in her back pocket until she pulled out a cell phone. "I know it's sudden, and I know it's crazy. But Halloran didn't have much family and the ones that are left don't have anything to do with her or Hyde, so there are no relatives that can or are interested in taking him. I offered, but I'm gone so much for work and my track record isn't exactly spotless, so they turned me down as fast as they could. I also had some bad habits and liked the wrong kind of men when I was younger. Luckily I got myself straight before it was too late." She gulped. "I very easily could've ended up like my friend."

She blinked at me then turned her attention back to her phone. "It may be crazy and hard for you to believe, but you have a son, and if you don't do something soon he's going to end up nothing more than a case number in some social worker's file."

It was my turn to shake my head. I wanted to tell her to leave. I wanted to tell her she was crazy and talking nonsense, but I had never been the type of man to run away from the messes I created or my responsibilities. So when she thrust her smartphone at me I took it from her like it was going to bite me.

I held the little device in my hand and stared numbly at the picture of a very pretty blond woman with her arms wrapped around a little boy in torn jeans and a Transformers T-shirt. He had wavy dark brown hair, big eyes that were a clear, calm dark green, and a smile missing a few of his teeth. He also had a very familiar dimple indenting his chubby cheek. He was tall for a little kid, and as I gazed at the image before me I couldn't help but feel like I was looking at a photo from my own childhood. My hand went numb and the phone tumbled to the ground.

Echo didn't say anything. She just bent down to pick up the device and held it out in front of me. "There are hundreds more if you want to see. The resemblance is startling, isn't it? That's why I freaked out when you first came out of the house. It's like looking at Hyde in the future when he's all grown up. He looks just like you. He just turned five, so you can do the math if the picture isn't enough to convince you that he's yours."

He did look just like me. He really fucking did.

I ran a hand over my beard and considered her thoughtfully. "Why didn't your friend ever find me? Why didn't she ask for help?" The idea that a part of me, a tiny human that I had helped make, had been out there in the world all these years without me knowing had some of that old rage and resentment I struggled to keep a lid on churning deep in my guts.

"I told you, she went back to the guy she had been with. I don't think she really knew who Hyde's dad was until he was born. It was pretty obvious when she had him, though, that it wasn't her boyfriend since he was Mexican and Hyde obviously isn't." The girl flinched and shoved her phone back in her pocket. "The boyfriend beat her so bad when she got out of the hospital she almost died then. That forced her to clean up her act for a while because she didn't want her newborn to be without a mother, but the older Hyde got the more Halloran started to slip back into her old ways. She probably could've tracked you down, introduced you to your son, but she was more concerned with chasing the next high and keeping her newest man to be bothered doing something that might benefit her kid. Like I said, Halloran was sweet and kind, but she wasn't a very good mother. I mean, I think she tried to be, she just didn't know how. Hyde has had a pretty shitty time of things in his few short years. You could make such a huge difference in this boy's life, Mr. Fuller. He's a great kid, outgoing and funny. You would never know what he's been through. He deserves a real home. He deserves a parent that will love him and take care of him."

I braced a hand on the top of my hammer and blew out a heavy breath. I felt like the entire world had shifted around me and had started spinning in the other direction.

"I have a kid?" I wasn't sure the words came out or if I just thought them, but they felt so bizarre and foreign on my tongue.

She nodded again and this time her expression was full of sympathy and knowing.

"Look, I know this is a shock. I know you might go back in that house and do nothing because you think I'm a liar or a crazy person, but it was a chance I had to take because the last person that should be forced to suffer for his mother's poor choices time and time again is that little boy. He makes me wish I had lived a better life, had been a better person from the start just so I could help him out."

"My history isn't exactly one that's going to win me any awards or make anyone think I'm prime father material." I was all too familiar with the sins from the past having a lasting effect on the here and now.

"Maybe. But don't you think you should at least try? Are you going to be able to live with yourself if there is even a slim possibility that Hyde is yours and strangers are given responsibility for his care? I've been in the system. It isn't pretty and most of the kids that come out of it end up in jail or way more messed up than when they went in. If you can stop that, why wouldn't you?"

I knew she was right because Rowdy had spent his youth orphaned and then his teenage years in foster care. He wasn't messed up per se, and had never been in jail, but whenever he mentioned his past it wasn't full of happy memories and sunshine and rainbows.

I sighed again and lifted my hand to rub it across the back of my neck. "Okay, lady . . . I mean Echo, I won't make any promises, but I do have a client slash acquaintance that practices family law, so I will reach out to her and see what she thinks I need to do. I imagine the first step would be proving the boy is mine legally. I don't suppose your friend put me on the birth certificate?"

The brunette tugged on her lip again and shook her head in the negative. "It's blank. I pulled it right after the funeral when the state came and took Hyde. I was hoping to find a name, but like I said I don't think she really knew who the father was and she was so scared of her man at the time there was no way she was going to put another man's name down. All I had was her mentioning you when she saw you on TV. I actually went to the tattoo shop and asked them for the name of the person that had done the renovations. The tiny blonde with all the tattoos at the front desk didn't want to hand it over without a reason why. I told her I was looking to hire someone to renovate my condo. I don't think she believed me. Luckily one of the guys that works there had your card and handed it over."

I knew exactly the kind of attitude that tattooed and tiny

blonde could throw, so I was grateful that one of my boys had stepped in. Even if this lady wasn't on the up-and-up, I owed it to myself, to the kid, and, sadly, to the girl that had helped me drown my sorrows in booze and sex when I was feeling so lost and alone to find out if the little boy really was mine.

"Like I said, no promises, but I will talk to the attorney and see what she thinks needs to happen. Okay?"

The woman nodded and I could see the relief flash across her face. "I guess that's more than I had hoped for when I initially decided to search you out. You honestly could've just thrown me off the property without hearing one word I had to say, so I'm considering the fact that you listened a win regardless of what happens next." She gave me a wobbly smile. "Thank you."

She turned and started to walk away back toward a little hybrid car that I just noticed was parked behind my truck in the driveway. I called out to her before she was halfway across the yard.

"Echo." She stopped and turned to look at me over her shoulder with raised eyebrows. "If I give you my cell number, can you text me a picture of the kid?" I shrugged. "It might help me explain the situation to the lawyer a little better since I'm not always so great with words."

She tilted her head to the side a little and narrowed her eyes at me. "I will on one condition."

"What's that?"

"Call him Hyde, Mr. Fuller. He has a name."

I swore softly under my breath. I purposely hadn't been using the kid's name. It made it all too real. Made him all too real.

"Can you please text me a picture of Hyde, then?"

"I'd be happy to."

I rattled off my number and she pulled her phone out to pop it in. She said nothing else as she made her way to her car and climbed in and left. I was just walking back into the house, my mind racing a million miles an hour, when my phone dinged with several messages.

I told myself to just wait and look at them after work, that it could wait, but I found myself sitting on the dilapidated steps of the cottage and scrolling through the photos.

They were all of a little boy laughing and playing. In every image he was smiling and happy. He appeared to be carefree and light of heart, which was amazing considering the things that Echo had mentioned he had been through. He was too young and innocent to have to navigate not only the sudden death of his mother but the shock of being put into the care of strangers as well. I didn't know for sure that he was mine even if the resemblance was uncanny, but I was about to really ruin any shot I had with Sayer Cole by asking her to help me find out.

If she thought I was an undatable ex-con before this, she was really going to steer clear of me when she found out there was a strong possibility that I had fathered a child during a forgotten night of drunken sex with a woman I couldn't even remember.

It didn't matter if she wasn't ever going to be interested in me the way I was interested in her as long as she helped me help the kid.

Right now Hyde, and whatever I could do to help him out, was my top priority, not convincing the lovely lawyer to go to bed with me . . . even though I wasn't one hundred percent ready to take that dream off my agenda just yet.

CHAPTER 3

Sayer

R ough day?"
   I was sipping on a lemon-drop martini and trying to rub
my temples where a dull throb has been pounding since lunch. I
blushed when Quaid commented on the gesture and wondered
how bad my lack of sleep really had me looking. I was typically
put together in a way that could almost come across as harshly
professional. I didn't mess around when it came to my job and
being a pretty woman in the legal world was always a disadvan-
tage when it came to being taken seriously, so I made sure to
have on a practiced and poised demeanor at all times.

"Rough few weeks. I haven't been sleeping well and I'm in the
middle of not one but two custody cases that are unbelievably
time-consuming. One day I'll have a client who really has the
best interest of their kid at heart."

I forced a lopsided grin and watched as Quaid pulled the knot
of his tie that rested loose at the base of his throat. He really
was outrageously good-looking. Several women at the bar kept
glancing over their shoulders in our direction, and the waitress

had almost dropped his Scotch on the rocks on his lap when she delivered it because he smiled at her. His hair was cut trendy and sharp, shorter on the sides and longer on top and styled like he was going to be in a magazine shoot for something expensive. Quaid was name brand all the way and not ashamed to show it off. His eyes were an unusual shade of blue that shifted between faded denim and gray. His gaze was calculating and focused. Nothing about him was relaxed or at ease, and while he dominated his space and oozed self-assurance, it was in a much more in-your-face kind of way than Zeb did.

I wanted to kick myself.

I was hanging out with Quaid specifically to keep my mind off Zeb, and yet I was having a hard time focusing on what was a lot of hotness encased in a very expensive suit across from me.

He lifted a golden eyebrow at me and picked up his drink. He grinned at me before putting the glass up to his lips and I wanted to have a serious talk with my vagina for not even kind of taking notice or perking up.

"I could never do family law. The kids are too hard, the emotion tied up in those cases seems exhausting. I deal with adults trying to manipulate the system and the law every day. Watching them do that to their own kids, using them as pawns . . ." He shook his head and I think I heard one of the women at the bar sigh dreamily all the way from across the room. "It's too much bullshit."

"Well, I couldn't deal with people who are guilty getting away with things they shouldn't be getting away with. I don't have enough faith in a random selection of jurors to make the right decisions when it comes to law. People are too easily swayed by charm and pretty words."

He lifted his other eyebrow to join the first. "You don't trust the system?"

It wasn't a popular opinion among my peers, but I had seen too much, had lived too long with what happened when the system failed, to put all my faith in a flawed construct. I finished my drink and shrugged. "I trust the system to fail, which is why I do what I do. Some of these kids have to have someone who will fight for them no matter what. The system can fail, but I won't."

Quaid's mouth pulled tight and he leaned back in his chair as he considered me thoughtfully. It was a good look. Piercing, intent, probing, I bet it worked really well when he used it to pick apart a witness on the stand, but I knew all the lawyerly tricks he had in his bag because I used them, too. I grinned back at him and waved the waitress over to order another drink.

"So what about someone who is just unhappy and out for blood? What about someone who just wants to make another person suffer? How are you helping in that situation? Are you fighting for the right and the just then?"

I was smart enough to know he was talking about his ex-wife. It was no secret in the legal community of Denver that she had taken him for a ride and that he had been lucky to escape with anything left to his name. They had been high school sweethearts, and when things went south they *really* went south. There were rumors of infidelity on both sides, but nothing had ever been brought to light, and because my firm was the best at what we did, Quaid escaped with both his reputation and fortune intact. He still had to pay through the nose monthly for maintenance, but overall we considered the settlement a win on our end. Apparently he didn't share those thoughts.

"Everyone deserves representation. Isn't that what the illustri-

ous system is built on? I don't handle a lot of divorce cases myself
for that very reason, but I do know how ugly they can get. Happy
people don't split up, so by the time the marriage has dissolved
I think everyone involved is already looking for somewhere to
place the blame and looking for an outlet for all that hurt."

He chuckled, but there was no humor in it. "Been married
before?"

I shook my head. "No. Engaged, and it ended amicably, but
I see it every day in my office. Something that is supposed to
bring couples closer, make them happy, ultimately makes them
the most miserable they have ever been."

"Tell me about it." The bitterness in his voice was impossible
to miss.

He muttered something else I didn't hear and put his panty-
dropping grin back on just in time for the waitress to slosh half
my drink on the table as she put it down.

I rolled my eyes at him. "Really?"

He chuckled. "Women like me."

"I bet they do." Why wouldn't they? He was gorgeous, smart
as hell, well-spoken, charming, exuded wealth and confidence,
and that smile was lethal. I was a fucking idiot for not responding to any of it. I would punch myself in the face if I could. Why
couldn't I get my act together?

"Not you, though. I mean you obviously like me well enough,
but you don't *like* me. Can't say I've ever had a woman cancel on
me more than once."

My hair was braided and pinned up in a coil at the back of my
head, but if it had been down I would be twirling it nervously
around a finger. A bad habit my father had hated. I had spent my
entire youth doing anything to avoid his disapproving looks and

cutting words, but some of my less attractive habits he had been unable to scorn out of me.

"I've been busy. My caseload is full, I was in the middle of a renovation on my house, and I've been trying to spend as much time with my brother as I can." It was complicated to explain to people why I was obsessed with being around Rowdy and being a part of his life, so I went with the half-truth that I told anyone who asked me about it. "We didn't get to spend much time together growing up and I feel like I'm making up for lost time now that my father is gone."

The promise of having someone, anyone, who I was tied to, who I could call family and rely on, the thought of not having to be just me, myself, and I anymore, made me determined to find a place for myself not only in Denver but in Rowdy's life. Luckily for me my little brother was a kind and caring man, and after a rough start he had welcomed me into his fold with open arms. My long-lost sibling was the greatest thing that had ever happened to me.

"Well, thanks for making the time for me tonight even though I think we had different ideas about what this date was about."

I cringed a little and awkwardly picked up my martini as he went on.

"You're really a lovely woman, Sayer. You're driven, intelligent, and dedicated to your job. We have a lot in common, I think, and I was hoping there was more of a connection between us. I think there could be, but you don't seem interested in letting it take root."

I chugged back the rest of the drink so hard that it made me cough and had my eyes watering. I was mortified at the spectacle

I was making of myself, but Quaid didn't so much as flinch and his gaze never wavered.

I put a hand to my chest and wheezed out that I would love a glass of water when the waitress stopped by to gape at me and ask if I was okay.

"Quaid." I started coughing again and wanted to crawl under the table and die. It took a full glass of water and five minutes in order for me to reply to him. "Your divorce was only finalized a few months ago. You can't possibly be ready to get into a new relationship."

A smirk played across his mouth and his eyebrows dipped down over his eyes in an undeniably sexy way. "Who said anything about a relationship? You're attractive, busy, and independent. You don't need me for anything other than sex. We're both single and we get along. I thought it would be a great arrangement until the first time you bailed on me. I get the feeling that even though you are very discreet, there is someone else in your life. And no, I am not talking about your brother."

Good Lord, could this get any more embarrassing? Yeah, there was someone else in my life, only he had no idea I was infatuated with him or that I was wearing out my vibrator because of my idiotic crush on him. Not that Quaid needed to know any of that.

Instead I told him, "There isn't anyone else, but that isn't an arrangement I would ever be comfortable with, regardless." I fiddled with the collar on my shirt and heard my father reprimanding me in the back of my head. "I'm kind of old-fashioned and boring when it comes to relationships, Quaid. Friends with benefits isn't something I have the ability to navigate." And if he took me to bed and was bored out of his ever-loving mind,

I didn't want there to be a chance in hell of that kind of gossip making the rounds in the courthouse. It would kill me.

"Fair enough. I kind of got the hint when you canceled on me for the second time."

I smiled at him. "But I do like you in the normal way and I really do enjoy spending time with you. It's nice to have someone who I can talk the law with."

It was his turn to roll his eyes. "Of course you normal like me, not naked like me. Like I said, all women like me one way or another."

We shared a stilted laugh. I was terrible when it came to men. That was one thing that was all on me and I couldn't blame on dear old Dad. I could never figure out how to be invested in them and still keep myself separated and safe. No one wanted to date or make love to an ice sculpture and pretty much that was all you got with me. It was the only way I survived growing up under my father's critical eye. When you're made to feel like the worst sort of idiot, the biggest kind of failure, for showing any type of emotion—even tears at your mother's funeral—you learn pretty quickly that if you don't have feelings then they can't be destroyed. Quiet disapproval and endless disdain could land just as heavily as a balled-up fist when it was all that was given to a child.

And now Zeb Fuller was not only threatening to melt the icy shroud that made me feel safe, he was also making it impossible not to feel things. So many hot, bright, and addicting things. It was no wonder I was equally terrified of and obsessed with the man.

The rest of the evening passed with easy camaraderie and friendly banter about the legal system. I wasn't lying. I really did like Quaid and I appreciated his quick wit and effortless flirting even though I didn't return the interest, but it was when my phone buzzed with an incoming text message as I was walking in the front door that all the attraction and lure I wanted to feel for Quaid flared to life because Zeb's name flashed on my phone.

He sent a message asking if I would be home on Saturday. I was so frazzled for a second I almost typed back *YES* in big, bold, shouty caps. When I calmed down I sent him back a reply that I had some work to do but he could swing by around lunch.

I didn't even think to ask why he needed to see me and he didn't elaborate, responding back with a brisk *See you then*.

At two in the morning the night before he was supposed to swing by, I gave up trying to sleep and went into my office to see if I could at least use my restlessness to get some work done, which really meant I sat at my desk and watched hours of *Buffy the Vampire Slayer* on Netflix without accomplishing much of anything besides wondering what Zeb could possibly want with me. It only took a few episodes before I decided that I was absolutely team Spike. I mean, hot, British bad boy, how could I not pull for him and Buffy to get over their obvious differences and find everlasting love?

I didn't have high hopes for getting any kind of sleep, but when I finally dragged myself to bed around five, after some stern nudges from Poppy, as soon as my head hit the pillow my body gave out and my mind finally shut down on me. There were no visions of a handsome bearded man and no endless fantasies of all the things I wanted that man to do to me . . . or fantasies of all the things I really, really wanted to do to him. There was just darkness and finally blissful, dense, consuming sleep. I had hit the wall and there was nothing left for my psyche or body to give.

When a soft hand landed on my shoulder sometime later I could have sworn that my eyes had just fallen shut. I jerked up in the bed and blinked at Poppy while I tried to figure out what was going on. I was confused for a second because the entire room was flooded with sunshine and she was dressed for the day. I was also surprised she was in my room and that she had voluntarily touched me.

"What time is it?" I pushed a messy handful of hair out of my face and stretched my arms up over my head. I groaned as every bone in my neck popped at the motion.

Poppy nervously fiddled with the end of her long braid and told me, "It's twelve-oh-five. Zeb's been downstairs for the last ten minutes waiting for you. I told him you haven't been sleeping very well and he offered to leave and come back another day, but I didn't think you'd want that, so I decided to come wake you up."

At first I just stared at her like she was speaking Spanish, then I swore and threw the covers off of me.

"You've got to be kidding me? I finally fall asleep after months of sleepless hell and I almost miss the visit of the person keeping me up in the first place? Un-freaking-believable." I never normally would have admitted that Zeb was the reason for my insomnia. That's how unsettled I was. There went those pesky emotions again.

I scrambled out of bed and paused when I caught sight of myself in the full-length mirror that was mounted on the closet door. My hair was a wild mess around my head. It looked like an entire family of squirrels had moved into the mess overnight. My face was scary pale and my eyes were way too big in my face, making me look startled and almost frightened. I had on the stretchy tank top and comfy yoga pants that I always wore to bed, but it was the last outfit I wanted Zeb to see me in. I didn't want to keep him waiting any longer than I already had, so I decided the sleepwear was going to have to do even though the idea of appearing as anything other than perfectly groomed and put together in front of him made me want to vomit. It felt like I was going into battle without armor.

Frantically throwing on a loose T-shirt to cover up the points on my chest that were also apparently excited to see him, I dashed around until I found a brush in the bathroom and ripped it through my hair until the tangled heap was smooth enough to put up in a ponytail. I wrapped a bandanna around my head and hurriedly slapped on some blush so I didn't look so much like an extra from *The Walking Dead*.

Poppy watched the frantic spectacle with a smile on her face while she shook her head at my antics. "Sorry. I would've woke you up sooner, but I was talking to my sister on the phone and lost track of the time. I didn't realize how late it was until the doorbell rang. I panicked for a second thinking it was a stranger that I was going to have to open the door for and try and talk to until I remembered you said Zeb was coming over. If it helps calm your nerves, he looks as uptight and stressed out as you're acting right now."

That gave me a moment's pause as I was headed out the bedroom door. I looked at Poppy in question where she was perched on the edge of the bed. "He does? Did he say why he's here?"

She shook her head. "Nope. He just came in and said it was nice to see me and that I looked pretty as a picture, but he did it without smiling at me. When I told him it would just take me a minute to go and get you, he muttered that he would just wait in your office."

That was odd. Zeb was always charming and laid-back. He was quick with a grin and one of his booming laughs. He typically went out of his way to put Poppy at ease and never seemed ruffled or keyed up about anything. If he was being abrupt and distant with her, then something was definitely off and this wasn't a friendly visit at all.

I took a deep breath and ran my sweaty hands over the thin material of my pants. "Okay. Well, I guess I'll go find out what's up with him, then. Thank you for waking me up."

"No problem. You look better. You obviously needed the rest."

No, I was pretty sure what I needed was to let the man waiting for me downstairs to fuck my brains out so I could stop dreaming about it, but I would rather have my tongue cut out with a dull knife than admit that.

I took the stairs two at a time and practically jogged across my living room into the room at the front of the house that Zeb had converted into an office for me. The door was propped open slightly, so when I hit it going full speed it flew open and crashed into the wall behind it with a loud bang.

The sound made Zeb whirl around from where he was looking out one of the big windows behind my desk. I flinched when I saw his reaction and told myself to calm the hell down. I plastered what I hoped was a friendly smile on my face and made my way much more slowly across the room. I shivered when his dark green eyes settled on me and felt secret places in my body get tight and start to tingle.

"Hey, Zeb. How are you?" It sounded forced and strained to

my own ears and I could tell he heard the tension in my tone as well when his dark eyebrows dipped over his leafy-colored gaze.

"I've actually been better." He sighed and I saw his gaze slip from the top of my head to the tips of my bare toes. I wiggled them involuntarily when his gaze seemed to stay stuck on the brightly colored appendages. Since everything I wore was typically black, taupe, or gray with an occasional neutral color snuck in, I liked to have my pedicure be as loud and as outrageous as possible. My toes were hard to miss, but when they made the corner of Zeb's mouth twitch inside of the facial hair that surrounded his mouth, it made my heart rate kick up. Even his smile was rugged and tough looking.

"Poppy mentioned that you seemed a little tense when you came in, so I figured this isn't a social call. What can I do for you?" I kept my tone level and as professional as it could be considering I wanted to purr and rub up against him. Professional I could handle. Heated and aroused just by being around him I had no clue what to do with.

He heaved a sigh and walked around to the front of my desk. He propped his backside on the edge and crossed his arms over his broad chest, pulling the thin material of his T-shirt tight and making his biceps bulge. It was an eye-candy feast that I would have appreciated much more fully if I hadn't noticed the muscle ticking in his cheek under the facial hair that covered it and the emotion in his eyes that darkened them from a deep green shade to one that was almost black. Sensing things were going to get serious really fast, I walked over to shut the door I had just thrown open and then took a seat in one of the cream-colored chairs I had bought to match the rest of the sedate decor in the office. I had to look way up at him when I sat down and I could see his struggle with whatever it was that had brought him to my door stamped clearly across his strong features as we watched each other silently.

"I didn't mean to rattle Poppy. I know she's sensitive and has every right to be. I thought I was holding it together better than I am, but something about actually admitting out loud what I'm about to tell you really has me on edge." He blew out a long breath and looked me straight in the eyes. "I fucked up, Sayer. I mean, I really and truly fucked up and I think you are the only person that can help me fix this mess that I made."

Startled by both his harsh words and the rawness with which he poured them out, I leaned back in the chair and curled my hands around the arms. "Are you talking about my professional help?"

I was asked for legal advice all the time, so I would gladly hand over any knowledge that I had that might benefit him in any way. In fact, it made me want to breathe a sigh of relief. Business, the law, cold hard facts, I could handle with ease. It was anything that required dealing with someone on an emotional and personal level where I tended to fall apart and drop the ball. When you shut your emotions off to survive, it is nearly impossible to turn them back on, even for someone you care about.

Zeb chuckled, but there was absolutely no humor in it. "Yeah, I need your professional help and maybe your personal help, too, considering you know what it's like to find out you have a long-lost family member that no one bothered to tell you about. You know what it's like to have your world turn upside down in the space of a few seconds."

I reared back a little and took a minute to get my thoughts in order before asking, "You have a sibling your family never disclosed to you, too?" It seemed highly unlikely, but I was missing a piece of the puzzle here and he didn't seem to be in any hurry to hand it over. I couldn't believe he'd found himself in a similar situation to the one I was in when my father died and his will revealed that I had a brother. The bastard couldn't even be bothered to tell me himself. Ever the consummate Svengali, toying with the people he was supposed to love like we existed for nothing more than his amusement. His games and ploys had been exhausting, but his last one had failed. Thank God. I was so lonely growing up, so sad and isolated, that when I found out about Rowdy, I dropped everything in my old life in Seattle and hightailed it for Colorado as quickly as I could. It was the one time in my life when I acted without thinking. It was the one time I had let myself feel . . . until that fateful day I met Zeb.

I made it no secret that I considered Rowdy to be the greatest thing that had ever happened to me, so if that was what Zeb was talking about I could walk him through the ups and downs of it all.

He pushed off the desk and started to pace back and forth in front of me. I was trying to figure out what exactly was going on as he brooded before me, but I couldn't stop my eyes from tracking the way the muscles in his shoulders and back bunched and flexed under his T-shirt each time he reached the end of the rug and turned around to walk back the other way. The man was hot even when he was troubled and it made me feel a little bit like a pervert for not being able to control my fascination with him.

"Not a sibling . . . a son." He stopped in front of me as the words dropped like a bag of bricks between us. "There is a possibility I fathered a child as soon as I got out of prison. I might have a five-year-old son out there."

I felt my jaw drop a little and I was glad I had taken a moment to add some artificial color to my face because whatever heat had worked into my cheeks by being around him had surely leached out with his revelation.

"A possibility, but you don't know for sure?" It was what I would ask any client in the same situation. "Is someone coming after you for child support?"

He shook his head and picked the pacing back up. "No. It was a one-night deal and the mother didn't even know who the father was until the baby was born. She passed away recently and the little boy is currently with Child Protective Services. The woman's friend tracked me down claiming I'm the boy's dad and begging me to keep him out of foster care. I don't really remember the girl or the sex, but I do recall the day since it was the day of my release and the timing fits. The little boy just turned five according to the friend that found me."

I frowned and fought the urge to get up and grab his arms to get him to stop moving so that I could talk to him without having to crane my neck.

"So a stranger dropped all of this on you with the mother out of the picture and you just bought the story at face value?" He had to be smarter than that.

My skepticism finally brought him to a halt as he stopped in front of me and looked down at me. I sucked in a surprised breath that whistled through my teeth when he bent down slightly and held his phone under my nose for inspection.

"No. I thought she was nuts and threatened to throw her off my jobsite until she showed me a picture of the boy." I stared in shock at the image on the phone of the mini Zeb. "That kind of proof made me listen to what she had to say."

Without thinking, I snatched the phone out of his callused hand and touched a finger to the adorable little face looking back at me on the screen. "He looks just like you."

Zeb snorted. "I noticed. Which is why I'm here."

I couldn't stop looking at the little boy, so without looking up, I asked him, "There are no other relatives? No grandparents or aunts and uncles who could take him in while we figure out paternity?" I winced when I realized I said "we" like this was a problem we were going to find a solution for together. For all I knew, Zeb just wanted some advice or the name of another good attorney. The thought of anyone else helping him navigate the tricky family court system made the hair on the back of my neck rise up.

"According to the friend that brought the information to me, the mom was living a pretty dangerous lifestyle. She hadn't been in contact with her family for years. The little guy has no one, and if he is mine then I need to do the right thing by him and I need to do it as quickly as possible."

I gulped and handed the phone back when he stuck his hand out for it. I put my own hand to my chest because my heart was beating so fast I thought maybe he could see it through my skin and layers of clothing.

"That's very admirable, Zeb."

"No, it's not. If he's mine I should've been taking care of him all along. He shouldn't be in this situation because I was too drunk and disgustingly miserable to use a condom one time. It's not his fault that his mom was an addict and made terrible decisions. No kid should have to suffer because of the shitty choices the adults in their lives might've made. He deserves better than this."

I agreed with him, but I also thought he was being kind of hard on himself. I knew far too many men who, were they in the same situation, would have ignored the revelation of a child they fathered and pretended like nothing had happened.

Since the conversation had turned serious so fast I no longer felt comfortable sitting down while Zeb loomed over me. I got to my feet and took up his original pose leaning against the glass-topped desk. I set my hands down next to me so I could rap my fingernails against the surface. It was another unconscious habit I had that my father had abhorred. He hated it so much that I had a burning memory from when I was fourteen of him scolding me, chastising me, and sending me to sit in my room during the middle of a fancy dinner party he had held at our house when his firm won a major case. It was mortifying to do a walk of shame in front of his colleagues and their families over something so small, something so seemingly insignificant. My father had ignored me, glowered at me for days on end. He told me I wasn't fit for company, and that I had no manners and that he had raised me better than that. His disapproval crawled all over me like angry bugs whenever I did something he didn't like. I learned to behave like nothing he said or did bothered me. I shivered a little as the image of his sneer and scowl whispered across my memory. I immediately stopped tapping my fingernails.

"So what do you want to do here, Zeb? Do you want to find out for sure if the child is yours, and if he is do you want to try to appeal to the state for full custodial rights? What's your plan?"

He moved so that he was facing me and we stared at each other for a long, silent moment. He took a step forward until the tips of his worn Red Wings were almost touching my brightly colored toes. He dipped his chin down so we were eye to eye, and I stopped breathing as he reached out and put his hands on top of mine. He towered over me, but my breasts still hit the center of his chest and he was bent just enough that all the parts of him that I dreamed about in the dark were pressed tightly against me. I could see a thick vein on the side of his neck throbbing. This was the closest I had ever been to him and I could tell the proximity was going to do nothing for my sleeplessness. He was everywhere and yet not close enough.

"My plan is you, Sayer."

I opened my mouth and then closed it again. I felt my eyebrows shoot up and a flush start to work its way up my throat. His eyes were so dark now it was almost impossible to see the pupils and every breath he exhaled I took in. I could taste his tension and my own across my tongue. The flavor of each was very different and had its own tang.

"What does that mean exactly?" My voice was thin and shaky and there was no real hiding the way my body reacted to his nearness. I longed for the layers of my professional garb, but instead the thin material of my bedtime outfit put the way my entire being flushed and the way my nipples tightened into noticeable peaks on full display.

He noticed.

Zeb took a step closer and ran his rough hands up my arms until they curled around my shoulders.

"I want you to help me, Sayer. I need you to get me through this. I need you to help me help this little boy even if it turns out he isn't mine."

His eyes drilled into me and I felt like I was being welded to the spot. I nodded slightly. "Of course I'll help you, Zeb. I'll get started on the paperwork we need to file to figure out paternity on Monday. You're going to need to get a DNA test and we'll have to petition the state to get one done on the little boy." I did a lot of pro bono work for families in the community and this was a case I would be happy to handle free of charge even though I knew Zeb made enough to afford my regular rates.

He sighed and I was stunned when he dropped his forehead so that it rested against my own. I could feel the brush of his beard against my face and I wanted to whimper at the surprising softness of it. I also wanted to rub my face against it like a cat.

"No, I don't think you get what I'm asking you. I want you to help *me* because it's *me*, Sayer. Not because it's your job and what you do."

His deep voice rasped across my skin and I felt like I had been thrown into an alternate universe all of a sudden, a universe where all I could do was feel things. I tentatively put a hand in the middle of his wide chest and was surprised to realize that his heart was racing and pounding just as erratically as my own.

"Obviously the fact that it's you and we know each other makes things more complicated on a personal level. Why would you think otherwise?" I was having a hell of a time concentrating because he took another step closer so that we were pressed even more tightly together and moved his hands up so that he was grasping either side of my face. His palms were rough and I wanted to lean into them.

"How about the fact that you spent three months dodging every move I tried to lay on you, or maybe it's the way you laugh off or ignore any kind of compliment I toss at you. You went out of your way to keep things between us strictly professional the entire time I was working on this house, but you can't deny that there is something there between us when we get close to one another that is completely unprofessional. I want your help, Sayer, but I want you, too."

I frowned at his words and lifted my hands to wrap around his wrists. I wasn't at all surprised when my fingers barely touched. Everything about him was so big and hard. He really was the epitome of what a man should be, and I had no clue what to do with any of it or the fact that he had just come out and told me I wasn't the only one suffering from what felt like a fatal case of lust.

"I thought you were just being friendly. You flirt with everyone. I thought it was habit, and I didn't want to make things awkward since you had so much work to do on the house." Not to mention I didn't want to try to explain to him my baggage and my chronic case of overthinking every move I made. Zeb was a nice guy. He wouldn't fuck me without getting to know me, and it made my stomach turn to think of him knowing any part of the real me, the me that walked on eggshells every day, the me that was constantly waiting for the other shoe to drop, the me that spent her entire life praying she had finally reached the level of expectation set out by the very man she hated most. He wouldn't like her very much. No one did.

He pulled his head back and his eyebrows snapped down low over his eyes in a fierce scowl. His mouth pursed into a tight line and I could see his jaw twitching under his beard.

"You thought I was trying to get you into bed out of habit? That I have no control around a pretty girl and just want to nail whoever happens to be in the vicinity? Jesus, Sayer, what kind of asshole player do you think I am?"

I dug my fingers into his wrists and scowled right back at him as his pulse kicked into my touch. "I don't think you're an asshole or a player at all, Zeb, but I also have no experience with men like you."

"Men like me? What does that mean? What kind of man am I?" He was getting angry and frustrated and I couldn't blame him. It was hard for me to explain why he was everything I wanted but everything I could never have. We were on two different levels when it came to our personalities and I knew there was no way someone as passionate and expressive as he was would ever be interested in someone as reserved and closed off as I was. Where I was the frozen tundra when it came to emotional availability, he was the blazing heat of the desert. I could see the fire of his annoyance in his gaze as he waited for my shaky explanation.

"You're a man who is sure of himself and confident. You're a man who is used to having women fall at his feet. You're a man who is exciting and interesting." I lifted an eyebrow at him. "You're a man who is tattooed and drives a cool vintage truck around, you're a man who doesn't mind getting dirty and can create things for a living. All of that is the total opposite of everything I've ever known, Zeb."

His eyebrows went from the deep frown over his nose to shooting up on his forehead and disappeared under the dark fall of hair that rested there. A grin that could only be described as wicked slashed through his beard and his hands tightened where they were still holding on to my face.

"I thought you were going to say a man with a past. A man that has been to jail. I thought you were going to say a man with my history is the kind of man you have no experience with. You surprised me."

If I was a different type of woman, I might have smacked him for that kind of ignorance. "Where you have been doesn't define who you are, Zeb. I told you when we first met that I understand that people make mistakes."

He grunted and moved his face closer to mine. "And here I am on your doorstep with another one. You want me to teach you about a man like me, Sayer? I'm pretty simple to figure out."

I didn't believe that for a single second, so I opened my mouth to tell him. There was never anything simple about passion. I didn't get a chance to utter a sound because before I got a word out I suddenly knew exactly what it felt like to be kissed by a guy with a beard because he dipped his head and devoured my mouth with his.

It felt phenomenal.

His lips were soft and warm when they landed on mine and the brush of his facial hair had just enough of a rasp against my skin to make me shiver all over. He was still holding on to my face, so he tipped my head back. While I was still trying to get my head around the fact that this was actually happening, his tongue invaded my mouth, and I thought I was going to pass out from the devastating pleasure of it all.

I had been kissed before. In fact, I liked kissing. I liked the press of mouths together and the way you could tell what kind of man you had on your hands by how skilled or terrible he was at such a simple act. I liked that kissing was intimate and involved without having to have all your cards on the table. But more than any of that, I liked that kissing spoke to exactly how into you the guy laying it on you was. If it was a peck on the cheek or a brush of lips, it meant there was no spark. If there was a closed lip press and no tease of the tongue, it meant he found you attractive and kissable but probably wasn't going to put forth the effort to be worthy of you. If there was a little nibble of teeth and the swirl of a tongue, there was promise and potential.

Then there was whatever it was Zeb was doing to me. It felt like a conquering. A victory. A battle fought and won. It felt like he was trying to make it so that I would never be able to kiss anyone else in my life without having to compare it to this moment, to the feel of his hard mouth contrasting with the soft scrape of his beard against my skin. It was more than a kiss, it was a sensation overload, and it was making all the crystalline barriers I had in place crack.

His lips were firm and unyielding as they pressed into my own. His tongue danced across mine as his teeth scraped delicately across my lower lip. I felt it everywhere and all I could do was hold on and let him devour me while I whimpered and shook against him. I think I kissed him back. I really wanted to be kissing him back, but I was so lost in the sensation, so caught up in the fantasy becoming reality and it all being so much better than I was prepared for, I might just have stood there like an unresponsive dope.

When he finally pulled back after tasting what felt like every hidden spot I had in my mouth and across my tongue, he was breathing hard and his dark green eyes were glassy with desire and something deeper.

"Men like me are about action, Sayer. We're much better at doing than saying." He let go of my face and took a step back from me. There was no missing that the front of his faded jeans had gotten much tighter. God, I wanted to rub my hands over that impressive bulge. "I've wanted you since the first day I saw you at the Bar sitting with Rowdy."

I cleared my throat before trying to speak. My head was still spinning from his assault on my senses and my libido was trying to take over my common sense.

"Zeb . . ." The word squeaked out even though I tried for collected and cool. "I like you and I think you're incredibly attractive, but you don't know me and I don't really think you would be interested in me if you did. Obviously there is an attraction here, but I can't act on chemistry alone. I'm not built that way." Even though I wished sometimes that I was. "I can still help you out with your situation with the child. We'll figure everything out together, so don't worry about things being weird. We can forget about this kiss and focus on what's important."

I would never forget that kiss . . . not ever.

He growled at me like an animal. He put his hands on his lean hips and narrowed his eyes, which had lightened back up to their normal mossy color.

"Sayer, do you want to go on a date with me?" I opened my mouth to tell him of course I did but that it wasn't a good idea with all the other things he suddenly had going on in his life. I also didn't want to bore him to death and risk having him find out just how unappealing I really was. Before I could speak he held up a hand and pointed his finger at me. "Don't give me a bullshit lawyer answer or tell me what you think you should say. Just tell me yes or no if you want to go out with me?"

Put that way, real and on the spot, there was only one thing to say to him without lying through my teeth. "Yes, I want to go out with you, Zeb." Even though I knew it would almost certainly end up a disaster.

He grinned at me and I felt my knees get weak.

"Okay, then I'll make it happen. We'll go on a date and you'll see you can totally handle a guy like me . . . I think I'll enjoy that part of it." He took a step toward me and I was startled when he pulled me into a one-armed hug. I instinctively wrapped my arms around him and squeezed back as he told me, "Thank you. I knew you were the person that was going to save me."

That was a lot of pressure and I had a moment of panic wondering what would happen if I let him down in court or on a date.

"We'll figure it out. I'm really good at my job and the reason I got into family law in the first place was to help kids." Because no one had been there to help me. "By the way, what's his name?"

"Hyde. His name is Hyde."

Of course it was. A mini Zeb wouldn't have anything but a cool and unusual name.

"I'll take care of you, both of you." My voice was muffled by the fabric of his shirt, but I was sure he heard it because his arm tightened around my shoulders.

I was already getting too close, melting a little bit into him. I was making promises I couldn't keep. That was what happened when emotion started to bleed through the cracks.

CHAPTER 4

Zeb

I was out of my damn mind.

I was supposed to be begging her for help. I was supposed to be trying to do the right thing. I was supposed to be full of dread and embarrassment at the consequences of my past actions. I wasn't supposed to feel the burn and sharp twist of desire that blazed through me every time I got near Sayer. That hadn't been part of my agenda when I went to her for help. There simply wasn't any stopping it.

Maybe it was the fact that it was the first time I had ever seen Sayer outside of her typical, severe-looking work wear. If there was such a thing as being tragically flawless and ferociously immaculate, then those were conditions that she definitely suffered from. She was always so tailored and put together. Sometimes she didn't seem real, more like a life-size doll without a hair out of place and a face full of perfectly subdued makeup still intact after a full day's worth of work. She was intimidating not only in her carefully crafted beauty but also in her consummate perfection.

Seeing her standing there with messy hair and dressed in rumpled clothes that she obviously slept in had pulled my head from all the cloudy thoughts about the possibility of impending fatherhood and immediately launched it into all kinds of filthy and sexy thoughts that involved putting her in even more disarray with my mouth and hands. God, I wanted to touch her, to taste her. I wanted to know if she felt as cool as she looked and just what it would take to get her to melt, to thaw her out and turn her into nothing more than liquid and want in my hands.

The kiss had been a solid start.

Hell, the way she kissed me back, arched into me and got all soft and pliable at just the touch of lips to lips, let me know she would have zero trouble rolling with anything I wanted to lay on her. Even if it was clear she had her doubts about that. As perfect as Sayer appeared to be on the outside, it was becoming obvious that all of that perfection cracked and splintered a little bit below the surface. She had a shell around her, but it was much thinner and more brittle than I think she was aware of.

Now that I had admitted the truth to Sayer, which felt like jumping off a cliff without knowing what was waiting below me, I had a few more people to tell about my current, questionable situation. I knew my sister and my mother would support me no matter what the outcome of the paternity test was, but I dreaded seeing the look of disappointment in their eyes when I came clean. They would be frustrated and exasperated that I had once again made a rushed, drastic decision that led to an outcome that could stick with me for the rest of my life.

I watched my mom's heart break in half when the judge laid down the sentence after I pled no contest to the aggravated assault and additional charge of child endangerment. She cried harder than I had ever seen her cry and that included the night my dad walked out on us for good when I was just a kid. I never wanted to put her through that again, and depending on the outcome of the looming test, my guts twisted into knots at the idea that I could cause her that kind of pain and disappointment more than once in a lifetime. All I wanted to do since getting out of prison was make my mother proud. That was why I worked six days a week and made sure to keep my nose clean and my easily ignited temper in check.

My sister, Beryl, was a little different. When I went to jail she had wanted to fight harder to keep me out than I had. She was in court with a broken nose, black eyes, and her arm in a sling, and was recovering from a head injury that had put her in the hospital for a week. She was ready to tell anyone that would listen that the only reason I was in trouble in the first place was because her boyfriend at the time, my niece's deadbeat father, had nearly beaten her to death. There was no way she could stop me once I learned how badly she was hurt, and I hadn't stopped to think for a second about what it would mean for me that I had attacked her abuser in plain sight of not only her but of my then three-year-old niece. Beryl couldn't believe I was the one facing a prison sentence while that asshole she used to be involved with got to walk free. She also couldn't believe that because her daughter, Joss, had witnessed the beatdown I had delivered, I was the one looking at a child-abuse charge. Beryl felt that it was all unjust and disgustingly unfair, but there was nothing she could do to help me when I decided that instead of dragging everything through court and subjecting her and Joss to a trial, I would just take my punishment and serve the time. I was going away regardless of any argument put forth, so I wanted to do it as quickly and painlessly for those that I loved as possible. Maybe it was guilt and remorse for losing it so drastically in front of Joss, or the fury that I hadn't known what was happening to my sister, but I just wanted it all to go away. It was the hardest decision I had ever had to make until Echo showed up on my jobsite claiming I fathered a child.

Beryl had hidden the violence and abuse she suffered at her ex's hands for years, but like all abusers a time had come when he had gone too far. With the evidence so brutal and blinding right in my face, I had lost my shit and taught the guy a lesson he would never forget about using his hands on the fairer sex, especially someone I happened to love beyond measure. He had beaten and hurt my sister, so in return I had nearly killed him with nothing more than fists and the rage behind them. I was out of control, and honestly once the haze of fury had dulled, I understood I had crossed a line and did deserve to be punished for my lack of control. My temper was always something I struggled to keep in check, it still made my heart hurt that sometimes I could still see threads of fear in my sister's eyes when she looked at me and saw the dangerous man I could be if pushed too far. For the last seven years I worked hard to be respectable and repentant because I never wanted to be that guy again. I didn't want my family or anyone I cared about to look at me like I was a bomb about to go off.

When I told Beryl about Hyde I knew her reaction would be to wrap me up in a hug, hold me tight, and tell me that everything was going to be okay. She would prop me up and help me fight to make things right if Hyde was indeed my kid, but behind her support and encouraging words there would be that sisterly knowing that scolded me for not thinking things through. While she appreciated me riding to her rescue and always told me how guilty she felt for not leaving the dickhead sooner so that years of my life weren't given up for her, she still never let me forget that there was a better way for all of us to have handled the situation with her ex. My actions had cost us all a heavy price in the end.

Sighing and shoving my shaggy hair off my forehead, I wheeled my fully restored, 1950 International farm truck into my mom's driveway and parked it next to my sister's little hybrid that was already taking up half the space. I had grown up in a suburb of Denver called Lakewood, and my mom still lived in the one-story brick rancher that she raised me and Beryl in. It was a quiet, family-friendly neighborhood that Mom had relocated to not long after Dad left. Even after all the time and circumstances that had passed, pulling into the cracked cement driveway that led to the garage still felt like coming home. I had offered to move my mom into one of my properties, to upgrade her home for her, but she wasn't having any of it. Beryl even bought a town house a few miles away, which made life easy for her since Mom picked my niece up and watched her after school until Beryl got off of work from her job as a bank teller. Mom insisted she wasn't going anywhere, and that her house was just fine the way it was. I honestly couldn't complain. It was nice to have a solid base, a place that never shifted or moved and that always felt welcoming and warm. My mom had always made sure we knew where home was and that had been one of the key factors in driving me to create that kind of place for others.

I loved working with my hands and getting to be my own boss. But handing over the keys, walking away from a family knowing that I had given them a place that could be their home base, their security, fulfilled me in a way that was hard to put words to. I always felt like what I did was so much more important than driving nails into wood or slapping some paint onto walls, and that was why my crew was all made up of guys that needed a second chance and a way to give back.

Every single guy that worked for me was either an ex-con or an otherwise at-risk individual. I was the captain of the second-chance crew and I couldn't be happier about it. I wanted all the guys I took under my wing to know that there was life after a major mistake, that making the most of a second chance was the only way to get ahead, and I wanted them all to see how important something like home really could be. I also wanted to give guys the opportunity that they might not get anywhere else to learn a tangible skill they could take with them wherever they ended up in life. There had been a failure or two along the way since I started recruiting the unrecruitable, but for the most part the guys were overly grateful for having honest work in an environment that wasn't about judging the sins of the past.

I didn't bother knocking on the metal storm door since the front door was open and I could hear the infectious sound of childish laughter floating from somewhere inside the house. It was the weekend, which meant plenty of family time. We usually all got together on Sundays for either brunch or dinner depending on my work schedule, but Beryl always swung by on the weekends and spent a couple hours catching up with Mom and letting Joss play with the neighborhood kids that made up her circle of friends.

I prowled through the empty house and followed the sounds of laughing and screeching to the backyard. I could see my mom's dark head bent toward my sister's as they talked quietly about something while a group of kids including my adorable niece played tag. A grin tugged at my mouth as I tiptoed my way through the kitchen and dining room until I reached the sliding glass door that led to the concrete patio they were sitting on.

Joss caught sight of me and I saw her lift her arm up to wave at me, but I shook my head and put a finger to my lips, indicating she should keep quiet while I crept up on her mom and grandmother. My boots squeaked on the laminate floor that Mom refused to let me rip up and replace, but the noise wasn't loud enough to draw attention. Joss giggled as she watched my approach, and when I got to the glass of the doors I gripped the metal handle and yanked it open while shouting "BOO!"

I chuckled uncontrollably as the glass in Beryl's hand went flying and as my mom leaped out of her chair like it was on fire. She spun on me and smacked me playfully in the center of my chest. I rubbed the spot playfully as she scowled up at me.

"Zebulon Fuller! Are you trying to give an old woman a heart attack?"

My mom was far from old. In fact she looked good and young enough that if it wasn't for the few wrinkles around her eyes she could easily pass for my older sister instead of my parent, so I didn't bother replying to that nonsense. Instead, I grunted and bent down to scoop Joss up as she ran at me. I wrapped an arm around her as she grabbed on to the end of my beard and pulled. It was something she did every time she saw me and it always made me smile. I gave her a smacking kiss on the cheek and made sure to rub my whiskers on her face as she giggled.

"Uncle Zeb, stop!" She wiggled until I put her down and dashed back to play with her friends.

I sighed dramatically and walked over to take one of the

remaining seats at the patio set across from my sister. "How quickly I'm forgotten."

Beryl was still frowning at me and wiping her damp fingers off on her jeans. "She's almost eleven. Just wait until she's a teenager and the boys she's running to hug are the ones she wants to date."

I let out a low growl at that and jerked when something freezing and slippery suddenly slipped down the back of my T-shirt. I leaned forward in the chair and practically pulled my shirt off over my head in order to fish out the ice cube Beryl had just dropped down the collar.

"You suck."

"You're the one that made me spill my drink. Jerk."

We glared at each other for a second until my mom snorted and had us both turning to look at her.

"I kept waiting for the day when you two won't argue like you did when you were little, but at this point I don't think I'll live long enough to see it. Zeb, it's Saturday, why aren't you working?"

I contemplated tossing the dripping piece of ice back at Beryl but instead dropped it back on the ground. I stroked a hand down my beard and looked at both of them solemnly.

"I'm in the middle of a situation and I needed to ask a friend for some help with it, so I took the day off. I also need to tell you guys what's going on. It's a conversation we need to have in person."

My mom put a hand to her mouth and I saw it shake a little. Beryl's eyes sharpened and she reached out a hand to put on my tense shoulder.

"Are you okay? Are you in some kind of trouble?"

I cringed involuntarily and shifted my gaze to the kids playing in the yard. "Some kind of trouble, I just don't know what kind yet."

"What happened?" Beryl kept her voice low and I could see worry filling my mom's eyes. They were the exact same color as my own so I knew by the way they darkened that she was already expecting the worst and that made my heart squeeze and my breath lock up in my lungs. That was exactly the reaction I was dreading. I was back to having her look past me and seeing only the things I was capable of. I was used to being judged, but it hurt a little more when it came from someone you loved unquestioningly.

"A girl showed up at my jobsite this week and gave me some news that flipped my world upside down."

Beryl's fingers curled into my shoulder. "What happened to the lawyer you were all hung up on? The one you worked yourself to death trying to impress by building her your dream home?"

I shook my head slowly and bent to put my elbows on my knees so I could hold my head in my hands. She knew me too well. Sure the house was Sayer's vision and her ultimate dream, but the work I put into her Victorian, the way I agonized and labored over every part of the remodel, meant I left a part of myself in the structure. Sayer's home *was* my dream home and she didn't even know it.

"This isn't about some girl, Beryl . . . well, it is but not like that. Sayer is actually the friend I went to see to ask for help. She's a family attorney . . . which I may need because there is a good chance I might have a family."

"What?!" The whispered exclamation came from my mother

followed by a whole slew of surprised curse words from my sister.

I pressed my fingers into my temples and sighed again. "Like I said, this girl showed up on my jobsite and dropped a bomb. She was pretty shaken but managed to tell me that her friend that had recently passed away identified me as the father of her child. A child that is currently on his way into foster care."

"Oh, Zeb." My mom's voice was soft and I couldn't bring myself to look her in the eyes.

"You can't just believe some stranger, Zeb. Where's the proof? This is ridiculous." I knew Beryl would immediately go into defensive mode, and while I appreciated it, the proof was pretty clear when the child in question had my face.

I pulled out my phone and pulled up the image. Without a word, I put the phone down in the center of the table and waited for my family to take it all in. Tears immediately shined over my mother's eyes, and for once Beryl seemed to have nothing to say.

"The proof is in the picture. I didn't *just* believe her, and there are things about her story that add up and make me believe the boy could be mine. When I got out of prison I wasn't in a good place. It was almost as hard to come home as it was to go in. Before I saw you guys after more than two years of being away, I needed a minute to get my shit together. That minute was full of some reckless choices on my part. Choices that very well could mean the boy is mine."

My mom picked up the phone and I saw her hands shake. "This looks exactly like your picture from the first day of kindergarten, except you had on a *Star Wars* T-shirt."

"I know, Mom."

I finally looked up at my sister, who was staring at me with a

mixture of compassion, aggravation, and that soul-deep understanding that we were ultimately in this together.

"What did the lawyer say?"

I couldn't stop the little snicker that slipped out as I sat back
up in the seat and laced my fingers behind my head. "Before or
after I kissed her?"

"Zeb!" My mom gave me a hard look and my sister just shook
her head.

"Really? You thought 'hey I may have a child floating out
there in the world somewhere' was a good pickup line? I hope
she kicked you in the balls."

"She told me that she would work on getting the state to put a
paternity test in place first thing tomorrow, though I think we all
know what the outcome is going to be. There is no doubt in my
mind that the boy is mine." I wiggled my eyebrows. "And then
she kissed me back."

"Okay, and once the paperwork proves paternity, what happens next? Have you thought any of this through, Zeb? Are you
really ready to be a dad full-time? What about your company?
You work all the time." They were the same questions that had
been chasing themselves around in circles in my mind ever since
Echo had ambushed me, and my answer always ended up being
the same.

"Of course I'm not ready. I have no clue how to be a parent
or how to take care of a child, but this isn't about me. That kid
needs me. There is no reason for him to be caught up in the
system when I'm here and can take care of him. He's my responsibility." And these were the last two people in the world that
would ever question how seriously I took my responsibilities in
life.

"Okay, then. You just let me know what you need me to do. You know I'll support you any way I can, Zeb." Beryl reached out and ruffled the hair on the top of my head just like she used to do when we were little kids. "And for what it's worth, I think you'll make a wonderful father no matter how it happened to come about. No one loves as fiercely as you do, little brother."

My mom reluctantly put the phone back on the table so I could reach out and slide it back toward me.

Beryl and I both watched her as she remained silent and on the verge of tears for long-drawn-out minutes. I kept waiting for her to say something, anything, and just when I was going to break the silence with an apology of rushed words, she got up and walked around the table and stopped right in front of me. I had to swallow hard to keep back the emotion that welled up in me. There was no disappointment or censure in her dark green gaze, none of the judgment that I feared with every breath I took. There was only open and endless love.

She bent down and wrapped her arms around me in a hug that felt like everything I wasn't aware I needed since hearing the news a few days ago.

She kissed me on the top of the head and whispered, "What's his name, Zeb? What's my grandson's name?"

It took me a minute to find my voice and to get my arms to move so I could hug her back. I had to clear my throat around all the feelings that seemed to be clogged there before I could answer her.

"His name is Hyde." I really needed to start with that instead of just calling him the kid or the boy. He needed to be real and solid. He needed to be more than just a fuzzy and cloudy idea of a thing that would forever change my life. He was a tiny, little person. He was my tiny, little person and I needed to get not only my head wrapped around that but my heart as well.

"Hey, what's going on? Why is Grandma crying and hugging Uncle Zeb?" Joss's tiny voice was concerned, so my mom pulled back and gave me a teary smile.

"Your uncle just told me a secret that made me happy, is all. They're happy tears."

Joss's delicate features curled up and her eyes narrowed at all the adults gathered around the table. "Secrets aren't nice."

Beryl reached out and tugged on the end of her daughter's ponytail. "Some are. Some are just a surprise that you have to wait for the right time to share."

Joss's mouth puckered and she crossed her arms over her thin chest. She had her mother's fight and stubbornness in her without a doubt.

"Is it a secret about my birthday? Am I getting the puppy I want?" Her petulant tone made me laugh and had Beryl sighing.

"Not everything is about your birthday, Joss. It's still three months away and I told you that I think we're gone from home too much to take care of a puppy right now."

Miniature dark eyebrows that matched Beryl's perfectly shot up, and I saw the spark of mischief light up my niece's blue eyes right before she threw her mom under the bus.

"Well, if the secret isn't about my birthday, is it about that guy, Wes, who's been coming over for dinner all the time? Did you tell Uncle Zeb and he told Grandma? I bet that would make her cry happy tears. She's always saying you need a man friend."

My sister screeched her daughter's name over my laughter. I stuck my hand out and Joss gave me a miniature fist bump right before running off as my mother called Beryl's name in much the same tone as the one my sister was using to holler at my niece.

"You have a boyfriend?" My mom sounded incredulous and delighted at the same time. Beryl was pretty and smart, but her experience with men had left her standoffish and overly protective of both herself and her daughter. There had been a short-term guy here and there over the years but no one that seemed special enough to keep around. Whoever this Wes was, he was already miles ahead of any other guy that had been on the track if Beryl had let him not only into her home but around Joss.

My sister flushed a hot red and fiddled anxiously with the ends of her long hair. "I have a friend who may be more than that, yes."

"Why didn't you say anything? Why haven't we met him?" My mom was going into full-on mother mode and all I could do was sit back and watch. Beryl glared at me as I grinned at her, grateful some of the focus was now off of me.

"Yeah, why haven't we met him?" I couldn't keep the teasing humor out of my voice.

"Ugh. Because I'm not sure what I'm doing with him. I met him at work. He's a customer at the bank. He asked me out for coffee and I turned him down. The next time he came in he asked again, and again, until I said yes. He's persistent and funny. He's really nice and has a good job. He's a natural with Joss, and really I think he's too good to be true, so I'm just waiting for the prince to turn back into a frog or for him to show his true colors. If I introduced him to you guys, that would be admitting that I want him to stick around. I'm trying really hard not to get attached."

It was my turn to reach out and put a hand on her shoulder

for a comforting squeeze. "Nothing wrong with hitching your wagon to a proven winner, sis."

She leaned forward and buried her face in her hands. "Ugh . . . don't say that. It'll just make it harder when it all falls apart."

Neither one of us had ever been very lucky in love. The first man my sister gave her heart to hurt her physically and the first girl that I thought I was going to spend forever with hadn't been able to handle the dire consequences I faced after I exacted justice from my sister's abuser. But despite all of that I felt like I needed to remind her that "Some things are built to last and won't fall apart no matter how much force or stress is put on them. Look at those old beauties I work with every day. They've been around for over a century, and while they might be weathered and worn they're still standing."

She grunted at me and rose up from the chair. "I don't know that I'm built that way and I have my kid to think about." She pointed a finger at me. "And so do you. You might want to re-think putting the moves on the lady lawyer if she's the one that you think can help you get custody of Hyde. I know you like her, Zeb, but your priorities are about to get dropped and shuffled around with that little boy being at the top of the list. For once you're going to have to stop and think about what happens if you act on your feelings without regard for the fallout. If you start something up with the girl and things don't work out, what will that mean for you and your son?" She reached out and flicked me on the forehead right between the eyes. "For once use what's in there and not what's in there." She poked a finger into the center of my chest where my heart was thudding steady and true.

I swatted her hand away and got to my feet, which meant I

was towering over her. "I think I need to figure out how to let both have a say. Letting one or the other rule all isn't any way to live." I could see it in the pretty lawyer I was currently obsessed with. Sayer was a good woman, but she did things in a deliberate and very careful way that was the exact opposite of how I plowed and thundered my way through life. Her brain was fully in charge of her actions and reactions.

At least it was until I put my hands on her.

When I touched her maybe it wasn't exactly her heart that was fully in control but there was no doubt her body was eager to tell her brain to take a backseat for once. I kind of hoped that if I played my cards right I could get her heart to have as much say as her brain did. I didn't want to think about the logic in Beryl's warning about things going south with Sayer while I needed her to help me iron out the situation with Hyde. I couldn't think about going through any of this without her there to show me the way. I needed more than her help. I needed her and the calm confidence she exuded when it came to assuring me she could handle helping me get my son where he belonged.

I was a man that constructed and refurbished things for a living. If I was intent on one woman, on having not only her but a life with her at the center of it, then there was no way I was going to build anything that wasn't one hundred percent indestructible even if that meant getting in there and knocking down some walls and pulling up some of the existing structure. Sayer Cole was a project I couldn't wait to get my hands on.

CHAPTER 5

Sayer

I was sitting at my desk aimlessly sifting through what seemed like an endless sea of paperwork and case files when there was a light tap on my office door. I pushed the paper that was full of words my tired eyes had blurred together away in frustration and told the person on the other side of the door to come in.

Carla Dragon was an amazing paralegal, and the only one on staff who hadn't been on my last nerve over the last few weeks. I knew I was extra tense and not nearly as focused as I usually was ever since the state had agreed to have Hyde's DNA tested against Zeb's. I knew that I shouldn't be as personally invested in the outcome as I was, but every day that passed I felt like I was waiting for a giant hammer to fall while we waited for the results to come in. I felt like the answer was almost as important to me as it was to Zeb. Which meant experiencing more emotions that were setting me off-kilter and making me decidedly uncomfortable.

Zeb called pretty much every other day to see if there was any word even though I told him repeatedly I would let him know as soon as the paperwork hit my desk. His anxiety and investment in the outcome of the test only served to fuel my own unease, and I could tell he was chomping at the bit to make things happen, to move things along so that he could get access to the child. I admired it, and him, but there was a tiny little piece of doubt that nagged at a place in my chest because even though I talked to the handsome contractor nearly once a day, he hadn't brought up getting together for that date he'd asked me about.

Logically I knew the timing was off and that we both had far more pressing things to handle at the moment, but the old uncertainty I had spent a lifetime fighting against because it had been ruthlessly drilled into me that I wasn't enough, wasn't worth time or effort from anyone, needled me no matter how hard I tried to push back against it. Zeb wasn't ignoring me or dismissing me, but the memory of how it felt when someone you cared about did, pricked at my skin.

"Hey, you doing okay? This is the third night this week you're at your desk well after the rest of the partners have left for the day." Carla entered the office and took a seat across from my uncharacteristically cluttered desk. My gaze went to the manila folder she had in her hands and narrowed. Carla was a lovely young woman with a sharp mind, quick wit, and a laser focus on the career path she wanted. It didn't surprise me she was also working late. I knew that currently she was happy being a paralegal at one of the top family law firms in Colorado, but she made it known that eventually she wanted to be the one sitting behind the big, messy desk pushing case files around. She worked full-time for us and also had a family. I had no idea how she was going to make law school happen, but I admired her drive and her confidence that she could handle it all. I needed a little bit of that can-do attitude for myself.

In Seattle my life had been structured, rigid, and painfully predictable. When I uprooted myself, threw caution to the wind, and came to Colorado, I was operating completely in unfamiliar territory. I was scrambling in pretty much every aspect of my life outside of work, because everything was so unfamiliar. I had a family I didn't need to beg for affection. I had someone in my life who knew how to love and be loved without games. I had feelings threatening to overwhelm me where a man was concerned, and I had someone relying on me to be strong for them, to help them heal when I was nothing more than an ugly and open wound myself. I never felt like I was doing any of it correctly outside of the courtroom, but I tried.

"I'm just playing catch-up. I'm not sure how I managed to get so far behind on things, but I am."

She lifted her eyebrows at me and tilted her head to the file I had open in front of me on top of the mess of the other ones. "Could it be the fact that you haven't looked at anything other than that case file for the last two weeks? Every time I'm in your office it's open on your desk and you're staring at it."

There was no missing the black-and-white mug shot of Zeb or the angry downturn of his mouth in the image. It was well before his face was covered in fuzz and I couldn't get over how young he looked and how furious he seemed in the image. That wasn't the Zeb Fuller I knew and dreamed about at night, but it was a version of Zeb that existed and could prove very difficult to deal with when it came to fighting for his kid. The idea that passion could be so wild and dangerous taunted me.

I knew all about the assault charge and the fact he had pled no contest and served his time. The hiccup and the surprise in the mix was the additional charge of endangering the welfare of a child.

The police report was vague and so were the notes from the public defender who handled Zeb's case. But from what I could piece together, Zeb had gone after his sister's boyfriend and hurt him badly enough to put the guy in the hospital for several weeks. The attack on the other man had happened at the sister's apartment and well within the view of the sister's then three-year-old little girl. The arresting officer claimed the child was terrified and crying. He claimed she wouldn't even look at him or stop screaming when he came to intervene in the situation, thus prompting him to add the endangerment charge. It wasn't uncommon for the police to level that charge upon physically violent parents who fought each other with no regard to how their actions might end up affecting the mental well-being of their kids. It was slightly more unusual for the charge to fall on a relative of the child, especially one who didn't share the home with the minor, and in Zeb's case it was going to make going before a judge decidedly more complicated.

"He's a friend, so the case is more personal. I'm tied up in it a little more than I probably should be."

Carla flashed me a knowing grin and leaned forward with the envelope she had in her hand. "He's a cute friend. I can see wanting things to be *very* personal with him." I rolled my eyes at her and reached across the mess in front of me for the envelope in her hand. My heart skipped several beats and then decided to start doing the tango when I saw the name of the lab the state used for all of its testing on the label.

My reaction must have been telling because Carla laughed a little as she climbed to her feet. "I was on my way out but had to drop a divorce amendment in the mail to go out tomorrow and caught the delivery guy just as he was dropping this off at the front desk. I knew you would want it as soon as possible."

"Oh, thank you." My fingers curled around the envelope like there was something precious and easily breakable inside. The contents inside of that simple manila covering were life changing. It seemed like they should be wrapped in something much more substantial than paper.

Carla walked across my office toward the door and paused at the threshold.

"Aren't you going to rip into it? I thought you would be tearing into the results like a wolverine, as distracted and hung up on this case as you've been the last few weeks."

I looked from the envelope to the paralegal and slowly shook my head in the negative. It was common for the attorney representing the questioning party in a paternity case to first look at the results and then figure out the best way to break the news, good or bad, to their client. In this particular case I knew Zeb needed to be the one to break the seal on the envelope. He needed to be the first person to lay eyes on the results to verify if little Hyde was in fact his. I felt it deep down in my guts that taking the results to him and letting him uncover the answer on his own was the right way to go about it.

"No. In this case I think the client needs to see the results first."

"That's different from how you normally handle paternity cases." There was questioning in her tone as I moved some files around and searched for my cell phone in the wreckage on the top of my desk. I needed to take twenty minutes and clean everything up so I could put my mind and my work space back in functioning order.

"Like I said, this client is a friend and things are unorthodox all around." Including the irrational way my body and every-

thing that throbbed and pulsed deep down inside of me leaped
to life from the first instant I'd laid eyes on Zeb.

"Right. It's personal. Be careful with that, Sayer. Making anything that has to do with the law personal is a recipe for disaster.
How many clients have you had to talk off the ledge because
love wasn't enough to fight against protocol and judge's orders?
You're a great attorney and it looks like your friend needs you to
be that more than anything else." She told me good night and
left my office door open since I was now officially the last person
left in the upscale building in Lower Downtown Denver.

I tapped the corner of my phone on the open case file that had
Zeb's too-young face staring up at me in black and white. Even
that harsh image had my heart kicking against my ribs. Carla's
warning had merit . . . too much of it.

If the results that I held in my hand were, in fact, positive for
paternity, then Zeb needed me to be his legal representative way
more than he needed me to be a woman with a ridiculous crush.
I was going to be more useful to him in a professional capacity
than I would be in a personal one, and as much as it made my
insides dip and dive toward my toes, I realized that was how I
was going to have to approach my dealings with him from now
on. I needed to bring back the ice queen—the way I'd been when
he was working on my house. Somehow I needed to ignore the
inadvisable lust and remember that, really, we were just two
people with very little in common and not a chance in hell of
having a functioning romantic relationship.

I flipped the folder closed on that face that was following me
everywhere, picked up my phone, and hit Zeb's contact info.
The phone rang and rang, which I thought was strange, as anxious as he had been for any news about the results. Usually I

was running to catch his calls or to call him back, so the fact that my call went to voicemail made me frown and had immediate thoughts of what—and who—could be occupying his time running around like angry squirrels in my mind. Frustrated and slightly disgusted with myself, I tossed the envelope on top of the now closed case file and told myself I was leaving Zeb here, in my office, along with hundreds of other cases that were on my desk and in the filing cabinets behind it.

I was pulling bobby pins out of the coil of my hair, peeling panty hose off my legs, and kicking my heels off so I could put on my hot-pink Vans, courtesy of a shopping trip with my brother's oh-so-hip and stylish girlfriend. They were quirky and casual, and before I moved to Colorado I never would have worn them. Even when I moved out of my father's house for college. It wasn't until I took the leap, took the risk to come to Denver and find Rowdy, that I could take itty-bitty baby steps toward not analyzing how every single decision I made would ultimately affect me. I could wear pink shoes because they were cute and not worry about getting looked down upon for that choice. Only my father could take something as simple as a pair of shoes and turn them into a reflection of a person's worth and perceived shortcomings.

I was gathering up my laptop to put in my bag when my phone shrilled from the spot where I had tossed it. It was startlingly loud in the quiet of my office, and when I saw Zeb's name on the display it made me groan out loud into the empty space as I felt my pulse kick in response.

I plowed my fingers through my now loose hair and put the phone to my ear. As soon as I answered I heard heavy breathing and a lot of background noise.

"Hello?" I asked it questioningly as Zeb's deep voice hollered out orders to someone who obviously wasn't me.

"You need to have someone get out in the drainage ditch next to the driveway with a magnet. I don't want the neighbors on my ass about nails in their tires. They're already pissed I had you guys work late the last two nights. Hello? Sayer, is that you? Did you call me? Is there news?"

He sounded just as keyed up and anxious as he always did when we spoke and I wanted to curl up in a ball of shame for thinking anything different just because he wasn't able to answer my call. I leaned forward and put my forehead on the edge of the desk with a solid thunk.

"Sayer? Are you okay? What's going on?" Great. Now he was worried about me because I was acting like a dolt.

I sucked in a deep breath and told myself to get it together. "I'm good. I'm still at the office and just happened to get some last-minute mail. It's something I think you'll want to see. I was going to offer to bring it over to your place, but it sounds like you're still working, too. You can swing by my office in the morning if you want."

He got really quiet on the other end of the phone and I could hear the guys on his crew in the background and the sound of cars as he breathed low and steady in my ear.

"Zeb?" I didn't want to ask if he was okay because I knew he wasn't. His life was going to change even if the adorable little boy who looked just like him was, in fact, not his. Even if Hyde wasn't his son I had a feeling that knowing the little boy was caught up in the system with no family and no one to look out for him wouldn't sit well with him. Zeb was a fixer by nature and this little boy was most definitely on his project list.

He cleared his throat and I could picture him pacing back and forth as he pushed his free hand through his too long hair where it flopped over his forehead. Whoever would have thought being unkempt was so unbelievably sexy?

"Did you look at them? The results, I mean . . . am I a father?"

I put a hand to my chest as my heart squeezed like it had a fist around it when his voice broke on the last word. So much for keeping it all professional from here on out.

"No. I didn't open the envelope. I figured that was something you needed to do. I know how worried you've been."

He barked out a laugh so ugly and harsh it made my skin rise up in goose bumps. "Worried? Fuck being worried, Sayer. I feel like the world has stopped spinning, like every goddamn thing I do or say is all backward because I can't think about anything but the kid. It's been weeks and he's still in foster care, alone and probably terrified. He needs to know he has family. He needs to know he has me." He swore some more and then sighed. "I ran into a problem with the install of the new electrical system at my current job and then my buddy Asa asked me to look at a space he's thinking about investing in, so I'm a week behind on this renovation. I've been pushing the guys hard this week, and I still have some things I need to finish up tonight. I hate to ask since the jobsite looks like a tornado blew through it, but would you mind swinging by here on your way home with the results? If not I can come by your place later and pick them up. I don't think I have the patience to wait until the morning."

I picked the envelope up off the desk and tucked it into my purse. "I'll come to you. Just give me directions."

His sigh of relief was audible as he rattled off an address in a part of Denver I wasn't exactly familiar with called the Highlands. I jotted down the information and told him I would see him in a few. But not before carefully asking, "Zeb, do you want to maybe call a friend or someone in your family? I know you've been waiting for what seems like forever to see what this test says, but when you see it, when it becomes real, you may not want to deal with it on your own."

I had seen the way earth-shaking news sent someone into an emotional tailspin more than once. I wanted to make sure Zeb had all the support he needed to soften the blow.

"You're going to be here, right?" His deep voice was extra raspy and the goose bumps that followed the way it dragged through my ears had nothing to do with unease this time around.

"Yes. I'll be there."

"Then you're the only person I need while I find out if I am Hyde's father. Honestly, if the results are negative I think my mother might take it harder than me. She's already calling the little guy her grandson. I don't want to disappoint her." There was an edge to his voice when he said it.

I nodded even though he couldn't see me and pushed my hair over my shoulders. It was tangled and all kinds of wavy and messy from being twisted and tied up all day.

"Okay, then. See you soon."

He grunted his good-bye, and I had a brief moment of panicked indecision about whether I should put my heels and panty hose back on so that even if I wasn't feeling particularly professional where he and his case was concerned, I could at least look it, but then decided he had been waiting long enough for this paperwork and my own insecurity and ridiculousness wasn't a good enough reason to keep him waiting any longer.

I shut my office up, made my way down the elevator, and

waved good-bye to the guard who kept an eye on the building after hours.

The directions that Zeb had given me led to an area of town that was actually really close to the lower part of downtown and just across the interstate. It was a neighborhood that was obviously in the middle of some serious gentrification, if the polished new storefronts next to the abandoned and broken ones were any indication. It was the kind of place that Realtors referred to as up-and-coming and it was obviously a neighborhood that could pay off big-time for an investor who knew what they were doing in the tricky housing market. When I pulled up in front of the cottage that matched the address that Zeb had given me, it was clear the man knew what he was doing.

His cottage was the ugliest house on the block. It was in a sorry state of disrepair and looked dilapidated and on the verge of falling in on itself. It was made to look even worse by the cute, obviously well-loved and well-maintained homes that surrounded it on either side. Kids played noisily in the yards on either side of the disaster and watched me curiously as I pulled in behind a mud-splattered Jeep. When I climbed out of my own car and headed toward the front door of the ramshackle home, I noticed that the tires on the ostentatiously masculine vehicle came almost up to my waist. It had to be Zeb's. Anyone else would look ridiculous driving such a grotesque beast around town. He was the only one big and bearded enough to pull it off.

I didn't even have to lift a hand to knock on the door. As soon as my bright pink tennis shoes hit the top step, the wrought-iron-and-glass storm door swung open and I was pulled inside by hard hands. I hit the center of a sweaty and strong chest covered in a thin layer of cotton. I returned the nearly smothering embrace and patted a back that was covered in ropy, work-hardened muscle, telling myself that petting him and clutching at him would be poor form under the circumstances even though I really, really wanted to.

"It's gonna be fine. I promise." My words were lost somewhere in his rock-hard pecs, but he must have heard me because he pulled back with a start and let me go.

Eyes the color of pine scanned me from the top of my tousled head to the tip of my shoes. When they landed on the bright pink sneakers encasing my feet, he grinned.

"Those don't go with your outfit at all, Sayer."

I huffed out a breath and tried not to drool too much when I noticed he still had on a tool belt that was tugging the top of his faded jeans down on his lean hips. There was a strip of taut, tanned, dark hair–dusted skin showing in the gap between his waistband and the hem of his T-shirt. I wanted to fall to my knees and lick all around it. That was a testosterone overload and my lady parts were ill equipped for the sensual assault the image had on them. God, there was something so undeniably sexy about a man who was good with his hands. There was something that made every girlie part of me pant and come to attention knowing he could break stuff with his brutal strength and then just as easily fix it back up.

"I was headed home. Standing in court all day in heels is awful. I'm not like Salem, who picked these out, by the way. I need to give my feet a breather." I shrugged. "But thanks for noticing."

He chuckled and guided me farther into the torn-up house. Walls were missing, parts of the floor were ripped up, lighting fixtures dangled from wires in the ceiling. He was right. It did look like a tornado had hit the place.

"They look cute. You could be wearing SpongeBob slippers and still pull it off, Say. I was just trying to break some of the tension. Shit is stressful right now, ya know?" He looked over his shoulder and reached out a hand to catch me as I tripped over a floorboard that wasn't all the way nailed down. Thank the Lord I'd taken the heels off. I would have ended up on my face and then died from the embarrassment. "Sorry about the mess. I bought the house at a city auction. It was slated for destruction, so I snapped it up for next to nothing. But the price reflects the current conditions. It's a fucking catastrophe, but when I'm done it's going to be the nicest house on the block, and with the way people are flooding into this part of the city, I'm going to make my initial investment back tenfold." He pulled me to his side as I tripped again, and chuckled into the top of my head as he stepped through a blown-out wall into what once must've been the kitchen. "This is the only room that isn't filthy and has a place to sit. Mostly because we haven't started working on it yet."

There was what appeared to be an ancient kitchen table covered in a splattered and stained painter's tarp and some sorry-looking metal folding chairs placed around it. Zeb worked the thick leather of his tool belt through the buckle and then caught the whole thing in a hand as it dropped. He thunked the contraption down on the table, making everything clatter and I shivered a little because even the sound of that was sexy. He plowed his hands through his hair and bits and pieces of plaster and sawdust went flying in every direction.

"I'm sure it will be amazing when you're done. I've seen first-hand how talented and how skilled you are." I sat down gingerly in one of the chairs he pulled out for me and gulped a little bit when he bent down so that his face was right in front of mine as he grinned wolfishly. I wanted to blurt out that he could eat me up anytime and anyplace he wanted. Those foreign feelings he stirred to life in me were frightful in their blatant want and need.

"Oh, Sayer, you ain't seen nothing about how skilled and talented I can be . . . at least not yet." He pulled back as I blinked at him stupidly, and propped a hip on the table next to me. "But that's for another time." He held out a hand and wiggled his fingers in a "gimme" motion. "Let's have it."

I dug around in my purse and pulled out the long envelope. I held it out to him and watched as his broad chest expanded out as he sucked in a deep breath. He stroked his beard, something I noticed he did when he was thinking hard on something.

"It seems so innocuous, doesn't it? Like it's just a normal piece of mail and not something that can change the direction of my life forever?"

I was a little bit surprised that I had had pretty much the same thought when Carla handed it over to me moments ago. I tucked some of my hair behind my ears and told him, "You would be surprised how important some pieces of paper end up being to us. We work ourselves to the bone for a degree we can hang on the wall. We pick the ruler of the free world by poking a hole in a paper ballot. Some people search endlessly for the right person so they can get a much-coveted marriage certificate, and don't even get me started on the importance of the papers that someone leaves behind after they are no longer with us." His eyes shifted to deep and dark forest green at my words. "When I got my hands on my father's will, my whole world changed. Those papers were everything to me, so I understand why these are so important to you."

When I got my first important piece of paper—my high school

diploma—my dad stood stiffly at the graduation, his mouth pulled taut with displeasure that I had had to share the title of valedictorian with another student. I should have been the best in my class, and honestly I think the only reason he didn't get up and leave was because of how it would have looked to the other parents in the auditorium. When I failed the bar exam the first time I took it, I thought he was going to flat-out disown me. I could drown forever in the ways I had seemingly let him down over my lifetime. I could have used a hug, some form of reassurance, and all I got was contempt. It was all I ever got from him.

My dad's will was another piece of paper that changed my life forever. In it he finally disclosed the fact that he had fathered another child, a child he wanted me to split his estate with. A child he had never had anything to do with. A child he had abandoned and left to fend for himself. A child I was instantly and immediately obsessed with because his existence meant I was no longer alone. It was a simple piece of paper that my dad had left behind that had finally given me a family. A piece of paper that had brought someone who loved me and treated me with kindness and care into my life when I so desperately needed it. I would never undervalue the power of something that seemed so harmless as a simple piece of paper when I knew how powerful it could be.

We stared at each other in silent understanding until he took a deep breath and started to work on the top flap of the envelope.

"I thought I was ready for it to say anything . . . either positive or negative, but now I feel like I can only accept one response."

I reached out and put a hand on his forearm as he worked the stack of papers out of the sleeve. His big hands were shaking and his eyes had shifted to a shade that was almost black.

"It'll be okay whatever it says. We'll make sure of it. There are options, Zeb."

He nodded distractedly as his eyes furiously scanned the paperwork. His lips pursed in the framework of his facial hair and his cheeks went pale and then immediately flooded with a bright pink heat. His gaze shifted to me and wordlessly he handed me back the paperwork.

I took it from him but didn't look at it. I couldn't tell by his reaction if he needed me to hug him or slap him across his face.

"What does it say? Are you Hyde's father?"

He just stared at me silently, his heavy breathing whooshing in and out as we watched each other. I was getting ready to read the results for myself when he suddenly whispered, "I'm a dad. I have a son." His voice was so rough, so full of emotion and feeling, that it almost hurt me to hear it. I had trained myself to feel nothing, or barring that to be strong and keep it to myself. Yet here was this giant of a man feeling everything at once, and I had never seen anyone look more bewildered or happy.

"Zeb?" It was part question and part concern.

He turned to look at me and again he stated, "I'm a father. That little boy is mine."

"Congratulations. I can't wait to introduce you to your son."

The corner of his mouth kicked up and a dark spark flared to life in his gaze. I couldn't help myself when I saw that tiny flash of his teeth—all professionalism flew out the window.

Instead I got to my feet, put the positive test results down on the messy table, grabbed his whiskered cheeks in my hands, and I did something I had never done before.

I kissed a boy.

Meaning I initiated it. It was so out of character, so opposite to how I normally behaved, again I felt like someone else was inside of me, controlling my actions. It was like the Sayer before Denver didn't even exist.

I pulled him to me, planted my mouth over his, and kissed the shit out of him. It was one of the greatest and boldest moments of my life, right next to moving and tracking down my brother. If the way he responded was any indication, Zeb was all for my acting like someone I absolutely was not.

CHAPTER 6

Zeb

I was in shock.

I was consumed with equal parts elation and terror.

I was internally freaking out, but on the outside everything was focused on the fact Sayer had pressed her soft and clever mouth to mine. My reaction to her kiss and the hot, thick way it made my blood start to churn was so much easier to think about, so effortless to hand myself over to, instead of the other, more daunting emotions hovering on the periphery.

Hyde was mine and that would change my life, but in this moment, in this brief second, I could simply kiss Sayer and put my hands on her like I had been dying to do for what seemed like forever. She felt like the only thing that was nailed down, fused, and unmoving in my new world. I wanted to cling to her, hold on to the security that her no-nonsense and matter-of-fact demeanor poured over me. But more than any of that, I wanted to tangle my tongue around hers and fill my hands with her endless amounts of soft skin. I wanted to thank her with my hands and mouth for not looking at me like I had failed, like I had screwed up again. I made a mistake that I was going to do everything in my power to fix, and she understood that. At least the way we tried to ravage each other made it seem like she understood it.

I wasn't a bad guy but I was a flawed one, and for her to see that, accept it unquestioningly as she pressed up against me like she couldn't get close enough, made me want to devour her.

I deepened the press of my mouth against hers and put my hands around her narrow waist so that I could spin her so that she was the one with her backside propped against the edge of the table and I was leaning all the way into her.

I was dirty from a day of hard work but she didn't seem to mind dust and grime as her fingers tangled in the messy mop of my hair or as my rough hands left fingerprints on her clothes as I started to pull at the hem of her silky shirt where it was tucked into the top of her skirt. She kissed me back with equal fervor, her quick tongue darting across mine and her teeth pausing to sink into the curve of my lip when I pulled back just a fraction to make sure I wasn't tearing her delicate skin up with my beard.

She looked good with her blue eyes hazy with lust and too big in her face. When she flicked her tongue out to lick across the damp arch of her upper lip, I groaned and stopped trying to be considerate of her fancy outfit and shoved my hands briskly up the sides of her rib cage until my fingers encountered the edge of satin and lace. I would bet good money that this woman wore underwear that cost more than my Jeep payment every month, and my dick twitched at the idea of getting to see her in nothing but that. I was already hard from just being around her, but feeling the velvety press of her skin against my own was enough to have blood pumping and throbbing into my cock and making the situation behind my zipper decidedly uncomfortable.

She watched me silently as I brushed my thumb along the edge of her bra while I tried to read her reaction in that ocean-colored gaze. There was heady passion floating around in there, but it was at war with obvious uncertainty. She wasn't telling me to stop and her chest was rising and falling just as fast as mine was, but there was a hint of desperation in her hold on my hair, and once I had pulled back from the kiss, she didn't move or initiate another touch or kiss.

I grinned at her and used the edge of my thumb to breach the barrier of lace that was keeping me from the sweet swell of her breasts. Sayer was on the tall side for a woman, which was nice when we were all lined up like this, and where my fingers were trailing a dangerous and forbidden path she was all soft and pillowy. She had more than a handful hidden behind that bra that I was sure was just as fancy as the rest of her clothes even though I couldn't see it.

"You going to tell me to stop?" My voice was rough with desire and everything else that was coiled up inside me and looking for a place to go.

She let out a shuddering breath and her hands moved from their death grip on my hair to rest lightly on my shoulders. She blinked those cerulean eyes at me and stuck her tongue out to lick at her lips again.

"Eventually, so you should probably kiss me again so I forget that this is totally inappropriate and that I need to put an end to it right now."

She didn't have to tell me twice. I placed the hand that wasn't creeping up her full breast in the center of her back and pressed her so that she was bent into me and I had full access to not only her welcoming mouth but to the elegant curve of her neck and the delicate shell of her ear as that satiny river of blond hair fell to the side. I quit playing around and shoved her bra up and out of my way so that I could rub the now pointed and prominent peak of her nipple with the center of my palm. It made her whimper and I made sure I put my mouth over hers to eat the sound up.

She was pliable and liquid, melting into my touch and wrapping around me like she no longer had bones or any sort of structure to keep her upright. I was the only thing holding her together and straight and that made me growl in deep satisfaction. I would craft her, mold her into something that was made up of nothing more than desire, want, need, and satisfaction if she gave me the opportunity.

I shifted my hand inside of her shirt so that I could get my fingers around that nipple that was now stabbing me in the hand with impatience. I wanted it in my mouth so bad I could already taste the sweetness drifting across my tongue. I pulled back from the greedy heat and press of her mouth so I could not only see how my touch affected her but also so I could breathe and try to get some space, because as much as I wanted to, I knew there was no way I was getting my hands or my mouth under her skirt tonight. There was no denying we had a spark, some kind of tension that pulled and guided us toward one another, but Sayer wasn't the kind of woman that would let a guy throw her on a grungy kitchen table and go to town. At least I didn't think she was, but then her hand slipped from my shoulder and started skating down the center of my chest right toward where there was all kinds of trouble waiting for her behind my belt.

The caress of her fingers through the light cotton of my

T-shirt felt better and burned hotter than I could ever remember fingers dragging across my naked skin feeling. This woman could unravel me with very little effort and that was a startling revelation considering I needed her so badly in more than one area of my life.

I brushed my fuzzy jawline across her cheek and had to smile when it made her giggle. It sounded so light and happy that I did it again just to hear *her* do it again. When her fingers stopped at the heavy buckle of my belt I sucked in a steadying breath and gave the nipple I was still playing with a sharp little tug before pulling my hand out of her bra and pushing back to put some space between us.

I traced the curve of her ear with the very tip of my tongue and got a full-body quake from her in response. I made a mental note to remember Sayer had a thing for ears and whispered, "I don't know what your stopping point with all this is, but if you get my pants open I bet it's going to go a lot farther than you anticipated. While I'm okay with that, something tells me you might not be. I want to fuck you, Sayer, but I think we can do better than a kitchen table that might not even hold us up. Not with the way I want you and all the things I want to do to you. I told you I would take you on a date; you should let me do that before you get your hands on my dick."

She made a noise that was part squeak and part moan of distress. She lifted both her hands to the flat plane of my belly and pushed me back a little. I took a step back and she stepped around me, tugging on her bra and putting her shirt back where it rightfully belonged as she moved.

She twisted her mane of hair around her hand and shoved it behind her shoulders. Her cheeks had the smallest hint of pink on the crests and I could see the slight redness my beard had left on her neck and chin. The marks should have made me feel bad, but they didn't. They made me want to smile and beat my chest while declaring that she was mine to whoever was around to listen. I had put my marks on her, so that made her off-limits to anyone else.

"Sorry. I lost my head a little. You do that to me." Her voice was quiet and I could tell she was embarrassed, like admitting that she returned my heady interest was something to be ashamed of.

I sighed and reached out a hand to catch her arm as she reached for her purse. She looked up at me and my guts tightened when I saw something cloudy and unpleasant moving across the clear sky blue of her gaze. I would've been scrambling to reassure her if any of that cloudiness had my name written on it, but I could see whatever was working in her head was all her.

"You do that to me, too, Sayer. You know that, right? My world just got a whole lot more complicated, and you're the only thing that makes that more manageable. I need you."

Her nostrils flared out a little bit and she gave me a sharp nod. "You do need me . . . to do my job, and I will. I told you we would get through this, and we will. I won't let you down."

Her words sounded like some kind of affirmation she practiced in the mirror. It made me frown.

"I need you, Sayer. All of you."

She just shook her head at me and patted my fingers where I was starting to squeeze her arm with more pressure than I intended.

"Don't worry, Zeb, you'll get the best of me." She shook me loose and took a few steps toward the front door. "I'm going to get a petition together to get you a visit with Hyde sometime this week. It'll probably have to be monitored and at a court-sanctioned location like a CASA facility."

She had pulled her lawyer pants back on and was talking to me like I was a client in her office and not like a guy that had nearly bent her over and fucked her on this rickety kitchen table.

"What the hell is CASA?" I crossed my arms over my chest and leaned back on the table, annoyed and sexually frustrated. I should've just let her put her hands down my pants.

"CASA stands for Court Appointed Special Advocate and they have locations all over the city to make visits with complicated custody less hard on the child and often on the parents. Colorado actually has some really amazing institutions in place to help children who end up in the system."

I grunted. "As long as I get to meet the little guy and spend some time with him before things really get moving I don't care where it takes place or who is looking over my shoulder."

The idea I was going to be face-to-face with my son, with the tiny little person I had helped create, made all that happiness and doubt flood right back to the surface.

"I'll set it up. Seriously, Zeb, congratulations. This little boy is very lucky to have you in his corner."

I narrowed my eyes at her as she wrinkled her nose a little bit while running her fingers over the burn my whiskers had left on her throat.

"I'm lucky to have you in my corner, Sayer."

She nodded absently and moved her fingers to the tiny marks of red on her chin. I chuckled a little, which had her turning her attention to me with a lifted eyebrow.

I lifted both of my own eyebrows up at her and let them fall in an obvious leer. "Just imagine what that'll feel like when I get my face between your legs. This is nowhere close to being done between us."

My words made her blush, but she didn't argue. "I'll get in touch when I hear back from the court. Things are going to start moving quickly now that we have paternity established. Well, as quickly as the legal system ever moves. I'll see you soon."

She left and I let out a deep sigh and turned to pick my tool belt back up off the table. It seemed like I still had a shitload of work to do . . . on the house and on the girl.

And on my life now that I had a son I was bound and determined to share it with.

I WAS ON pins and needles waiting to hear from Sayer the rest of the week. My mom and Beryl were both over the moon at the news, though I don't think either was surprised. When I told them that Sayer was working on getting a meeting with the little boy in place, I think they were both as excited and as anxious as I was.

Sayer called right before the weekend and told me that she got the order from the court and that I could see Hyde, but it would have to be supervised and monitored at a court-approved location. My heart lodged in my throat and I couldn't come up with anything to say to her. All I could do was grunt like a Neanderthal.

She asked if I could get an afternoon off work the following week and told me she would get everything scheduled. Since she was my attorney she was supposed to be present for the visit, but she assured me that this was something she did all the time, so both she and the CASA representative would be as unobtrusive as possible so that my time with Hyde would be uninterrupted.

When I finally found my voice to thank her, it was almost a squeak as I asked if I was allowed to bring Hyde something. I didn't know much about kids, especially five-year-old little boys, other than when I had been one myself, but I figured it couldn't hurt to break the ice with some kind of trinket. When I was five anything that had wheels and made noise made me the happiest kid on earth . . . actually those things made me a pretty happy adult, too. Sayer told me she would have to check with the CASA rep and that she would get back to me. We set the date for Wednesday and I spent every day leading up to it in alternating states of elation and soul-deep panic. I was sure I was driving Beryl crazy calling her every five minutes to ask her what should I do, what should I say. I couldn't believe I was so torn up worrying if a five-year-old would like me or not.

Finally, after call number thirty she put Joss on the phone, and my niece told me to stop worrying because all kids liked me. I laughed and asked her how she knew that and her reasoning was so innocent and simple it put some of my fears to rest.

She told me that because I was so tall and so big I seemed like a superhero. She told me I could pick her up and carry her around no matter how big she got and that I always made her laugh. She said my hugs were the best and that my beard tickled when she kissed me and then she reached her little hand right into my chest and poked my heart when she told me that I had kept her and her mommy safe when her daddy was mean to them. She told me all kids needed someone that made them feel safe, so of course Hyde would like me. When she handed the phone back to Beryl I could tell my sister was crying, and honestly I could feel the burn of tears in the back of my own eyes.

Sayer called the day before I was supposed to meet my little

boy and told me she had cleared it with the CASA person and
Hyde's foster mom that I could bring him a little something for
our first meeting. She warned me not to go overboard since he
was going to have to return to the foster home after our meeting and that meant he was going to be around other kids that
would be jealous if he came rolling in with something fancy and
expensive.

That was how I found myself in the toy aisle of Target thirty
minutes before they closed staring aimlessly at rows and rows
of brightly colored boxes. I had no clue what was appropriate or
what Hyde was even into and that made me want to pull my hair
out. Finally, my gaze hit on a box of Legos and it clicked.

Maybe he liked to build things like I did. There were enough
blocks and pieces to the set that even if there were a bunch of
other kids at the house he was staying at, they could share and
play together. I grabbed a couple different designs and went
home knowing good and well I wouldn't sleep a wink until the
meeting tomorrow. Instead, I stared at the ceiling and alternately
thought about the little boy and the woman that was the key to
making him a permanent part of my life.

I couldn't think about one without the other invading the
thought the next second. They were both so important and in-
trinsically tied together in my life at the moment that separating
them seemed impossible, and I wasn't sure that I wanted to. If I
did win full custody of Hyde he was going to be part of the deal
if Sayer ever decided to let me into her life. She couldn't have me
and not have him and I wondered if that was part of the reason
she had reverted to putting up her professional mask every time
we talked now.

She was always polite, always reassuring, but none of the

playful attraction that floated between us before was present in her tone and she made sure all our conversations were brief and to the point. She was making me crazy, but I couldn't figure a way around it and frankly had to keep my focus on my kid and not my dick.

When the day of the visit arrived I skipped work in the morning, leaving my foreman, Azzy, in charge of the crew. Azzy was a good kid who survived a really nasty upbringing. He had spent his formative years in juvie and most of his young adulthood behind bars. We had met in Canyon, and when he got out he looked me up. The guy had no construction knowledge and I knew how hard it was for anyone, but especially someone of color with a criminal history, to find a good job and someone willing to give them an honest shot at a future. I hated being judged for my past mistakes but knew I could have it so much worse than I did. Azzy had a fierce resolve to never go back to prison and a noticeable dedication to making something of himself. Since I had hired him on he had also proven to be a quick learner. Over the last few years I had been entrusting more and more responsibility and workload to him. In fact, after I had blueprints drawn up and a bid squared away, I was thinking about handing that entire build over to the young guy. Azzy was ready for something to be all his, and I knew Asa would get it when I explained my reasoning for handing the project over to my protégé.

I dressed in a pair of black Dickies and put on a lightweight plaid shirt that had pearl buttons up and down the front of it along with white piping across the shoulders. I traded my Red Wings for a pair of black Frye boots and tried to tame my typically unruly hair with a handful of goop and a comb. I cleaned up all right but no one was ever going to hand me the key to the city and there was nothing I could really do about the tattoos on either side of my neck or the ones that marked the back of each hand, so I knew I would still get *those* looks. The ones that stated that no matter how respectable my career was, or how much money I had in the bank, or how nice the car I drove was, I still looked rough and would always be an ex-con.

Figuring this was as good as it was going to get, I climbed into the Jeep with my Lego haul and headed to the address Sayer had given me. The CASA building looked like any other business on the side street where it was located. It wasn't until I went inside and had to go through security and pass through endless pairs of suspicious eyes that I realized how different it was. There was a reception desk and I signed in and looked around the little wait-ing area for a familiar face. All I saw were men who looked de-feated and women who looked scared. This was obviously an establishment that was the worst-case scenario for some and that just made my nerves jangle even more.

I didn't want to be Hyde's worst case. I wanted to be his best option in the crap hand he had been dealt in his life so far.

A door next to the reception desk opened and Sayer came through it and strode toward me. I was stunned stupid for a second at the sight of her. I had seen her in her lawyerly garb plenty of times while I was working on her house, but some-thing about seeing her all buttoned up and sharply pulled to-gether on my behalf was startling. All that golden hair was tied up and pulled away from her face. I wanted to shove my hands in it and pull it all free. Her eyes skimmed over me and the corner of her lightly painted mouth kicked up in a grin.

"You look nice. Are you ready to go back? This is Maria, she's our CASA contact. She'll be in the room with you and Hyde for the next hour. Don't be alarmed if you see her taking notes, and you need to know all your visits here are going to be both recorded and filmed. So far, all Hyde has been told is that you're an old friend of his mother's. No one feels it's time to explain to him that you're his father just yet. We want him to get comfortable around you first. Are you okay with all of that?"

I just nodded stiffly. What else could I do? "Whatever you need me to do."

She gave me a full smile and it settled some of the sharp and pointy things that were jabbing at me under my skin. When she reached out and put her hand on my elbow, I finally felt like I could breathe normally.

"We just need to fill out some forms and then we'll go back. Hyde is in the room playing with another rep." I nodded again, it kind of felt like that was all I was capable of doing at the moment.

Sayer must have seen my panic and my fear because as she reached out to hand me a stack of paperwork she took a step closer and told me under her breath, "He's a happy little boy, Zeb. He seems sweet and wasn't at all curious or afraid when his current guardian dropped him off. He just wants to play. He'll be happy to see you. It's all an adventure to him." I exhaled so hard I was surprised I didn't blow her over.

"Thank you for that."

She gave me a little wink and patted me where she was holding on to my arm. "In person the resemblance is even more obvious." She pointed to her own cheek. "He even has your dimple."

I felt my eyebrows shoot up. "How do you know I have a dimple?" I started growing the beard when I was in prison because getting razors behind bars was a hassle I didn't want to mess with. When I got out, the thing was long and unruly, but trimmed up and maintained, it was pretty awesome, so I decided to keep it. As far as I knew, no one I hung out with now had ever seen me clean-shaven, including Sayer.

Her smile dipped a little bit and she pulled her hand off my arm as I scribbled my name and birth date across the pile of paperwork. She cleared her throat and looked away from me as she muttered, "In the mug shot in your file you don't have a beard. I noticed the dimple when I was looking over everything before filing my motion with the court."

My mug shot. Shit, she had seen my mug shot. It made my teeth clench together with an audible click. No wonder she had started to pull back from me. There was no getting around the fact I had served time for an unarguably violent act. With the evidence of that right in her face, why would she want to give me a shot at being something more to her? She came across as so cool with all the baggage I dragged around with me but how could she ignore the contents of it when they spilled right in front of her over and over again? They didn't make a strong enough lock to keep the contents of my past secure.

"Are you ready to go back?" She handed the papers over to the woman she had introduced as Maria and I tilted my chin down in the semblance of a nod.

"As ready as I'll ever be. Let's do this." I wish I felt as certain as I sounded.

"Okay. Follow me."

We walked down a long hallway and then entered a room that looked like a preschool. There were a bunch of little tables, art supplies, and a padded rug on the floor with numbers and letters on it. In the middle of all of that there was a dark-haired little boy lying on his belly, kicking his tiny feet up in the air behind him as he made car noises while he pushed a big plastic dump truck in front of him.

Time stopped.

The world stopped.

I stopped.

Everything that had ever mattered to me, everything that had ever seemed important to me before this moment, before I laid eyes on this little person that was so very much a part of me, seemed wholly insignificant and unworthy. Green eyes that matched the ones that stared at me in the mirror every day flicked up to me and a toothy smile with a gap on the bottom flashed as the little boy climbed to his feet and raced over to where I was frozen to the spot as I watched him with my heart in my throat.

"Hi. I'm Hyde. Are you a giant? Are those Legos? I love Legos. Do you want to play with me?"

I stared down at a tiny carbon copy of my own face and told myself to get my act together. I was never going to get another chance to make another first impression on this little man that was suddenly everything to me.

I crouched down so that I wasn't towering over him and held out the box. "Hi, Hyde. My name is Zeb. I'm not a giant, but I am pretty tall, so it can seem that way, and the Legos are for you. I would love to play with you."

Green eyes blinked slowly now that I was at eye level and he tilted his head to one side while he considered me thoughtfully for a second.

"You knew my mom?" I heard the tremor in his voice and it nearly killed me.

"I did. I only met her once, but she was very nice. She was a good friend to me when I really needed her to be."

He nodded solemnly and reached for the Legos I was still holding, which he promptly set down on the ground next to his sneakered feet once I handed them over. "She could be nice sometimes, but not always. Did you let someone draw on you?" He pointed a finger at my neck, where an old-timey pocket watch was inked onto the skin, and I turned my hands over so he could look at the swirling ink that covered the back of each. I stayed as still as could be as he reached out a finger to poke at the design.

"I did. These drawings don't really wash off, though. I get to keep them forever."

His lips twitched and that dimple we shared deepened in his cheek as he grinned. "Okay. Can I touch your face?"

I couldn't stop the bark of laughter that snuck out. It looked like Joss was right about the beard. Kids did like it.

"Sure. My niece says it tickles when I kiss her."

I heard a strangled choking sound behind me and cast a glance over my shoulder to see Sayer blushing furiously and coughing into her hand. Apparently Joss wasn't the only one that thought it tickled during kisses. I was forced to turn my head back around when small hands grabbed both of my cheeks and ran down the sides of my beard.

I stared into the eyes that were so like mine and fought down the urge to pick the little boy up and never put him down. That dimpled grin flashed at me again. "I like it." I heard a chorus of soft sighs behind me from the women in the room, but this time didn't take my eyes off of the little boy.

"I'm glad."

He nodded like he somehow understood the importance of this playdate just as much as the adults in the room did.

"Okay, let's play." He looked at the women standing behind me. "Do you guys want to play with us, too?"

God, he was a gem, just like Sayer had told me. He was sweet, considerate, and so welcoming that I had no idea how anyone could have chosen drugs and abusive relationships over him. He was nothing but light.

Sayer's soft voice floated over us as I moved to open the boxes of colorful blocks for him.

"Thank you, Hyde, but you should play with Zeb. He's here just for you. He's been waiting for a really long time to play with you."

"Really?"

The wonder in his tone made my fingers twitch as my hands fought to curl into fists. How could such a wonderful child ever doubt his importance? It made me want to break things. Lots and lots of things.

"Really, buddy. It's just me and you. Let's make something awesome."

"Cool!" His excitement was infectious as he flopped back down on his stomach on the rug in front of me. I folded myself into a sitting position on the floor in front of him and looked over at Sayer.

She had her hand over her mouth and her eyes were locked on us and I could see the same determination in those bright blue depths that I knew was shining out of mine.

Hyde was mine. He was going home with me and it didn't matter what we had to do to make that happen.

This little boy would never, ever have to question if he was wanted again. He was more than wanted and the sooner I could tell him that the better.

CHAPTER 7

Sayer

I felt like I was watching my kid graduate or achieve some other major life accomplishment as Poppy walked out the front door of my house with Rowdy. She wasn't a shut-in exactly, but it was close. Poppy would go to the grocery store or make a run to Target, but she never left to do anything fun. She definitely didn't search out interaction with other people, especially people of the opposite sex, so the fact that she was voluntarily and eagerly going to have dinner with my brother one-on-one felt like a momentous occasion. I may have even gotten a little teary-eyed when Poppy told me she would be fine when I asked her if she wanted me to tag along just in case. It felt like her road to recovery was finally getting less steep. Regardless of the terrain, I was so happy that she had so many people willing to make the trip with her, and I wanted to hug my brother for being so amazing and refusing to give up on his childhood friend.

I wasn't the least bit surprised when as soon as Rowdy and Poppy pulled out of the driveway my phone rang. It was Thursday night so I knew Salem would be hanging out with her tight-knit group of girlfriends and that an invitation to join them would be coming my way. I often tried to make sure I kept my Thursday nights free just for that purpose because I enjoyed spending time with Salem's group of girlfriends very much. The young women were all colorful, funny, smart, and maybe, most admirably, they were all deeply in love and protective of the men that made up my little brother's chosen family. They were also very kind and welcoming, never making me feel like the odd one out even though I knew I didn't exactly fit in with the group.

While I could admire and appreciate the beautiful art that covered so much of their skin and could listen endlessly to the tales of motherhood and relationship trials and tribulations, it wasn't anything I could relate to. I couldn't even imagine how that kind of body modification would have gone over as I was growing up, and now, as an adult, I was so deeply entrenched in my professional world that I couldn't see a place for it. Not to mention those kinds of permanent colors were terrifying to a person who was only brave enough to hide them on her toes and then cover them up with nude pumps.

I also had no clue what it took to raise a child while working or going to school full-time, to give of myself so fully to someone else while trying to still be successful and happy. To me, Salem and her friends were superwomen, and I was so lucky they included me and seemed to genuinely like me. It also tugged at my heart how they had all rallied around Poppy and tried to guide her gently, yet firmly back into life. Their concern and kindness went well beyond the fact that she was Salem's sister and could be attributed to the fact that they were all simply amazing women who wanted another woman to heal and be healthy.

Then there was the way they were with their men. All of

them, Salem included, had fallen for strong, difficult, complicated men. They all had spouses and lovers who took some work
and yet they never complained or asked for anyone easier. I think
that was what drew me to them the most. I couldn't get enough
of listening to the way they talked about the challenges and rewards they had in loving the men they did. It was beautiful. It
was special. It was heartbreaking because I doubted that I would
ever have someone be as passionate or as willing to fight for me
through the chilly walls I had erected to keep myself safe and
insulated for most of my life.

I thanked Salem for the invite but declined mostly because I
didn't want to do my hair or put on real pants to go out. We chit-
chatted for a few minutes and I could tell she was just as emotional and just as hopeful as I was that Poppy had not only left
the house but had done so on her own with a man. We shared
a moment of sappy love over how wonderful Rowdy was and
I dropped a hint that was as subtle as a sledgehammer that my
brother would make a wonderful father. She laughed but there
was an extra sparkle in her voice even over the phone, and if I was
the betting type I would put down good money that I would have
a beautiful little niece or nephew to dote on in the near future.

When I hung up I was suddenly faced with a house that was
far too quiet and a mind that was far too noisy. The idea of someone fighting for me, being passionate and invested in me, of
course meant I started thinking about Zeb. If I had been infatuated with the man before, there was no stopping the precipitous
and out-of-control slide of my feelings into something deeper,
bigger, and more layered as I watched him get to know his son.
Seeing the tender and careful way he handled the little boy was
way too much for my heart and my ovaries to take.

It didn't matter that he was Hyde's biological father, or that the boy was smitten with him, the court had a procedure to follow and questions were already being asked about Zeb's criminal record. We were scheduled to have our first hearing in front of a judge on Monday, and I knew he was a nervous wreck about it. There was nothing he could do to change his past and it seemed entirely unfair that it was going to have such a huge impact on his future. He needed me to be at the top of my game, to have my legal ducks all in a row to fight this fight for him. The idea of failing Zeb and little Hyde ripped at me, and now it was the possibility of not coming through for the green-eyed duo that kept me awake at night instead of sweaty, sexy dreams.

While the professional distance was necessary and should have been in place from the beginning, it didn't stop me from wishing things were different and longing for the date that now seemed like nothing more than a collection of empty words. My father had hammered into me over and over again that the only thing I should strive for was perfection, for flawlessness in my schooling and then in my business. To him, that was where my value had always been, in tangible and external manifestations of success. Wanting something or someone for myself on a personal level was frivolous and selfish and I had denied myself that luxury over and over again. It was one of the reasons I was no good with men. I didn't know how to be with one just because I wanted him.

My entire life I had sought out partners whom I could take home and who could withstand my father's scrutiny. They had to look right, act right, and come from the right background. How they made me feel, how they treated me, how we were together when the lights went out were all secondary to how my father would perceive them. It was all show and never an actual relationship. Nathan was the prime example of that. The one time my father seemed to approve of anything I did was when Nathan put a ring on my finger. It didn't matter that we bored each other silly and lacked any kind of passion or heat.

As though my intense and swirling thoughts had pulled Zeb into the vortex of self-pity I was lost in, my phone vibrated in my hand with a message from him as I wandered aimlessly through the empty rooms.

I shivered at the sight of his name and then silently scolded myself for having such a powerful reaction to only his name on the screen. His message was simple but for some reason it felt full of more meaning and emotion than the three words staring up at me indicated.

Can you talk?

I bit my lip and decided how to answer. I didn't talk to my clients after office hours were done for the day and I was already having a really hard time keeping the professional and personal lines clear where he and this case were concerned. I sighed and tapped out:

I can. Do you want me to call you?

I had started this process as his friend first and it wasn't fair to him that my heart was pulling itself apart because of his situation. He was probably nervous and scared about what was coming next week, and I was the only one who could put some of that at ease.

There wasn't a response for a long couple of minutes and I hated that all I could do was stare at my phone and pace back and forth while I waited to see what he was going to say. I was acting like a smitten teenager and it was ridiculous. I snorted at myself and headed into the kitchen to pour myself a glass of wine when the phone rang, making me jump. I wasn't prepared for him to call me right that moment and had a bout of anxiety about answering the call before I told myself to man up and swiped my finger across the screen.

"Hey. Everything all right?" I heard a car honk its horn wherever he was calling from, and he mumbled something that wasn't directed at me before answering.

"Fuck no. I'm freaking out over this court date on Monday. I can't think straight and I'm screwing things up left and right, which isn't good when you deal with power tools most of the day." He sighed and I so wanted to give him a hug. "I ordered the wrong color paint for the living room in the house I'm working on and the painters sprayed it today. It's blue . . . like really goddamn blue, and now I need to fix it so my guys don't kill me. I have to go get a layer of primer on the walls so the paint crew can go in and respray tomorrow. I've been working my crew like crazy because I've been missing so much work lately and this may be the last straw. I'm gonna have to work all night. I need you to tell me everything will be all right, Sayer. I'm going out of my mind over here."

I didn't want to lie to him, so I huffed out a breath and told him, "The case has some challenges, Zeb. We've talked about those, but the court advocate has seen how great you are with Hyde and it's obvious the best place for him is with you. We just need to convince the court of that and you need to leave that to me. That's why I'm your plan, remember?"

He swore again and I heard his car door open and shuffling as he got in. "I just wish I didn't have that arrest staring me in the face every time I think about possible reasons the judge could keep Hyde from me."

I squeezed my eyes shut as his remorse over his past misdeeds heavily laced his words. "All you can do is be thankful that no matter how bad the circumstances might've been that led you there, they did, in a roundabout way, lead you to Hyde. I see the way you look at him, Zeb. There is no regret there even if the path to him might have been bumpy."

He sighed again. "You're really good at this lawyer shit, Sayer. If I haven't said it enough, thank you. I don't know what I would do without you."

I put a hand over my eyes and squeezed my temples with my fingers. His words pulled at so many different parts of me. I could feel those emotions that he called to pushing at all the things I tried to keep them tied down with.

"I'm happy to help. It's not often I know for a fact that the parent fighting so hard for custody is the absolute right choice for the child. We are doing the right thing here, and you just have to have faith that the court and the powers that be will see it. One battle at a time, Zeb. That's all we can tackle, okay?"

He was quiet for a long moment, but I could hear him breathing and then finally he grunted a little bit and replied, "Well, then the battle I need to tackle right now is those god-awful walls. Thank you for talking me off the ledge. It's impossible not to hope for the best when I talk to you."

Maybe it was the overwhelming quiet of my house or it was the wistfulness in his voice. Or maybe it was the fact that no matter how hard I tried to keep a clear divide between the two of us, I was always going to be too eager to cross over it when an opportunity presented itself.

Like a goddamn fool.

Calling myself every kind of name for fool there was in the book, I blurted out, "I'm not doing anything tonight, and Poppy went out with Rowdy, so if you need an extra set of hands to help with the paint I can swing by the house." I wanted to groan. I was the least handy person in the whole world and I don't think I had ever even held a paintbrush, but the idea of getting to spend some one-on-one time with him was just so tempting that I ignored all of that and secretly hoped he would ignore it, too.

He chuckled a little. "Are you serious?"

I shrugged even though he couldn't see it. "Sure. Why not?"

"Well, I'm not going to turn down free labor, especially when that free labor looks like you. Do you even own anything that you won't be pissed to get paint on, Say? What I do tends to get dirty." His voice dropped a little bit and there was a husky timbre to the words that made me shiver.

There was a double entendre there that was impossible to miss and it made all of my skin heat up from the inside out. Not to mention no one had ever shortened my name before. I wasn't exactly the cutesy nickname type. My father wouldn't have approved and as such I was always just "Sayer." Zeb's shortening of my name felt intimate. It felt far more familiar than I should be allowing myself to get with him. Still I didn't say anything other than "I'm sure I can find something. I'll change and head over."

He told me thank you again and I was eternally grateful no one was around to witness the way I ran up the stairs so fast that I tripped, or the way I started pawing through all the clothes in my closet like a deranged person. Things fell off of hangers and off of shelves, ending up in piles on the floor that got tangled around my feet and had me tripping all over again. Finally, out of desperation, because I really didn't own anything that was worn out or already stained, I decided that what I wore to the gym would have to be good enough. I left on my stretchy yoga pants that I had changed into after work and added a tank with a built-in bra—both were colored a sedate gray—and shoved my feet into my running shoes. Those were black with hot-pink stripes on the sides. Overall it was as boring and uninteresting as the stuff I wore to the office, but at least I wouldn't cry if I had to throw any of it out if it ended up paint spattered and ruined.

I yanked all of my hair into a messy braid at the back of my head and practically ran out the front door. I told myself to calm down the entire drive over, lectured myself sternly that appearing this eager and excited to see him outside of CASA or my office would send the wrong message. I could be his lawyer and his friend. I was strong enough, my heart cool enough from the deep freeze I kept it in, to put all the heavier, denser things I felt for him to the side and simply enjoy some casual time in his company while I offered a helping hand. I was just a friend helping out another friend.

Yeah, right. I wasn't buying it, which meant Zeb would see right through me.

Despite the embarrassment that my out-of-control hormones were bound to cause, I strolled past his gigantic Jeep with my head held high and my breath trapped deep in my lungs. The front door was propped open and there was light and music coming from somewhere inside the house.

I picked my way carefully over the still littered and messy

floor because the lighting was faint and only coming from the front room of the house. Even though things were still torn apart, it was amazing to see how much work Zeb and the guys had put into the house in just a few short weeks. In places where there had been holes, there were now openings to other rooms and I could see they had started on the kitchen. All the old stuff was gone, leaving blank walls and a clean slate for Zeb to do his thing.

I followed the twangy, bluesy sound of whatever he was listening to into what I assumed was the living room of the house. I expected him to already be hard at work on the "god-awful" blue walls—really they weren't that bad. I kind of liked how bright and cheery they seemed, but he was sitting on a white bucket, focused intently on his phone. There was a slight smile stamped on his mouth, and I had a moment in which I was tempted to turn around and run back to the car and head home. I didn't want to intrude, but while I waffled, his head suddenly snapped up and those green eyes pinned me on the spot. Some of my indecision must have shown on my face because he held the phone up and told me, "My niece keeps texting me from my sister's phone. Beryl has a new boyfriend that she isn't ready to introduce to the family, so I've been covertly bugging Joss for info."

I cleared my throat a little. "That isn't very sneaky if you're texting her on her mom's phone. Your sister is guaranteed to see it."

He chuckled. "I want her to see it. My sister hasn't dated much since all that stuff went down with her ex. I want her to be happy, and if this guy is the one to do it, I want to meet him. It's my brotherly right."

I walked farther into the room as he climbed to his feet. "Zebulon and Beryl? Your mother named you both after famous explorers."

He lifted a dark eyebrow at me and his grin got wider within the beard that covered the lower half of his face. "Not many people pick up on that. I think she wanted great things for us. Too bad she just got stuck with a couple of normal kids. What about you? Where did 'Sayer' come from? That's pretty unusual."

I blinked up at him stupidly as he moved even closer to me. I wasn't prepared for the way his very innocent question threw me headfirst into a place I rarely visited since my father had died. I inhaled a sharp breath and winced at the way it made my nostrils flare. "It was actually my mother's maiden name—Abigail Sayer. I think passing it on to me the way she did was a small way for her to keep a part of herself alive after my father took over her whole life." I never talked about my mom. It was too hard, and all those things I tried so hard not to feel threatened to overwhelm me when I thought about her.

His eyes narrowed a little bit as he considered me thoughtfully for a second. "I know your dad passed away not too long ago, but you've never mentioned your mom. Is she still around?"

This was the last thing I wanted to be talking about, but considering I knew each and every single thing about him and the mistakes that had shaped him, I figured I could give him a brief glimpse into the train wreck that was my own past. I shifted my weight on my feet and let my eyes drift to the worn floorboards under the soles of my tennis shoes. "My mom died when I was a teenager. She committed suicide." She left. Abandoned me knowing good and well the kind of monster she was leaving me with. A monster she had loved up until her dying breath. A bastard she had begged for love and affection until it killed her.

To this day the memories still burned and the image of her blue, unmoving, and so obviously dead in the bath where I found her was etched forever into my mind. It never went anywhere, holding on to me just as tightly as the way my father had chastised me for crying hysterically at her funeral. I was making a scene and it was undignified. He was already mortified at the disgrace my mother had caused him by taking her own life, he wouldn't abide by his child embarrassing him further. He told me to stop crying, so I did—forever. Instead of questioning how he handled me, or my mother's passing, I had clear recollections of everyone at the funeral, friends and family telling my father how proud they were of him for handling the death so stoically and how impressed they were with how well behaved I was. I was conditioned and trained to be that way.

"Shit. I'm so sorry." He took a few steps closer and I lifted my head to meet his intense gaze.

"It's okay. I mean, it's obviously not okay, but I deal with it and now I have Rowdy and Salem—and Poppy was an added bonus, so it kind of makes up for all that I lost back then." It did and it didn't, but I couldn't really dig into all of that with him. That would be like rolling over and showing him my soft underbelly and I was already way too exposed where this dynamic man was concerned.

He didn't look like he believed me, but he didn't push. Instead he walked over to one of the windows in the room and picked up a plain white bag off the ledge. I hadn't noticed it before, but now that it was in his hands I couldn't miss a heavenly and obviously greasy and bad-for-you smell coming from within.

"I was so behind today I didn't get lunch, so I figured I would grab some brats from Home Depot while I was there getting the primer. I picked you up one if you're hungry and not scared of hot-dog-cart food. There's also some beer and a few sodas in the cooler in the kitchen."

I'd never had hot-dog-cart food before, so I didn't know if I was scared of it or not. Again it was not something pre–Denver Sayer even had on her radar. Whatever he had in that bag smelled better than any five-star dinner I had ever eaten, so I held out my hand and he plopped a warm, silver-wrapped concoction into it. He motioned to another white bucket and I gingerly sat down while unwrapping my food. Immediately sauerkraut and mustard slopped down on my lap, making me swear and causing Zeb to laugh at me. I narrowed my eyes at him but was surprised that his amusement at my expense didn't make me immediately freeze up. I asked around a mouthful of food, "How come you don't drive your cool truck during the week?"

Both his eyebrows shot up and I had to wait while he finished chewing to answer me. "My cool truck? The International? I know about a hundred sixteen-year-old boys that would disagree with you about the Jeep not being cool. Especially here in Colorado."

I shrugged a little and gave up trying to be delicate with the messy sausage. I was sure I had yellow all over my face, but I didn't care. The Brat was delicious. Seattle Sayer had no idea what gloriousness she had been missing hidden in a hot dog cart.

"I like the old truck. It's pretty and it's so neat to see something like that restored and well loved."

"I do love it. That's why I don't drive it to jobsites. Too many nails and other stuff getting carelessly tossed around. I try and baby her."

I made a face. "The truck is a her?"

He laughed again and cleanly polished off the rest of his brat. I was amazed he did it all without getting anything on his face fuzz. That was real talent right there, I thought begrudgingly as I continued to make a mess all over myself.

"Sure. She's classy, elegant, made of sturdy stuff, expensive as hell to keep running and keep pretty. She's only good to me if I'm good to her, so obviously she's a girl."

I rolled my eyes and then wiped my hands on the outside of my pants when I finished off my own dinner. Briefly I thought my dad would be horrified at the action but I shoved that thought down and instead focused on Zeb and only Zeb, "How long did it take you to restore her?"

He shrugged, got to his feet, and moved to pry open the massive bucket of white primer he had been using as a chair. "My buddy Wheeler sold the body to me for next to nothing when I got out of prison. We went to high school together and I think he knew I needed something to keep me busy because the only kind of work I could find right after being released was shit work for shit pay. Every week I would give him a few bucks here or there and he would find me a part or a piece of the motor and we slowly but surely got her all together. It was one of the reasons I knew I had to find a long-term way to support myself. Just because I had a record didn't mean I wasn't a valuable employee or a hard worker. I got really sick of being treated like a second-class citizen because of one mistake."

His eyes cut to mine and all I could do was nod in sympathy as he poured the liquid into trays and fished a couple of roller brushes out of a plastic bag.

"I actually met Rowdy through Wheeler. He had done a bunch of Wheeler's tattoo work, and when I told Wheeler I wanted something to remind me not to do stupid things that would cost me years of my life again, he recommended Rowdy and the Marked shop. Rowdy was the one that recommended me to the guys that own the tattoo shop when they decided to open and renovate the new location downtown. It all seemed very meant to be, ya know?"

I did know. Everything was tied together with thin threads of fate, and when one loosened or tightened it was surprising how impactful it could be. Kind of like how I had ended up here with Zeb now.

He motioned me over to the wall and showed me how to roll the primer onto the surface in a wide W pattern and then how to go back and fill in the spots. I must have looked as clueless as I felt because he was patient and calm while he went over his careful instructions with me a second time. After I felt like I got the hang of it all, I asked him, "So what tattoo did Rowdy give you to remind you to think first and act second?"

He held an arm out and pointed with the roller to a broken hourglass that covered the entirety of his forearm and hand, all the sand pouring out of it and falling into bricks that built up a wall that circled his wrist all in a seamless flow. He flipped his arm over and showed me the tipped-over birdcage on the back of his hand and the swarm of black crows that were lined up on a barren tree all inked in black on the opposite side. "All kinds of reminders of how hard it is to be locked up while life moves on for everyone else without you. He did a great job."

I nodded and turned my attention back to the wall. "He's very talented. I'm proud of him. I think it's amazing that he found a way to make a living off of something he really loves. It's amazing the way he gets to leave his mark on people for the better."

He made a soft noise. "It must run in the family."

That was one of the nicest things anyone had ever said to me, and if he wasn't careful I was going to drop the roller and jump him. I muttered a soft thank-you but refused to take my attention off the task at hand. My resolve was already paper-thin . . . throw in his kindness and it became nonexistent.

We spent the next hour or so in silence steadily working our way across one wall and onto the next. The repetitive motion and the sound of the roller across the wall was surprisingly soothing, as was whatever music was coming from Zeb's phone. It wasn't quite country and not quite rock, but something that was the best of something in-between, and I really liked it. We worked mostly in silence, just muttering a question here or there, and then there was the point where Zeb asked me if I cared if he took his shirt off. It was hotter than hell in the old house with no working air-conditioning even if it was late fall, so of course I told him it wouldn't bother me. I was lying.

It bothered me . . . in the best way possible.

When he crossed his arms and peeled the cotton of his shirt over the seemingly endless amount of rippling muscles that adorned his chest and stomach, it made my mouth go dry. It felt like he was moving in slow motion, revealing more skin, more ink, inch by inch just so he could tease me with hints of his work-hewed body. I wanted to lick my lips and then lick him but that would let him know I was watching like a greedy voyeur. He was hard and colorful everywhere. I was having a hell of a time keeping my gaze off of all that decorated and defined muscle, so eventually I gave up and kept checking him out whenever he wasn't looking in my direction.

Out of the corner of my eye, I watched the wings of the big

firebird he had inked across his rib cage flex and move as he worked toward the top of the wall. I was also trying not to watch the way the pinup girl seductively sitting on a hammer taunted me with the words "hit it hard" every time his massive biceps flexed. There was ink and color everywhere on him and I wanted to soak every single inch of it in. I was so absorbed in trying to covertly check him out instead of what I should be doing that I missed that spot where I thought I had left the paint tray and ended up tripping over the stupid thing, which, of course, made a huge mess and had white primer oozing all over me and the floor. To make matters worse, the noise startled me so much that I lost my grip on the roller, which went flying like a weapon where it ended up hitting that pinup girl on his arm right in her smug face.

"Oh my God! Zeb, I'm so sorry." I immediately got to my knees and tried to keep the spill from leaking off the tarp he had laid down before I got there. "I didn't want to make more work for you. This is a disaster."

"Sayer . . ."

"I mean, seriously, who does that? Ugh . . . I'm not normally such a klutz." I wasn't listening to him, but I heard him say my name again. My hands were covered in white and so were my clothes. The stuff was everywhere and I realized I was making a bigger mess than I had started out with. It was his fault for being so . . . distracting, and sexy, and masculine, and simply perfect in all his rugged glory . . . Gah, of course I couldn't focus on what I was supposed to be doing and had made a mess.

I felt a heavy hand fall on my shoulder and I looked up at him in exasperation. He was grinning at me and I forgot whatever I was going to say when he reached down and swiped a finger down my nose. It came back covered in white. "You have paint everywhere."

I groaned and got to my feet, looking down at my paint-covered hands. "I know. I'm sorry."

"Don't be. The room is almost done and it was just an accident. The floors haven't been laid yet, so even if you did get some primer on the subfloor it's not a big deal. Okay?"

I didn't really believe him, but I wasn't sure what else to do, so I lifted my shoulders and let them fall uselessly. "Okay."

He took a step closer to me and put his finger under my chin so that I had no choice but to look at that darkening green gaze. "You know what *is* a big deal?"

Without thinking I put my wet hand on the center of his chest and watched as my handprint covered the place where his heart was thudding heavy and strong. He felt so vital and real, like everything I had had my hands on before him was just make-believe.

"What?" My voice came out more of a whisper than anything else.

"We hung out, I bought you dinner, we talked about our families and shit. We shared. This was a date, Sayer. Maybe not the best first date ever but it was still a date, so you know what that means."

I did? I was still trying to get my head around the fact that it really had been kind of a date when his head lowered toward mine and my lips tickled as his beard got close enough to brush against them.

"It means we went on a date, so now you should absolutely put your hands on my dick . . . a lot. My gentlemanly tendencies only reach so far and with you they have about reached the end of the line."

I gulped a little. "Oh." That sounded like so many different kinds of dangerous and delicious. I never asked him to be a gentleman, and frankly one of the reasons I was so attracted to him was because he seemed so rugged and untamed by the conventions I was used to and bored to death by.

"Yeah, oh . . . which I fully intend to make you say over and over again while I'm as deep inside of you as I can get."

When his mouth settled over mine, it was an entirely different mess I was suddenly worried about. There was going to be no cleaning up the wreckage that was going to be left of my heart and body when this man was done with me and that felt entirely like a great big deal even though I was helpless to stop it. It was one mess I intended to embrace and not apologize for even if that went against everything I had ingrained deep down within the very core of me.

CHAPTER 8

Zeb

The primer splattered all over the tarp on the floor was a minor catastrophe compared to the tragedy I saw brewing in Sayer's eyes. I wasn't going to give her time to think about what I was doing, about what we were doing.

I also wasn't going to give the nagging voice in the back of my head that told me that I needed to finesse her, needed to handle her with kid gloves, the chance to get louder than the blood roaring in my ears.

When her back hit the wall and some of the wet primer smudged away with the impact, it became crystal clear why I had ordered the wrong color for the walls in the first place. The bright, blinding blue on them peeking back at me over her head matched perfectly the ocean-colored gaze that was locked on mine and filled with a thousand questions.

I couldn't stop thinking about her. It didn't matter how pressing, or how complicated the other stuff in my life was at the moment, Sayer occupied most of my waking and sleeping hours. The way she frosted over like an ice storm, and then thawed out like a warm spring day the moment I touched her, tore at me. I was caught up in the tempest of this woman and I was in no hurry to get myself free of her.

After my first visit with Hyde, she'd created an obvious emotional distance between us, and as frustrated as that made me, I really wasn't sure how to broach the subject without seeming like my priorities were all screwed up. I wanted my son more than anything. The need to have him with me, to be the one to care for him, was bordering on obsessive, but that didn't make the want and the need I had for her any less. I wanted them both and I wasn't sure how to go about telling her that without seeming greedy, so I let her drift off like a storm cloud. I let her put on her professional mask that seemed shatterproof, and I told myself I could tackle my attraction to the pretty lawyer after I had my kid in my home, where he belonged. I didn't like it, but we had been dancing around one another for months and months now, so I figured a little more time and patience wouldn't kill me. I was wrong.

We were covered in paint, but Sayer didn't protest. Instead she kissed me back and tunneled her fingers in the shaggy hair at the back of my neck, for sure leaving a trail of white paint all over me, while I continued to eat at her mouth and pressed my bare chest into hers. The thin cotton of her top did little to keep the points of her lush breasts from rubbing across my skin, and I knew that even though she deserved a four-poster bed and silk sheets, she was about to get rough and raw up against a wall. I had told her we could do better, but now I wasn't so sure, because as she whimpered into my mouth as I started to pull on the edge of her top, I couldn't remember anything ever being more amazing or all-consuming than even this simple touch with her.

I wasn't nearly as covered in the white primer as she was. I had the drying spot on my arm where she hit me with the roller and a few spots on the back of my hands and across my chest where she had touched me, so I was careful when I started to pull her top off not to get any more of the stuff on me. I wanted to touch her—*everywhere*—and that meant I needed to keep my hands as clean as possible.

When I pulled back from her hungry mouth our eyes locked as the stretchy and tight material cleared the top of her blond head. I sucked in a breath because she was so pretty and perfect she almost didn't seem real. Girls like her, with wide blue eyes, a perfect pink blush, skin softer than a flower petal, and a set of breasts topped with the sweetest, perkiest pink nipples weren't for guys like me . . . at least not normally. She was even more flawless seminaked, ruffled up, and flushed than she was in her power suits with her professional cloak firmly in place. I was careful not to break delicate things that I knew would cost a fortune to replace. I knew just how to handle them . . . and how to handle her if the way she moaned and pulled at me with impatient hands was any indication.

I grinned at her as her fingers tightened in my hair. I bent my head so that I could nip at the curve of her jaw and lifted my hands so that I could brush the pads of my thumbs over the crest of both straining tips. "Do you have any idea how badly I wanted to taste these the last time I was this close to you? I bet they're as sweet as they look."

Her eyelids fluttered a little and I saw her bite down on her bottom lip. She shivered in my grasp and I could see that indecision that was so weighty start to creep into her eyes as she watched me. Her chest rose and fell against my own, which had my dick kicking painfully behind my zipper. I wasn't going to let her doubt interfere with what had been so long coming, so I dropped my head and pulled one stiff peak into my mouth. She was tall, even in her running shoes, and I couldn't remember any other time I had lined up with anyone else quite as well. I still had to bend down, but the new position meant I could pull her hips tightly into mine and that there was room to work one of my hands under the elastic top of her workout pants.

She moaned and I heard her head thunk back against the wall as I gripped her naked backside and ground my erection against her soft center. I was happy to find that there was nothing, not a single stitch of clothing, between my questing fingers and her baby-soft skin.

I brushed my beard softly across her chest and scraped the edge of my teeth lightly over the velvety nipple I had trapped between my lips. "No underwear?" To say I was surprised was an understatement. She seemed far more proper and buttoned up than that. I let my fingers glide over the firm swell of her ass and then danced them around the front under the stretchy fabric. I wanted to give a little cheer of victory when she moved her leg to the side to give me more room. She had to know where my final destination was and she was all but giving me the green light to keep going.

I moved my mouth to the other breast and her hands fell from my hair to my shoulders. Her fingernails bit into the taut skin there and she was breathless when she replied. "I wasn't planning on anyone finding that out. I couldn't find anything else to wear that seemed suitable. I don't keep things around that I can ruin, because I never really get dirty."

She was wrong about that. She was about to get all kinds of dirty, and not just because she was covered in paint.

"Getting dirty is fun, Sayer." I put my mouth on the pulse that was fluttering like a trapped bird on the side of her neck. I let my teeth sink into it at the same time as my exploring fingers found that hot, damp place between her legs. I leaned in closer to her and her entire body jerked as I slid my fingers through her slick outer folds. Not only did the woman look flawless, she felt that way, too. Silky, hot, slippery, and smooth. She was made up of all kinds of tempting things I couldn't wait to feel around more than just my fingers.

She gasped my name and I heard the question in it. There was no answer I could give her other than that this was bound to happen, so I just moved my head up to kiss her again and let my fingers slip all the way inside her grasping body. It was a hold I never wanted to pull away from.

I ravaged her mouth, knowing my facial hair was again going to leave its mark. I pulled her leg up around my hip so I could go deeper, feel more of her around me as she throbbed and pulsed in time with our synchronized heartbeats. I rubbed my chest against hers and sighed into her mouth when I felt her hands start a quest of their own.

Her touch was featherlight, barely touching my skin as she worked her palms over the tattoos on my pecs, down across my ribs, pausing a second to rub across my tense abdomen, and then tentatively hitting my belt buckle. My cock strained against the denim and metal of my zipper, but since my hands were otherwise occupied, it was up to her to set it free and move this from dirty to downright filthy.

To encourage her I put my thumb on her clit and pressed

down hard. When she gasped into my mouth and her whole body jerked, I grinned in satisfaction as she started to work on my buckle. Her inner walls were quivering around my fingers and she was lava hot. Her breathing was getting more and more jagged, so I kept up the pressure on that little center of pleasure right at the heart of her until she had my pants all the way undone and was working on pulling them down and out of the way. She was getting all liquid and pliable around my twisting fingers and her breath was starting to come in short, choppy pants against the side of my neck. She was so close to the edge, but I wanted to be inside of her when she went over. I wanted all of that pretty perfection wrapped up tightly around me and hammering against me.

She was reaching for my dick, but I pulled my hand out of her body and out of her pants and caught it in my own. While I liked the slide of her paint-covered palm across my chest, if she got that shit on my cock it was going to be game over, and if that happened I knew there was a chance I was never going to be able to have her like this again. Once I was in, she was going to have a much harder time pulling on that goddamn mask of hers when she was around me because I had already seen all the kind, thoughtful, passionate things she was trying to hide underneath it. Maybe it was selfish to want her with the same desperation that I needed her for other things in my life, but she wanted me just as bad and I knew I could make her need me, too.

"That's a different kind of dirty than I'm after, doll." I leaned forward so that the entire lengths of our bodies were pressed together and my dick was trapped against the soft skin of her stomach. I felt a drop of moisture bead up at the tip and she must have felt it, too, because her eyes went wide in her face. I put her trapped hands on the wall over her head and leaned down so I could whisper in her ear, "In the next minute your pants are coming off, my dick is coming all the way out, I'm getting suited up, and then I'm going to be so deep inside of you that all those fears, all that hesitation you're watching me through, won't have any room to fit. There's only going to be room for me and the way we feel when we're together."

Her pale eyelashes fluttered a little bit and some of that bright flush that had filled her cheeks disappeared. I could see her brain starting to work again, starting to tell her all the things I was refusing to listen to behind my own rampaging desire. We both knew she deserved better than a hard fuck up against the wall, but knowing and doing were two separate things and it was well past time I started the doing with this complicated and irresistible woman.

"That wasn't a warning, Sayer. That was a promise." She opened her mouth to say something back to me but I knew I wasn't going to like whatever it was, so I bent forward to kiss her again and used the hand that wasn't keeping her hands trapped to dig my wallet out and find the condom that had been languishing away in there since the first time I saw her. It took some teeth to get the wrapper open and some patience to get my jeans down while putting the latex in place with one hand. I was afraid if I gave her too much time to analyze, she'd bolt, so I worked quickly as I kept her pinned to the wall with my body.

Since our height similarity had all the best and needy parts of our bodies all lined up and rubbing together nicely, I decided to take advantage of the situation and gently nudged her around so that she was facing the wall like I was going to strip-search her and frisk her. She had her hands flat and slightly above her head as I stepped up behind her. She looked over her shoulder at me with a lifted eyebrow and now the curiosity in her gaze was more heated and less terrified. I smiled at her as the impeccably heart-shaped curve of her backside was bared and filled my hands. She was so soft and yet there was strength there as I ran my hand up the slight bow of her spine and wrapped the rope of her braid around my hand. I pulled her head back a little as I kissed her shoulder and worked my way up to her mouth. I had to pull her hips back and bend her over slightly so I could get the tip of my now aching erection lined up with her slick opening.

I moved my hips just the slightest bit to drag my hardness through her soft folds. It made both of us groan and I felt tremors start in her legs and it made my gut go tight.

"You ready for me?"

Her eyes drifted closed and she turned her head back around so that she was facing the wall away from me. She dropped her forehead so that it was resting on the back of her stacked hands and whispered, "I don't think I could ever be ready for you."

I knew she was talking about more than the thick slide of my body into hers. I also knew the catch in her breath had as much to do with that innate hesitancy she had around me and the pull that vibrated between us as it did with the way I filled her all the way up. Her body clenched around mine in a squeeze that made my balls ache. I blew out a long breath and pushed into her until my front was resting against the elegant bend of her back even though it had white paint smeared all across it. I buried my face in the curve where her neck met her shoulder, wrapped my hands around her rib cage so I could fill my palms with the heavy swell of her breasts, and started to move.

There was no other girl I could have this way. No other girl that fit me, matched me, lined up with me like that's what she had been put on this earth to do. There was no other girl that not only moved with me, but moved *on* me in the most perfect back-and-forth that had ever been created. I could feel every stretched-out inch of her from the inside out, could feel the heat and the friction we generated, and every time her heart beat or her lips let out a whimper of delight I felt it all along my pistoning cock.

She burned on me and I thrust in and out, in and out. She fluttered across me as I tried to catch my breath and to appreciate the beauty of the moment. I'd never had much, but what I did have I cherished and took excellent care of. Sayer fell firmly into that category. She was like the best treasure, the greatest gift I had ever been handed, and I absolutely planned on appreciating every single part of her.

She said my name again and turned around to look at me and the blue in her eyes was so bright it felt like it could light up the entire room. I grunted as her body pulled on mine, and captured both of her nipples between my fingers. I tugged on them harder than I probably should have, but it made her bite her bottom lip, which of course made me want to bite her bottom lip. I was inside of her as deep as I could go and I knew things weren't going to last much longer for either of us.

It was my turn to say her name on a broken sound as I smoothed a hand down across her belly and aimed right for the honeyed spot between her legs. She was drenched and opened wide to accommodate the insistent length that was pounding in and out of her. I found that hot button of pleasure and started rubbing firm circles around and around with my index finger. I made her entire frame tighten up and the walls inside of her that were milking my dick in the sexiest of caresses clamp down and hold tight. The drag and pull in and out of her as she locked up in pleasure made my blood thunder and my balls draw up tight.

I kissed her on the back of the neck, continued to hammer into her, and moved my lips to the delicate shell of her ear so that I could tell her, "I changed my mind. This is the greatest date that has ever happened in all of time."

She let out a gasp that could have been a laugh but in the next instant she went loose and liquid all around me. She threw her head back so hard that I had to jerk back to avoid getting a broken nose, and one of her hands clamped down on my wrist as she continued to come all across my cock and fingers. Watching how beautifully she broke apart for me was enough to have me letting go and slipping over the edge of completion myself. Everything I felt for this girl rushed out of me so fast and hard that I was barely able to stay on my feet once it was all said and done.

We were both panting, sweaty, stuck together, and covered in sex and paint. I'd never seen such a lovely mess, one I never wanted to clean up.

When I pulled out of her she immediately pulled her pants back up and turned around so that she was leaning with her back against the wall. She had white streaks on her naked breasts and flecks of paint on her flushed face. Her eyes darted around like she was looking for the shirt I had long ago discarded, and when she didn't immediately see it she heaved a huge sigh and sort of wilted and folded herself down the wall until she was sitting with her back against it. Behind her was a clear imprint of a female body, including where her hands had been left in the wet paint. Damn if I wasn't going to hate covering that up before the crew showed up in the morning. It was proof that this was all real and not the best dream I had ever had.

I turned away so I could get the condom off and situated myself back in my jeans. I found my shirt where I had tossed it earlier and hers where I had literally chucked it across the room. I handed her the flimsy item of clothing and then sank down on the floor next to her. Some of the primer she had spilled had dried up, but most of it was still in a puddle on the tarp, which immediately soaked into my jeans.

I looked at her out of the corner of my eye and could see the wheels turning in her head. She was thinking again.

"Sayer. This has been headed straight for us since the beginning." I leaned over so I could bump her shoulder with mine. She pulled her braid out from where it was trapped behind her and fiddled with the ends of it.

"I usually try to avoid impending disaster, Zeb. I'm a problem solver, not a trouble maker. I'm supposed to be helping you make your life better and helping you get what you want, not making it more complicated."

I sighed. "We are not a problem and this isn't trouble. How can you not think the way we are together doesn't make both our lives better? Are you really going to tell me that wasn't the best sex you've ever had?"

She threw her head back so that it hit the wall with a thud. "*We* might not be a problem, but I sure as hell am. I need to go." She climbed to her feet and made a face when her shoes swished in the spilled primer. "I'll see you in my office before court on Monday."

I ground my teeth together when she purposely didn't respond to my question about the sex. She might not want to admit out loud how amazing we were together but the evidence was all over—the red marks on her skin, the bite marks on her neck, and the nail marks she had left on my shoulders.

I grabbed her hand as she started to walk away from where I was still sitting. "You can put the lawyer mask on and tie it on as tight as it'll go, but I know what's under it, Sayer, and even if I didn't, I still would've had you up against the wall. You are more than one thing to me and I want all of them."

She looked down at my hand; it was the one that had a skull tattooed on the back of it with a set of screwdrivers underneath for the crossbones. Her eyes flicked back up to mine and I could clearly see the storm clouds hovering over the sea. I didn't want to let her go, we needed to talk about this, about what was going on between the two of us, but I could see if I pushed her she was going to break apart and I didn't want that. She was strong and resilient, and I was just starting to get hints of why she had to be that way. The more she opened up about her past the more I understood why she shut down and pulled away when I asked her about it. I didn't want to be the thing that made her shatter. She might be a problem solver but I was Mr. Fixit. I didn't break things, I repaired them.

So quietly I almost didn't hear her she told me, "I'll see you before court." She shook off my hold and was gone before I could get to my feet.

When I did get up it was to turn around and stare aimlessly at the impression her body had left on my wall.

The woman was good at leaving an impression, on more than just my wall. I think my heart was starting to have a Sayer-shaped spot in it and I wasn't entirely sure how to feel about that given the current chaotic state of my life.

CHAPTER 9

Sayer

I couldn't remember a single time in my life when I had forgotten to be me as thoroughly as I did the moment Zeb touched me. There was no second guessing, no worrying about the outcome and inevitable fallout of handing everything over to him. There was only the moment and being consumed by all the feelings and emotions that he brought to life in it. It was enough to get lost in, enough to blur common sense and a lifetime of warnings about what happened when you opened the door to those kinds of attachments.

When he handled me, moved me, invaded my mind and body, there wasn't room for doubt, fear, or anything else. He took up too much space and the way he made me feel, the way we felt together, was so much bigger and more expansive than all the other things that typically filled me up. There was no room to worry about what would happen after, to think about the fact that I was spread out naked and exposed, revealing any and every flaw I had to him. He was everywhere, took all the accessible air and capacity my body had to give him. All I could do was respond and melt in his skilled hands and across his insistent heat.

Sex had always been a chore, something I had to get through to make whoever my partner was happy. It was what was expected, so I complied. I instinctively knew it wasn't going to be that way with Zeb. Even in my dreams, sex with him was explosive, unforgettable, and intense . . . but dream sex didn't hold a candle to real sex with him. Real sex with him was transformative and wholly terrifying. His touch made me feel like a different woman, a desirable woman, a fascinating and intriguing woman with so much more to offer him than my skills in the courtroom. It made me want to let the reins slip on all those emotions I kept such a tight hold on.

I couldn't handle feeling so out of control, so absorbed in the emotions and passion that he brought out with nothing more than the brush of callused fingers and the touch of soft lips surrounded by rougher facial hair on my skin. It terrified me, the swell of feelings, the rush of desire toward him, toward us together, so I ran like a coward.

I wanted nothing more than to collapse in a heap in my walk-in shower when I got home. I still had paint all over me and there was no mistaking the large handprints that were smeared across my skin in places. It was a visual reminder that I had royally screwed things up and needed to figure out a way to put them back to rights as quickly as possible. Unfortunately, as soon as I came through the front door, Poppy was waiting for me and couldn't wait to tell me all about her adventure out with Rowdy. Apparently it had all gone so well that when my brother asked her to accompany Salem and him on a quick weekend getaway to the trendy ski town of Breckenridge, she had agreed to go.

I plastered a stiff smile on my face and told her how proud I was of her and the steps she was taking. Admittedly my mind was elsewhere—namely up against a wall with a big, tattooed body covering it—so I missed it when she asked me to go with her. I must have blindly agreed because the next thing I knew I was embraced in a warm hug, which I returned with tears in my eyes. Poppy had been living with me for months and I could count the number of times she touched me on one hand with most of my fingers left over. I didn't have the time or the desire to go to the mountains for the weekend, but if it made her happy I could get on board with the spur-of-the-moment vacation.

That was another thing I would never have been willing to do in my life before Denver. Spontaneously leaving town to spend time with people who loved me and cared about me was such a foreign concept. Almost as foreign as having the best sex of my life up against a wall with a guy covered in tattoos and paint. I didn't recognize the parts of me that were changing now that I had a new life, and that made me nervous. It felt like the new parts that had been unleashed were all about being spontaneous and out of control. It felt like every risk that was presented was worth taking and that any repercussions were incidental. I hated that. I knew that repercussions could kill.

When I finally did make it to the shower an hour or so later, it was much more difficult to scrub him off my skin than I thought it would be. I had fingerprints and tiny little abrasions from his beard all over my chest and across my shoulders and neck. I could still feel him all over me and it made that place between my legs that had been focused on him from the get-go feel all achy and needy. I was used to the hollow feeling of desire that nagged at me when I thought about Zeb; what made me slightly frantic and almost violent as I tried to wash him away was the lingering pulse that throbbed in my chest, low and insistent, right where my heart was at.

I could work through wanting Zeb on a physical level, could handle being attracted to him in all his masculine and unrefined sexiness. There was no getting around the fact we had a physical attraction happening no matter how ill-advised it might be. What made me want to turn tail and run back to Seattle was the idea that I wanted more. I didn't want to want more. I didn't want my heart to trip over itself when I watched him with Hyde. I didn't want to feel scrambled and out of sync every time he called to talk to me or anytime I had to be in the same room with him. I didn't want to compare every other man I saw to Zebulon Fuller and find them lacking because, come on! Who could really compare to all that brawn, beauty, and genuineness?

Zeb was too vibrant, passionate, and real to allow for anything other than an equal give-and-take. When he realized how dead on the inside and untouchable I was, he was going to have no choice but to walk away from me because he deserved someone who *could* give him everything and more. I had a feeling that watching him walk away would shatter my poor, brittle, and underused heart into a million, irreparable pieces. I really, really didn't want that. With Rowdy's help I had just started letting the rusty thing work again after so many years of keeping it shut off.

Of course, I suffered through a sleepless night and was less than enthusiastic when Rowdy and Salem showed up to pick Poppy and me up on Saturday morning. Rowdy nudged me with his elbow when I stopped by the trunk to toss my weekender bag inside and looked at me with lifted eyebrows.

"Everything okay? You seem pretty quiet this morning."

I helped him shut the lift gate and leaned a hip against the bumper of his SUV. There was no one else on the planet I would rather talk to than my little brother, but considering that everything that had me all twisted up revolved around one of his closest friends, I wasn't sure how much to share. Old fears that he might judge me, or look down on me for my recent choices, raised their ugly head and made me stiffen next to him. Rowdy had never been anything but accepting and loving toward me after the awkwardness of our first meeting was out of the way. But the thought of someone else I loved, someone else who was supposed to love me, finding fault in me and my actions was almost crippling.

"Just worried about court on Monday. I care about all of my clients and their cases, but it's a little different when it's someone you know on a personal level as well." I did what I always did when I felt my feelings start to slip. I slapped on my professional mask and locked everything down in a deep, dark place where no one, not even me, could touch it.

A crooked grin pulled at his mouth as he clapped me on the shoulder. "Don't worry. You're the best, so everything will work out the way it's supposed to."

He was always so optimistic, so go with the flow. It was an inherent difference in our personalities and it always made me slightly envious that, even though his childhood hadn't been any kind of picnic in the park, he still had escaped the soul-crushing existence of living under my father's roof.

"I hope so. I don't think I can even beginning to wrap my head around failing Zeb or that little boy. You should see them together, Rowdy. They belong together."

He started to move around the side of the car and I followed suit. He looked back at me over his shoulder and his expression was knowing. "Then you'll make sure they end up together, Sayer. That's all there is to it."

If only it was that simple. I let the subject drop and climbed into the backseat so I could sit next to Poppy. She was chattering on and on to Salem about something from when they were younger, so I dug my phone out of my purse and couldn't decide if I was relieved or crushed that there were no missed calls or messages from a certain bearded contractor.

Swearing under my breath, I turned the device off and put it back in my purse. When I lifted my head back up I noticed Rowdy's gaze, the exact same blue as my own, watching me intently in the rearview mirror. Salem had also turned her head to the side and was looking at me curiously. To complete my humiliation, Poppy was also gazing at me with curiosity bright in her tawny-colored eyes.

"What?" I know I sounded surly, but I couldn't help it.

"Why don't you tell us what?" There was humor in my brother's voice, so I did the only adult and mature thing I could think of and kicked the back of his seat. He grunted at me, which had the Cruz sisters laughing at us.

"It's a work thing." I grumbled the lie out and Poppy laughed softly at me.

"Sure it is. Just like you coming home covered in paint last night was a work thing." I frowned at her and slumped down in my seat.

"That was work. Not my work exactly, but still work." At least it had been until I ended up naked and fucked. I sighed a little. I'd never ever actually been *fucked* before Zeb. Seattle Sayer had never dated men that were the kind to fuck, and again I could kick her for all that she had missed out on. I sure as hell had never had sex up against a freshly painted wall with my ass sticking up in the air and now I knew what I was missing.

I wanted to be numb to it all. Wanted to chalk it up to raging hormones that had hummed around Zeb since the beginning. I wanted to be detached and calm so that I could tell him it was a mistake that we shouldn't make again. I wasn't any of those things.

Nope, despite my best effort to keep a lid on them, my feelings, where Zeb Fuller was concerned, were leaking out through every crack they could find in my icy exterior. They were oozing, flowing, liquid, and as hot as lava all over me.

I was heated up and flushed thinking about it and annoyed that he had seen all of me on display and I had gotten only a fleeting glimpse of his wide, tattooed chest, his narrow hips, and the line of dark hair that dusted below his belly button and pointed right at his cock. That was something else I wanted to see. He felt *huge* but I wanted to touch it, put my hands and mouth on it, and see if my impression was correct or if it had just been the position he had me in. I wanted to know him inside and out the way it felt like he now knew me. All the guys before him had been careful, deliberate . . . boring. Just like I was. They didn't *fuck* and neither did I . . . well, neither did I before last night. Another new part of me to be terrified of and that I needed to try and control before she got me into trouble.

I sighed and fought the urge to fan myself with my hand. I was supposed to be working on forgetting about last night, not reliving every caress, imagining every growled sound of satisfaction over and over again. Working my way out of this problem was proving to be particularly difficult and it was putting me in a bad mood. I'd spent a lifetime having no moods and here I was turning into a basket case because of a boy. My father's scorn would have whipped across me like a thousand lashes if he could have seen me now.

I wondered if Rowdy could tell because I saw him exchange a look with his beautiful girlfriend and then he dipped his chin down in a little nod at whatever unspoken communication passed between the two of them. That kind of connection, that tie to another person, seemed so dangerous to me that it made my heart squeeze painfully tight in my chest. They could hurt one another with such ease.

"No work this weekend. We wanted everyone to get together so that we could all celebrate." Salem's voice was husky with emotion, so I sat up straighter in my seat and looked between her and Poppy.

"Celebrate what?" I assumed it was the fact that Poppy was out and about in the world, well on her way to reclaiming her life as her own, but the spark in Salem's dark eyes and the tender way Rowdy reached over to put his hand on her leg spoke to something larger than that. I felt my mouth fall open and my hands clapped together as soon as the words "We're having a baby" came out of her scarlet-painted mouth.

"I knew it!" I leaned as far forward as my seat belt would allow to try to hug her, and settled for smacking Rowdy on the shoulder so he didn't wreck the car if I strangled him in my excitement. "I knew it was coming and I'm so excited for you guys."

I looked over at Poppy and felt the smile on my face dull slightly at how pale and panicked she looked as she huddled in the corner. I reached out a hand and immediately pulled it away when she flinched. "It's great news, right, Poppy? We're going to be aunties!" I loved kids. Loved their innocence and joy. I loved that for the most part they hadn't been tainted by the atrocities the world could level at them. It was part of the reason I went into family law against my father's very clear wishes. Kids who didn't have the luxury of being innocent didn't have a shot because the adults around them were twisted and broken. Those kids needed someone to fight for them. They needed an advocate . . . just like I had when I was little and alone with a mentally unstable mother and an emotionally unavailable father. I had no one, so I was going to be that someone whenever I could for any child who came my way.

The young woman nodded woodenly and I could see the sadness start to engulf the joy in Salem's midnight-colored eyes as she watched her sister's reaction to the happy news.

"Poppy . . ." Poppy jerked at the sound of her name and I watched her gulp a few times and suck in a few deep breaths. She put a shaky hand on her chest and looked away from her sister so that she was staring right at me instead.

"It's okay. I'm okay. I just need a minute." A tumultuous smile moved across her stiff mouth. "I'm happy for you, I really am. It's just a big change and it reminds me of . . ." She trailed off and Salem gave a stiff nod.

"I knew it was going to be a little rough for you to hear. That's why Rowdy and I wanted to do it with just the family and someplace that wasn't tied to any bad memories. I know you're happy for us, Poppy, even if it hurts you to feel that way."

Poppy could only nod stiffly and I watched her drift back inside herself and the memories that weighed her down, which was heartbreaking considering how far she had come in the last few months. I didn't know every single detail of Poppy's past

beyond the abuse, abduction, and extremely violent and physical end to her own personal nightmare at the hands of her ex-
husband. From her reaction to Rowdy and Salem's news, there
must have been other tragic chapters to her story that I wasn't
aware of. It made the fact that she was making so much progress
even more impressive and the fact that she had shut back down
and folded in on herself once again that much sadder.

We made the rest of the trip in relative silence. I decided it
was for the best to let Poppy work through what she was thinking and feeling on her own while Salem and Rowdy carried on
a low-voiced conversation in the front of the vehicle. Feeling the
oppression of everyone else's emotions made my skin too tight
and the air in the car thick and heavy. I turned my phone back
on and gave an audible sigh because even though I didn't want
to feel, I did, and I was relieved that there was a missed text message from Zeb on the screen. All it said was:

See you on Monday.

But it was enough to loosen the tightness in my chest and to
have the air trapped in my lungs moving more freely.

I couldn't decide what to send back to him. Everything I
thought of seemed too personal, too involved, so I decided on:

Yes you will.

I left it at that and focused on spending the weekend with my
family and appreciating the fact that we were growing and getting more people to love and protect. It took Poppy the rest of
the ride, checking into the swanky hotel and spa, getting settled
into the room we were sharing, to break free from the zombie-
like state she had been in.

Once we were alone in the room she sank to the edge of the
bed, looked me dead in the eye, and told me about the baby she

had lost when she was just a teenager. I knew she and Rowdy had been close when they were younger, but I hadn't known my brother fancied himself in love with the wrong Cruz sister for most of his youth. He was so convinced that Poppy was the one that he followed her to college and then had lost his scholarship when he attacked the father of Poppy's unborn baby because the guy had hurt her and caused her to miscarry. After Rowdy left her and school, she moved back home to her parents because she was alone and afraid, which then ultimately led to her ending up in the abusive hands of her ex. The poor thing had been abused by more than one man who claimed to love her, which made her hesitation around the opposite sex all the more clear to me as the words came pouring out of her.

It all came out in a rush that was flavored with hiccuping sobs and a torrent of tears. I knew she was shaken up when I sat next to her on the bed and she actually allowed me to put my arm around her shoulders and comfort her. I wanted to cry, too, but instead I made soothing noises and told her everything would be all right. I offered comfort to my clients in a professional capacity all the time. This was the first time in my life I wanted to open myself up and offer comfort and reassurance on a personal level. I wanted her to know I was there for her beyond a roof over her head and a safe place to stay. I wanted her to know I cared, and that stunned me so much that we were both shaking as we huddled together and let our emotions run their course.

I wasn't sure how long we stayed like that, but when it was all out of her she pushed her caramel-colored hair out of her face, took a deep breath, and told me she needed to get cleaned up so she could go and tell Rowdy and Salem she really was happy for them. I nodded and took a minute to get myself back under control.

Poppy seemed weak and fragile on the outside, but she never stopped fighting, never gave up when all the bad things from the past tried to drag her down. She felt everything so fully, so intensely, that it paralyzed her with the force of it and I had to admire that. Instead of dealing with the entanglements and thorns that pricked at me from before, I denied feeling anything. I shut myself down and closed myself off so that there wasn't the kind of pain Poppy was dealing with. She was a thousand times stronger than I would ever be.

Rowdy and I decided to leave Poppy and Salem alone to have a heart-to-heart, which meant we ended up in the bar with a couple of frosty craft beers and some tortilla chips and green chili in front of us. It took exactly five minutes of small talk before Rowdy laid into me about what was really going on with Zeb.

"So you want to tell me what's really up with you and Paul Bunyan? I mean I know you're helping him out with his kid but there's more going on there, isn't there?"

I snapped a chip in half with my teeth and narrowed my eyes at him, and only partly because he called Zeb by such a ridiculous nickname. Sure the guy was big and looked like he could fell an entire forest with one swing of his ax, but he was far too handsome and far too well-spoken to get saddled with the silly moniker. "What makes you say that?"

"Besides the fact that you were checking your phone every five minutes in the car, how about when I called him last night to see if he wanted to go get a beer at the Bar and he told me he couldn't because you were coming over to help him work on his latest flip. You aren't exactly handy, Sayer. You had to call me to come hang all the pictures and curtains up in your house when he was finished with the remodel, so that tells me 'work' probably means something else."

I groaned a little and picked up my beer. "I don't know what I'm doing or what any of it means. I'm deeply invested in helping Zeb get full custody of his son and that's all it should be. Anything else involving me and him is a terrible idea. Honestly, I have no clue what to do with him outside of the courtroom, so I'm pretending nothing is going on in between bouts of throwing myself at him and running away."

He snorted at me and picked up his own beer. "How's that working out for you?"

I scowled because there was humor laced liberally through his tone. "Not very well."

"Because it's been brewing from the very beginning. Zeb has been interested in you since day one; it just took you a while to recognize it. Once you did there was no way in hell that he was going to let you ignore it."

Oh, Zeb had no idea how good I was at ignoring things. I was a master at denying I felt anything. It was my second greatest skill next to practicing law. He wasn't going to get a choice in the matter if I really put my mind to pretending nothing was going on between the two of us.

I tucked some of my hair behind my ears and looked at Rowdy unwaveringly. "I'm not good with passionate people, Rowdy. I don't know how to deal with someone who acts on what they feel, or how to handle someone who takes what they want with no regard for the risks. The fact that he jumped both feet in with Hyde even before knowing if the kid was his petrifies me. That kind of investment in another person, that level of unconditional love . . ." I shook my head sadly. "I don't think I'm wired to return those kinds of feelings, and that will ultimately lead to a disaster. Someone will end up getting hurt and I lived with enough hurt when I was younger to last a million lifetimes. I don't have room inside for anything else, which means I'm immune to all the things he stirs up, and that isn't fair to him. He should have someone who is just as passionate and invested as he is."

His eyes that were an identical match to my own widened and he set his beer down on the table with a thunk. He leaned closer to me and bit out, "That's bullshit, Sayer. It's utter bullshit and you know it."

I blinked in surprise at the vehemence in his tone. It went completely against his laid-back personality to get so heated, especially at me. "Why do you say that?"

"Because as soon as you found out about me you dropped everything and moved your life here. You had no idea how I would react, if I was a nice guy or a complete asshole, and yet you took that leap blindly. You didn't know a thing about me or my life and yet you were determined to be my family even when I acted like a dipshit when we first met."

I sucked in a sharp breath and sat back in my chair a little bit as his words sank in. He wasn't finished leveling the hard and uncomfortable truth as he saw it at me, though.

"Then you helped Asa out for me without blinking an eye. That fancy-ass lawyer friend of yours wouldn't have even looked at his case if it wasn't for you, and then not even a month later you took in a stranger. You moved a scared, broken girl into your home simply because I love her. You have done more for Poppy than either Salem or I have been able to do, so don't try and tell me you don't invest in people as passionately or as wholeheartedly as Zeb does because it's bullshit."

I couldn't think of a valid rebuttal, which annoyed me to no end, so I sat back in my chair and glared at him. "Are you sure you didn't take any law classes while you were in college?"

He wiggled his eyebrows up and down at me in his usual cavalier way, and I fought the urge to throw a chip at him. Going after Rowdy was the first completely out-of-character thing I had ever done. It was a compulsion, a craving for family and a place to belong and be loved, which was something I never had before. I couldn't resist the pull any more than I could resist the draw and tug of endless attraction between me and Zeb. When I took Poppy in it wasn't just because she was important to Rowdy, and he had become so very important to me . . . no, it was because I saw so much of myself inside the broken shell of the young woman. I knew exactly what it felt like to have someone try to strip you of your value and humanity. I knew all too well what it felt like to never measure up to someone who was supposed to love you unconditionally and yet all they did was tear you down. My father had never been uncouth or out of control enough to raise his hand to me or to my mother . . . but his words and his pitiless, dismissive actions . . . those nasty suckers had fallen just as heavily as the mightiest of blows. Poppy had her whole life ahead of her. I didn't want her stuck in place and stuck unmoving from the past's embrace like I was. I didn't want her to shut off her heart. It was too beautiful and needed to be shared with someone who would cherish it. She deserved that.

"If you don't put yourself out there to risk the hurt, then you won't ever feel the pleasure either. There is no good without the bad, Sayer. Just look at the way I came into this world."

We both got quiet for a second as he sucked in a sharp breath. "My mom was young, too young, when she had me. Your dad was older, knew better, and was married, with you at home when she got knocked up. The only two people that can tell us what actually happened between the two of them are gone, but we both know that whatever the circumstances were, my mom was taken advantage of and left to deal with the consequences on her own."

I gulped a little because I never wanted to admit to him just how manipulative and hateful my father could be. I didn't want to think about the man who had raised me taking advantage of a helpless teenage girl, but it was impossible not to when the proof was sitting across from me sipping a beer.

"Regardless of the hurt my mom may have suffered, she loved me. She took amazing care of me and never let me go a single second without knowing I was loved and the center of her entire world. She focused on the joy I brought her, not on the pain that she had to go through to end up with me in her life. You have to be wounded in order to heal."

Rowdy's mom had been killed during an armed robbery when he was just a little boy, so I was surprised he had such bright and clear memories of her. My mother had killed herself when I was slightly older and yet most of the things I remembered about her were fuzzy and covered in a tint of gray and sorrow. There was no joy and pleasure when I thought about her, only sadness and resentment. I wanted her to be stronger for herself, but more than that I had longed for her to be stronger for me.

"Some wounds go so deep and reach so far down into the basic parts of who we are that they can never be healed, Rowdy. They just bleed, fester, and trickle really nasty stuff out of the person bearing them forever."

He shook his head and I was amazed that the styled front of his hair didn't move so much as an inch. I guess it took a lot of skill and a lot of product to keep that modern-day James Dean look in place.

"You're wrong. You know how I know that you're wrong? Because I used to think the same thing. I had a heart that was broken and, I'd thought, beyond repair. I was hung up on what I thought I always wanted instead of what I actually deserved. The wound might be deep, so deep that you feel it all the way to your bones, and that means you get comfortable with the pain, the hurt becomes familiar, and you don't know what to do without it. But then someone else comes along and sees you suffering and it hurts them to watch you ache within the walls of that pain. Your wound wounds them and you realize really fast that maybe you weren't able to heal the hurt on your own, maybe you are, in fact, immune to how shitty it feels, but for them and with them you work to get better because that person makes you realize that you shouldn't be comfortable or complacent with something that feels awful no matter how used to it you are. It just takes the right person to see it. No one except for Salem was able to put my heart back together and she had to fight to position each and every single piece in the place it was supposed to be. She healed me not only for me but for her as well."

The sentiment was so sweet, so brutally honest about how he felt about his girlfriend, that it made a heavy ball of emotion form in my throat. Mostly to break some of the feelings that were sneaking up on me that I wasn't sure what to do with, I lifted an eyebrow and jokingly asked him, "Aren't you supposed to be doing the brotherly duty thing and warning me away from a guy with a criminal record and a history of sleeping around? Isn't he the last kind of guy who we should be talking about fixing what's broken inside of me?" It was a silly question to ask considering Zeb fixed broken things for a living, but houses weren't people and it would take more than some new paint and refinished floors for the ice that surrounded my insides to fissure and thaw.

"If Zeb is the right guy then he's the right guy and none of that other shit matters. At first when I saw him watching you it made me really uncomfortable, but not because I don't trust him or think he's a good dude. I'd just gotten you and I don't think I was ready to share you with anyone else yet, but now that you're obviously here to stay and I get to keep you forever, I want you to be happy, Sayer."

Deciding to change the subject because I wasn't sure what happiness really looked like or how I went about getting it for myself, with or without Zeb in the picture, I asked him when the baby was due and when they would know if it was a little boy or girl. His excitement over impending fatherhood was contagious. I knew he and Salem would make wonderful parents, and when the sisters joined us a few minutes later, both looking emotionally wrung out but finally at peace with one another, the weekend that was meant to be a celebration finally started.

None of us came from families that taught us to love and to care about others. All of our backgrounds were fractured and cracked. It was a flat-out miracle we had all found one another and through fight and persistence now had a solid foundation of real family and love to rebuild on. My niece or nephew would never know what it felt like to be unwanted or unloved. He or she would never have to worry about living up to unrealistic expectations and being judged harshly for any of the struggles and failures life liked to test us all with. That baby would know what a real family and what a real home was like, and just like that, I felt the edges of that wound I pretended I didn't have, and had told Rowdy would never heal, start to tug themselves closed somewhere deep inside of me.

CHAPTER 10

Zeb

I wasn't this nervous when the cops slapped cuffs on me and hauled me off to lockup.

I wasn't this nervous when the judge issued my sentence and I learned that I was going to be locked up for a minimum of two and a half years of my life.

I wasn't this nervous when my high school girlfriend, who had eventually become my fiancée and then ex-fiancée after I had gone away, told me that she thought she might be knocked up when I was only sixteen. It was a false alarm, one that you would have thought taught me a valuable lesson about birth control, but no, it was another lapse in judgment when it came to women and sex that had me walking into the massive Denver court building with Sayer looking serious and ready to fight tooth and nail at my side.

In fact the only other time I had been this nervous was that first day I got to meet my son. It was overwhelming how important someone I had just met could be and how vital that little boy had become to not only my future but my happiness as well.

Every chance I got to see him I took it. It was tricky scheduling visits around his current foster-care situation and my work schedule, but I did it, and so far I had been fortunate enough to get a few hours each week with the little boy. Every time I saw him he took a bigger chunk of my heart with him when I had to say good-bye, and I could tell he was getting more and more attached to me as well. After our last visit he had wrapped himself around my legs and refused to let go. It took both me and Maria, plus a promise of an extra visit, to talk him into letting go.

The pep talk Sayer had given me for an hour in her office had done little to settle my jangling nerves. She was the perfect mix of feminine and fierce in a black pants suit that was tailored to her long and lean frame perfectly with some kind of pale pink lacy thing poking out behind the lapels, but the more she told me that it was all going to be fine, the less I wanted to believe her. She was trying to be confident and reassuring, but we both knew what was at stake. She kept telling me to answer the judge's questions honestly, that I needed to keep my cool if they asked about my prison sentence, and that I simply needed to show the court how much I wanted to have Hyde in my life. I needed to convince the judge I had what it took to be a father. Over and over again she told me nothing was going to be off-limits, so if I had any skeletons hidden deep in my closet she needed to know. They were going to judge me, my biggest sore spot, but she told me repeatedly they wouldn't find me lacking. It was nice to hear coming from the woman I wanted more than almost anything but it didn't make my nerves any less taut.

Sayer mentioned that she had been before this particular judge in the past and that he was stern but ultimately fair. She told me he was going to grill me about anything and everything and that all I had to do was give him factual and succinct answers. I reminded her that I was an open book and had hidden nothing from her since the beginning. Telling the truth about who I was and where I had been sounded so easy because I never tried to hide it. Declaring all my faults and putting every mistake I had ever made on display in front of the person that would ultimately decide if I should be a father or not amplified every insecurity I had. Sayer tried to tell me over and over that it would all be fine and I wanted to believe her, but I could see that she was just as nervous as I was in the way she couldn't stop fiddling with things in front of her and the way her toes kept tapping under her fancy desk.

All I could do was nod at her and assure her that I understood how much was riding on what happened today and how I presented myself to the judge. For this initial meeting, it was only me and Sayer, plus Maria from CASA, going before the judge. She told me that moving forward she would also plan on involving my mom as well as Beryl in the proceedings if the court needed any kind of character witnesses on my behalf. She was hoping it wasn't going to come to that, but I wasn't so sure. I had cleaned myself up but there was no hiding some of the outward trappings that would always mark me as a man that had done and paid for things that would never make a good impression on anyone. I could have shaved my beard off, put on a suit and tie, found some fancy wing tips, and made a big production about how hard I had worked to turn my life around since getting out of jail, but I decided that I needed to be truthful not only with the court but with myself. There was no getting around my past, it had made me who I was today, and I was proud of that man. That man would take care of his son to the best of his ability, he would love him, and he would care for him and make sure the boy never wanted for anything. I could do all of that whether or not I was clean-shaven and polished up. Plus I liked the way Sayer's eyes roved over me and lit up with a spark of hunger when she saw me. She liked the man I was, too, and if I was good enough for her then I was good enough for the judge. She didn't need me spit-shined, and that made me even more determined to break through those walls she kept stacking back up around herself whenever we spent time apart.

She hadn't brought up the other night, and I figured it wasn't the time or the place to force the issue, so I silently followed her and her fancy, imported sports car across town as we left LoDo and headed toward the courthouse on Capitol Hill. She parked the car and we walked around the massive building toward the front doors. She moved fast on those tall heels she had on, but I didn't mind bringing up the rear because the view was nothing short of heart-stopping. Pulled together and proper might not work on me, but it sure as hell worked on her and there was no end to all the dirty thoughts that raced through my head as I imagined pulling that suit off of her elegant limbs piece by piece.

I let out a grunt as I ran into her back as she suddenly came to a stop. I was too busy checking out her ass to notice that she had stopped moving, so I wrapped an arm around her middle to keep my bulk from knocking her over as I plowed into her. I was going to ask her what the deal was when I noticed a tall blond man in a suit and a young woman with bright pink hair having an argument in the center of the sidewalk. It was kind of a funny sight considering how different the two individuals looked until I realized that was exactly how opposite Sayer and I appeared to anyone on the outside watching the two of us walk toward the building.

Their voices were raised, and the young woman was calling the debonair-looking man every filthy word in the book plus some inventive ones I had never heard before. The guy shook his head as the petite young woman, who I now realized I recognized, took a step forward and poked him in the center of his chest with a finger. The blond man threw his hands up in the air in obvious exasperation before turning in our direction. He knew Sayer, which didn't surprise me at all, everything about the guy screamed litigation and prestige. He made his way over to where we were standing without saying good-bye to his colorful and agitated companion. When he reached us his gaze purposely dropped to where my arm was still wrapped around Sayer. She made a little noise in her throat and stepped out of my hold, which had my hands curling into involuntary fists at my sides. The guy gave me a disinterested once-over and obviously wasn't impressed with what he saw. He turned his full attention to Sayer, effectively dismissing me.

He pushed some of his hair off his forehead and flashed a smile in a toothy, smooth way that made me want to cram my fist in his face and knock every one of his perfectly straight, perfectly white teeth down his throat.

"I thought women liked you. It doesn't look like that one is very fond of you, Quaid." There was quiet humor in her tone, a familiarity between the two of them that grated across my nerves.

The other attorney chuckled. "Yeah, she's one of my more challenging clients without a doubt. She needs to learn to listen to me or she's going to have a rough go at it." His gaze skipped back over to me and I felt my teeth grind together in the back even though I made sure to keep my expression bland. It wouldn't do me any good to beat the man to a bloody pulp steps away from the front doors of the courthouse my first time before the judge who would determine my son's and my future. "She's a pain in my ass and a spoiled brat, but I don't think she deserves to serve hard time. I just did my damnedest to get her charges dismissed."

I lifted my hand and ran my thumb down the edge of my mouth and lifted my eyebrows up. "Avett is a good kid; she just fell in with a shitty crowd. She definitely doesn't deserve to end up in jail for what went down at the Bar. She has a good family that will look out for her. Obviously if they're paying your bill."

The other guy reared back a little and Sayer turned around to look at me with wide eyes. I shrugged. "Avett is Brite Walker's only child. Brite used to own the bar my buddy Asa Cross works at and Avett worked in the kitchen there for a few months. She hooked up with a junkie and somehow ended up driving him to the bar the night he decided to try and rob the place. She got picked up on an accessory charge, and I know Brite freaked out and has been doing everything in his power to keep her out of jail."

Sayer cleared her throat and pointed between the two of us. "Quaid Jackson, this is my client Zeb Fuller."

Her client? That was how she introduced me to the slick bastard in the thousand-dollar duds? It made my spine stiffen as I stuck my hand out. It annoyed me even further that the other lawyer had a firm and all-business handshake. I wanted him to be a weasel, mostly because he looked at Sayer the same way I looked at her . . . fascinated and hungry. He wanted under her fancy pants suit as much as I did.

"I actually handled a case for Asa a couple months back. You keep some very interesting company, don't you, Mr. Fuller." It wasn't really a question, so I didn't bother to answer him. I knew for a fact good people could be found on both sides of the law and that wasn't something I needed to prove to anyone.

Sayer shifted her weight again and let out a small sigh. "I actually know Asa, too. That case turned out to be a setup, didn't it? He's involved with the cop who arrested him now, and I've met Brite several times. He's a lovely man who I'm sure wants nothing more than to help his daughter, which is why you were so highly recommended to him. I'm sure you have her situation well in hand. We really need to head in. It was nice to see you, Quaid."

She turned to look at me over her shoulder and inclined her head toward the big building. I went to step around the other man when he reached out a hand and grasped Sayer's arm. He smiled at her again and I really, really had to fight down the urge to physically remove his hands from her.

"I have a dinner party coming up with the partners in a few months. I was going to call you to see if you wanted to go with me, but since we're both here now I figure it doesn't hurt to throw the invite out in person. I'd love for you to be my date for the event, Sayer."

Oh, the dude so wanted to die. He may have asked Sayer, but he was watching me out of the corner of his eye and I couldn't stop the growl that slipped out. I crossed my arms over my chest and narrowed my own eyes back at him. I wasn't typically one for male posturing, but she had called me her "client" and that still stung.

She shot me a look over her shoulder and I could see how uneasy she was being caught between the two of us. She shifted her weight on her feet and I saw her shake her head just a little bit in the negative.

"No. Thank you for asking but I already told you that I'm not interested in pursuing that kind of relationship with you. I'm sorry, Quaid."

His smile never wavered, but he stopped looking at me and focused on her. "I'm a lawyer, it's my job to try to persuade people to see things my way. I'll see you around." He finally let go of her arm and his attention shifted back to me. "Good luck today."

I bit out a terse thanks and stiffly followed Sayer into the building and through security. We didn't say anything to one another, which was probably for the best. All I wanted to do was ask her how in hell she could call me her client and leave it at that. Was that really how she saw me after everything we had been through together in the last month? It made me want to grab her and fuck some sense into her. I sure as hell wasn't only a client when I was buried deep inside of her and she was whimpering my name over and over again as she came.

The courtroom was uncomfortably familiar, and I told myself not to panic over what had happened last time I put my fate in the hands of the system. This was an entirely different situation, and yet I felt like I had so much more to lose this go-round. Sure, my freedom was valuable and I missed it terribly when it had been taken from me, but that felt like nothing compared to the painful ache that engulfed me when I thought about having to leave my boy in the system. He belonged with me. We belonged together and I needed to believe that the judge would see that and that Sayer would do her thing and make sure everything worked out the way it was supposed to.

We took a seat on one side of the room and I nodded at Maria, who offered me a little smile. I was happy to know the court-appointed advocate seemed to be in my corner; now I just needed to convince the man that entered the room with his black robe billowing behind him after he was announced. I sat back down next to Sayer once he gave the order to proceed and took a deep breath as he looked down at me from his bench over the edge of his wire-rim glasses.

"We're here today to discuss the sole legal and physical custody of the minor child Hyde Bishop, correct?"

Sayer got to her feet and addressed the man that held my entire future in the palm of his hand.

"That is correct. Paternity testing came back proving that Mr. Fuller is the boy's biological parent, and he has been attending court-supervised visitation with the child for the last month. There is no other immediate family and we can't see any reason for the child to remain in foster care when he has a biological parent willing and eager to give him a permanent home."

The judge looked at Sayer in much the same way he looked at me and then flipped through several of the papers that were spread out in front of him on the desk.

"The mother is deceased?"

"Correct."

"And I'm going to assume you have done your due diligence

and looked for family on the mother's side to inquire about caring for the child?"

My jaw tightened and I blew out a heavy breath through my nose. Even if Hyde did have family on the maternal side, they had left the little boy alone and scared in the system for months. They didn't deserve him.

"Yes. The child's mother was estranged from her family and had some problems. Her lifestyle left a rift in the family. The family on the maternal side wasn't interested in taking the boy in. I have the paperwork in the file from my conversations with them."

She looked at me out of the corner of her eye and gave me a small reassuring nod that made some of the bands of tension surrounding my chest loosen.

"Mr. Fuller, how is it that you had no prior knowledge of the child?"

I felt a little bit of heat work up into my neck and was grateful that my beard covered it up. I reminded myself to be honest, no matter how bad it might make me look. I had made mistakes and I needed to own up to that.

"I wasn't in a relationship with his mother. I met her at a particularly difficult time in my life, and we were just two strangers that took solace in one another. I never saw or spoke with her after the one night we spent together. I didn't know about Hyde until after she had passed away. A friend that was concerned about what was happening with him actually tracked me down."

He looked at me over the rim of his glasses again. I broke out in a cold sweat and told myself not to flinch under his steady gaze. I wanted to appear as confident and as steady as I could.

"Is that a common occurrence for you, Mr. Fuller? Do you

often have encounters with women whom you never speak to or see again?"

Sayer stiffened next to me, and I sat up straighter in my seat and met the guy's stare with one of my own. "I've been single since the girl I was engaged to left me. I date, and yes, I have had encounters with other unattached women that didn't last more than one night. However, I was raised by a single mother and have an older sister and I have a ten-year-old niece that I adore. I know how to treat women with respect and reverence, even if it is only for a brief amount of time."

He didn't so much as blink as he returned his attention to the papers in front of him. I gave Sayer a questioning look and she mouthed, "It's okay," before she reached out and gave my leg a little squeeze. That felt like a lot more than an attorney trying to soothe her client.

"Your sister is the reason you found yourself in trouble a few years back, correct?"

I stiffened and nodded. "Yes. She was living with a guy that liked to use her as a punching bag. He went too far with his abuse one night, and I flew off the handle. My sister was hurt so badly that she ended up in the hospital. I attacked him in their apartment, which led to me being arrested and serving a prison sentence."

"I can see that you served a little over two years on the assault charge."

"I did. But I haven't gotten so much as a speeding ticket since I was released."

"I also see that your niece witnessed all of this." It wasn't a question and I saw the corner of his mouth tighten and felt Sayer stiffen next to me.

"She did. I thought she was with her grandmother at the time. I didn't know she was home when I went over to confront my sister's ex. One of the first things I did when I got locked up was enroll in every kind of anger management program they had because I never wanted my niece to see me lose my temper like that again. It scared her and it scared me. I know what I did wasn't right, and I'm sorry every day that Joss has to live with the memory of what I did to her father."

Sayer stood back up. "It's been more than five years since Zeb was released from prison. He subsequently started his own very successful company and stayed on the straight and narrow. There are no other transgressions on his record and he has all the familial support anyone could ask for when planning to be a full-time parent."

"Your client has no other children, and by his own admission is looking at being a single parent, considering that he is currently unattached. Do you understand the kind of commitment you are facing by being the child's sole legal and physical guardian, Mr. Fuller? I'm questioning whether or not the gravity of the situation you are asking the court to weigh in on is clear to you."

Of course it was fucking clear to me. Why else would I sit here and let some stranger pick apart not only my sexual history but the entirety of everything I had screwed up in my life?

"Mr. Fuller is very aware of the seriousness of the situation, Your Honor. He has followed every direction decreed by the court and by the court advocates as he has gotten to know Hyde. He has followed all the rules set out before him, all in pursuit of making sure he had the opportunity to know and raise his son."

The judge looked over to Maria, who was sitting slightly off to the side, and she climbed to her feet and walked up to the podium that was next to the table we were sitting at, and introduced herself for the record. She looked over at me and then back to the judge.

"Hyde is a sweet, smart little boy, Your Honor. He has taken to Mr. Fuller, and it is my opinion that they have bonded in a short amount of time and that the child would indeed be better off in the care of his father than remaining in foster care. Mr. Fuller has shown nothing but compassion and kindness toward his son and it is obvious when you watch him with the child that he is deeply invested in the boy. Mr. Fuller is the kind of parent I wish all the kids who came through my door had. Most of them aren't that lucky, Your Honor."

He asked a few more questions and Sayer walked him through my income for the last couple of years; all of it was tense, and I couldn't tell which way the guy was going to go in his determination. He rose suddenly and told us to take thirty minutes while he went into chambers to review all of those papers he had been moving around on his desk.

Maria walked over and squeezed me on the shoulder and told me good luck and then left me alone with Sayer. She turned to me with a soft smile on her lips and her heart in her eyes. She was proud of the way I had handled the judge's needling and my honest assertion that the only place Hyde needed to be was with me.

"You're doing great."

I sighed and pushed my hands through my hair, messing up the strands I had ruthlessly styled earlier in the day. "It doesn't feel like it. It feels like he's looking for a reason to tell me I can't have my son."

She shook her head and reached out to put her hand on my

leg again. This time I covered it with my own and gave it a squeeze.

"That's his job. He has to poke and prod. He's looking for any sign that you're going to fold or break under the pressure. He's purposely trying to get a reaction out of you. He only has Hyde's best interests in mind, so he doesn't care how uncomfortable or how angry he makes you. He's trying to get an adverse reaction and you aren't giving him one."

"I want to give him something, namely the middle finger. What twenty-five-year-old do you know that hasn't had a one-night stand? I didn't expect him to pick my sex life apart."

She tugged her hand free and sat back in her chair. She bit the corner of her lip and started moving her own papers around. "I never did."

Well, that made me even more uncomfortable and also slightly relieved, because if she was using the word "never," that meant I was absolutely going to get another shot at her and that delectable body. I wanted to tell her I was glad she hadn't been as careless with herself as I was over the years when the judge was announced again and we had to rise back up as he came back into the room.

My palms started to sweat and I shifted nervously in my seat as the man who was about to say the most important words I had ever heard took his own seat on the bench. He took his glasses off and leaned forward on his arms a little bit. He was staring intently at me and it took every ounce of self-control I had not to squirm under his scrutiny.

"Mr. Fuller, I think you have made tremendous strides in setting your life on the right path in the last few years. I do believe your desire to have custody of your son comes from a sincere and genuine place, but that being said, I have some concerns. The child already went through the trauma of losing one parent, and I'm hesitant to hand him over to another one who has proven and documented anger issues. If you lose control of your temper in such a significant manner again, Mr. Fuller, that opens the child up to the possibility of suffering the loss of another parent."

I made an involuntary noise of protest, which had the judge holding up his hand before I could launch into an argument.

"I think some time is needed. Time for Hyde to adjust to you being his father and sole caregiver and time for you to realize how significantly a child is going to change your life. I want you to enroll in a level-two parenting class and agree to further anger management counseling, and then we will move toward full custody of the child. For now I'm going to order that you can have four unsupervised visits a week outside of a CASA location. After the initial four weeks have passed, we can move to four overnight visits in your home for another four weeks. We'll set another court date after the eight weeks have passed to see where we're at, and I would strongly encourage you to look into attending some family counseling with the boy. The transition is going to be trying on you both, but I ultimately think you are the parent the child deserves, Mr. Fuller."

His gavel hammered down on the desk and we all stood up as he left the room. I fell back into my chair and ran my hands roughly over my face. I gazed at Sayer and tried to tell what she was thinking about the ruling, but she seemed coolly stoic and nearly impossible to read.

"Did we win?" I breathed the words out and leaned toward her.

She turned to look at me and like the sun parting through the clouds on a rainy day, her face split in a bright smile. It was so sunny and full of light I had no idea how she could come across as chilly as she often did. She was full of warmth when she let it out. When she showed it, it was so electric and blazing that I just wanted to bask in it.

"It's a lot of work on your part, but yes, the fact that he granted overnight visits right from the get-go is an absolute win. I thought we would be looking at at least six months or more until we reached that point. You were authentic and sincere. He could see how much you love Hyde and that's all that matters. I'm very proud of you, Zeb."

I reached out and caught one of her hands between both of mine. She tugged on it, but I refused to let it go as she looked down at me.

"Thank you. I know I tell you every time I see you, but I really couldn't get through this without you."

Her smile faltered a little, and when she pulled on her hand this time I had to let it go. I climbed to my feet and followed her out of the courtroom and back out onto the busy sidewalk in front of the building, all the while wondering and being increasingly annoyed that she wasn't saying anything to me.

When we reached where she had left her Lexus she pulled the driver's door open and tossed her bag inside while mumbling, "You'd be fine without me, Zeb. You are doing everything you're supposed to be doing, and anyone with eyes can see you'll jump through all the hoops the court might ask you to jump through if it means you end up with full custody. There isn't anyone fighting you for your rights to Hyde, which also makes things a little bit easier to navigate. We have an excellent case. You've got this."

I let a growl slip out from between my teeth at her flippant tone and nonchalant attitude. Everything about her body language and words screamed that she was having this conversation with her *client,* not with *me.*

"No, *we've* got this." I stepped around her door and crowded her into the opening of the car. I put my hands on the roof on either side of her shoulders, caging her between my arms and forcing her to look up at me as she reflexively put her hands on the center of my chest. "No one else would keep me as calm, would tell me to just be honest and myself with the judge, and believe that was enough. No one else would tell the court that I was the best option for Hyde and mean it like you do. No one else in the system cares if that boy ends up with me or not like you, Sayer. I couldn't do this with anyone besides you. It's as much your fight as it is mine and you're lying to yourself if you think any different." No one else simply believed in me like she did. Why couldn't she see how desperately I needed that?

"Zeb . . ." She said my name like she was gearing up for one of her lawyerly rebuttals, and since I refused to have her put more walls and more space between us than she already had, I stopped the protest forming on her lips with my own. I bent my head the few inches I needed to quiet her reservations with my own type of persuasion.

At the first brush of my tongue against the rigid seam of her lips, she stiffened, but it only took a little more probing and leaning into her more fully to get her to open up. Her hands slid around my sides and curled into the fabric of my shirt as I twisted my tongue around hers and devoured every reservation she might have about how important me and my son might or might not be to her. There wasn't any kind of clinically cool detachment to be found as she reverently kissed me back and tilted her head slightly to the side so I could get a better taste. She wasn't kissing her client. Hell no, she was kissing me, and she was loving every single second of it.

She made a sweet and hot noise in the back of her throat and the only thing that stopped me from tumbling her back in the car and crawling all over her was the fact that her phone rang from somewhere in the car, which shattered the moment and had her pulling free of my demanding lips and grasping hands with a gasp. Her eyes were wide and rushing pure liquid blue like a mountain stream. Her lips were strawberry-stained, damp and plumped up in an inviting way, as she pushed at my chest a little, encouraging me to give her some space.

"I have more meetings and another court appearance today. I have to go." She tried to turn her face away from mine, but I put my finger under her chin and kept her gaze locked with my own. I leaned forward and lightly brushed my lips across her cheek. I was rewarded by the way she shivered all along where we were pressed together.

I couldn't stop the rushed words from falling out of my mouth as she made every effort to leave. "If you've never done a one-night stand, and if you aren't the type to fuck and run, then you owe me another night, Sayer. Let me take you on a real date."

She blinked at me like a regal-looking owl for a minute and then reluctantly shook her head no. "I don't think that's a very good idea."

"Why not?" If she threw our working relationship up between us like a wall I was going to smash through it with my bare hands. I knew the barrier was there, but I could see the longing and hesitancy in her gaze, so I knew the thing wasn't built to last or to withstand my determination. I narrowed my eyes at her as she pushed me back even farther and moved her hands to the top of the car door like she was going to shut it and close me out. I put my hands over the top of hers and leaned in so that we were almost nose-to-nose and repeated, "Why not?"

She sighed and looked down as her phone rang again. "Because who I am around you isn't the person I normally am. When I'm with you someone else seems to take over my body and brain, but eventually the real me is going to show up and I can't imagine she's someone you're going to want to spend time with. I don't even like to hang out with her most of the time. We had the one date you promised, the one date I dreamed about forever, and it was the best date I've ever had. It was perfect and I want to keep the memory of that forever and not risk messing everything up by giving you the opportunity to see what I'm really like. It's what's best for both of us in the long run."

I was so stunned by her response I loosened my grip on the door, which allowed her to fold her tall frame into the driver's seat and pull the door shut. She looked at me through the glass that separated us as I watched her dumbly. She gave a little wave and pulled out of the spot like she hadn't just knocked me stupid with her words.

The real her? What kind of nonsense was that? I knew all about her, the girl in the frozen kingdom that was forged of silk and steel. I knew that the girl could burn white hot and smolder when she forgot that she wasn't supposed to react to me as a man. Just her "client," my ass. I had the memories and the hard-on to prove otherwise.

My mind was whirling from the high of my appearance in court and from the low of Sayer's rejection. One thing was clear: getting my son in my life on a permanent basis wasn't the only thing that was going to take a hell of a lot of work on my end. If I wanted the girl, whatever version of her I could get my hands on, then I was going to have to fight for her as well. I swore under my breath as I headed back toward the International. She was made of more than soft and hard things. Made of more than fire and ice. She had rivers and valleys of scars and damage that ran so deep and wide inside of her that I wondered if she even recognized what they were since they had taken so long to reach the surface. I could see them through the perfect veneer she liked to hold up for the world, and none of it scared me. A little wear and tear, even when it was on someone's heart and soul, wasn't worth walking away from what I knew could be the most important restoration project of my life.

CHAPTER 11

Sayer

After that day in court—or rather what transpired outside after the hearing—I worked like a madwoman, burying myself in cases so I wouldn't think about Zeb. Still, even though it had nothing to do with me or my job, I found myself wanting to check in on Hyde and see how he was adjusting to spending more time with Zeb. Somewhere during the last many weeks, the little guy had fully slipped under my defenses and was rubbing up on the opposite side of my hidden heart right across from his father.

Hyde's foster mother was a nice woman and let me swing by when I was finished at the office for the day. Her house was tidy, considering she had around seven kids under her roof, and I could see that Zeb's son had genuine affection for her. I couldn't help but smile when he immediately took my hand like we were forever friends and dragged me into the kitchen so that he could show me all the cool things he had learned to build with the Legos Zeb had bought him. It only took a glance to see that his father had clearly been adding to the collection. There were Legos as far as the eye could see.

It made my heart thump so heavy and loud I could no longer ignore its existence. It was there, demanding to be seen and heard no matter how badly I wanted to keep ignoring it.

"Want to build a castle?"

"Sure. Let's build a castle." I sat at the table for twenty minutes moving blocks around with him, forgetting my reason for being there and just enjoying his infectious, youthful enthusiasm, when I looked over at the rather impressive structure he had in front of him. It was tall and colorful and seemed surprisingly sturdy for something built by such small hands. "You did a good job with that, kiddo."

Hyde beamed up at me and I wanted to hug him to me and never let him go.

"Zeb showed me how. He said you can build as tall as the sky as long as the foundation is solid."

I jolted at the reminder of why I had told myself I was here. "Zeb is a smart guy and he would know all about building things to make them last. Sounds like you have fun with him."

The little boy looked up at me with familiar green eyes and his gap-toothed grin widened. "I get to see Zeb a lot now. It's neat. He always plays with me and I get to ride in his truck."

I sighed a little, propped my elbow on the table, and put my chin in my hand. "He does have a very cool truck."

Hyde laughed and the sound wrapped around me more tightly than the past ever could. That sound alone was more validation that I was where I was supposed to be and doing what I was supposed to be doing than a kind word from my father ever could have been. I didn't ever think much about kids of my own but this kid, this kid with his shaggy dark hair and forest-colored eyes, I couldn't imagine a future without his happiness and joy being a part of it. He was going to have a shot. He was going to have love. He was going to be accepted and forgiven throughout his lifetime, and that was everything. I would never have been able to be a part of that if I hadn't acted out of character, hadn't embraced my desperation for something more than I had, and come to Colorado.

"Does he take you for a ride in his truck, too?" Hyde's eyes widened in fascination as I pushed forward a structure that could pass for a blocky castle.

"No, but I've seen it, so I know how awesome it is. You're lucky you get to ride in it. I'm jealous." I made a funny face at him that had him laughing and holding his sides as he wiggled in his chair.

"If you ask him for a ride I'm sure he'll give you one. Zeb's really nice. He's a giant."

If I asked Zeb for a ride it wouldn't be happening in his truck, or maybe it would, but either way it wasn't the kind of ride Hyde was talking about.

"He is kind of a giant, but that's a good thing. No one messes with a giant."

The little boy nodded and pushed my haphazardly constructed castle back toward me. "And you're a princess."

I couldn't stop a snort from escaping. "Sorry, buddy, not even close."

His eyes widened in his face and he flashed that adorable grin at me again. He was going to be a heartbreaker and Zeb was going to have his hands full when the little guy got older.

"You're pretty like a princess. You have fancy shoes like a princess. You're nice like a princess. You grant wishes like a princess."

I lifted an eyebrow at him. "Princesses grant wishes?" I think he was getting his Disney references confused, but he was five, so I wasn't in a rush to correct him.

He nodded so vigorously I thought he was going to topple out of his chair. "I wished for someone to come take care of me when my mom went away and you showed up with Zeb." He looked down at the collection of Legos and then back up at me. I was blinking to combat the tears I felt burning at the back of my eyes. "You granted my wish."

I gulped, hard, and reached out across the table so I could touch his cheek. His skin was so soft, so delicate. I admired this little boy who'd suffered so much and still had a heart of gold. Again I thought how brave it was for people who'd been hurt, who had been kicked around by life and the people in it, to allow themselves to feel all those things and to still have hope.

"I'm glad I got to grant your wish for you, Hyde. You deserve to have lots and lots of people in your life taking care of you."

The somber moment was broken by another one of the foster kids running in buck naked and screaming at the top of his lungs. I knew it was a simple cry for attention, something all kids needed, so I invited the rest of the kids in the house to play Legos with us, and by the time I left, an entire city was taking shape on the kitchen table.

Hyde was happy. He was well adjusted, and he obviously loved Zeb. I told myself I could leave it all alone, there were no more questions to be asked, and that my part in their budding relationship was done.

It wasn't that easy. It never was.

The entire way home I fought back tears because while my job was everything, while I now had a family I could lean on and things outside my office that required me to be present and available, it suddenly didn't seem like it would be enough. Kids were never something I thought would be for me. When my father was alive I knew having one wasn't an option. I could never subject a defenseless child to what I had endured, and frankly none of the men I dated ever inspired the urge for home and hearth in me. Not even the one I was supposed to marry. Now my father was gone, my life was my own, and there was a man . . . a man who was all man and so much more . . . who inspired *everything* inside of me.

It made me want. It made me feel. It made me nervous and it made me very, very afraid.

I was exhausted when I finally pushed open the front door of my house, so it took me a minute to realize something was off. I tossed my laptop case on the couch and scraped my fingernails over my scalp as I pulled my hair loose from where it was tied up. I was too tired even to change my shoes, so I stepped out of my heels and stripped off my blazer, carelessly tossing it on top of where my computer case had landed. A pair of stretchy pants and a giant glass of wine were calling my name even if nothing had really worked to relax me since walking away and leaving Zeb staring after me in the parking lot a couple days ago. The stunned look on his face and the way it bled into anger haunted me, but I kept telling myself it was for the best. He deserved more than a woman with an irreparable heart.

I was halfway up the stairs and had one arm out of my mint-green blouse when my nose twitched and I realized a delicious aroma was coming from my kitchen. Considering neither Poppy nor I could cook much beyond scrambled eggs and bacon, it brought me to a stumbling halt.

"Poppy?" I called my housemate's name questioningly, pulled my other arm free of my shirt, and draped it absently over the stair railing. I didn't typically run around the house half dressed, but I was tired and whatever was cooking in my kitchen smelled heavenly. In fact, my belly rumbled loud enough that I could hear it, which would have been mortifying if anyone else had been around.

When Poppy didn't answer me I padded toward the kitchen to investigate. I called her name again and I felt a tingle of concern at the back of my neck when there still wasn't a reply. I was contemplating pulling my houndstooth-check skirt off and leaving it in the middle of the living room as I rounded the corner and stuck my head into the brightly painted kitchen. The sight that greeted me had me snapping up straight and automatically moving to cover myself up, even though the massive man standing at my stove had seen everything the lacy bra was covering up and then some.

Zeb had on a blue-and-red plaid shirt, jeans that were so faded they were white and frayed at the seams, and a smirk that made my legs quiver and the place between them clench in an involuntary reaction.

"Nice outfit. I bet that led to a good day in court." His emerald gaze drifted over my barely covered chest, which was rapidly turning red, and his smile grew more predatory as he watched me try to make sense of what was happening.

"Where's Poppy? What are you doing here?"

He turned back to the stove, so that I was staring at his broad back in surprised shock. He looked good standing in my house, at my stove. He looked like he belonged there, like he had created this space for himself, and it made my heart kick and my body tighten in longing.

"Poppy is staying the night with Salem and Rowdy as a favor to me. I called her and asked her if I could come over and cook you dinner. I told her she was invited, but when I showed up she had a bag packed and Rowdy was already here to pick her up. She's a smart girl and very sweet and Rowdy knows exactly what I had in mind. I consider the fact he didn't punch me in the face as him giving me his seal of approval to date his sister."

I let my arms fall to my sides since he was no longer facing me and shifted awkwardly on my bare feet. "Why are you cooking me dinner, Zeb? I thought we agreed that we were going to keep things strictly professional from here on out. You in my kitchen has nothing to do with your case."

He turned back around with a wooden spoon in his hand and my mouth watered at the sight. It hardly had anything to do with the thick tomato sauce that was clinging to the surface. "We didn't agree on shit. I asked you if you wanted to go on a date, you said no even though you wanted to say yes, and then you ran away. So I decided instead of going on a date I would bring the date to you." His dark eyebrows shot upward and a sexy grin tilted up the corners of his mouth. "It was nice of you to dress for the occasion."

I shook my head at him but didn't bother to try to cover myself up again. I liked the way his eyes got darker and darker the longer he looked at me. It made me warm all over, and that was a feeling I wanted to wrap around myself and never let go of. I pointed a finger between the two of us as he stuck the spoon in his mouth and winked at me. "We aren't doing this."

I wanted to sound stern and definitive. I didn't. I sounded wistful and sad.

"It's already done, Sayer." He turned and put the spoon on the stove and I watched him crank the heat off. When he turned back around he prowled toward the island in the kitchen that separated us and narrowed his gaze on mine. "You let me in, just a little bit, but I'm a big guy, Say. I have no problem shoving the door all the way open. Now you have two choices: we can sit down and eat this awesome spaghetti I just made . . . clothing optional, or we can go to bed . . . clothing not optional." His eyebrows snapped low over his mesmerizing eyes and a muscle twitched in his cheek under his beard. "I'm good with either one as long as you realize the second option is happening regardless."

His words made me quake like the earth was shifting, like the ground wasn't solid, like all the things that kept me anchored and secure had suddenly broken loose and become insignificant. No one had ever pursued me. No one had ever chased me. No one had ever stuck with me after I pushed them away because I was really, really good at freezing people out. The men in my life were practical, found through convenience or placed there by my father. I dated them because I was supposed to, because it was easy.

But not Zebulon Fuller. He was here, in my kitchen, looking like he was ready to fight not only me but whatever else I might throw in his path. I put a hand to my chest and tried to hold it steady. My heart and my mind wavered forever at war but my body always agreed with him . . . it was done.

"I tried to explain to you why this won't ever work out between us, Zeb. I had a long day at work and I don't have the

energy to fight you on top of it. Do you think I enjoyed telling
you that, that I like being the kind of girl who knows that she's
going to end up hurting a really nice guy? It makes me feel terrible, but it's true, and it's easier for me to head you off at the pass
than it is for both of us to crash and burn later on. Why collide
when we can walk away uninjured?" I wanted to choke on the
words.

"That's your truth, Say. It isn't mine. Neither of us knows
what is going to happen beyond this moment."

His expression turned thunderous as he leaned forward and
braced his arms on the counter. His biceps bulged and the fabric
of his shirt pulled tight across his shoulders. He was so powerful, so big in my space. He really had forced his way inside and
I had no way to get him out. I knew that the hole that would be
left behind if I did manage to exorcise him from my life would
be unfillable and infinite.

"My truth is that I like the woman you are with me and I
like the woman you are in court. I like the woman you are with
your brother and the way you fought to be his family. I like the
woman I first met at the Bar that didn't judge me when I told her
I had been to prison. I like the woman that lets a scared young
woman use her house as a sanctuary and leaves a bright red wall
in her kitchen to make that same young woman happy. I like the
woman who looks at my son and sees that he is everything and
is willing to fight for him just because I asked her to. My truth
is that you could never be anything other than fascinating and
amazing, Sayer, and I fucking *hate* that you think you are anything else than all of that. So again you have two options, dinner
or bed, which one do you want to pick?"

Was there really any choice, after all those heart-wrenching and soul-stretching words he had just thrown at me? I felt like I couldn't breathe. My vision narrowed and all I could see was the glimmer of jade and the pulse at the base of his throat making the ink that lived there jump. My fingers curled into a fist on my chest and I blinked once.

"Bed . . . but dinner smells really good, so I want that, too . . . but later." My voice was whisper thin, but there wasn't a hint of hesitation in it. I wanted him. I wanted to be the person he had just described. I wanted to be more than I typically felt like I was. There was only warmth and anticipation that sizzled and popped bright and hot under my skin as he prowled around the big island and stalked toward me. He kept coming until the tips of his boots were touching my naked toes and I sighed when his rough fingers reached up and tangled in my hair on either side of my head.

"I would tell you where the bedroom is, but you already know." I sounded breathless and not at all like me . . . well, the me I usually was. I totally sounded like the me I was when I got within touching distance of this persistent and hard man. The me that was taking over more and more of my life.

"Doubt we're gonna make it to the bed, Say." He growled the words low in his throat and his hands tightened on the sides of my head. My nipples pulled tight and ached as they hit the lacy fabric of my bra. I put my hands on his lean hips and let my half-naked body absorb the heat that seemed to effortlessly emanate from his enormous frame.

"Oh." The word feathered across my lips and they made his eyes twinkle and that smile that transformed him from burly to sexy flash across his face.

"I like it when you say that. I like it better when you moan it when I'm buried deep inside of you and you're squeezing me tight."

My insides fluttered and I felt my eyes widen. "Zeb . . . the things you say." I bit my lip and looked up at him from under my lashes. "I don't know what to do with that." Because his words made me feel . . . feel so many things, and I couldn't stop the rush of emotion. I was turned on but it was more than that. I felt desired. I felt wanted. I felt needed. I felt valued. I felt worthy . . . I felt loved.

He chuckled a little and lowered his head so that his lips could brush against mine. I never wanted to kiss anyone who wasn't him again. Even that light touch had my knees weak and my center going liquid and soft.

His lips ghosted across the curve of my jaw and trailed up my cheek until they brushed against my ear. His deep voice was heavy with seduction and promise as he told me, "You don't have to do anything with the words because they're the simple truth. You inspire them just by being you, Sayer."

His mouth was on mine, his tongue was tangled with mine, my bra was gone, and his callused fingers and rough palms were working the hem of my skirt up my thighs. It was a whirlwind of sensation and all of my senses exploded and filled up with Zeb. I could taste the spicy tomato sauce on his tongue. I could feel his heart where it tip-tapped against my own and my hands delighted in digging into all the hard muscle that stretched taut across him. He was a tactile fest and I wanted to stroke him, hold on to him, dig into him so deep that he couldn't ever get rid of me. I could hear our labored breathing as he backed me out of the kitchen and the light groans and moans that escaped both of us when his hands curved over my backside as he shoved my skirt up around my waist so that he could pull on the lacy panties that matched my abandoned bra. I could smell that scent of wood and work that clung to him no matter what and all I could see was green bleeding into the endless black of desire in his gaze as we hit the stairway in the living room that led up to my bedroom.

Maybe if I was more graceful, more familiar with these kinds of situations, I wouldn't have stumbled. Maybe if I was used to mind-blowing sex and wanton desire, I could have pulled away and taken his hand while leading him seductively up to my lair. Maybe if I was confident and poised in my sexuality, I wouldn't have teetered and faltered, I wouldn't have tripped and fallen just like my heart was bound and determined to do every time I was around this man.

But I was just me, the girl who was so overwhelmed by him, by the things he made me feel, so my knees were weak and I lost my balance when he pressed into me and I landed with a grunt on my exposed backside. Suddenly having my skirt shoved up around my waist and being mostly naked in the middle of my house seemed less sexy and way more silly. I groaned and went to drop my head in my hands in embarrassment because only I could ruin such a sexy and heated moment in such a gloriously inept way, but I didn't get a chance because Zeb's hands were on my waist and he was urging me up another step as he fell to his knees before me. I never in my life thought that being man-handled would be a turn-on, but the way he effortlessly moved me where he wanted me made my skin prickle in arousal and had me clutching his wide shoulders as his hands skimmed the last scrap of lacey undergarment I was wearing down my legs.

"What are you doing?" I felt like all the control, the purpose

I held on to, was fraying and unraveling all around me. Instead of making me panic, the feeling was fuzzy and filled me up with something soft and indulgent. It felt decadent and lush.

"I told you we weren't going to make it upstairs."

His deep voice was even huskier than normal, and I shivered at the way it rumbled out of him. His eyes gleamed at me like polished stones, and when he shifted so that he was directly between my spread legs, I could see his erotic intent reflected back at me. I wasn't the type of girl to let a guy go down on her without several dates and a strong sense of comfort built into the relationship. It was too intimate, too open and raw, so it generally made me too tense to enjoy, but here I was on the stairs in the center of my house, not caring that the lights were on, the windows were open, and I wanted it. God, did I want him to lower his head and fulfill all those dark and dirty promises his eyes were making me.

I leaned back on my elbows on the stair that was behind me and whimpered a little bit when he tickled the inside of my thigh with his work-roughened fingers as he put one of my legs over his shoulder. Thank God for yoga and mornings at the gym. Even with him a few steps below me he was still so tall and so big, so it was a stretch and it burned . . . in a really good way.

I was pretty sure I was blushing the brightest red possible, even in those hidden, sweet places he was now staring directly at. I gulped a little bit and squeezed my eyes closed as tightly as they would go.

"You are flawless. You know that, right?" I felt his words right before the damp press of his lips hit the inside of my knee. The soft brush of his facial hair had goose bumps chasing his mouth as he kissed his way up the inside of my leg. I'd never felt flawless, just honed and polished to a perfect shine that reflected back what I thought everyone wanted to see. With Zeb's mouth on mine and his hands touching me like I was something rare and precious, that shine was starting to dull, to get marked up, and all the rust and tarnish that went way down inside of me was starting to show.

One of his hands curled around my hip and the other made me jolt as his fingers dipped between my legs and danced between folds and into places that were already wet and aching. I muttered his name on a drawn-out sigh and shifted so that I could wind my fingers into the thick mess of his dark hair. I wanted to hold him to me forever, and if I thought the tickle of his beard against my lips was addicting I knew that I would never recover from the way it felt rubbing against the sensitive skin at the apex of my thighs. It was rough and springy. It scraped across my skin at the same time as his fingers stroked inside my body and his clever tongue landed on my clit.

I think I screamed. I probably screamed because he chuckled against my throbbing center and continued his overwhelming stimulation. I was pulling on his hair, urging him closer and closer even though he was invading all my private places in the most devastating ways possible. He added another finger to the wetness he was coaxing out of me and the gentle nip of teeth. It had my hips arching up off the step I was sitting on and my legs quaking where they rested next to his head. There wasn't any place to hide from him or the feelings and emotions he had coursing through me. It was a lot to process and I was shocked that I wanted more. I was stunned when the words flew out of my mouth between pants and his name. I asked him to destroy me, to own me, to push me over the edge and leave me shattered in the aftermath.

I didn't use those words exactly, but when I told him "more," and "deeper," and "harder," I think he understood the message.

Suddenly he had my hips in his hands and was lifting them up to his face. The sheer strength this required made me melt, and when he barked at me to touch myself right before his tongue filled up the empty space his fingers had left, I thought I was going to evaporate into nothing. He was fucking me with his mouth, his hands were hard on my skin, leaving marks I knew I would stare at with a mixture of awe and pride in the morning, and I was letting my own fingers drift over that intense spot of pleasure with a deftness I had never, ever known myself to have. The thought of all the times I had done this to myself while thinking of him, while imagining him doing this very thing to me, was enough to have me convulsing and enough to have pleasure rushing across my fingers and flooding his quick tongue with desire. He groaned deep in his chest, a heavy rumble of satisfaction, and it was so hot. We were so hot and I couldn't believe it. There was nothing cold or icy crawling up my spine, just languid satisfaction and the need to make him feel as good as I felt.

He let my legs fall limply to his sides and bent forward to place a kiss right above my belly button. I sighed at the abrasion of his beard against my skin there and shivered from the wet kiss of what was left of my orgasm where it clung to him and now to me as well. It was sexy as hell and I wanted to touch his lips where they smirked and shined at me.

"Flawless." I wasn't sure what to say to that, so I decided not to say anything at all.

The fabric of my skirt was still all twisted around my waist and I wanted it gone, so I sat up and started to wiggle out of it. Once it was in a heap on the stairs at my feet and I was totally naked, I finally managed to find some composure, rose to my feet, and held out a hand that he immediately clasped in his own.

"You know how amazing my bedroom is since you built it. We might as well put it to use."

He lifted an eyebrow at me and rose to his feet. The bulge in his pants was unmistakable and so was the hungry look in his eyes. Walking buck-ass naked in front of any man, but especially a man as confident and secure in who he was as this one was, would typically rank up there with all of my worst nightmares, but there was something heady in the air around us, something languid inside of me after all of his wonderful, wild words, that made me feel powerful and in control in a totally different way than I normally was.

Thankfully my room wasn't a tornado of discarded clothing and scattered shoes like it usually was after I got ready for work. I hit the light by the bedside and turned to face the mountain of delectable man that had followed me into the room. He was already pulling his shirt off and stripping out of the white tank top he had on underneath. My fingertips tingled with the desire to trace the endless miles of ink that covered his chest and my mouth watered when his muscles rippled and flexed as he pulled his wallet out of his back pocket and tossed it on the unmade bed over my shoulder. It was my turn to lift an eyebrow and he just shrugged.

"We're gonna need it later, and if I work things right, my pants aren't going to be on hand."

He made me laugh. He made me do a lot of things I didn't typically do, and for the second time in my life I kissed a boy. I took charge, stepped into him so that our bare chests pressed together, and wrapped my arms around his shoulders so I could kiss him. He rested his hands on my hips and didn't push, didn't rush me, just let me lean into him and taste and explore. It was intoxicating and I just wanted to taste him and feel him pressed against me forever. I pulled back when my lungs felt like they were going to burst, but since I was being bold, owning the confidence that he somehow siphoned into me, I reached for his belt and started working on getting him as naked as I was.

"The bed is right there and you said clothing wasn't optional if I picked option number two, so you need to catch up, Zeb."

He laughed and it sounded a little strained as he took a step back from my eager fingers so he could kick off his heavy boots and drop his pants and boxer shorts in a pile on the floor. His cock was hard and pointed up at his washboard belly as he moved back toward me. The sight of all that male perfection made my mouth water and I couldn't stop myself from licking my lips. He groaned when he watched the action and grabbed his substantial erection in his fist and gave it a couple pumps.

"I've never wanted anyone so badly that it hurt, Say. Only you."

I put a hand on his chest and twisted so that I could guide him down on the edge of the bed as he reached for me. I put my hands on his shoulders once he was sitting with his legs spread and leaned forward so I could kiss him again.

"I don't want to make you hurt. I've been trying to avoid that from the start."

It was my turn to fall on my knees before him, a position that usually made me unsure and anxious, but before this man made me feel beautiful and strong.

"Not gonna last very long with you naked and your mouth on me." His voice was raspy as his hands wrapped the long strands of my hair through his fingers.

I breathed out and his dick twitched in response. I put my

hands on his rock-hard thighs and looked up at him from under my lashes. "I just want a taste, Zeb."

His jaw locked and his skin flushed. "Whatever you want, Sayer."

I just wanted him in all the different, lurid ways I had been dreaming about since I'd first met him. I took a deep breath because again this kind of intimacy normally freaked me out and I generally treated it as a chore. With that turgid, restless erection right in my face, twitching and moving the closer I got, there was no room for anything but anticipation and willingness. Nothing I did with Zeb or for Zeb felt like something I *had* to do. I wanted to do it and I wanted to do it over and over again.

I dragged my tongue along the throbbing vein that ran along the underside of his cock and was rewarded with a deep groan. He was salty and, like all of him, somehow woodsy and earthy. When I reached the plump head he was already leaking out his pleasure and I swirled my tongue around it with a delicate twist. His hands got harder in my hair and pulled me farther down his impressive length. I complied with his silent command and wrapped my fist around the base of the straining erection. His hips shifted on the bed and I heard his breathing turn ragged as I sucked and pulled him farther and farther into my mouth.

He muttered my name and I couldn't recall ever hearing anything sound as sweet. The feeling of being in control of such a big man, of owning the things that were happening to him, the knowledge that I was the one in charge of his pleasure, was turning me on all over again. I wanted him and the fact that he wanted me just as badly, the fact that I could feel it and taste it, burst across my tongue and did more to defrost the parts deep down inside of me that I thought would never warm up.

I was using my hand in tandem with my mouth to wring him out and string him taut. His breathing was loud in the quiet of the room and every part of him I was touching was marble hard and tense to the point of shattering. He was holding on to my head and guiding me farther and faster down his length when he suddenly swore and yanked me off of him. I squealed in a very unsexy way as he picked me up and tossed me into the center of the bed and crawled up and over me. He kept himself propped up with one arm while he scrambled for his wallet with the other.

"I want inside, Sayer. That's where I belong."

I couldn't argue with this because I was starting to think he was right. Plus I was all achy and empty again and I wanted him to fill me back up. I curled my hands around his back and flattened my palms against the wide plank of muscle that flexed under my touch.

"Whatever you want, Zeb."

Those dark green eyes shone at me as he positioned himself at my entrance and slowly made his way inside the welcoming stretch of my body. We both let out a whispered sigh and his mouth fell over mine.

"Everything, Say. I want everything."

I didn't have anything to give, let alone everything, but I wasn't inclined to try to stop him from trying to take it. I kissed him quiet so he couldn't speak anymore and arched up into him as he started to move over me. I felt like he was doing the same thing to my body that he had done to my house, changing things, rearranging them, making it his own, and creating a space inside that only he could fill.

He was everywhere. His mouth on mine, his breath in my lungs, his chest rubbing tantalizingly across my nipples, his hips hammering into mine, his body making mine move across the bed with the force of his thrusts as his hands skipped over every part of my skin that he could reach.

He wasn't gentle with me and I loved it. He fucked the way he did everything else in his life. With unrestrained passion. With purpose. With determination. With single-minded focus on his goal . . . in this case, it was obvious his goal was to make me mindless with pleasure. His beard rubbed across my throat and his teeth nipped into my skin.

I whimpered and moved my legs up around his waist when he clutched my thigh with one hand. The new position drove him deeper and pushed us closer together. Every time he pulled out slightly and slammed back in, I felt him rub against my clit in the most delicious way. I refused to just hold on for the ride. There was no way I could just take what he was giving and not be wholly invested in the sensations we were both drowning in. I put one hand back in his tangled hair and the other on my breast and squeezed the pert tip until it hurt in a really pleasurable way.

Zeb grunted as he watched me and I felt his big body tense up above me.

"One of these days I'm just gonna watch you. Nothing has ever been that pretty." His words were the end for me.

I gasped his name and pulled on his hair. His fingers dug deeper into my thigh and his pace picked up until I felt him jerk and heard him mutter a few broken, filthy words as he found his own release inside my pliant and satisfied body. I fluttered around him and caught him when he collapsed on top of me with a sigh.

His fingers rubbed up along my rib cage and his voice was

lazy in my ear as he told me, "I'm so fucking happy you picked option two."

It made me laugh, which was hard to do with a naked giant pinning me to the bed. I stroked my hand over the stark and violent-looking image of the Norse god he had inked on one entire side of his ribs. I assumed the god was a depiction of the mighty Thor because of the hammer the image was wielding. The tattoo was powerful and huge, just like the man sporting it.

I was going to tell him how wonderful it all was, how happy I was that he had brought the date I'd claimed not to want to me, when my stomach remembered the abandoned dinner in the kitchen and roared loud enough that it made him push up and look down at me in surprise.

I would have been mortified but he was still buried deep inside of me, and when he chuckled at me I felt it everywhere.

"Let me clean up and get situated and I'll feed you. I don't want you to tell me no the next time I ask you on a date."

We groaned in unison as he pulled out and I shifted around on the bed as he headed toward the bathroom. I was going to tell him that there would be no dating, that all of this was a fluke. When there was space between us I could think and the reality of things was as bleak and as barren as it always was. I wanted him to understand that what happened when I was with him was something magical and that it would eventually fade, but as I watched his toned backside flex as he disappeared into the bathroom I decided I just wanted to enjoy the view and that I would worry about the reality of who I was and how she had no idea how to be with who he was later.

CHAPTER 12

Zeb

I had my hands full of Sayer's plump, firm breasts and her long, silken hair was tangled all over my chest where her hands were planted and it hung on either side of my face as she bent forward so that she could rock on my very happy dick even faster. She made a strangled noise in her throat as I trapped her puckered and flushed nipples between my fingers and her eyelids fluttered in a way that let me know she was getting close to coming.

Her typically pale cheeks were flushed a pretty pink and her mouth was damp and looked well loved, and her normally sleek hair was a mess from my hands and rolling all across her king-size bed for hours. She looked good all put together and ready to take care of business. She looked way better like this—messy, wild, out of control, and totally lost in the moment, caught up in how good we could make each other feel. This was the Sayer I was pretty sure I was well on my way to being in love with and I was really grateful she had started showing up more and more.

I grunted as her fingernails bit into my skin and moved a hand up to the back of her head so I could draw her down for a searing kiss. She came easily, folding into me like soft butter, so I shifted her so that she was stretched out underneath me so that I could watch those limitlessly blue eyes burn as I pushed her over the edge with a single, hard thrust. I wanted her to know it was me, only me, that could make her go off like that. I was the one she melted for. I was the one she let inside. She sighed in pleasure as she kissed me back and I felt her inner walls start to milk my cock with desperate little motions.

She still wouldn't go out with me when I asked her on a date, but if I showed up at her house, she always let me inside and she never kicked me out of her bed. A few days ago I had asked her to come over to my place and was surprised when she readily agreed. My condo was nothing to write home about, basic in all the ways a condo typically was, and when she mentioned it, I had a hard time dancing around the fact that I had already built my dream home . . . she just happened to be living in it. I distracted her from that conversation by putting her on the kitchen counter and wrapping her legs around me, which, of course, led to a bout of vigorous kitchen sex. It took me a few nights to realize that to her, if we weren't actually going out, actually participating in any kind of social activity other than all the sex we were having, then we weren't dating.

I tried to talk to her about it, tried to get her to see that I was in this for so much more than her delectable body and the mind-blowing sex, but it was her turn to distract me from the conversation by pulling my dick out and sucking it so far into the back of her throat I was amazed she didn't choke on it. Needless to say, I couldn't think much after that, but the conversation still needed to happen, but it could wait, unlike the orgasm that I felt coiling up at the base of my spine as I hammered into her. Our pubic bones collided and I could feel her sweet spot quiver and her whole body tense up.

She put a hand on the side of my face and combed her fingers through my beard. It was a new thing she seemed to like to do, and while it should feel comforting and sweet, all it made me want to do was bury myself inside her as far as I could go so that she felt me everywhere, every day, in every single move she made while we were apart. I growled at her and sank my teeth into the top of her shoulder with just enough force to make it sting. She garbled something that I'm sure was supposed to be words and then her body clamped down on me like a velvet vise and I felt her pleasure and mine collide and merge into one intense flood of completion. I couldn't remember a time when I ever got off at the same time as the girl I was with. I was never that in sync with anyone, never that caught up in the moment and feeling what they were feeling as intensely as my own desire. It had happened more than once since I started sleeping with Sayer, and each time it felt more important, more significant than the last.

I swore down at her and she giggled up at me as I rolled to the side so I didn't crush her when I collapsed. I brought her with me and she wiggled on my dick, which had me growling at her. I was so over the latex that kept me from being able to stay inside her forever and enjoy a minute where I could just hold her and marvel at how perfect she fit me. That was another conversa-tion I wanted to have but was leery of how she would react. She seemed bound and determined to keep me close but with enough room that she could duck out if she felt like she needed to. I didn't want to push too hard, considering being here, in this house I built for her, in her bed anytime I asked, was a huge victory. I might not be all the way through those icy barriers she had, but I was tunneling my way into the core of her nicely.

I pulled out of the heat that she still had me wrapped in and bit back a grin when a frown pulled at her face. I liked the way her golden eyebrows puckered in annoyance at the loss of me. I leaned forward so I could kiss those little lines and told her I would be right back.

It was a good thing she had a master bath attached to the room. One morning when I was running particularly late because of shower sex—totally worth the hitch in my schedule, by the way—I had scared Poppy half to death by bursting into the kitchen half dressed and hurried. The timid young woman was getting more comfortable having me in her space, but clearly she wasn't at the point where a big, half-naked man was something she was ready to deal with. I thought she was going to burst into tears, and I wasn't sure how to make the situation any better. Luckily Sayer had heard Poppy's shriek of terror and had come down to smooth things over. She was so good with the fractured young woman, so kind, so caring, I was baffled how she thought she was going to hurt me.

I made a concerted effort to stay dressed and move more carefully around the Victorian when I knew I might run into the other woman. It broke my heart a little bit for her, but Sayer assured me that the fact that Poppy hadn't run and barricaded herself in her room after the encounter was huge progress. I was skeptical but decided to believe her.

I crawled back into the bed and pulled Sayer on top of me so that she was sprawled across me like a sexy, naked blanket. I pulled the comforter up over her waist and ran my fingers up and down the knobs of her spine while she traced over the tattoo on my shoulder with her index finger. She did that a lot. It was almost like she was trying to commit the images to memory through touch or something. By now I was convinced that she could draw spot-on images of them if I asked her to, given how much time she spent studying them and touching them.

"Did you tell Hyde?" Her voice was sleepy and sluggish against my chest. I twisted my fingers in the ends of her hair, and as usual the silky strands clung to the calluses I had there.

I'd had two long weekends of unsupervised visits with the little boy, with two more to go before he could start spending Thursday through Mondays with me. I wanted to tell him I was his father before he came to stay with me, but every time I had him all to myself, I chickened out or couldn't figure out a way to give him such important information in a way that was easily digestible for a five-year-old.

"No. He wanted to ride around in the truck and eat pizza today. I'm pretty sure he thinks I'm just his playtime buddy. I couldn't do it. He was having such a good time, and I feel like when I tell him, that's gonna change how he sees me." I'll admit it. I was scared to death of a five-year-old. I already loved him so much, was so attached to the little guy that I was terrified that when I told him what our relationship really was he would feel betrayed.

She yawned and then lifted her head up and rested her chin on her hands, which she stacked up over my heart. "You're running out of time if you want to tell him before the overnights start." She lifted her eyebrows up. "Speaking of the overnights, you might want to ask your sister or someone to help you make that condo a little more kid-friendly before he comes to stay with you."

I tugged on her hair and she scowled at me. "What's wrong with my condo?"

She rolled those ocean-colored eyes at me like I was clueless. "Nothing is wrong with it for a single guy. Everything is wrong with it for a five-year-old. He needs to have someplace that is fun, a place that is all his own. Before you get full custody, the court very well may send a social worker out to check out the living conditions. Your condo is nice, but it doesn't scream 'family.'"

I moved one of my hands and propped it behind my head. She watched the way the motion made my bicep flex and her gaze got all kinds of stormy and appreciative.

"And I think you're worrying about nothing. Hyde adores you. He can't wait for your visits and he talks to his current guardian about you nonstop. It might take some time for him to process the fact that you're his father, but he's bright and he cares about you so much. You guys will figure it out together."

I let go of her hair and tickled the base of her spine where she had two really cute dimples that I was now intimately familiar with. I liked to dip my tongue in them and make her squirm and wiggle while she tried to figure out how low I was going to go as I licked her like a lollipop.

"I hope you're right, and what do you mean by 'single guy'?" I palmed one of her ass cheeks and gave it a solid squeeze so that I made sure I had her attention. "Two of us in this bed right now, Say. Two of us in bed at my condo. That makes for me being decidedly unsingle. It's been that way for a while now."

She wiggled a little on top of me as I brought up the topic I knew she didn't want me to broach. She dropped her head so that her cheek was on her hands and I was looking at the crown of her head. "You know what I meant, Zeb."

I grunted and gave the tight ass cheek I was fondling a smack. She yelped and jerked her head back up so that we were eye-to-eye in the dimly lit room.

"No, Sayer, I don't know what you mean. I'm with you even though you refuse to admit it, so I am not some single guy. I'm not fucking anyone else, have no desire to fuck anyone else, so you are it. *This* is it." I was annoyed and she could tell because I could see the war waging between what she thought she should say to that declaration and what she was actually feeling. Terror and joy did battle and crashed like angry waves in her eyes as she gazed down at me.

"I . . . I'm not sure what to say." Well, at least she wasn't trying to litigate her way into some bullshit response about how we could screw each other's brains out but not be anything more because she was scared of hurting me. That would've really pissed me off.

"Just admit that neither one of us is single at the moment, Say. That's all I want to hear."

She gave a breathy little sigh and closed her eyes. "Neither one of us is single, Zeb."

It was a small victory, but one I would gladly take, and since I was gaining ground I figured I would go for the gusto. "And since neither one of us is single and neither one of us is fucking anyone else, how about we work something out so that I don't have to buy stock in Trojan?"

That startled a laugh out of her and I wanted to pound on my chest in primitive pride. She cuddled back into me and her hair slithered all around me in an erotic caress that had my dick tightening up and twitching underneath her.

"I have an IUD, so we're good." She said it so offhandedly, so blasé like she hadn't just given me the keys to the only kingdom I wanted to get inside without a suit of armor for protection.

Her declaration made me and my impatient cock very happy. I slipped my hands all the way under the covers and between her legs. She jolted a little and peered up at me curiously as I dipped my fingers inside her soft opening. She wasn't protesting, but she wasn't spreading her legs to let me in any farther either.

"Really?" She sounded dumbfounded. I had been all over her for hours, but she just gave me the green light to go in bare and that was like dropping a lit match into a puddle of kerosene.

I rolled her under me for the second time that night and rubbed my aching dick between her plump folds until I felt them start to warm up and her body start to react to the gentle ministrations.

"You just told me I could have you raw, uncovered, and you didn't think that meant I was going in? I told you, Say . . . I want inside and I want to leave parts of myself there so you can't shake me loose."

Her mouth rounded in a little "oh" and her hands curled around my arms as I sank into her heat and let her burn all along me. It was sweet as heaven and hot as hell. It was everything and more. It was a place that was all mine and that I was never going to let anyone else anywhere near.

I started to move, slower, more deliberate than I usually did when I was inside of her. I wanted to savor every drag, every pull of flesh against flesh. I wanted to memorize every squeeze, every tiny tremble of pleasure. I wanted to remember every pulse and throb as I retreated and invaded over and over again. I wanted to leave a mark and I wanted to leave with marks of my own, our straining bodies imprinted on one another and linked in intimate ways no one else could see.

This wasn't me fucking her or her fucking me, this was making love. This was coming together. This was the kind of sex that made lovers fall in love. This was the kind of sex that neither one of us was going to be able to live without once we tasted how intense and profound it could be.

I came before she did this time . . . I mean, give a guy a break. I was inside her with nothing between us, she felt like she was made just for me, and I had ridden her hard and merciless before this bout of lazy lovemaking. She whimpered when I filled her in a hot rush and I watched as she turned her head to the side and squeezed her eyes shut. There was a lot of emotion welling up there and I knew it was easier for her to hide from it than to face it.

I grabbed her chin in my hand and forced her to look at me as I rocked into her one last time with a languid glide of my hips. "Sayer . . ." Just her name. That was all it took. Her name spoken like it was everything to me because it was. She broke apart under me in rippling waves.

I knew she was going to be spent both physically and emotionally after she came down from her orgasm, so I wrapped her in my arms and turned to the side so that her back was to my front and I was surrounding her.

I kissed her on the back of the head and muttered a soft "thank you." What else was there to say? What she had given me felt like a gift.

She breathed out and my heart kicked hard when she gently put her hand over the top of mine where it was possessively curled around one of her breasts.

"Tell Hyde, Zeb. You're going to be an amazing father and he deserves every minute of that."

We were both quiet after that and eventually I felt her go lax and knew she was asleep. All I could think while I held her was that there was no *falling* in love with this woman, there was only *being* in love with her. She had owned me from the very start; now I just needed her to take possession and keep me forever.

"You are such a coward." I threw a handful of the little pellets I bought Hyde to feed the giraffes with at Beryl and laughed when she smacked my arm in retaliation. Fall was rushing headlong into the colder winter weather, so I had a heavy canvas coat on over my shirt and barely felt the blow.

"I'm not the one with the secret boyfriend that's too afraid to introduce him to the family." I watched as Joss took Hyde's hand and practically dragged him across the walkway toward where the wolf enclosure was. It wasn't the first time my niece had been to the big city zoo in the center of City Park, but it was Hyde's. His little face was alight with wonder and he couldn't seem to take it all in as Joss delighted in showing him all her favorite animals. Both the kids were bundled up, and even though he was five years younger than her, Hyde was almost as tall as my energetic niece. He really did take right after me.

Beryl snorted and tapped her fingers on the white Starbucks cup she clutched in her hands. "Wes actually really wants to meet you and Mom. He sort of gave me an ultimatum the other day."

I lifted an eyebrow at her and chuckled as Hyde pressed his nose against the glass so he could get a better look at the animals. Everything he did tugged at my heart and made me even more anxious about what his reaction was going to be when I told him the truth.

"What kind of ultimatum?"

"He told me that he wasn't going to be a dirty secret anymore, that if he was going to be part of my life, he deserved the chance to know the other people that love me as much as he did. I sort of freaked out and told him it was over."

I sighed and cut her a sideways look. "You didn't really?"

She nodded and looked up at me. "I did." She sniffed a little and I reached out to put an arm around her shoulders.

"I'm sorry. I know you liked him."

She laughed and shook her head.

"I love him. I was going to call and tell him that I made a mistake and ask him to forgive me when Mom called and said she couldn't wait for brunch on Sunday and that she was so excited to finally meet Wes. The stubborn bastard called her and ratted me out and outmaneuvered me. He worked around all my fears and got himself exactly where he wanted to be."

I had to admire the man's persistence. "Well, I can't wait to meet him, then."

She nudged me in the ribs with her elbow. "It's the same Sunday you're bringing Hyde to meet Mom, so hopefully she'll be distracted by his adorable face and not embarrass me too much."

I wiggled my eyebrows at her. "Don't worry, sis, I can embarrass you enough for the both of us." My mother had been chomping at the bit to get her hands on the little guy, but I still wasn't a hundred percent sure how to describe all the new adults that were going to be a part of his life to him. I kind of wanted to wait until he knew I was his dad before I broke the news that he also had a grandma who was dying to smother him in love and affection. Holding her off while I made sure Hyde was ready had been a Herculean feat.

This time her nudge almost knocked me over, so I let her go and she pointed toward the kids with her cup.

"He loves you already. He'll be fine when you tell him. You didn't need to call me and Joss in for backup, though I'm so happy we finally got to meet him. Joss is obsessed with having a cousin now. If you don't tell him he's ours forever, she will. You know my kid and her mouth."

"I know . . . it's just . . ." I trailed off, not sure how to put my fears into words without sounding like the coward she had accused me of being.

"It's just that you want him to like you, and you want him to still be your little buddy, but, Zeb . . ." Her tone got stern in that older sister way that meant I better listen to what she had to say. "As a parent, there are times when he's not going to like you very much at all. So you better get used to it now. It's your job to do what's right for him, not what's easy."

I lifted a hand to rub it across my beard and moved to tuck my hands in my pockets. "I know. Sayer keeps telling me pretty much the same thing."

That brought Beryl to a halt as the kids skipped ahead of us to go look at some mountain goats.

"How are things going with the lady lawyer? I didn't realize you were seeing her outside of the courtroom—officially anyways."

I shrugged. "She's making me work around her." I looked at her out of the side of my eyes. "Sound familiar?"

She blushed a little and pushed some of her dark hair out of her face, and the nippy wind suddenly kicked up. I felt it sting my ears and frowned at Hyde. He needed to put a hat on if we were going to be out in the cold much longer.

"Have you talked to her about it? Why she makes you work around her? I told Wes about Joss's father, about what happened with you and how it changed me, how it changed my relationship with all men, and I think that's part of the reason he refused to give up. I also told him about our dad leaving. I never really thought it mattered, but the older I get the more I wonder if that's part of the reason I fell for the first guy that told me he loved me even though he smacked me across the face five minutes after saying it."

I swore under my breath at the question and at the memories her words stirred to life. "She won't talk about much. I know her dad was an asshole. I don't think he used his hands on her or anything, but she always shuts down when I try to bring the past up. Her mom committed suicide when she was a teenager and I think all of that has led to her being pretty closed off, but when we are alone together, when I get inside, she's the warmest, sweetest, most thoughtful and caring person I've ever met. I just wish I didn't need a crowbar to get at it all the time."

Beryl let out a low whistle and reached out to pat my arm. "You know that words can hurt just as much as hands if they are wielded effectively. She could have those walls up for a reason. Just like I did." She gave me a sad smile. "And losing her mother like that . . . the girl comes with baggage."

She didn't just have baggage, like I did. She had a *vault* full of secrets and emotions she was keeping under lock and key. She didn't realize I was willing to throw every tool I had at my disposal at her fortress, even if I had to pull out the dynamite and blast my way in.

"She doesn't talk about it and she runs off when I try to get her to open up."

Beryl sighed heavily again. "Falling in love after you've been hurt so badly is terrifying. You better lace up some tennis shoes and prepare to chase after her if you plan on keeping her around."

I laughed a little and switched my attention back to the kids.

"Mom, I'm cold." Joss hollered the statement from where the kids had paused a few yards ahead to wait for us. She grabbed Hyde's hand and they started walking back toward us.

Beryl tossed her cup in the trash and put her hands in her coat pockets as I took mine out so I could hoist my son up in my arms. His cheek was freezing as he pressed his face next to mine so he could rub his face into my beard.

"I'm cold, too." He sounded sleepy and I hated that I was going to have to take him back to the foster home he was currently staying in until I could have him with me.

"I know, buddy. We need to get you a hat." I rubbed a hand over his dark hair and felt even more of my heart settle in his tiny hands.

He pulled back from where he was cuddling into me and looked at me with a miniature scowl that so obviously matched my own I had to fight down a chuckle.

"You don't wear a hat, Zeb. If you don't, I don't. I hate hats."

I glared at my sister as she hooted out a laugh. The boy had inherited more than my coloring and my height. It seemed like my stubbornness and natural defiance were coursing through him as well.

"I do when it's cold. I just forgot it today, and when I tell you something like that, you need to know it's for your own good, Hyde. If you're cold and a hat will keep you warm, then I'm gonna make you wear a hat even if you don't want to."

He seemed to consider it for a second, matching green eyes

locked on mine in an unwavering battle of wills. I thought I was
going to have to explain that I didn't want him to catch a cold
and that everyone wore a hat in Colorado in the winter, some
even when it wasn't winter, but just as fast as his defiance flared
to life it quieted back down and he nodded at me solemnly.

"Okay, Zeb. If you want me to wear a hat so I won't be cold,
then I will." His eyes widened and a crooked smile that was
missing a tooth flashed across his face. "Can it be a Batman hat?"

I snorted out a laugh. "It can be whatever kind of hat you want
as long as you wear it."

Joss heaved a dramatic sigh and asked if we could go get pizza.
I was going to say no since I fed Hyde pizza the last time I had
him for a visit, but apparently five-year-olds could eat pizza every
day and his eyes lit up at the prospect.

It was a short drive to a pizza shop on Colfax, and as we all
piled into a booth it ended up being the kids on one side and the
adults on the other. I was really happy my niece had decided to
take Hyde under her wing. He seemed at ease with her and I
thought that maybe spending more time with my family would
ease him into understanding I was his father and he wasn't alone
anymore. I was still trying to figure out the best way to tell him,
the easiest way to explain the situation, when I heard Joss tell
Hyde:

"I don't see my dad, but that's okay because I see my gram and
Uncle Zeb all the time. And my mom has a man friend named
Wes that is really nice. He watches cartoons with me and helps
me do homework."

Hyde nodded sagely like he understood all those words and
reached for his plastic cup that had the lid on it.

"I never had a dad, but I had lots of uncles."

Beryl was leaning forward to derail the touchy subject when Joss turned to the dark-haired little boy and blurted out the words I had been struggling with for weeks. "Uncle Zeb is your dad, so you have a dad now. The best dad ever."

I opened my mouth in shock as Beryl barked her daughter's name in horror. I was gaping at my son like a fish as he turned wide eyes in my direction.

"What? It's true. Why am I getting yelled at?" Joss huffed out the words, but I barely heard them as my son continued to watch me like he was afraid I was going to disappear in a puff of smoke before him.

His head cocked to the side and he lifted his cup to his lips so he could slurp on his soda. When he was done he leaned forward a little bit and asked, "For real?"

I wasn't sure he really understood what it all meant, so I nodded. "Yeah, for real. I'm your dad, and I've been working really hard so that you can come stay with me all the time really soon."

I waited for him to cry, or to ask a million questions. I waited for him to be happy or upset. I waited for him to do anything, but he just stared at me and continued to play with his cup.

Beryl asked him if he was all right and he nodded without saying anything. I thought I should grab him and go, but the pizza came and he devoured a massive slice, still without saying a word. Joss was pouting because she was in trouble for speaking out of turn, and I knew Beryl was concerned about the anxious tension that was rolling off of me in waves.

We finished and paid the bill. I told Joss I wasn't mad at her because she looked like she was going to cry and told my sister

I would call her after I had Hyde settled. Really I meant I would call her after *I* was settled but that was neither here nor there.

Once I had the little boy strapped into his seat in my truck, I climbed behind the wheel and started across town to take him back to his temporary home. I was watching him out of the corner of my eye as he stared out the window.

"You okay back there, buddy?"

"Yeah." He was quiet for a second and then he said my name softly. "Zeb?"

I plastered a smile on my face and nodded encouragingly at him when he twisted to look at me.

"You're my dad?"

"That's right."

"And I can come live with you?"

"Eventually. There are some things I have to do first, but I'm working really hard to get them all done."

He stuck out his bottom lip like he was thinking really hard and then he stated so chillingly and matter-of-factly that it made my heart clench. "My mom died. I don't want you to be my dad if it means you're going to die."

"Oh, Hyde." I had to take a moment to get my composure back so I could answer him. "Your mom did some things that were really dangerous. I don't do any of those kinds of things, so my chances of dying are really slim. I have you to take care of, so I promise to do my very best to stick around as long as possible, okay?"

He was quiet for a long time but eventually sucked his lip back in and flashed me that uneven grin.

"Okay." He leaned back in his seat and looked out the

windshield. "Will you still play with me and let me ride in the truck?"

I wanted to laugh but instead it came out as a wheeze of relief. "Yep. We can play every day and we'll go for a ride in the truck whenever you want."

He clapped his hands and grinned even wider. "If you're my dad, does that mean when I get bigger I'm going to be a giant, too?"

That made me laugh for real. "Possibly, but you have to be a friendly giant if you get this big."

"I can do that."

And just like that, it was settled. I was his dad, he was my son, and we were a team from here on out. It was a good day and I needed to thank my niece and her big mouth and total lack of filter for doing what I, a grown-ass man, a giant according to my kid, hadn't had the balls to do.

From the mouths of babes.

CHAPTER 13

Sayer

I scowled at the pretty saleswoman dressed fairly similarly to my own after-court outfit as she cruised by where Zeb was shaking his head at the price of bedding for a kid's bed. She'd already asked once if she could help us find anything in the sprawling department store located inside the upscale Cherry Creek Mall. And I had already told her once that I knew exactly where we needed to go, so I could only assume her return appearance had more to do with the way Zeb's ass looked in his faded jeans and the way his flannel shirt pulled across his shoulders than it did with any actual desire to help.

When she caught my dirty look she scampered off just as Zeb tossed the package containing the sheets with a thread count no little boy would ever appreciate back on the shelf. He crammed his hands through his wavy hair and turned to me with a frustrated huff. I saw an older lady who was looking at bath mats in the same section jump and scuttle to another aisle like Zeb was the Big Bad Wolf and he was getting ready to blow the whole place down. I liked the way he looked, more than liked it. He looked like he could take on the entire world and win, but that was apparently intimidating to the average high-end shopper. I rolled my eyes and turned to him as he put a hand on my elbow and started to lead me out of the linen section.

"Don't they have sheets with trains on them or superheroes? Who spends five hundred bucks on a pair of sheets that the kid is gonna outgrow in a few years when he needs a bigger bed?"

His frustration was kind of cute. "I would. I won't even tell you how much the sheets on my bed cost."

He shifted his eyes to me and moved to wrap his bulky arm across my shoulders. The same older woman gave a sniff of disdain as we walked by and it was the saleswoman's turn to give me a dirty look as we swept by on our way back into the belly of the mall.

"I like your sheets." There was humor and innuendo laced together in his tone. "But your bed could be covered in sandpaper, and as long as you were naked on top of it I wouldn't even notice."

"Ouch." I muttered the word softly but couldn't stop the rush of pleasure that followed his sweet statement.

He chuckled at me and let his gaze skip over the rest of the fancy stores and their modern lettering and minimalist window decor. "I'm not going to find stuff for a kid's room anywhere in this mall, am I?"

When he texted me and asked me to go with him to find stuff to get Hyde's room ready, I initially wanted to tell him no. It felt too intimate, too permanent. It felt like not only was he crafting a place for himself in my everyday, but was working to make a specific space for me in his very busy and complicated life as well. I was so close to the edge with him. I hovered so close to letting go and falling all the way in with him. I was hanging on to that precipice with only my fingertips and it was so scary. At the place where there was nothing and it was barren and empty, I knew I was safe even if it was aching alone. I knew if I let go of the ledge the drop could kill me, that the impact would shatter me, so I kept clawing and clinging to familiar ground to keep myself aloft. As hard as I was holding on to the cliff and not wanting to give in to every emotion he pulled from me, Zeb was constantly there below, tugging, dragging, urging me to crash into him and into every promise of love and forever I could see he wanted to give me.

When I hesitated he told me that he had already asked Beryl, but Joss was home sick and his mom had plans for dinner. He insisted he needed a woman's touch to help him get things right for his son's homecoming and I couldn't resist, but the only place to shop that I was familiar with in Denver was Cherry Creek. As soon as we pulled into the parking lot it was clear his dirty Jeep didn't fit in with the Mercedes and Audis littering the parking garage and our trip into Nordstrom's had only solidified the fact that where I shopped wasn't exactly Zeb's cup of tea. Even if the girls who worked there liked the rugged eye candy he provided.

"There's a Bed Bath & Beyond on the other side of the mall. I bet they have sheets with trains on them." In hindsight we probably should have started there. The chain store was much more Zeb's speed and more kid-friendly in general. "I told you I'm not good at decorating and stuff. I'm beige and pastel all the way." Beige and simple colors weren't offensive. If a color could be offensive. According to my father, it could be. According to him, everything was worth judging and finding fault with if that meant he could use it to make someone else feel poorly about what they liked or found pleasure in.

Zeb tugged me closer and dropped a kiss on the top of my head as several people moved out of our way. He commanded space and people seemed to automatically give it to him. It was impressive to watch and sent a little thrill down my spine knowing that I was fortunate enough to be the one he was making that space for.

"You only think you're beige and pastel. You like color and you like things that are different and fun; you just hide them in places where you think no one will notice."

I scowled a little and pulled away from him. He didn't let me get very far. As soon as there was room between us he reached out and caught my hand in his. I couldn't remember a single time in my whole life when anyone had held my hand. Not my father, not my mother, not Nathan . . . no one except Zeb, and it rattled me to my core. All at the same time I wanted to pull free and clutch him so tightly he would never let go. That hold I had on what I knew from before loosened even more. I was clinging by fingertips now.

"What are you talking about? Everything in my house is muted and neutral. Everything I own is a basic, plain color. Even my car is gray."

He snorted at me and squeezed where our hands were locked together. "But I bet you a million bucks that your underwear is bright purple or blue and that your toes are painted some crazy color with a design on them. Your workout clothes are black and gray, but every single piece of them has some neon strip or some splash of color in the design. Not to mention you could've paid someone to cover up that red wall in your kitchen or you could've bought a new building or an updated home instead of sinking a fortune into restoring and customizing that old beauty. You have your own flare, Sayer. It's subtle, but it's there, and it's beautiful if someone is smart enough to look for it."

I almost pulled us both to a stop so that I could really process his words. I had never considered the little things in my life that I did just for me, for the little piece of joy they brought me, as "flare." I considered them guilty pleasures, ones I still had a hard time believing I was getting away with, ones I was waiting for a dead man to tell me were frivolous and wasteful. I never noticed Zeb noticing them.

He tugged on my hand to get me to pick the pace back up and looked at me over his shoulder. "And don't think for a second that I haven't noticed that you can't keep your hands off my ink. Not that I would ever complain about it, but most chicks like it at first and then get bored with it because it just becomes part of the scenery. Not you. It doesn't matter how many times you see it or have your mouth on it, you always want to explore it, absorb it. You more than like color, Sayer. You savor it and worship it."

God, did his truth undo me . . . every single time.

I blew out a deep breath and looked at him out of the corner of my eye because I could feel him watching for my reaction.

"Growing up, everything had to be just so. My father was particular about every minute detail of my life. To start off with, he always wanted a son and was disappointed I was a girl from the second I was born. That was the first in a laundry list of disappointments I burdened him with throughout my life. What I wore, how I did my hair, what kind of makeup I used, who my friends were, what my room looked like, everything was subject to his approval and nothing ever lived up to his standards. He hated everything about me and everything I did, so by the time I was ten or eleven I figured out it was easier to just keep everything bland and neutral. He had a harder time picking apart beige and cream. Ivory and black and white became staples and made it so that I could fly under his radar for the most part." I shook my head a little as we finally reached the brightly lit store. "I carried a lot of that over into my adult life as habits, but I guess as I got older the bits and pieces of things I liked for myself worked their way into my everyday without me really noticing it."

I gave him a lopsided grin. "And I actually really like that poppy-colored wall. I'm keeping it even after Poppy moves out."

He let go of my hand and put a palm on my lower back as he ushered me into the store in front of him. Quietly, so that only I could hear, he asked, "What happened with your mom, Sayer? If your dad was that nasty and controlling, why didn't she step in and stop him? Why did she stay with him? Why didn't she protect you from him?"

Those were questions that had tormented me and helped me keep my heart encased safely in ice to this day. I couldn't help my fingers from curling into my palms and digging in so hard that it hurt when I answered him.

"She loved him. She really, truly loved him, and it killed her. It never mattered how mean and terrible he was to her. She tried every single day to please him, to be the perfect wife and to make me the perfect daughter. All she wanted was his approval, some form of affection and kindness, and he knew it, so he delighted in purposely stringing her along and tormenting her." Memories churned and slipped out of the iron hold I had them in. They twisted around all the emotions Zeb had unleashed inside of me, and they made my guts hurt and the place where my heart was supposed to be throb painfully.

"He had affairs and told her she wasn't as pretty as his mistresses. She would starve herself, she would work out endlessly. She changed her hair, got plastic surgery, and he mocked her, told her she could never be perfect. He wanted a son since she screwed up with me, but she was sick, not just in the head, and couldn't maintain a pregnancy to full term. He considered her worthless, but she still tried time and time again for him. Her life was nothing more than trying to reach an unreachable finish line where he would finally love her as much as she loved him. She died because she knew she was never going to make him happy and she couldn't live with the fact. She left me with him, knowing how he was and what he was capable of. I don't think I'll ever forgive her for that." I was heartless. I was cruel. I was a terrible person for feeling that way, but it was true. If I forgave her, it meant the floodgates would open and there would be no holding back all the painful, ugly, agonizing things that lurked inside the dark. If I let them free with forgiveness there would be no more ignoring them, and I wasn't sure I was strong enough to survive that.

Zeb didn't respond as he guided us toward a section of brightly colored kids' bedding. Already I could see a set with both Superman and Batman logos as well as a set with a train on it. Zeb zeroed in on a set that had a bunch of vintage cars and trucks printed on the fabric and went to town picking out a matching rug and curtains for the room. It was fun to see his excitement and my heart turned over knowing that Hyde had a father who loved him and would never put him through the kinds of horrors I had lived through. My truth was a lot more unpleasant and a lot harder to digest then Zeb's.

I complied when he asked me to pick out another set of bedding for the room. I went with a wildly colored geometric pattern that had shapes going in all directions. It wasn't cars and trucks, but it wouldn't clash too badly with all the other stuff he had decided on and it was busy and fun. It served the purpose of making the space more kid-friendly so that both Hyde and any court inspector who might swing by would know that Zeb was rearranging his life for his little boy.

The price tag on the haul was completely reasonable and the cashier who checked us out had a nose ring and dreadlocks and barely blinked an eye at Zeb in all his tatted-up and bearded glory. I silently chastised myself for taking him to the pricey department store in the first place. The mistake made me feel stupid and disjointed. So did the lingering silence between the two of us as we trekked back to his Jeep.

He threw the bags in the back and then walked over to open my door for me. The Jeep was splattered in mud and various other dirty things from being parked outside his jobsite, so he wouldn't let me get in without a boost up. He laughingly told me he couldn't afford to replace my pantsuit if I got it dirty, and now I was wondering if that was something he was really worried about.

He put a hand on the door handle and one on the indent at my waist. He bent his head a little so that we were almost eye-to-eye and told me softly, "Your dad was an asshole and I wish he was still around so I could kick his ass, but your mom . . ." He shook his head slowly from side to side. "Sometimes who we love can't be controlled. I watched my sister struggle with it for years. She hated what her old man did to her, but she loved him, too. If you let all those things you did to survive your dad and all that resentment you have toward your mom fill you up, you'll never have room inside for all the things you actually want to feel. All that valuable real estate is taken up by things from the past and there's no room for the future to build on."

I pulled my eyes away from his as he wrenched open the door and put both hands on my waist to help me inside the vehicle. When he climbed up next to me on the driver's side, I let out a little sigh and muttered, "I'm not sure the ground is stable enough to build on whether or not the past gets cleared out."

He craned his neck to back out of the spot and reached over to put a hand on my thigh. "It just takes someone with the know-how to do it. Lucky for both of us, I'm a certified expert at building on shaky ground."

That made me laugh a little bit and I laced my fingers through his as he pulled out of the parking garage. I looked around when he turned in the opposite direction he would need to take to drop me back off at my house.

"Where are we going?"

"I'm starving and I want a drink. The Bar is only a few blocks down on Broadway, so I thought we could stop and have a quick bite to eat." His green eyes flashed at me and a wry grin pulled at his mouth. "Don't worry, I won't consider it going on a date since you seem allergic to the idea."

I balked a little. It wasn't that I didn't want to go on a date with him; it was that the idea of dating him made all of this seem so much more real. Right now I had myself convinced it was just sex and business. Eventually, the business would be over, when he had custody of Hyde, and the sex would be harder to come by, and I doubted he would keep putting forth the effort to see me. Emotions didn't have to be involved if we were work associates and fuck buddies . . . at least if I had done this right from the beginning they wouldn't have been, but I screwed up. Big-time.

"It's just a burger and a drink, Say. I didn't ask you to marry me."

I blinked when his words hit me, and realized I had turned into a statue in my seat. I swallowed hard and shifted a little bit.

"Okay. Sorry. I didn't mean to freak out."

"But you did. Eventually, you're going to have to spend time with me outside of the bedroom and the courtroom, Sayer. I have a five-year-old coming to live with me really soon and that means I'm a package deal. Spending time together is going to take on a new meaning with Hyde underfoot."

He squeezed my thigh and I tried not to panic at his revelation. He was going to put in the effort. What the hell?

I cleared my throat. "We'll cross that bridge when we get to it, I guess."

"Why does that feel like you using some kind of lawyer tactic to avoid the subject?" He sounded annoyed, but we were already in front of the little dive bar, so I didn't bother to explain that I was indeed trying desperately to change the subject. We worked really well naked and tangled together. I wasn't so sure how any of that translated to real life, and just like that my grip on the ledge tightened and I pulled myself a few inches up from the danger zone of love and longing.

"Let's go inside and eat. I'm hungry, too, and I love Darcy's BLT. We can talk about what happens next later."

He grunted at me but came around to help me out of the Jeep nonetheless. When I was standing in front of him with his hands at my waist, I wasn't surprised at all to see him bend his head down and kiss me—hard. He always did this when I put off a conversation that he wanted to have about the current state of our relationship. It was like a physical reminder that he was letting things slide, but only for now.

"Eventually there won't *be* any more laters, Say. There will only be right now and you're going to have to decide what you want to do with it."

The Bar was packed and we were enveloped in noise and revelry as soon as we pushed the doors open. A large man with beautiful skin that hovered somewhere slightly beyond the golden hue of a deep tan gave Zeb a fist bump and nodded at me. He was as beautiful and fierce looking as Zeb, so I returned the nod and decided not to trip over words by saying hello. His eyes were the most unusual shade of light blue that bled into an iridescent yellowish gold on the outer rim. I'd never seen anything like them and it was hard for me not to stare every time I was around him. I'd met Dash Churchill a few times when I had stopped by the Bar for a drink with the girls, and while he was always polite he was never what I would consider friendly, even when he instructed me to call him Church in that slow and thick Mississippi drawl of his. The same could not be said for the little-redheaded flurry of sass and fun that was Dixie Carmichael. The long-standing cocktail server for the place was everyone's best friend and didn't hesitate to throw her arms around me and Zeb, though he had to bend down quite a bit so the petite woman could reach.

"Oh my gosh, I haven't seen you guys in forever. It's crazy in here tonight, so you might have a tough time finding a place to sit." Her eyes widened.

Zeb rubbed his hand over his beard and scanned the busy bar. "What's going on tonight?"

Dixie shrugged which sent her strawberry-colored curls dancing. "The band is one of Jet's finds. Whenever he sends a group in they pack the house, and Asa isn't here to tend bar because he's trying to move into his new house, so it's just Danny, who is pretty new, and this totally new guy Zack. They're both okay but not as fast as Asa is. I should call Rome, but with Cora being pregnant and about to pop I'll only do that in an emergency."

She rattled off the list of familiar names that made up the group of men and women my brother claimed as his own. I nodded like I was following along and tapped Zeb on the shoulder. "You try and find a table. I'm gonna go wash my hands before we eat." I needed I minute to pull myself together as well. My mask was slipping and the woman trying to peek out from behind it was starting to take over my entire life.

He nodded and moved away as I started to push through the crowd of people blocking my way to the restroom. I was brought up short by a light touch on my elbow. Dixie's dark brown eyes gleamed up at me with all the romance and heart I was lacking.

"So you and the mountain man, huh?" The question was innocent and not all at the same time.

"I'm helping him out with some things and that led to us spending a lot of time together." That was about as much of a lawyerly no-answer as there was when it came to the status of my relationship with the big, bearded man.

Dixie giggled, and really the only person who could get away with giggling like that as an adult and still make it look cute and sexy was this little firecracker of a woman. "He's wanted to spend time with you for a long time and I always thought the feeling was mutual. Well, whatever it is, good for both of you. I love it when good people find each other even if they don't seem to fit. That makes it even better in my book."

Her gaze shifted toward the burnish-skinned bouncer and then back to me.

"Make each other happy. That's all that matters. I have to go pick up an order and yell at the new guy to get his ass in gear. If Zeb finds a seat I'll take a Coors Light to the table for you."

And just like that, she scurried off, and I resumed my battle to get to the ladies' room. I had never been to the Bar when it was so crowded, and I wasn't sure what kind of crowd it actually was. There seemed to be a lot of young, college-aged kids milling about who I assumed were here for the band that was playing later. There was also a big group of men and women dressed similarly to me who had clearly stopped by for an after-work cocktail, and then there was a hodgepodge of other folks who looked like they had just randomly chosen any old bar to stumble into off the street.

I picked my way around noisy patrons and pushed into the bathroom. I had to wait in line once I was inside, and for once I didn't feel like the odd man out because I knew the woman in front of me was wearing a Mauro Grifoni pantsuit that was way more expensive than anything I typically wore to work. It was also a really pretty shade of slate blue, and before it was my turn to disappear into a stall and do my business, I bookmarked the page on my phone where I could buy one for myself. Slate blue was pretty and it was colorful. Slate blue wasn't a neutral color at all, and if I went ahead and bought it there would be no hiding it as a guilty pleasure when I wore it.

I was putting my phone back in my purse when I bumped

into someone in the narrow hallway. I put my hands up to brace myself and looked up into the hazy and obviously drunk gaze of the man I ran into. He was half in and half out of his suit. His shirt was unbuttoned to the middle of his chest even though he still had on a tie knotted up toward his throat. He swayed on unsteady feet and took me with him since he was still holding on to my arms.

I gave him what I hoped passed for a friendly grin instead of a grimace and repeated, "Excuse me," as I tried to shake him off.

"Aren't you a pretty thing . . . and so tall. I bet your legs are fucking incredible."

I recoiled automatically at the slurred come-on and put some real effort into trying to pull free from him. I was annoyed that other men and women coming in and out of the bathroom didn't bother to say anything to him.

"I have someone waiting on me. You need to let me go—*now*." I put extra emphasis on the last word and gave him a solid shove in the chest. He grunted and curled his hands tighter into my arms, which made me yelp. I was going to have a collection of bruises left over from this encounter for sure.

"I don't want to let you go. I want to give you a kiss." He was so sloppy and drunk that all the words smooshed together and we almost fell again as he leaned toward my face.

Fed up, I put a hand over his puckered lips and pushed back as hard as I could. "Gross. Let me go."

I gained a little ground but when the man realized that he wasn't going to get to put his mouth on mine, he gave me a teeth-rattling shake that had my head snapping back. I let out a yelp of surprise as he screamed at me that I was a stuck-up bitch and I should be glad anyone wanted to kiss my stuck-up ass.

I was going to reply that there was someone in this very bar who was more than happy to kiss my stuck-up ass all the time when that someone was suddenly there and the drunk guy ended up shoved against the wall with two hundred and fifty pounds of furious Zeb Fuller in his face.

Zeb wasn't yelling. He wasn't throwing punches. He was simply holding the guy up off the ground by his shirt and threatening to do really awful things to him in a quiet and deadly voice. Only they weren't exactly threats. They were promises, and the drunk businessman could tell. His eyes zeroed in on me over Zeb's shoulder asking for help. I sighed and took a step forward so I could put a hand on his coiled shoulder. He felt like a predator about to pounce and go for his prey's throat.

"Zeb, let him go."

"He has his hands on you. He made you scream. He's not walking out of here without bleeding."

It was all growled through teeth as he shook the man similar to the way I had just been shaken. I'd never seen him like this . . . well, that wasn't true. He looked an awful lot like he did in that mug shot in the case folder on my desk, and that had panic rearing up and putting me in a choke hold. He couldn't go down that route again.

The idea of Zeb going away, of him losing everything he had worked so hard for because of me, had done what thinking about my mother and talking about my father hadn't been able to do. The gates were open, the plug was pulled, the walls were down, and every single fear, desire, want, dream, nightmare I had ever had rushed forth. It wasn't feeling one thing, it was feeling all the things I had repressed for so long, and it was enough to take me to my knees. I stopped breathing, stopped thinking, and let the flood of everything I had tried so hard, for so long, to pretend didn't exist carry me away.

Zeb had too much to lose and I refused to be the catalyst for it. I couldn't cost him or Hyde a future. If I did that I would deserve every awful, hateful word my father had leveled at me. The contempt and scorn that had been my everyday would finally be earned and I couldn't abide by that. Not for a second. Ancient words about worth and value, about not being enough, started to drag icy fingers along my spine. I knew what it was like to grow up without an ounce of love and there was no way I would ever put Hyde in that position. I would never make Zeb sacrifice like that for me.

I curled my hand over the thick muscle as much to keep myself steady as to make it possible for me to talk directly into his ear. My voice was shaky and raspy but he was so intent on the man he wanted to hurt I doubted he could tell. "You have too much at stake to be tossing this guy around like a rag doll. You don't want someone to call the cops. That's the worst thing that could happen when you're this close to getting custody."

The guy gurgled as Zeb crammed his forearm into his neck and cut off his airway. "He had his hands on you."

"I know, but I had the situation under control." I hadn't really, and now I was even more out of control than I had ever been. But there was more at stake here than this drunk idiot and Zeb's natural instinct to protect those he cared about. My bruises would fade, but if he lost Hyde over something stupid . . . I could never live with that kind of consequence. "Let him go. Please." I was begging and on the verge of tears. I could feel the desperation to get him out of here pulling at me with grasping hands.

I felt the tiniest bit of tension loosen in his shoulders and suddenly he stepped back and let the disheveled man fall to the floor in a shaken and terrified heap.

"Keep your hands to yourself, asshole."

The guy blinked up at us dumbly and then slowly nodded. I put a hand on the center of Zeb's back and wanted to cry when he shook off the touch. This is why emotions were dangerous. They hurt so much and there were too many of them to handle. I could feel mine cresting and breaking all around me. He stalked through the crowd with me hot on his heels until he found Church.

"Some drunk idiot just manhandled her in the hallway. He was shaking her and had his hands on her. He wouldn't let her go."

Church stiffened and nodded, his unusual eyes solemn and intent on the direction in which Zeb pointed. "His shirt is halfway open and he has a red tie on. The fucker is lucky I didn't strangle him with it."

"I'm on it. We'll eighty-six him. Do you want me to call the cops?"

"No." I poked my head around Zeb's back and shook my head frantically. "I'm fine. Don't call the police."

"Are you sure?" Church crossed his arms over his chest, and had the situation been different I would have taken a moment to appreciate the way they bulged under his tight, black T-shirt. He really was an extraordinarily beautiful and intense man.

"I'm sure. Let's just go, Zeb."

There was an exchange of masculine grunting and glaring that apparently communicated things that went beyond my knowledge and then I was whisked away and cloistered in the front seat of the Jeep and enveloped in a stony silence as Zeb seethed next to me. I could only take it for a few minutes before I blurted out, "I'm sorry."

His head whipped around so fast I was shocked the Jeep didn't run off the road. "For what?"

I shrugged. "For everything." For not handling this better. For thinking I could do this and end up unscathed. For not being able to be as passionate and loving as he was. For not being brave enough to trust him to breathe life back into my mistreated and shriveled heart like he had done to my house.

"I can't stand to see men with their hands on women. It's a hot button for me." I knew it was. It had to be after what happened to his sister.

"It was fine. I was fine. I was handling it. You have too much at stake right now to come riding to the rescue like that."

He growled low in his throat and I saw his hands go white on the steering wheel.

"When you say shit like that, it makes you sound like my lawyer, not my lover. Whenever someone hurts you, threatens you, or makes you afraid, I'm going to interfere, Sayer. I care about you . . . I lo—"

I cut him off before he could finish the thought. I couldn't hear that. If I let him say it the flood would wash me under. I took a deep breath, collected the tattered pieces of my shell around me, and prepared to do what I knew I should have done from the start to keep us both safe. I reached over and put a hand on his leg and waited until he turned his head to look at me.

"I *am* your lawyer, Zeb. I want what's best for you and your son." It looked like later had descended upon us sooner than either one of us had thought. I knew how to be his lawyer and give myself fully to that. I wasn't going to let him risk anything for me. Not his heart. Not his child. Not his future . . . nothing, not when I couldn't offer him anything in return.

He was deathly silent as we made it the rest of the way to my house, and when he pulled in the driveway and shut off the engine, I knew this good-bye was going to hurt worse than any other kind I had ever said before.

His green eyes were dark with prickly, painful things and I could feel their impact all over my suddenly too sensitive skin.

He blew out a breath that was so heavy as it landed on my skin that it felt like it was loaded with every hope and dream of his that I had taken away.

"So that's it? You want to be my lawyer? You want to figure out every problem you have on your own and handle anyone that tries to hurt you by yourself, even though I'm right here? I know I have a lot to lose if I get myself in trouble, Sayer. I understand that there is a lot at stake; what I don't get is how you can ignore that you're one of those things I'm trying my damnedest to be better for." His eyebrows shot up. "You've seen me, just me, from the very beginning, Sayer. Why is it so hard for you to believe that I've seen you, all of you, as well?"

He was going to make me cry. I bit down on my lower lip and reached for the door, but before I could push it open he was there. He was always there, in that spot right in front of me that seemed to belong only to him.

He put his hands on either side of my face and I felt him rub his thumbs over my cheeks. I was surprised at the moisture that followed the trail he left.

"I don't know what else to do here, Say. I built you a house. I made love to you. I gave you all the colors and helped you celebrate them. I melted you over and over again. I want to tell you how much I care about you . . . you tell me what else I can do?"

The world.

This big, tough man had given me the world and I couldn't do anything with it. For once, it was my hands that were too cold, while my heart felt like it was burning up inside my chest. So many feelings. So much fear. It was all too much to grasp as I flailed around inside the torrent. I reached out for the only thing that seemed stable, that seemed rooted to the ground. I reached for him.

I curled my hands into his shirt, I pulled his mouth down to mine. I whispered to him that I wanted him to come inside with me one last time, and I did it all knowing Zebulon Fuller would be the first and last boy whom *I* ever kissed because I was changing, slipping and sliding into a person who wasn't before or after but who was a confused and jumbled mess of both. He should have something better than that. I was half a woman lost in the horrors of the past and half a woman just now figuring out what she wanted and needed in a life that was her own. He deserved someone whole and so did his son.

He destroyed me with openness and stark honesty. I destroyed us by not having any space inside of myself. Even with the emotions I was purging and choking on leaving a hollow and empty space, I still couldn't find room to hold all of those wonderful things he was trying to give me.

CHAPTER 14

Zeb

She kissed me good-bye and I followed her inside. This was one of those prime opportunities for me to practice thinking long and hard about the consequences of my actions before I dove recklessly into the deep end. Too bad I wasn't going to stop and do anything other than fall even harder for her.

It was stupid. Probably even stupider than spending a night with Hyde's mother when I was off balance and unhinged after two-plus years without an ounce of freedom. Both experiences would end up leaving forever marks on who I was and how I loved. I knew Sayer was going to break my heart and I was willingly letting her do it. She was as cold as she had ever been on the outside, her skin like ice everywhere we touched. On the inside she was an inferno, a raging storm of too many emotions, making her typically clear eyes cloudy and wild. Again I thought she was a tempest, a gale that was going to wreck me and ruin me, and I wanted her to lay me to waste.

Everything I had ever felt for her, good, bad, uncertain, clean, and dirty, flared up into burning-hot points that wanted to pierce through my skin in order to get at her. She was going to completely melt for me now because there were no more icy walls holding me back from the very center of her. I'd done the hard work, made room for myself and my boy in her life, rearranged a space that was just mine; now it was up to her to figure out how to get rid of all that other junk so I could rightfully claim the rest of what was mine.

I undid the buttons on my flannel as soon as her bedroom door was shut behind me. I would leave her in this house I had built just for her and I would leave as much of myself behind with her as I could, so even if she wanted to, she couldn't forget me and couldn't ignore what I knew we meant to one another.

I watched with heavy-lidded eyes as she pulled her blazer off and turned toward me as she peeled off the rest of her clothing. She was beautiful and this was all so tragic. I told myself to turn around and walk out before things got even more complicated and fucked up between the two of us. But then her shirt cleared her head, and her bra hit the floor, and her hands were suddenly under the T-shirt I had worn under the flannel in defense against the diving fall temperatures. Her touch was firm and far more direct than it typically was when she put her hands on me.

She liked to run her fingers over me, liked to explore and caress with a light touch. This felt more like she wanted to take something. Like she wanted to hold on to me even though she was the one pushing me away with both hands. Before I knew it, she had my pants undone and was shoving the denim and my boxers out of her way. Even if my head and my heart knew this was good-bye, my dick didn't seem to care about the impending heartbreak. It eagerly fell into her waiting hands as she looked up at me with those tumultuous eyes. It wasn't a pretty squall trapped in there. It was ugly and crashing. Beating against the inside of her in endless waves, and it almost killed me that this wasn't something I had the skills or know-how to fix. There was no repairing Sayer Cole. She had to tear it all down and rebuild from scratch.

I was already as bare as I could be for this woman. There wasn't anything else I could offer her or create for her, so I stepped out of her grasp, which made her whimper a little and my dick really pissed off at me, and put my hands on her shoulders so I could turn her around so that she was facing away from me. I wasn't sure I could get through this alive with those tumultuous eyes pleading up at me to make it all better. I had done all I could. Now it was all on her.

I popped open the fastener on her pants and skimmed the charcoal-gray fabric down her long legs. Just like I suspected when I bet her in the mall about her underwear, they were a deep turquoise in color and very much in my way. I got her out of those as well, still without turning her around to face me, and slid my hand around the back of her neck. Her hair was still all twisted and tied up on the top of her head, so the skin was exposed and made her seem slightly more vulnerable than she really was.

I kissed her naked shoulder. I licked the vein that was pulsing out my name as it throbbed on the side of her neck. I ran my nose along the sweet curve of her jawline and stepped even closer so I could whisper in her ear, "When this is over, and I'm on my way out the door, I'm going to tell you that I love you."

She went stiff where my chest pressed into her back and tried to turn around to look at me. I wouldn't let her. I curled a hand up under her arm and circled her rib cage so that I could fill my

palm with her breast. The delicate pink tip immediately puckered and dug into my skin. I used my hips to point her toward
the edge of the bed since my legs were still trapped half in and
half out of my pants. I had no intention of getting any more un-
dressed. I loved her, but I couldn't make love to her right now. I
was too pissed. Pissed at her. Pissed at myself for following her
inside when I knew it was going to end in sorrow. And just generally pissed off at the entire situation. We deserved to be happy.
We deserved to make this work. It infuriated me that I couldn't
just force things to be the way I wanted. I was used to my persistence and stubbornness getting me what I wanted.

She obeyed my silent command to get on the bed in front of
me on her knees. The position had that delectable ass up in the
air and her already slick and glossy entrance lined up perfectly
with where my cock was pointed. She crossed her arms and
rested her forehead on the bed, unable, I think, to look at me
after what I told her. I did love her. Whoever she was and whoever she decided to be, but I couldn't be *in* love with her until she
had the room inside of her to love me back.

I walked my fingers up and down her spine and palmed the
curve of her hip. I wanted to slam into her. I wanted to pull her
hair and use my teeth on all of that delicate skin. I wanted to
scrape my face across every pale inch of skin and leave marks on
it with my beard. I wanted to use my tongue to torment her, to
bring her to the brink of pleasure and then take it away like she
had done with all the love I had for her. I wanted to use everything that normally brought her pleasure to cause her pain. I was
hurting and I knew she was, too. The difference was she had the
power to make it all stop. All that pain and all that hurt was in

her hands, she just had to put it down and grab on to the other stuff I was trying to hand her, things like love and forever.

I dug the fingers of one hand into her hip and let the others trace those little indents at the base of her spine that I was infatuated with. I skated my touch along the plush curve of her ass and didn't play around when I reached her already hot and begging center. I dove right in, swirled several fingers around, and told her to hold still when she jerked a little at the sudden invasion of her body.

It wasn't very nice. It totally wasn't smooth or romantic in any way, but I was feeling pretty split open and nasty. A good-bye like this wasn't supposed to be easy on either one of us, I supposed.

She was so warm and soft under my touch. So much the opposite of everything that was locked up tight when she looked at me. She was supple and sweet as she moved in time with my stroking fingers. She moved to lift her head up and I knew she was going to look at me over her shoulder and I wouldn't be able to deny the connection, the pull to try and save both of us from drowning as the current inside her pulled us farther and farther apart. I let go of her hip and leaned forward to bury my hand in her hair. I pulled with little finesse, sending the tie and a million bobby pins scattering across the bed and the floor. The blond tresses fell in endless, kinky waves across her shoulders and into my waiting hand. I grasped a handful and used it to keep her where I wanted her, which was as far away from me as possible, even though my fingers were inside of her and my dick was happily rubbing along the crevice her perfectly formed backside offered up. I felt her mutter a sound of distress as my belt buckle hit the back of her legs, but I still didn't stop what I was doing to her. We could both be distressed as far as I was concerned.

She started to make little noises in her throat, and I could feel her body quicken and tense where I manipulated it. She was close to coming, close to letting me give her the one last thing I could, pleasure and memories, and I knew I would regret it if I gave that to her without being inside of her to share it.

I pulled my fingers out of her now dripping core and yanked her closer to the edge of the bed. That had her ass even farther in the air and it took very little effort to sink down deep inside of her scalding heat. I felt her muscles contract around me as my eyes nearly crossed at how good she felt. I might not like either one of us very much at the moment, but there was no denying I would always love this. Worshipping her body with my own was never going to be an ugly or brutal thing. There was no punishment when we joined together, only acceptance and beauty. I was an idiot to think otherwise.

Steam . . . fire and ice made steam. It boiled and percolated between us and bubbled viciously and fiercely.

I couldn't stand the distance anymore. Couldn't handle fucking her and not being with her while I did it. So I used the hold I had on her hair to pull her up so that her back was pressed into my front and so that when she turned her head to look at me, our eyes were only a few millimeters apart.

She was crying.

Big, fat tears rolling out of her eyes as we watched each other. I put one hand on her breast and squeezed and the other over her heart so I could feel it beat out my name in code. I slowed down the pace I was moving in and out of her. I slowed my fury down by lightly touching my lips to hers. I slowed my heart down by realizing those tears were the ice she was forever encased in melting. There was hope. It was small. It was fleeting. It hid behind so many other things that felt so much more important. But it was there and it wouldn't be ignored.

I kissed her for real. Kissed her with everything I had. Kissed her with the desperation and fear that I had felt the first time our lips touched. I kissed her with enough force and fury that I knew she had to make room for it. She kissed me back the same way. It was a collision of lips and teeth. It was a duel of tongues and pounding hearts. It was slippery and messy in all the best ways, and when I mimicked the motion my hips were making as I drove into her harder and harder, she groaned into me and clutched at the back of my head like I was her lifeline.

I wasn't. She had to save herself, but I would be around waiting on the shore to scoop her up when she did, when the storm she was caught in subsided and the howling winds that were whipping her emotions back and forth died down inside of her.

I rolled her puckered nipple between my fingers and then circled it with my thumb. She panted into my mouth and one of her hands fluttered over mine where I was still holding on to her heart. I caught her free hand and dragged it over the flat plane of her stomach until we were both at the apex of her thighs. I knew how to touch her now, how to make her go off and wilt with just the barest hint of pressure. I knew all her secret spots of pleasure and how to manipulate them to make her break for me.

"I still want to watch, but not today. Today I just want to feel. I want you to feel us together and understand what you're giving up."

She made a strangled noise in her throat as I told her to spread her fingers around where I was driving in and out of her body.

The added stimulation from her touch and the gentle squeeze she added had my eyes rolling back up in my head as I used my index finger to circle her straining clit. Everything between us was coiled so tightly and ready to snap that neither one of us really needed the extra stimulation, but fuck if it didn't feel good.

Her fingers had her spread wide and everything was wet and warm as I felt my heart rate kick up and as pleasure almost took me to my knees. I applied even more pressure, used a firmer touch than I normally would on that sensitive little nub that was singing under my fingers, and continued to eat at her mouth like it was my last meal.

Her fingernails raked across the back of my skull and she jerked her head back so that she could scream my name. She wasn't much of a screamer when we had sex, usually just urging me on with soft little mewls and whimpers that made me feel like I was king of the sheets. But the scream . . . God . . . the earsplitting, brain-rattling, throat-breaking scream was the prettiest sound I'd ever heard. My name never sounded better. She owned it now and I knew there was no way she could deny it after coming apart like that.

I let her go and she folded back over so that I could reclaim my maniacal hold on her hips and ride her hard. It didn't take long, not with my name still singing in my ears and her body pulling at me with desperate tugs.

I came so hard my vision went black.

I came so hard my knees shook and I almost fell across her back.

I came so hard I felt it in my back teeth.

I came so hard that I knew that she would be feeling me for days and days after I was gone because I would be feeling her.

When my breathing regulated itself and I could see again, I ran both of my hands up either side of her spine and through her now ridiculously tangled hair and shifted so I could pull out of her and kiss her on the back of the neck.

The despair was there again when I separated our spent bodies, but this time it didn't feel like it was going to crush me. I took a step back from the edge of the bed and hefted my pants back up as she rolled over onto her back and stared straight up at the ceiling. She was so pretty and mussed up and messy from my hands and mouth. Her chest was flushed, her breasts still had pink imprints from my hands, and where her legs were slightly spread we both glistened shiny and real as our good-bye leaked out of her body.

She lifted her hands up and wrapped them around her throat as she continued to stare at the ceiling. It was like she was trying to hold that scream in. But there was no going back. We both heard it.

"What almost happened today . . . I can't ever be the reason that little boy loses you. I can't be the selfish, thoughtless person my father spent my entire life trying to convince me I was."

I blinked, a little bit stunned at her quiet revelation, and bent over so I could pick my shirt up off the floor.

"You could never be thoughtless or selfish, Sayer. You don't have an ounce of that inside of you." I shoved my hands through my hair and stopped to tug on it hard enough to bring tears to my eyes. "You want to be the emotionless robot you had to be to survive your father and your mother's death, that is a choice you are consciously making when you know there are other options. That is what you are choosing when instead you could choose me, could choose us. I know it's a risk but it's a risk we would take together." I sighed at her as I yanked on my shirt, not even bothering to try and find my T-shirt. "I love you and you know it. What you choose to do with it is also your choice."

I saw her hands tighten reflexively where she was still holding her neck and I wondered if all those emotions she kept bottled up and trapped inside were rising up to choke her.

I took the step that was needed to have my knees touching hers and hunched over so that I could put my hands on either side of her head. I stared down at her as she continued to cry and gazed up at me with those liquid, thawing eyes. Parts of the iceberg were shearing off and the jagged edges were slicing her to bits.

I touched my lips to her forehead and whispered against her skin, "I choose you, Sayer. Lover, lawyer, and all the shit you are in between that, I choose it. I choose us. When you're ready to accept that, you come find me." I pushed up off of her and gave her a twisted grin that had no joy or humor in it. "I'll see you in court."

The gauntlet was thrown down, my last hand had been played. Now all I could do was love her and leave her.

I LIKED BERYL'S boyfriend. Wes was an easygoing guy and he didn't seem put off by my sour mood or the fact I had a five-year-old Velcro'd to my side. I was surprised how shy Hyde was when the whole family got together for brunch on Sunday. It could have been the way my mother burst into tears the second she saw him and that she couldn't stop rubbing the top of his head or bending down to hug him. Or maybe it was that after we all ate, my mom and sister presented him with an army of toys that were more than enough to make up for every Christmas and birthday we had missed with him. There was no way my condo wasn't going to be considered kid-friendly after I hauled everything home for him.

I kept asking the little boy if everything was all right and he would nod at me and not say anything. Finally, after everyone was stuffed with dessert, Joss dragged him away to go watch some Disney movie with her in the living room while Wes and I tackled the dishes in the kitchen. Beryl was torn between keeping an eye on the kids and making sure I didn't do anything to embarrass her now that she had officially brought her man home to meet the family. Around the fifth time she stuck her head in the kitchen to ask if we needed help, I made sure she caught me relaying the most embarrassing story I could think of from when she was in high school. It involved her sneaking out in the middle of winter to hook up with a neighbor, getting locked out of the house by accident, and almost getting frostbite because she was too scared to ring the doorbell to let Mom know where she was at. I told him my sister had always taken risks when it came to men and rarely did they work out. She glared at me as Wes laughed, but there was weight to my words under the humor and my meaning was clear.

Don't be a risk she regrets taking.

Wes handed me a stack of plates to dry and leaned on the counter so he could face me. "I've never worked as hard in my life as I have to get her to give me a shot. She's beautiful, but it was more than that from the very start. I knew she was special and she made me feel special by being around her. That isn't something you give up lightly."

No, it wasn't. It had only been a few days and I felt the weight and loss of walking away from Sayer with every breath I took and in every movement I made. She was settled in my bones, tied so irrevocably to my foundation that the absence of her made me feel like I was going to collapse in on myself. I was also back to being in one hell of a shit mood because of the untouchable blonde.

"And Joss." He shook his head on a laugh and his eyes lit up as he talked about my niece. "That kid is something else. The life in her is amazing and you never know what is going to come out of her mouth."

I snorted and put the plates down so I could adopt a similar pose to his.

"Usually something that shouldn't be coming out. She's trouble, and as she gets older it's only going to get worse. Beryl is going to have to be on her toes."

"Well, hopefully she won't be the only one. I plan on sticking around, Zeb. I'm in this for the long haul. I want them to be my girls."

I considered him thoughtfully and silently for a long time. I could tell my lack of response made him nervous because he shifted on his feet a little bit. I was a good six inches taller than him, probably outweighed him by a solid eighty pounds, and I knew that he knew about my past. But he never wavered or looked away. He just told me softly, "I'm not asking you to give them up, but I do want you to share them with me."

I dipped my chin down in a jerky nod. "As long as you treat them right and they want you around, I'm happy to share. Make my sister happy and try and keep my niece out of trouble, that's all I ask for."

He chuckled. "Neither of those things is an easy task, but I'm going to give it my best shot from here until eternity."

The guy really loved my girls, and I would be lying if I said it didn't sting just a little bit at how easy it seemed to be for them. I knew that wasn't the case; Beryl had been burned and turned just as badly as Sayer had been, but my sister wanted more, so she let the past go. Sayer seemed to be holding on to it in a death grip. If I could just get her to let go I could have everything I wanted: the girl, my kid, the dream house, and a life with all of those things tied together.

After the dishes were done we went and watched the rest of the movie with everyone. Hyde was curled up into my mother's side, and I don't think he had any clue that the simple gesture was making her cry. It was so small and yet so huge that he was here with all of us. He was ours and he fit right in.

He was still withdrawn and quiet when I bundled him up in his coat and brand-spanking-new Batman hat and loaded him into his seat in my truck. There would be snow on the ground soon and that meant my baby was going to have to go into storage for the winter. She was pretty, but she sure didn't like to get her wheels dirty and she was the only girl on the street that could make a child's safety seat look badass.

I reached across the bench seat and clapped my son on the back of his neck and gave him a little squeeze. He might not want to talk in front of everyone else, but I knew when we were alone he would spill why he was so sullen and remote today.

"Why so quiet, buddy? Grandma was so happy to meet you, and Joss talked about playing with you all week long."

He shrugged his tiny shoulders and kicked his feet like he did when something was bothering him. As if on cue, he sucked in his lower lip and looked out the window.

"You can tell me, Hyde. You can tell me anything, and if you don't want to tell me what's bothering you, that's okay, too, as long you know I only want to help if I can."

He was silent for a few more minutes and then turned so that he could look at me. "I'm coming to stay with you soon, right?"

I squeezed his neck again. "You bet. This is the last weekend where we hang out during the day and then you get to come stay overnight at my place. Not every day just yet, but that will happen really soon."

"Okay." His voice sounded thready and thin. When I looked down at him he appeared to be holding back tears.

"Hey, if you aren't ready for that you don't have to come stay with me, Hyde. I want you with me, but you have to be all right with it." That was some heavy stuff for a five-year-old, but I wasn't exactly sure what was wrong with him. "I'll wait until you're ready." It seemed like I was going to wait on everyone I loved to be ready for me.

He lifted a hand and rubbed it across his eyes. I palmed the back of his head and contemplated pulling over on the side of the road so that I could give him a hug.

"Are you going to leave me alone in your house when I come stay? My mom used to leave me alone all the time and it was scary. I hate the dark and I was hungry. Auntie Echo would come over and take me to her place so I wouldn't be scared. You take me places all the time now, and people are always around, so you can't leave me alone. I don't like to be alone."

Talk about a knife right through the heart. I did have to pull over because I was shaking so hard and was so full of regret and wrath that I could hardly respond to him. It took a solid two minutes of deep breathing and mentally talking myself off the edge before I could reply. I was so lucky he had survived his mother's neglect. I was beyond fortunate I even had a chance to love him and care for him.

"I won't leave you alone, Hyde. I won't leave you alone at my house or anywhere else. In fact, if you ever even feel alone I'll show you how to use my phone and you can call your aunt Echo, you can call your aunt Beryl and Joss, and you can call your grandma because even though I'm there, you still might feel lonely, okay?"

He nodded and sniffed up what I was sure was an epic amount of snot. He rubbed his eyes again and blinked lashes that were spiky with spent tears at me. "What about Sayer? Can I call her if I feel alone?"

The kid was going to kill me. "You want to call Sayer?"

He shrugged again but this time he had a smile on his mouth and that dimple that matched mine flashing in his cheek.

"She's really pretty and nice. She smells good and she plays with me. She's a princess and I like her."

I bit back a groan. She was all of those things . . . well, maybe not a princess, but that aside, I liked when she played with me, too. "I like her, too, and I'm sure she would be happy to talk to you if you were feeling lonely. She really wants you to be happy."

He nodded like a little grown-up and gave me a full grin. "She wants you to be happy, too. She told me."

I lifted my eyebrows up at him and pulled the International back onto the street so that I wasn't late dropping him off back at the foster home.

"She did? What did she tell you?"

"Hmm . . ." He kicked his feet again and laughed at me when I growled at him because he was tapping his chin like he was thinking hard about the answer. He giggled uncontrollably when I reached out and tickled his ribs with my index finger until he gasped, "Okay, okay! She just said that she was working hard to make sure I got to go home with you because it's what was best for both of us. She said I made you happy, which made me happy, which made her happy."

Five-year-old logic at its finest. "You do make me happy, kiddo."

"You make me happy, too, Zeb."

We just needed to get the third member of that happiness tripod on board with all the good things we were feeling so we could be complete.

"When did she tell you all of this?"

He shrugged. "When she came to the house to play with me. She's always dressed up."

Which meant she must have stopped by after work to see him. I didn't want to be jealous of my kid, but I kind of was.

She might not know it or be willing to admit it, but she was going to choose us . . . both of us. Her actions said as much.

Again that tiny spark of hope, that thing I was clinging to with every ounce of strength I had, pulsed bright.

CHAPTER 15

Sayer

It had been nearly a month since Zeb walked out of my bedroom, leaving me shattered and pooling into a puddle of misery that was entirely of my own making. I was drowning in every single choice that had led to that point, and every word he uttered to me as he walked out wrapped around me and cocooned me in his harsh truths.

I still had to talk to him about the case. The court had wanted Social Services to check out his place before Hyde went to stay the night, and I felt like a boulder dropped on my heart when he'd told me they could come up and that he didn't think I needed to be there for the visit. He answered every text I sent him asking about how Hyde was settling in with one word like: "fine," "okay," "good." Every email I sent asking if he had already talked to the school district and made sure Hyde's vaccination records were up-to-date was answered with one that had only the facts and copies of the documents I would need to show the court if they asked for proof about how proactive Zeb was being as a parent.

I understood that he had to pull away because I left him no other option. I understood I had given him nothing to keep fighting for, but the loss still hurt. I knew that space he made for himself inside my life and my heart wouldn't be filled with anything else and I became achingly aware that alone and lonely were two different monsters.

Even as bad as being alone felt, it couldn't hold a candle to feeling lonely.

Alone was empty and cavernous. It yawned wide inside of me, never ending, and the pain of it echoed hollow and dull.

Lonely was the exact opposite. Lonely filled me up to the point of bursting. There was so much of it that I had no clue about how it wasn't pushing through my skin. Lonely screeched loud and infinite between my ears. The shrill cry was an ugly mélange of blame, want, fear, and fury. There was also nothing dull about lonely. It poked hot, so hot, in every tender place it could find. It prodded all those wounds now open and weeping as they bled everywhere, and I was finally forced to do something about them or end up bleeding to death.

I wanted to be the girl who I was when I was with Zeb all the time. She was who I was choosing, and even with that decision made, I wasn't exactly sure what steps I needed to take to keep her around forever.

I knew I was going to have to put on my best battle gear for the final court appearance. It was the first time I would be seeing Zeb in weeks, and he wouldn't be alone. Both his mother and sister were tagging along to hear the final verdict, so I felt outnumbered even though we were all on the same side of this particular fight. I knew I needed to let the woman I was trying so hard to be take the lead if I was going to get through the hearing with my poise and professionalism intact. I bought a new outfit from the same jealous saleswoman who had been hovering over me and Zeb on the day we shopped for sheets, and took an inordinate amount of satisfaction in the fact that she begrudgingly told me the vibrant purple hue didn't look good on many people but I could pull it off. I thought her eyes were going to pop out of her head when I bought a startlingly yellow shirt to go underneath it. Maybe it was too much, too eye-catching, but I didn't care . . . and that felt freeing.

I also decided my long, simple hairstyle had to go. All I ever did with my hair was tie it up or pull it back. I wanted it unfussy. But I deserved some fuss. I wanted some fuss. I made an appointment to chop inches off, and while I was at the beauty salon decided to thread as many different shades of blond as I could find through the heavy mass. The end result was eye-catching and trendy. Far more showy and flashy than anything I had ever tried to wear before.

The mask was all the way off, and the woman who was facing the world without it might not have everything figured out just yet, but she was getting there. Even if it was through baby steps like colorful new clothes and a chic new hairdo.

When the day of Zeb's final custody hearing rolled around, I offered to do the precourt meeting in my office with everyone, as we had previously done, but Zeb turned me down and told me that he and his family would all just see me at the courthouse. He sounded like a stranger. None of his easy humor or sexy innuendo could be found anywhere in his deep voice. He was talking to me like all my other clients did and it stung. There wasn't a hint of our previous relationship or anything personal in his tone.

Having him turn my own tactics on me felt a little bit like being dropped into a deep lake with frigid water. The shock of the impact was jarring and my limbs quickly went numb. I deserved it but the chill still shook me. It was so much easier not to feel, to pretend not to care. The tide of emotions was free and there was no escaping them as they ebbed and flowed inside of me, drifting and rising around Zeb like he was the gravitational pull that controlled them.

When I got to the courthouse I saw Zeb's Jeep already parked along the street and it made my heart kick. I couldn't recall a time in my life when I wanted to see someone so badly. Not even when I moved to Denver and had started to search for Rowdy. I just wanted to look at Zeb. I wanted to see him and breathe him in. I wanted to be in the vortex he created around himself that felt so secure and safe. I wanted to hear his voice rumble and watch his hands stroke his beard while he thought about things. I missed all the big things about having him in my life, but the little ones, the special things that made Zeb, Zeb . . . I was dying for a dose of those.

I was walking around the front of the building when my cell phone rang. I paused to dig it out of my bag in case it was the office calling about something I might need before court, but I almost dropped it when I saw the familiar Seattle number flash across the screen. I juggled my bag back onto the crook of my arm and put the phone to my ear.

"Nathan?" I couldn't keep the shock out of my voice.

"Uh . . . hey, Sayer. Been a while."

That was the understatement of the year. I gave him his ring back, told him I was moving to Colorado to find my brother, and hadn't spoken to him since. It had been a year since I last heard his voice.

"Is everything okay? I'm heading into court for an important case. I don't have much time to talk."

He chuckled with no humor in it and I was reminded of why we would have never worked out. "You are always headed into court for an important case. Some things never change, I guess."

I didn't like that he was trying to belittle me or what I did, still, but I had broken the guy's heart, so I figured he was allowed to be a little bit of an ass.

"What do you want, Nathan?"

"Well, I know it's a long shot, but I'm in Denver for a few days to meet with a potential new client. I thought you might like to get a drink and catch up."

I nearly tripped over my own feet at his words. I tightened my fingers on my phone and looked toward the front of the building. It felt like I was standing at the crossroads of my past and my future, and if I took one wrong step I would end up losing one and falling dangerously into the other.

I paused for a second instead of blurting out an automatic acceptance to be polite. I hadn't particularly enjoyed hanging out with Nathan when I had been involved with him. It wasn't like there was anything wrong with the guy, he just hadn't been as interesting as my work, and I hadn't particularly missed him at all since we had been apart. It wasn't like I was dying to reconnect and spend an awkward hour while he asked what I had been up to and I had to explain that I was exactly where I was when I left Seattle except for the fact that I now had a brother I loved, a roommate I would protect with my life, and a man who owned me but I was too scared to love back. I blew out a breath and replied honestly and truthfully.

"No. I don't really want to catch up, Nathan." There was no guilt, no worry or recrimination, because the woman I was now, the woman I was when I was with Zeb, didn't need to feel bad for saying no. I didn't want to see him and there was nothing outside of my own knee-jerk reaction to do what would be the easiest making me. It was liberating to say no with zero concern as to what his reaction would be.

He sighed on the other end of the phone and I looked at the screen of my cell to see what time it was. I still had a few minutes, but what was waiting for me in the courthouse was way more important to me than Nathan's aggravation.

"God, Sayer, you're still as cold as winter."

I scoffed a little because I wasn't anymore. The woman I was now ran both hot and cold, felt everything, including annoyance that he was egotistical enough to think his time was more valuable than mine. "No, Nathan, I'm not. What I am is busy."

"You were always busy. That was what kept us from really connecting."

I sighed heavily and paused as I reached the front doors of the courthouse. What kept us from connecting was the fact that I hadn't loved him and he hadn't loved me . . . not the real me anyway.

A flash of pink caught my eye, and I felt my mouth drop open in stunned shock when I saw the same young woman who had been giving Quaid hell the last time I was here come barreling out the doors. She was very pretty up close, in a surprisingly delicate way that didn't go with her shocking hair color or the angry twist of her mouth. I couldn't make out the color of her eyes as she flew past me, but I could see her eye makeup smeared across her face and the distinct tracks of tears on her face. Quaid was hot on her heels, looking as polished and professional as ever in a severe gray suit, minus the fact that his hair was standing up on the top of his head in a thousand directions like he had been pulling on it. He didn't seem to notice me, and I was about to call out a greeting when I saw him reach out and pull the young woman to a stop by her arm. He spun her around, shouted something I couldn't make out, which made me want to interrupt because he was obviously about to lose his cool. However, when I started to speak Quaid yanked the woman up on her tiptoes until they were lined up and his mouth was on hers.

I blinked in shock at the sight.

It was there as Quaid pulled the struggling girl closer and as she reluctantly gave in and curled her arms around his wide shoulders. The color. The risk. The more than love that people needed to be together forever. The more that made people strive to be better for the people that honestly cared about them. Quaid and the pink-haired firecracker appeared to be so wrong together. His divorce had jaded him and made him hard. She was too young for him and seemed so disillusioned. Not to mention that she was his client . . . his criminal client, but I could see something special in the way he handled her even as she jerked away from him and then slapped him across his too handsome face before stalking off; there was more there between them. It was vibrant. It sparked with life and it made me envy what I had willingly walked away from.

I missed everything about being with Zeb.

"Sayer?" I had forgotten all about Nathan on the other end of the phone and ducked inside the building before Quaid could catch sight of me witnessing his heated moment with the girl. I was shaken a little and I wasn't really sure why.

"I'm getting ready to go through security. I have to go. I honestly hope that one day you meet someone who makes you want to do more, Nathan."

I didn't bother to explain beyond that. He muttered a sour-sounding good-bye, and I hung up so I could send everything through the X-ray and walk through the metal detector. I was nervous when I entered the room where Zeb and his family had been told to wait for me before the final ruling.

I tried to force it down but some of my anxiety must have shown on my face when my gaze locked on his dark green one because before I could rattle out a shaky hello, a lovely, dark-haired woman who could only be his mother was in front of me, forcing me to tear my eyes off him with her hand held out.

"Hello. I'm Melissa Fuller. I can't tell you how grateful we are for all the work you've done to help Zeb and Hyde. We can't wait to have him home for good."

Zeb growled from across the room and his deep voice rumbled out a gruff "This is my *attorney,* Sayer Cole." I didn't miss the emphasis that he put on the word "attorney." It made me cringe, even though that was the role I'd chosen to play in his life. It still prickled when he gave me what I wanted . . . or what I thought I wanted.

I shook the woman's hand and cleared my throat. Zeb was still staring at me from where he was propped up against the wall, but I ignored him and shook the hand of the other woman who came forward. She looked so much like Zeb that I knew she had to be his sister. When she introduced herself as Beryl and raked her eyes over me in a very speculative way, I couldn't help but feel judged, not in a bad way, but the woman was obviously assessing my worth. I wanted to blurt out that I *knew* her little brother deserved better than what I had put him through as of late, but instead I told their mother, "Zeb has had to do most of the work. I just put the wheels in motion. Hyde should be at home with his family. I was happy to have a hand in making it happen."

I looked at Zeb out of the corner of my eye, but he hadn't moved a muscle. I could see a muscle in his cheek flexing under his beard and his eyebrows were furrowed over his eyes like he was contemplating something really troubling. I wanted to rub the furious lines away with my fingertips. I put my bag on the table and told the women to take a seat so I could briefly explain what was going to happen once we went before the judge. I looked at Zeb and asked him quietly if he wanted to join us.

He just shook his head and stayed where he was, looming like a grumpy statue and filling the tiny space with waves of discontent and annoyance. He wasn't happy with me, which was fine. I wasn't very happy with myself either. But I was getting there.

When the women sat down across from me, I ran through what would happen if the judge decided he wanted to speak with them about Zeb's fitness as a parent. I warned Beryl that if she took the stand there was a very good chance that her history with Joss's father would be brought up, and how it had led to Zeb's arrest. I told her to keep calm, state the facts only, and to focus on how Zeb was with her daughter now. I told her to tell the court that she had no qualms about leaving Joss in Zeb's care and to focus on how far he had come since his time in prison. I gave her a little grin and told her that all she had to do was tell the judge why Zeb was a great brother and uncle, to which she replied, "Piece of cake."

I liked her immediately and it made me feel even worse for being the cause of the massive thundercloud that lurked in the corner of the room.

The woman nodded solemnly and continued to watch me like she was trying to figure out what made me tick. If she found an answer I was ready to beg her to share it with me because whatever mechanism had been used to wind me up and keep me going over the years felt broken and all the springs stretched out and sprung.

I turned to Zeb's mom and found her looking between me and her son with speculation bright in her green eyes. I tapped my fingernails on the table like I always did when I was nervous and didn't bother to stop when she finally landed her gaze back on me.

"If the judge calls you to the stand, it will mostly be to talk to you about taking care of Hyde after school until Zeb gets off of work. He'll ask you how many hours you anticipate caring for him, how you plan on juggling a five-year-old with your existing schedule, and he may or may not ask your opinion about how you think Zeb will handle fatherhood full-time. All you need to do is present a united front with Beryl and show the court how much a part of your family Hyde already is. The judge already wants him to be with Zeb, so this is about all of us convincing him he made the right choice."

She smiled at me and I caught a glimpse of where Zeb got his dimple. "Zeb's done a fantastic job with Hyde so far. He might be a tad more lenient than I was with him when he was that age, but he's learning." She raised her dark eyebrows at me and reached out to pat my still twitching hands. "Being a single parent is never ideal, though. It's nice to have someone else around to help handle the day-to-day trials and tribulations of raising a family."

I forced my fingers to stop and looked over her shoulder toward her son. Zeb was still watching me and his face had turned even stonier at his mother's words. He finally pushed off the wall and made like he was going to run his hands through his hair only to remember it was slicked back and somewhat presentable for court. He stopped short and huffed out a deep breath.

"Beryl and I turned out just fine, Ma. I promise not to ruin Hyde if it ends up being just me and him for the long haul."

She laughed and we all got to our feet when I mentioned that it was time to head into the courtroom. "Of course you won't ruin him, Zeb, and obviously there is no way on God's green earth that you and that adorable little boy are going to be alone for long."

She might have been speaking to her son, but she was looking right at me when she said it. She gave me a knowing look as she moved past me toward the door. It was Melissa Fuller's truth, and it was as heavy as a ton of bricks when it hit me.

Her meaning was clear. Get my shit together right quick or else someone not scared, and not searching, was going to step up in my place and there would be no one else to blame for everything I stood to lose this time but me. Zeb got more than his dimple from his mother; his forthrightness and in-your-face honesty, no matter how harsh it might seem, obviously had come from her as well.

Zeb paused before me on his way out the door and I gazed up at him with everything I had inside of me shining out of my eyes.

"Good luck today." My voice cracked and oozed longing at him.

His nostrils flared as he breathed out a heavy breath. He lifted a hand toward my face like he was going to cup my cheek but let it fall before he made contact. I wanted to cry as it fell away.

"I don't need luck. I have you. I like your hair, and you look really pretty today." His words wrapped around me and squeezed tight. I wanted to cuddle into that feeling and forget the ache of his absence that had been my constant companion the last few weeks. I let him walk out in front of me and took a second to bend over and rest my hands on my knees so I could catch my breath. Those goddamn feelings could pack one hell of a punch when they were free to do their thing.

When we got into the courtroom the mood was surprisingly optimistic. The heavy uncertainty that had reigned the first time we had done this was long gone. This all felt like no more than a formality. We followed all the protocols as the judge entered the room and I answered all the questions from the bench as we went over the home visit, Zeb's progress on the classes he had been ordered to take, and the details of everything the judge had handed down at the last hearing. The judge seemed pleased with Zeb's progress and asked him to get up and go to the bench. I nodded at him encouragingly and reminded him to simply be honest. It was what he was best at after all.

"How have the overnight weekends been going, Mr. Fuller?"

Zeb shrugged and then straightened up and spoke clearly and firmly. "There has been some transition. Hyde is really scared to be alone, and I think he's sensitive about being shuffled between my place and the foster home. He always asks me if I'm going to come back for him. And the kid would live on pizza alone if I let him, so there have been a few meltdowns when I wanted him to eat like real people."

That startled a laugh out of the judge, which made me smile.

"We work through it. My mom and sister have been great and Hyde's mother had a really good friend that he was close to. She's been by to visit him, so I think he knows we're all just trying to make him as comfortable as possible. I may spoil him rotten, but I figure I have a lot of lost time to make up for."

"What about the practicalities of transitioning the child into your care on a full-time basis: school, day care, health insurance? How are you doing on all of those things?"

"Hyde won't go to kindergarten until fall since his birthday is late in the year. I'm going to enroll him in the same district as my niece so that my mother can pick him up and watch him for me until I get off work. Joss already loves him and I would rather have him with family than in day care."

He looked over his shoulder at his mother and she gave him a nod. The judge watched the exchange over the rims of his glasses and made a note in the file he had open on the desk. "What about insurance?"

I saw Zeb's shoulders tense, but he answered the question truthfully. "Since I'm self-employed, that has been a tad bit trickier. I have to wait for open enrollment to sign him up on a policy, so until then I'll put him on Medicaid."

"What about my recommendation for counseling? You mentioned the child was having issues being alone and separated from you."

"My sister gave me the name of the doctor she took my niece to after the incident a few years ago. He didn't have any openings this month, but I set us up an initial appointment for a few weeks from now. I want to make sure Hyde is comfortable with the guy before I commit to anything on a long-term basis."

More scribbling but there was satisfaction stamped on the judge's face. This was all going really well and I hadn't had to do much of anything. I didn't think he was even going to call the Fuller women to the bench.

The judge nodded and scribbled some more notes. "How has the adjustment in your social life been, Mr. Fuller?"

Zeb's eyes darted over to me and then back to the judge. I forced myself not to start squirming as the judge followed the exchange.

"Haven't had much of a social life lately, Your Honor. I've been working and getting things settled for my boy. I'm waiting for someone special. I won't let anyone I'm not seriously involved with near my kid. He's been disappointed by the adults in his life far too much already."

The judge reached up, pulled his glasses off, and offered up a slight grin. "That is a very good answer, Mr. Fuller. In fact, I am very pleased with everything you have told me and all the steps you have taken to facilitate your motion for custody. Go ahead and have a seat. Counselor, can you approach the bench, please?"

I wasn't expecting this but kept my face blank so that I gave nothing away as I passed Zeb on my way up to the bench. He gave me a curious look, but since I had no idea what was going on, I just shrugged a little and took purposeful strides until I was in front of the judge.

He pushed the microphone in front of him to the side, crossed his hands in front of him, and leaned forward so that he was looking down directly at me.

"You've been in front of me several times the last few years for different cases, Ms. Cole. You are passionate, dedicated, and driven to do right by your clients. I like having you in my court-room."

I blinked in shock and shifted on my feet. "Uh, thank you, Your Honor."

"You fight for your clients with the obvious belief that you are doing so with their best interests in mind. In this case, I know the father is who you are representing, but I want to know that if it was the child you were fighting for, would you still be con-vinced the best place for him is in the care of Mr. Fuller?"

I opened my mouth and let it close again. It was unprece-dented for a judge to ask legal counsel their opinion on a matter like this.

"Your Honor, I . . ."

"I want your honest opinion, Ms. Cole. Should the child be placed in the care of your client on a permanent basis?"

The truth. My truth . . . finally. It was the easiest thing in the world for me to give it to this man who held Zeb's world in his hands.

"Zeb loves that boy and Hyde loves him back. They are a team, and while I recognize there is a learning curve for both of them, neither could ask for a better teacher. Zeb will never, ever give up on Hyde, no matter what issues from the child's formative years may present down the road. He will work endlessly and tirelessly to make sure that little boy never goes without, and there has never been a man more willing to open up himself and his home for anyone. Honestly, Your Honor, I wish I was as certain in all my cases that the child in question was going exactly where he or she was supposed to be."

The man's eyebrows rose up on his forehead. "Both of them

seem pretty fond of you as well, Ms. Cole. The reports from both the CASA representative and the social worker who visited the home mentioned both the father and son brought you up quite frequently in conversation."

I felt myself flush. "This case started out on a personal note and became more so as I got to know the people involved more intimately." Maybe it was a bad choice of words because the judge was going to know I meant that Zeb and I were involved sexually, but I didn't care. There was nothing to be ashamed of. The woman without the mask knew that as she stood there confidently and unafraid of judgment.

"It's rare that a child in the circumstances that Hyde found himself in has so many good people looking out for his best interests. He is very lucky."

I nodded a little stupidly. "He is, but so are we. He's a great kid, Your Honor."

The judge nodded again and reached for his glasses. "You are someone special, Ms. Cole. In this courtroom and, if I had to wager a guess, outside of it as well. Keep that in mind after my ruling."

I closed my eyes briefly as his words echoed Zeb's statement that he was waiting for someone special to be in his life. I took a deep breath to steady myself and went back to the table as the judge told me to have a seat so he could read his final ruling.

"As far as the court is concerned, Mr. Fuller has met all the requirements mandated by the court and provided enough evidence that he is willing and capable to assume fully physical and financial responsibility of the minor child Hyde Bishop. The court reserves the right to intermittently check on the welfare of the child for the first five years of custody, but beyond that you are free to raise your son as you see fit, Mr. Fuller."

He picked up the gavel, but before he brought it down he said, "On a side note, it does this often jaded court official good to see a man turn his life around, accept responsibility, and make self-less and caring choices. I didn't know you before, Mr. Fuller, but the man standing before me now is the kind of parent I wish all children had fighting for them."

The gavel hit the top of the bench, the judge left in a flurry of black robes, and I turned to Zeb with a huge grin as his mother and sister got up and slowly made their way over.

I wanted to reach out and touch him, to hug him and cel-ebrate with him. His eyes were shining bright and his smile was so infectious that I couldn't help but return it.

"You won." I whispered out the words around the lump in my throat.

His grin dimmed a little and he climbed to his feet. I went still as stone when he bent over and pressed his lips to the top of my head.

"Not yet, but the game isn't over yet." He straightened to his impressive height and looked down at me with serious eyes. "Thank you, Sayer. You gave me everything."

He walked away from me and threw his arms around his family. They all shared an embrace and I could hear his mom crying.

Victory was very sweet, but watching Zeb walk away with it because I wasn't ready to let him share it with me felt like the greatest loss in the entire world.

CHAPTER 16

Zeb

Hyde had been in my custody for two full weeks when Rowdy called and told me that everyone was getting together at Asa and his girlfriend Royal's new place for a housewarming party. He mentioned that everyone was curious about the little boy they had heard so much about from Sayer and that had been keeping me occupied. I hadn't really seen much of my friends since the whole custody case started and I knew there was a big part of me that wanted to go on the off chance that Sayer would be there. I agreed to swing by for an hour and refrained from asking my friend Rowdy if his sister was planning on making an appearance. I knew he had to know what was going on—or rather what was no longer going on—between the two of us, and if he didn't mention it I wasn't going to either. That was an open wound that didn't need salt poured on it.

Taking myself out of Sayer's life ranked up there with the hardest things I had ever done. Seeing her in court, listening to her tell the judge about all the love I had to give to Hyde and yet not being willing to take any of it for herself when it was so freely offered had me ready to rupture at all the places where I was barely holding it together.

When she told me that I won I wanted to shake her and ask her how in the hell she could say that when we hadn't spoken directly in a month. There was no winning without her being where she was supposed to be. She was supposed to be with me, with my son, and we were supposed to be a family. She was the one that had fought to make it so and she was the one walking away from the spoils of the war.

Hyde was playing in the living room when I went to get him to take him to the party. He had settled into being with me with relative ease, even though there were still some struggles at night. He didn't like the dark. He didn't like to be left alone. He didn't like to sleep through the night. I was getting used to waking up in the morning with a tiny body inhabiting the opposite side of my bed. He also didn't like it when I had to leave him with my mom while I went to work. Every time I came to pick him up in the early evening he ran at me like we had been separated for months instead of hours, like he was surprised I'd come back for him. It broke my heart that he felt so insecure, but all I could do was show up. I would always show up for him and eventually he would realize that he had nothing to worry about.

"You ready to go, little man?"

He turned to look up at me from the trucks he was pushing around the floor and furrowed his tiny brow. "Is Joss gonna be there?"

God bless my niece. She might be a handful and not know when to keep quiet, but she had taken the little boy under her tiny wing and the two of them were as thick as thieves.

"No. These are a bunch of my friends that all want to meet

you. There might be a little girl named Remy there, but she's pretty young, so I'm not sure she'll know how to play with you."

Rome and Cora's daughter was the spitting image of her pixie-like mother and a tiny tornado of activity.

"I'll take my trucks just in case." He got to his feet and held the plastic toys out to me.

"Sounds like a plan. Don't forget to grab your hat and gloves." Denver had nose-dived into early winter, and even though there wasn't snow on the ground yet, the temperatures were hitting below freezing on the regular. I was regretting every single time I ever gave my mother hell for trying to make me dress warm when I was a kid as Hyde grumbled all the way to his room. Little boys apparently hated being warm and it was an ongoing struggle to keep my little guy bundled up.

I put on my own coat and shoved the trucks into the pockets. I grabbed the keys to the Jeep and waited for Hyde to come barreling out of his room. He had his knit hat on and one glove and a puzzled look on his face.

"I only have one." He held up his bare hand for inspection as I lifted an eyebrow at him.

"Where did the other one go?"

He shrugged his tiny shoulders and shuffled his feet in the black Converses that matched my own.

"I dunno. I lost it."

I sighed and pulled the glove off his other hand. I was going to have to start buying those suckers in bulk. "You think you might've left it over at Grandma's?"

More shrugging. "Maybe. Are you mad at me?" His bottom lip trembled when he asked it.

I took his uncovered hand in my own and left the condo. "No,

I'm not mad at you. I lost my fair share of gloves when I was your age. I just want you to be warm, remember? It's my job to take care of you."

I made sure to keep my steps short and easy for his much smaller legs to keep up with. "I'll try harder."

I grinned down at him. "Thanks, buddy."

"Hey, Zeb." I stopped and hefted him up so I could put him in the Jeep. When we were eye-to-eye he asked me, "If your friends are going to be there, is Sayer going to be there? I miss her." Now that he was with me full-time she no longer stopped by to see him after work. I wanted to call her on it, tell her she was making the wrong choices all around, but I knew she had to figure out where she was going on her own. I continued to have hope but the past was still pulling at her hard and I couldn't do anything more until she worked her way free.

It was a gut punch.

I gave Hyde a little squeeze and worked him into his seat. "I don't know. She might be and I miss her, too."

"Call her. You said I could, so why can't you?" Again, five-year-old logic at its finest.

"Well, bud, I think she would want to talk to you if you called; me . . . not so much. It's complicated adult stuff that you don't need to worry about, okay?"

He didn't bring her up a lot but every time he did it was heart-wrenching. He was too young to have lost so much. He nodded and gazed up at me through his lashes. "Okay, Zeb."

I shut the door and walked around the Jeep to get in the driver's side. We were both quiet as I drove toward the suburbs where Asa had bought his new house. I knew Hyde was thinking because his feet were bouncing up and down and he was biting on his lower lip. I could read the kid like a book now and knew he was going to hit me with more questions I probably didn't have the right answers for. I tried to be honest with him. I tried to be as forthright and as compassionate as I could be, but life wasn't fair sometimes and there wasn't always a happy ending. I just hated to tell him that his mother fell into that category.

"Hey, Zeb?"

I looked over at him. "Yeah, buddy?"

"How come you're better at taking care of me than my mom was?" It was an innocent question but not innocent at all.

It all came down to realizing how much I had to lose if I didn't care for him the best I could. Hyde was the ultimate second chance, the pinnacle of proving I was a different man from the hotheaded kid who acted without thought. He wouldn't understand that, so I told him, "I had your grandma and your aunt Beryl to show me how to do it right. I also screwed up really bad a few years ago, made some really bad choices, and saw what would happen to me if I didn't figure out how to take care of myself and the people I love. I learned from my mistakes and I learned from people that loved me. I don't think your mom could do that. And I'm not always going to be better at taking care of you, kiddo. We're both gonna screw up here and there, but we're going to learn along the way and be better for it in the end."

He held up his bare hands and wiggled his fingers at me and I nodded at him because he got it. The kid was too smart and too aware for his own good. He shouldn't have had to live as much life as he already had in his short time on this earth. It was one of my goals to make sure he got to enjoy being a regular old kid from here on out.

"If Sayer wants to be the one to help you take care of yourself and me, that would be awesome."

I looked at him out of the corner of my eye and was treated to a giant, toothless smile. If I didn't know any better I would swear the little man was playing matchmaker.

"I'll keep that in mind."

Asa's house was easy to find with all the cars parked in front of it. I took Hyde's hand, which felt like a block of ice—thank you, missing glove—and led him to the front door. I didn't bother to knock since I knew everyone was expecting us and was enveloped in the atmosphere of celebration and family as soon as we crossed the threshold. Laughter rang out. There was football on the TV. There were deep voices arguing in a good-natured tone. This was a place full of family, laughter, and love. I had missed it and I was so glad me and my son got to be a part of it.

I hung our coats on the hooks on the wall in the hallway and retrieved Hyde's trucks from my pockets. I gave him one and held on to one since I still had his hand in mine as we made our way toward where I assumed the kitchen was, since that was where everyone typically congregated when we all got together. We were intercepted by a blond toddler before we made it even a few feet into the house.

Remy Archer was too cute for words in her pink-and-black dress and with her fair hair pulled up in a miniature ponytail on the top of her head. She was still baby chubby but surprisingly sturdy on her legs as she came toward Hyde with glowing blue eyes.

She pointed at one of the trucks he was clutching and announced in a very serious tone, "Mine."

Hyde looked up at me with questioning eyes and I showed

him the truck I still had in my hand. "You can let her have that one. You can take this one and go play with her."

He opened his mouth and I could see that he wanted to argue when Remy wandered closer and put one hand on the truck and the other on Hyde's cheek. It took me a second to realize she was poking at his dimple. He jerked back and scowled at the little girl, which made me laugh as he thrust the truck toward her.

"Take it." He sounded so disgruntled I couldn't help but feel sorry for him.

The toddler took the toy and smiled a toothy grin just as her very pregnant and very frazzled mother came around the corner. I saw Cora's multicolored eyes light up at the sight of us and a huge smile crossed her face when she saw Hyde.

"We were wondering when you were going to show." She put a hand on her round belly and scooted closer. "Oh my, don't you look just like your daddy? You're quite handsome, my little friend."

"I'm Hyde." He looked up at me and grinned. "My dad's a giant. So I'm going to be a giant, too."

Cora tossed her head back and laughed. "You're probably right about that. But don't be surprised to find there are a few giants running around this place today. It's nice to meet you, Hyde. I'm Cora and the little thief that took your truck is Remy. You can call her RJ if you want. She's harmless, mostly."

The little girl looked at her mom and gave her a grin like she knew exactly what was being said about her. I didn't envy Rome having to deal with that kind of handful as the little girl got older.

Hyde took the truck from me, and even though he grumbled about it, he didn't complain when Remy took his hand and started to totter off with him deeper into the house. Cora put a hand over her heart and sighed.

"Oh my. I think my daughter has her first crush. I can't blame her. He is adorable, Zeb."

I grinned and lifted a hand to rub the back of my neck. "He's a good kid. After everything he's been through . . ." I shook my head. "He deserves the world."

She half walked, half waddled toward me and I didn't argue when she wrapped her arms around me even though hugging her around her protruding belly was slightly difficult.

"And what about you, Dad? What do you deserve for giving him the world?" That was Cora. She was never one to beat around the bush or pull any kind of punches.

"I'm still working on that. It's been a little tougher than I anticipated."

She pulled away from me and I followed her into the house. The sound of voices got louder and I could hear Hyde talking about giants from somewhere close by.

"She left already. She was here with Poppy, but all the people and all the noise . . ." Cora shrugged a shoulder. "Poppy froze up and Sayer took her home. I honestly don't think she wanted to leave, but she's like a mother hen where that girl is concerned. I think it hurts Salem's feelings that Poppy leans so much on Sayer instead of her."

"Did she know we were coming?"

Cora nodded. "Rowdy told her. Zeb, that woman is in love with you and your son. She talks about Hyde the same way I talk about Remy. She lights up when she says your name and we both know she isn't the type that glows."

I sighed. "She can be."

Cora looked at me over her shoulder as we joined the revelry. "For you she can be. Not for anyone else. I don't know what happened between the two of you, but I do know that you shouldn't give up on her if she is who you want to be with."

"It's not about me giving up, it's about her giving in." I said it, but I don't know if she heard me because we were separated by a bunch of guys, most of whom were as big, if not bigger, than me.

There was a lot of back pounding. There was a lot of congratulations and at one point Rowdy handed out cigars that had *It's a Boy* written on the band. I took it all in stride and was happy that Hyde seemed fascinated rather than intimidated by all the colorful and exuberant people around him. He also seemed okay with the fact that wherever he went, Remy followed. She was stuck to his side like glue, which had Cora cackling and Rome frowning from my son to me in an entirely comical way. All I could do was shrug at him.

It was an onslaught of well-wishes and catching up. It was busy and fun, so when Rowdy cornered me when I was coming out of the bathroom I wasn't really ready for it. I should've known something was coming my way from him; after all, I would have done the same thing if I was in his shoes. I knew all about the brotherly need to protect and defend.

He was leaning on the wall with his arms crossed over his chest. I rubbed my hands on my jeans and tilted my chin up at him. "I did my best, dude. It's all on her now."

His blond eyebrows shot up. "Just like that?"

"Just like that." It really was that simple.

"Things seemed to be on the right track there for a while. You want to tell me what happened to fuck it all up? She's my sister, Zeb, and you're my friend. I feel like if I can help fix this, I should."

"What happened is I told her that I needed her to be more than my lawyer. I told her I needed her to be everything and she told me she couldn't. She's lost somewhere where she didn't matter enough to the people she was supposed to matter the most to and I can't help her find her way out of that."

He frowned a little and pushed off the wall. "But she's great with me. She fought to have me in her life even when I resisted, and she's amazing with Poppy. You can't tell me she doesn't love that girl like she's her own flesh and blood."

I rubbed both my hands over my beard and shrugged. "You're the only real family she's ever had. That asshole that raised her, and her mother, sure as hell don't count. She'll hold on to you for dear life because without you, she thinks she'll be alone . . . really and truly alone. And Poppy is like a bird with a broken wing. Sayer is nursing her back to health, but she knows one day she's going to be able to fly again, so she isn't worried about her leaving, she knows she's gonna go. With me she has to take the risk that I'll stay, that I'll be there no matter what, that I'll love her even if things aren't always easy. She has to trust that she's enough, more than enough, and I can't tell her that. She just has to know it and believe it. It has to be her truth."

He let out a low whistle and tossed his hands up in the air. "I was ready to give you some long-winded lecture on why she is amazing and how you just had to fight through the wreckage of her past to get to the heart of gold she has, but you just outbrothered me."

That made me snort. "I have a sister, too. I get it."

He reached out and clasped me on the shoulder and gave me a little shake. "By the way, Rome told me about the run-in at the Bar a few weeks ago. I know it could have been bad for you to get mixed up in anything physical with everything that was going on with the custody case, but thank you for keeping my sister safe."

I blinked in surprise. "Did Church tell him what happened?"

"Yes, but he also saw the tape. That guy was pawing at Sayer and she was terrified. You did the right thing." He gave me another little shake since I couldn't come up with a reply. "For what it's worth, I think you did the right thing before as well." He lowered his voice and leaned closer so that we were almost nose-to-nose. "Sometimes we have to suffer and give up a piece of ourselves to do the right thing for someone that we love. I've been there."

He pulled back from me, but I could still feel his words lying heavy on my shoulders. I didn't know the ins and outs of Rowdy's whole history, but I did know that he had done something similar to what had landed me in prison when he was younger. I had lost years of my life, he had lost a full-ride scholarship. I wasn't sure it was the same, but it made me feel a little bit better that he did indeed know where I was coming from, then and now. Just like with his sister, there was no judgment about what I could have done differently; only acceptance for the things I had done. It soothed some part of me that was always so frayed and worn.

We walked back toward the living room, where everyone was winding down. Hyde was sitting on the floor watching TV and Remy was curled up in a little ball next to him fast asleep. Rome stopped me with a hand in the center of my chest before I could grab my kid and say my good-byes.

"What's up?" I said. Rome Archer was one of the few men I had met in my lifetime that I didn't have to tilt my head downward to make eye contact with. And if that wasn't intimidating in itself, the scar that bisected half his face and the stern set of his mouth would be.

"My kid seems taken with your kid."

I chuckled. "She's two. I think you have a minute before you start worrying about her chasing boys around."

He grunted and turned to look at the two little kids. "He seems like a good kid. If he's anything like his old man, I don't mind her chasing him around. I won't let her catch him until I'm good and ready, but all that running around is the only thing that's finally wore her out."

I gave him a solid thump on the back because Rome wasn't the kind of guy you grinned at. "Thanks, man. I appreciate that."

"Saw what happened to your girl. Church was pissed. The Bar's getting busier and busier and he can't be everywhere at once. I might need to hire more help."

"Church is a good dude. He takes his job seriously."

Rome made a noise. "He takes safety, especially the safety of women, seriously. I doubt the drunk will be putting his hands on any more women anytime soon."

That made me ridiculously satisfied. I might not have been able to put my hands on the man, but I was glad someone else, someone infinitely more terrifying than I would ever be, had taught him a lesson in manners and how to treat a lady.

"Good. I'm gonna take Hyde and head out. I have to work tomorrow and have to drop him off at my mom's pretty early in the morning."

Rome nodded and clapped me on the shoulder. "It was good to see you. Don't be a stranger. Remy could use a playmate."

I agreed and picked my sleepy kid up and wrestled him into his coat and then into the car. I was almost at the condo when my mom called and told me she wasn't feeling well and asked me to see if Beryl could watch Hyde for the day. I reminded her that

Wes had whisked Beryl and Joss away for the weekend but told her not to worry about it. I would find someone to watch him, and if I couldn't I would just skip work.

Of course, being the ever-observant and wicked smart kid that he was, Hyde overheard the entire conversation.

"So what do you think, little man? Should I ask your aunt Echo to hang out with you tomorrow?"

He pondered the question for a second and shook his head in the negative. "You should ask Sayer. We can build more castles."

I'd had a feeling it was coming, so I blew out a breath and agreed to call her when we got home.

Hyde took his sweet time getting ready for his bath and then fought me like he usually did when I tried to put him to bed. I didn't mind him crawling in with me after he woke up in the middle of the night, but I always insisted he start the night out in his own bed. I turned the night-light on, curled up with him, and read him a bedtime story. His eyes drifted shut and he was nearly asleep when he mumbled, "You promised to call Sayer."

"I will." And I would, after he was asleep, so he didn't see me pacing around the house like a nervous wreck.

I peeled out of my clothes and plopped down on the bed before bringing her name up in my contacts. I hit the send button and held my breath until her sleepy voice came across the line. I hadn't even looked at the clock, but when I did it was only a little bit past ten.

"Did I wake you up?"

She let out a strangled-sounding laugh. "Uh, no. I haven't been sleeping very well. Is everything all right?"

I wondered if she wasn't sleeping because I wasn't there next to her. I really hoped that was the case. My dick went hard at just the sound of her voice. I shouldn't be the only one suffering because we weren't together.

"Everything is fine. I was actually calling for a favor. My mom can't watch Hyde tomorrow and my sister is out of town. He's really sensitive about who he's left with during the day when I go to work and when I asked him who he wanted to spend the day with he said you."

"Me?" She sounded shocked.

"Yeah, you. He likes you and he misses seeing you." He wasn't the only one under this roof that felt that way.

"Um, sure. Bring him over. I have a little bit of work to do from home tomorrow, but I can tackle it before you get here."

"Nice. He'll be stoked."

"Oh . . . yeah, well, I will be, too. I've missed seeing him."

I missed that "oh." I missed kissing it and sucking it in. I missed it wrapped around my dick as her mouth moved on me. I missed her screaming it in surprise every time I made her come for the second time. I missed the soft shock on her face when she said "oh" after every time she surprised herself.

"Yeah, oh. You can see him . . . and me . . . anytime you want to, Say. You just have to make that choice. I'll see you in the morning and have a good night."

She made a strangled sound in her throat and I could clearly see her putting her hand up to the base of her neck like she did when she was trying to work out how she felt about something. "You have a good night too, Zeb."

I hung up the phone and tossed it on the empty side of the bed . . . the side of the bed she should be on.

CHAPTER 17

Sayer

I had a motion I was supposed to be working on before Zeb showed up with Hyde, but obviously I couldn't concentrate to save my life. Instead of screwing up my entire case, I decided I would try and make pancakes for breakfast. I figured all little kids liked pancakes for breakfast, so I threw on a pair of jeans and a baggy sweater and ran to the store so I could buy the mix. While I was there I also grabbed some fruit and some snacks. My cupboard was most definitely not kid-friendly, in fact, it wasn't very adult-friendly either. I was running behind by the time I checked out and tossed everything into the car, so I was scrambling around the kitchen and staring at the clock on the stove instead of paying attention to what I was supposed to be doing with the pancakes.

It was premade mix, so it should have been impossible to mess up. Impossible for anyone but me. A plume of smoke wafted up from the top of the stove and had me coughing and frantically dumping the entire pan, blackened batter and all, into the sink and running water over it in the hopes that the smoke detectors in the house wouldn't go off. I burned my fingertips and I was pretty sure I had batter in my hair. I was throwing every dirty word I had in my vocabulary at the mess when a shrill sound echoed through the house.

At first I thought I wasn't fast enough with the disaster on the stove and the detectors were going off anyway, but then there was a pause before the noise started up again and I realized it was someone ringing the doorbell. I rushed out of the kitchen so fast I tripped over my own feet and landed on my hands and knees with a soft "oomph." I was freaking out on the inside and outside, but I needed to get my act together or the bell was going to wake up Poppy and Zeb was going to see what a wreck I was and not trust me with Hyde.

I pulled open the door just as Hyde was standing on his tiptoes to reach for the bell again. He fell back down on his feet and grinned up at me. God, he looked so much like the unreadable man standing behind him. I wondered if it was rude to stare at him all day long while I mourned the time we had spent apart.

"Hey."

"What's on your face?" Hyde pointed at his own cheek and I used the back of my hand to rub at the sticky batter that was stuck there.

I sighed and ushered them both into the house. "I tried to make pancakes for breakfast. It didn't go so well."

Hyde's grin got even bigger and Zeb lifted an eyebrow at me. "Why were you trying to make pancakes?"

I shrugged and tried to keep my eyes from hungrily eating him up. He was so close, but the distance between us gaped wide and vast. "I thought Hyde might like them for breakfast. I fig-ured they would be easy enough. I was wrong."

He shook his dark head and a reluctant smile pulled out his mouth. It made his beard twitch and his green eyes shine.

"You can pass the bar exam in not one but two states but not figure out how to make pancakes?"

I bristled a little and crossed my arms over my chest. "If I want pancakes I usually just go somewhere and have someone make them for me."

He chuckled at me and reached out to tug Hyde's gloves, coat, and hat off. "The little man isn't too fussy when it comes to breakfast, but if he tells you all I feed him is pizza, he's lying." Hyde made a face as Zeb reached out to ruffle his hair. "You're doing us a solid by hanging out with him all day, isn't that right, buddy?"

Hyde nodded vigorously and walked over to take my hand. I looked down at him and couldn't help but smile at that adorable face.

"If you want pancakes, Sayer, I'll help make them. I'm a good helper, aren't I, Zeb?"

"You are, bud. Hey, you be good for Sayer and remember if you go outside that you—"

Hyde cut him off before he could finish the warning. "Put on my gloves and my hat. I will."

Good Lord, they were so cute together. It had only been a few weeks and they were already so in sync. They made it hard to breathe. They made it impossible not to be in love.

"He'll keep himself entertained, for the most part, just play with him and hang out with him. He has a habit of pulling his gloves off and throwing them wherever they land. If you take him outside to play, keep that in mind."

I nodded and looked down as Hyde pulled on the hand he was still holding on to. "Let's make pancakes, Sayer."

I agreed and looked back up at Zeb, who was watching us with a look that was caught somewhere between eternal heartbreak and true love. It sucked every thought from my head and killed whatever I had been about to say to him.

"I'll see you guys later."

"Bye, Zeb." Hyde let go of my hand and ran at his dad. Zeb bent and caught the little boy seconds before he collided with his knees. He lifted him up and put a smacking kiss on his cheek.

"Your beard tickles."

It sure did. I flushed hot at the wayward thought. Hyde leaned in close to Zeb and whispered in the loud way all kids did, which meant I could hear every word he said.

"You're coming back for me later, right, Zeb?"

I inhaled so sharply it hurt. I saw Zeb's eyes flick over to mine before he shifted Hyde in front of him so that they were gleaming green eyes to gleaming green eyes. "I will always come back for you, Hyde."

The little boy watched him for a solid minute before giving him a far too serious nod and wiggling to be put down.

Zeb and I stared at each other and everything I wanted to say to him, everything I knew I should give him, lay there heavy and immovable between us. I wanted to do what Hyde did and run at him and trust him to catch me.

"Bye, Zeb. Have a good day at work."

He grunted a little. "Thanks, Say. I'll see you guys in a few."

I put my hand on Hyde's thin little shoulder and we both watched Zeb leave with longing in our eyes. Once the front door was shut, I nudged Hyde with my hip and inclined my head toward the kitchen.

"I think it's safe to go in now if you want to try for round two."

"Yeah. I'm kinda hungry." I turned to guide him into the still slightly scorched–smelling kitchen and looked over my shoulder at him when he started giggling uncontrollably.

"What's so funny?"

He put his hands on his tummy and tilted his dark head back and laughed so hard I could see all his missing teeth.

I pouted at him and playfully crossed my arms over my chest. "Come on, Hyde. Share the joke."

He kept giggling and pointed to my backside. "You made a big mess." I sure had, and watching his father walk out the door without being able to touch him, without being able to kiss him or hold him close, reminded me of that fact like a smack in my face.

Obviously I couldn't see my own butt, so I stopped in front of the stainless-steel refrigerator and turned around to see what had him in hysterics. On each back pocket was a perfect hand-print, obviously left over from my first attempt at the pancakes. I rolled my eyes and shook my head at my own level of disaster.

"I did make a big mess. I seem to do that a lot." I helped Hyde climb up into one of the stools that sat at the island. I found a clean bowl and spoon and put both in front of him while I measured out more mix and dug the milk back out of the fridge.

"Zeb says making a mess is okay as long as you also clean it up." It sounded like Zeb had taken to fatherhood like a duck to water.

"Your dad is full of good advice."

A little furrow worked between his tiny dark eyebrows as I added the liquid to the mix in the bowl and told him to go ahead and stir. I thought he was concentrating on the task at hand but when he spoke he surprised me.

"Everyone calls him my dad."

I propped my elbows on the countertop and put my chin in my hand. "He *is* your dad. I'm not sure what else we would call him."

He looked up at me and sucked his bottom lip in and then let it go with a pop. "He was my friend before he was my dad."

"You're right. He was and he's still your friend even though he is also your dad."

"Sometimes I want to call him Dad."

I sucked in a breath through my teeth. I wasn't sure I was the person he should be having this conversation with. "Try and get as many of the lumps out as you can." I pointed to one big blob of batter in the bowl and walked over so that I could lean on the counter next to him. "Have you mentioned to Zeb that you might want to call him Dad?"

He shook his head and I heard his feet thumping under the counter as he kicked them up and down.

"No. What if he doesn't like it?"

I reached out and put a finger under his chin and turned his face up so that he was looking at me. "Hyde, do you think Zeb is honest with you?"

The little boy considered me thoughtfully for a second and I tried not to cringe as he let go of the spoon and it slipped all the way into the bowl and was sucked up by the gooey batter.

"Yeah. Zeb doesn't lie."

"So if you tell him that you want to call him Dad, then you know he'll tell you how he really feels about it. I bet you a hundred bucks it makes him really happy and that he might even cry." It was a hedged bet. I knew I was going to win the bet and lose the money because there was no way that Zeb wouldn't at least tear up when Hyde asked that question. A hundred dollars would buy the little man a lot of pizza and make the emotional moment between father and son even more special.

I wiggled my eyebrows up and down, which made Hyde laugh. "Zeb won't cry." He sounded so sure of the fact. The adorable little boy had no clue just how much of an effect he had on his big, bearded father.

I stuck out a hand. "A hundred bucks says he does."

Hyde put his hand in mine and screwed up his face in concentration. "I don't have a hundred bucks, though. I only have ten quarters."

Could the kid be any more precious? The answer to that was a resounding "hell no." "You don't have to give me your quarters. If you win and Zeb doesn't cry when you ask him, all you have to give me is your best hug. Deal?"

He shook our joined hands vigorously and grinned at me. "Deal."

I tugged him closer, so that our noses were almost touching, and mock-whispered, "Do you want to know a secret?"

His evergreen eyes popped wide and he nodded so vigorously that for a second I thought he was going to slide off the stool. I put my lips on his baby-soft cheek and gave him a little peck.

"It doesn't matter to your dad what you call him . . . Daddy, Zeb, Zebulon, Old Man River, Mr. Giant, Captain Beardo, Paul Bunyan . . . all he cares about is that you're here to call him anything. He simply wants you, Hyde. No matter what, I want you to remember that, okay?"

He gave a jerky little nod and I pulled away and took the bowl with me over to the stove so that I could try again to make pancakes once I found another spoon. There was no way I was going fishing for the one that was at the bottom of the bowl. I would end up with batter in even more places than I already had it.

I had everything set up and was intently focused on my task when Hyde's voice drifted to me from across the room.

"How come you only have one red wall?" He had climbed off the stool and was standing in front of the poppy-colored wall, studying it with his head tilted a little to the side.

"Uh, your dad actually painted it for me. I have a friend who lives with me and he asked her to pick out a color to cheer her up. That was the color she chose."

"I like it. It's bright."

"I like it, too, and when the pancakes are done and hopefully not burned this time around, we can go wake Poppy up and you can tell her you like it. She'll be thrilled."

"Are you gonna have my dad paint more?"

I felt my spine go stiff at the stove as the butter melted and sizzled on the griddle. I wondered if he even realized that he had referred to Zeb as his dad. "No. I wasn't going to have him paint any more. Just that one wall."

He made his way over to me and I cautioned him to keep his hands clear of the top of the stove.

"Do you like it like that?"

I looked down at him. "Like what?"

"Everything so boring. The red wall is better."

I bit the inside of my lip and turned my head to look at it. "You're right. It *is* better."

And no, I didn't like the rest of the house being plain and boring. It was supposed to be soothing and comforting; instead I felt like the entire inside lacked personality and that every single neutral-toned wall mocked me as I walked by it. I sighed and pulled the pan off the heat.

"Let's go get Poppy and dive into our masterpiece, shall we?"

He followed me without argument.

Luckily Poppy was already up and in the living room when we went to fetch her. I should've known she wouldn't be able to sleep through the doorbell going off. Hyde took an immediate liking to her, and the three of us spent the rest of the morning eating pancakes, coloring on the back of computer paper, and playing band with overturned pots and pans. Hyde was quite the drummer, and I was surprised at how dedicated Poppy was to her role as lead air guitarist. I, by default, ended up as lead singer, which sucked for them since the only songs I knew the lyrics to were eighties heavy metal. After the second round of "Pour Some Sugar on Me," Poppy threw in the towel and claimed she needed a nap. Hyde also looked a little heavy-eyed, so I set him up on the couch with Nickelodeon on the TV. He was out before I could turn around and cover him up with a blanket.

I felt like I should run into my office and grab my computer so I could get through the work that was waiting for me, but all I could do was stand there like I was glued to the spot and stare down at the precious little boy. He was so sweet, so re-silient, considering everything he had been through. I had no idea how he had it in him to be so trusting and so open to love, but I was unendingly thankful that he was. I could learn so much from him.

I jerked when Poppy put her hand on my elbow and inclined her head toward my office. I followed her as quietly as I could so we wouldn't wake Hyde, and sniffed a little when I realized that

I had tears in my eyes that were threatening to spill over. All these feelings were so much and they were starting to leak out of me regularly now.

"I thought you were taking a nap."

"I was going to, but then I started thinking about something and I wanted to talk to you about it before I lost my nerve." She twisted her hands together and started to pace back and forth in front of me. She fluttered around like a little golden bird and it made me anxious.

"You know you can talk to me about anything, Poppy."

She audibly gulped. "I do . . . well, anything about me, but this is about you, Sayer, and it's hard for me to say, after all the wonderful things you've done for me."

She succeeded in catching me off guard. "Uh, okay, I'm listening."

She took a deep breath and was obviously rallying her nerve before she blurted out, "You would be a really great mom."

I blinked in shock because that wasn't what I was expecting. "Excuse me?"

She moved shaky hands to push her hair behind her ears and I saw her turn pink. "I know you struggle with the way your mom died and feel like she abandoned you, but, Sayer . . ." She reached out and put a hand on my arm. "You would never and could never do that to anyone. I watched you with Hyde all morning, and I can see how much you love him."

I put my hand over hers and gave it a pat. "He's just a little boy, Poppy. It's impossible not to care for him."

Her amber eyes sharpened as she narrowed them at me. "Really? Because if that was true, it would be his mother cooking him pancakes for breakfast and not you."

I opened my mouth to argue and then let it fall back closed because she did have a point.

"It's not just that. When you took me in without question because I couldn't handle being around men, even the man I trust most in the whole world, I thought you were my guardian angel. I wouldn't have survived without you, Sayer."

"No." I automatically denied my role in her ongoing recovery. "You're a fighter, Poppy."

She snorted delicately and lifted her caramel-colored eyebrows. "Am I? Because you threw me the life preserver months ago and all I've been doing is floating and hoping I don't drown. I haven't been swimming at all, Sayer, but you have loved me, protected me, sheltered me, and fought for me when I wouldn't fight for myself. You did everything for me your own mother couldn't do for you."

I jolted and jerked back from her touch as she stared at me solemnly. "Your father tried to convince you that you weren't good enough, that you weren't enough, but you are a better mother to that boy and to me than our own were. You care more for us than the people whose only job in the world it was to love us and keep us safe. So you need to start swimming, too, Sayer. After everything the past has tried to bury us under, we owe it to ourselves to be brave, to do more than float."

My mouth opened and closed like a fish. The tears that had been brewing while I watched Hyde with my heart in my throat started to fall.

"I . . . where . . . what brought this on, Poppy?"

She had shiny eyes as well but that brittle shell that she had been encased in since she first came to live with me was splintering and a new, vibrant creature was starting to emerge.

"Partly from watching you with Hyde today and partly from being around all those happy couples at the party yesterday. I miss my life. I miss my sister. I miss being able to hug Rowdy without having a panic attack. I want to be around for those babies and weddings. I want to be a part of my family again, so that means I need to learn how to be alone and be okay with it. I need to take control so that at some point in my life I can willingly give it up to the right person." She pointed a finger at me and wiggled it in a circle. "And you, you need to learn how to not be alone. You need to take the risk on that boy and on his daddy. You love so much more than your mother, and you have to know that you have so much more to offer this world than the person your father tried to mold you into. Let the way those boys love you and the way you love them be what defines you, Sayer. Be that woman, not the one your dad wanted you to be."

"Uh . . ." I wasn't sure what to say to her, but when she wrapped her arms around me and gave me the first real hug she had ever offered up since moving in, I couldn't do anything else but hug her back as we silently cried together. We did deserve to be brave, and we had survived so much. The marks that abuse had left on her were more visible and tangible than the marks a totally different kind of abuse had left on me. Both ran deep. Both hindered the way we lived and loved, but if she could overcome her circumstances, there was no reason I shouldn't be able to do the same.

She pulled back and wiped a hand across her damp cheeks. "I'm going to ask Rowdy to help me get a car and I'm going to go back to work." I must have looked shocked because she laughed a little bit. "It might not be tomorrow but soon. I'm also going to move out. I need to find my own place, which means you'll have lots and lots of empty rooms." She started out the door and looked over her shoulder at me. "Think about that."

She wasn't just swimming, she was paddling hard for the shore, and I needed to follow her lead. I was taking baby steps, and if I didn't want to lose Zeb and Hyde forever, I needed to start making leaps and bounds instead.

"Sayer?" The door pushed open and Hyde wandered in rubbing his eyes. His bottom lip was sticking out and his lashes were slightly spiky, as if he had been crying, too.

"You all right, kiddo?" He shook his head no, so I sat down in one of the chairs in my office and let him crawl up into my lap. I stroked my fingers through his hair. He put his cheek on my chest and sniffled. "You want to tell me what's wrong? You weren't asleep for very long but did you have a bad dream?"

He shook his head no and his soft hair rubbed against my chin.

"Do you miss your dad? We can call him for a minute and check in if you do."

Again he shook his head no and cuddled deeper into me.

"I'm out of ideas, buddy. You're gonna have to help me out so I can help make it better, okay?"

He huddled even farther into me and put his arm around my side. His damp lashes fluttered back closed and he let out a breath. "You weren't there. I opened my eyes and you weren't there. I missed you."

Jesus. If there was ever anything that the universe demanded that I be brave for, it was this little boy. There was no time to wallow in the past or fear the uncertainty of the future with those simple words soothing every single rough spot that was on my soul. Hyde didn't care if I wasn't all the way where I felt like I needed to be in order to be the kind of person he deserved in his life; he missed me because he cared about me. It made him cry because I was important to him and he trusted me. The stark truth in that pulled apart every thread that stitched my history together and unraveled the whole thing. He missed me and Zeb loved me.

The me that was awkward.

The me that was reserved.

The me that could be cold and detached.

The me that would try to make pancakes even though I didn't know how.

The me that took no prisoners in court.

The me that tried to do the right thing for the wrong reasons.

The me that would have messy sex against a newly painted wall.

They cared about all the different versions of me and all of them were enough to make an entire person worthy of their love. I kissed Hyde on the temple. "I'm sorry I left you alone. Poppy wanted to talk to me, and I didn't want to wake you up. I missed you, too, Hyde."

"It's okay." And it was. It really was okay. For the first time in what felt like forever, things actually felt like they were going to be okay. I finally knew exactly what I wanted and how to go about getting it. It wasn't going to happen overnight. I'd done a lot of damage to Zeb and his truth, but my foundation was finally steady, the ground under it secure. I still had some rubble to remove, but once it was all clear I was going to let him build whatever he wanted on the space.

Hyde took a real nap in my lap and woke up an hour later and wanted to go play outside. It took twenty minutes to get him into his hat and gloves, and once he was out there he realized it was really cold and wanted to come back inside. We ended up playing hide-and-seek and tic-tac-toe for hours until Zeb showed up in the early afternoon.

He seemed surprised that Hyde didn't rush to greet him but instead pulled him into the kitchen to show him all the pictures he had drawn that I had put on the fridge. Hyde was chattering a mile a minute and Zeb was staring at me like I had two heads. I smiled at him as he scowled at me and somewhere in our stand-off Hyde must have realized that he had lost the adults' attention because he tugged on Zeb's hand and whined, "Dad, you aren't looking at my picture."

Zeb's head jerked around so fast I was sure he gave himself whiplash and I saw his mouth drop open and his eyes blink rapidly for a second. "Did you just call me Dad?"

Hyde's eyes widened and he looked from me to Zeb and back again. I gave him a nod of encouragement and mouthed "it's fine" at him.

"Um . . . is that okay? Sayer said it's okay." Zeb turned his head to look at me and I couldn't keep the smile off my face. His green eyes looked like grass after it rained.

He got down so that he was on the same level as his son and pulled him into a tight hug. "Of course it's okay. I *am* your dad and I couldn't be prouder of the fact. You can call me whatever you want, Hyde."

The little boy squeaked inside the big man's embrace and there was a spark of envy that lit up under my skin. I wanted to be in that embrace as well.

"Are you crying? Sayer said you were gonna cry. She said she would give me a hundred bucks if you did!" Hyde pulled back and looked hard at his father's face. It was hard to see because of the beard, but sure enough, on Zeb's tanned cheek there was a single, glittery tear. Hyde threw his head back and laughed. He pointed at me. "You owe me a hundred bucks."

Zeb let go of his boy and straightened to his full height. He gave me a questioning look. I just shrugged. He could figure out I knew the odds and had weighted the outcome in Hyde's favor without me spelling it out for him. "I'm gonna give it to your dad to hold on to, but I promise to pay up."

"You two seemed to have a good day."

Hyde nodded vigorously. "I love Sayer."

I saw Zeb's Adam's apple bob up and down. "Good to know, little man."

I cleared my throat and pushed some of my hair over my shoulder. "Honestly, I adored having him here today. If your mom needs a break on the weekend while you're working, I would be happy to spend the day with him."

Something dark flashed across Zeb's face as he considered me carefully. "Seriously?"

"Seriously." I made sure he could see the conviction in my gaze.

He made a noise low in his throat and I saw his hands curl into fists. "Hey, buddy, why don't you go grab your coat for a minute so I can talk to Sayer real quick."

"Are you gonna get my money?"

Zeb barked out a laugh. "Yes. I'll get your money." Little feet scurried out of the room, and as soon as we were alone Zeb prowled toward me and backed me into the island until I was caged between his arms.

"You ready to choose us, Sayer?"

It reminded me of the time he backed me into my car after

court and kissed me stupid. I wanted to do the same thing to him, but we didn't have much time before we were interrupted by a five-year-old and it was obvious the wounds I left on him needed to be tended to.

I put a hand on the center of his chest and looked up at him with my newly thawed-out heart in my eyes. "I'm swimming, Zeb. I'm not at the shore yet, but I'm trying to get there. You've trusted me with Hyde this entire time. I just need you to trust me a little bit longer."

"Why should I?"

I fisted his heavy flannel in my hand and pulled him down so that we were nose-to-nose. "Because before I can choose you, before I can choose Hyde, I have to choose myself, and that's what I've been trying to do." I hoped that made sense to him because it was the first giant step I needed to take. "It's not that easy."

He huffed out a breath and it ghosted across my lips like a phantom kiss. "I've been waiting on the shore for a long time, Sayer."

"I know, Zeb. Please, trust me."

He pushed off the counter when Hyde came rushing back into the room. His eyes didn't give anything away and his mouth was unsmiling when he bit out, "You're still my only plan, Sayer. That never changed."

That made my heart swell because I had no intention of letting him down this time around either. We could both win and this time it would be a victory that lasted forever.

CHAPTER 18

Zeb

I wasn't sure what to make of Sayer's sudden revelation that she was trying to make her way to me through the viscous water of her past and I wasn't sure I could do what she asked and simply trust her. But when the weekend rolled around I found myself calling her and asking if she was still game for taking Hyde for the day. He hadn't stopped talking about her since I picked him up at her house, so I figured it couldn't hurt anything to let them spend the day together. She told me of course she would watch him, then caught me off guard by asking me what my favorite color was.

Obviously the answer was blue. Sparkling, turbulent ocean blue. She got quiet on the other end of the phone for a second and then told me she would come pick Hyde up and drop him off if that was okay. She said she had a few errands to run and would take him with her. I tried to warn her that a five-year-old, even one that was as well behaved as Hyde, added at least an hour onto the time it took to get errands done. She laughed it off and said they would be fine. I tried to warn her again when

I moved Hyde's car seat from my Jeep into her Lexus. She just smiled at me and told me it would be okay. She also looked at me like she wanted to pull all my clothes off and have her way with me right there in the parking lot of the condominium complex. It was all pretty confusing, and only head and heart were at war with what it all meant.

I sent her a text to let her know I was heading home from the jobsite. I had recently bought an old Victorian not too far away from where her house was and was working on switching it over from multiple apartments and living spaces back into a single-family home. It was a massive project, but I knew once the work was done, the return on my investment would be huge. I told her I could just come get my kid since I was so close, but she texted back *NO!* in all caps and said she would drop him off within the hour.

When she showed up at the condo both she and Hyde looked a little wilted and worse for wear, but my son's green eyes were alight with mischief and glee. He also had splotches of what looked like blue paint in his hair and on his hands. He hugged me around my knees and took off running for his room so he could ditch his coat and gloves.

Sayer also had blue streaked across her cheek and splattered in her pale hair. Her normally sharp appearance was nowhere to be found as she hovered in my doorway in stained jeans and a too-big-for-her sweatshirt.

"Did you guys get into a paint fight?" I reached out and plucked a colored strand of her hair up and let it fall.

She laughed a little and shook her head. "Kind of. We're work-ing on a secret project."

That piqued my interest, so I leaned against the door and crossed my arms over my chest. I had to admit it was a stroke to the old ego when her eyes widened at the motion. She stuck the tip of her tongue out to trace her bottom lip and I growled at her. I wanted to follow the trail of moisture with my own tongue and then bite on the lush curve that pouted out. Aside from my time locked up, this was the longest I had ever gone without sex and it was starting to make me a little crazy. Every move she made seemed like a come-on or like it was designed to entice.

"What kind of secret project?" My voice was gruff and I saw her shiver.

"You'll find out soon enough. Can I come get Hyde next Saturday, too?"

I wanted to tell her she could only have my son if she was willing to take me, too, but I understood whatever she was working her way through was thick and snarled. She was slowly picking her way through it, though, and all I could do was wait on the other side.

"Yeah. You can come and get him next Saturday. I think my mom actually likes having a day for herself. Do you want to come in and have dinner with us? I'll probably let Hyde order pizza."

She cocked her head to the side and then nodded. "Sure. I would like that."

The three of us spent the rest of the night eating pizza, watching some silly family-friendly movie, and laughing. I tried repeatedly to get Hyde to tell me what special project he was working on at Sayer's house and each time he just giggled at me and shared a conspiratorial look with Sayer while telling me over and over again it was a surprise. He also told me his favorite color was red, that Sayer's favorite color was green, and that Poppy liked purple. I wasn't sure what that had to do with anything, but when I walked Sayer out to her car when it was time for her to leave, I pushed her up against the side and trapped her between my body and the chilly metal.

"Your favorite color is green, huh?"

The corner of her mouth kicked up in a grin and she lifted a hand and put it on the side of my face. Her fingernails raked lightly through the side of my beard and it made my entire body go tight. "Your favorite color is blue, huh?"

I grinned back at her. "Touché. I hope you figure your shit out sooner rather than later, Say. I sure do miss the fuck out of you."

I pushed back from her car and watched her long lashes drop over her eyes. "I'm working on it," she said.

I sighed and my breath fogged up in front of me. "I know you are. Renovation takes time and there is always something unexpected behind the walls when you knock them down. I'll see you next weekend."

WHEN SHE SHOWED up the following weekend she looked different. She was dressed like she had raided the Salvation Army for their most used and abused jeans and I recognized the T-shirt she had on as the one I left at her house on our last night together. She seemed so much less polished and worried about being put together than she typically did. Even though her clothes were casual and even slightly sloppy, she still made it all look really good and I wanted to peel her out of it.

I let my gaze skim over her and told her, "Nice outfit. More secret projects on the agenda today?"

Hyde clapped his hands and squealed a little. "Yeah, Sayer, are we finishing our surprise today?"

"You bet, but I have a small stop to make before we do, okay, buddy?"

Hyde pouted a little bit, but I think the kid and I were in the same boat when it came to this woman. Any chance we got to spend time with her we were going to snap it up and hold on to it with greedy hands. I walked them to her car and helped get Hyde situated in the new car seat she had bought for him. It tugged at parts of me that were forever tied to her. She went and bought a car seat for my kid. That had to mean she was planning on keeping us around. Didn't it?

"I'll see you guys in a little bit. Be good." I wasn't sure if I was talking to Hyde or her, but either way the warning felt fitting.

When she showed back up at the condo later that evening, at first I didn't know it was her. I heard a car pull up and looked out the window to see who it was, but there wasn't a Lexus parked behind my Jeep. Instead, a brand-new, cherry-red Jeep Grand Cherokee was where she usually parked. It wasn't as tough looking and as masculine as mine, but it was still rugged and made for more than looking pretty. I thought it must be a neighbor until her blond head emerged from the driver's side and she walked around to let Hyde out on the other side. She had to heft the boy down from the height, and as they walked toward the front of the building hand in hand I knew that was everything I was ever going to want in my life.

They were perfect together.

They were perfect for me.

I couldn't ask for anything more and I would do everything in my power to keep them and to keep them safe.

I pulled open the door when I heard her quiet voice and Hyde laughing. They pulled up short when they saw me and I watched both their smiles turn just a shade brighter.

"New car to go with the new hair and new duds?"

She smiled and let go of Hyde's hand so that he could throw himself against me like he liked to do. I picked him up and mock-growled at him as he put both his hands on my cheeks. I almost died laughing when he growled back at me like a little animal.

"Sayer let me pick the color. Red. It's my favorite."

"I saw." I looked at her over her shoulder and she lifted her hands and let them fall.

"I never really liked the Lexus and the Jeep makes more sense for winter."

"You bought a Jeep?"

She shrugged again. "Yeah. I like yours."

I wanted to growl again, but instead I flashed her a predatory smile and muttered, "I like yours, too." I wasn't talking about the Jeep and she knew it. "Want to stay for dinner?"

This time she shook her head. "No. Not tonight. I have a few things I need to finish up at the house. But thank you, and I'll see you next weekend, if that's okay."

"It's okay, but one of these days I want my shirt back." I stared at her so that she knew I meant I wanted to peel it off of her while she was wearing it and get to all the pretty, pale, and pink things underneath.

"Soon. I'll see you guys next weekend. Bye, Hyde."

"Bye, Sayer. I can't wait for Dad to see the surprise."

"Me, too, kiddo." She smiled at me and both my heart and my dick responded. "Next weekend, Zeb. I'll see you soon."

She disappeared back down the walkway and I looked at my

son. "Waiting for this surprise is killing me, you know. I better like it." I was only half kidding around.

His little face got really serious and he leaned in close so that our noses were touching. "You have to like it. Sayer worked real hard. You can pretend if you don't so you won't hurt her feelings."

"I'll pretend. Just for you, little man."

"Good. Can we have pizza for dinner?" I groaned.

"How about we make tacos or something else?" I was going to have pizza coursing through my veins by the time the kid was old enough to buy his own food.

"It's the weekend. We get to have pizza on the weekend." His eyes twinkled at me and I knew I was going to cave in, even though the last thing I wanted to eat was another slice of pizza.

"Fine, we can order a pizza."

"Because you love me." He threw his arms around my neck and squeezed so hard I had to pry him loose.

"Because I love you." I put him down and pulled my phone out of my front pocket.

"Sayer loves me, too." I blinked down at him.

"Did she tell you that?" I was going to burn in hell for being envious of my own kid yet again.

He shook his head in the negative. "No, but she let me pick out the color of her new car, so she has to love me, right?" If only it was that easy to tell what the beautiful blonde had working under the surface.

I chuckled. "That seems like solid logic to me, little man. Let's get cleaned up and dinner ordered."

The next week passed in a blur. I ran into a major issue with the roof on the Victorian, which was going to be nearly impossible to fix, and the power was iffy at best, which meant my crew was working intermittently in the cold and pissed about it. Hyde also came down with a cold and was cranky for three days. I think by the time Saturday rolled around, my mom was more than ready for a break. When Sayer came to pick him up she was bundled up, so I couldn't see if she was still dressed like she was working for HGTV and she seemed far quieter and almost anxious as we made small talk. I told her Hyde was on the end of a cold, which had her going into a flurry of touching his forehead and fussing over him like he was going to keel over on her at any minute. She was so busy rattling on about how they would make chicken noodle soup and watch all his favorite movies that she didn't even tell me good-bye when she drove off.

It annoyed me all day until she sent me a text in the afternoon asking me if I minded coming to get Hyde after work instead of her dropping him off.

I replied that was fine and asked her if everything was all right.

She sent back a message saying everything was fine, she wanted me to come inside the house and take a look at something.

When I asked her what she wanted me to look at, she didn't respond. Needless to say, her silence and my curiosity made me hurry my ass up and had me hustling to get through the bathroom teardown I was working on. The guys were happy to call it a day a few hours early, so I texted her that I was on my way over and asked her if I needed any tools for what she needed me to fix.

She sent back a smiley face and the reply:

Just one tool.

Care to elaborate?

You'll see when you get here.

I parked my Jeep behind her fancier one and practically jogged up the front steps. I didn't have to knock because she was already at the door and pulled it open as soon as I lifted my hand.

She reached out and grabbed the front of my flannel shirt and hauled me inside, and before I could ask her what in the hell was going on, she pushed me back against the front door she had just closed behind us.

It had been so long since I tasted her, had her lips on mine, that my brain short-circuited. Her hands curled around my neck and she stood up on her tiptoes so that she could press into me. I wrapped an arm low around her waist and hauled her closer. I felt her breasts flatten against my chest and her knee work between my legs so that it rubbed against the erection that was stretching my jeans to extreme limits. She sighed against my mouth and twisted her tongue around mine until I pulled back with a gasp.

"My kid is walking around here somewhere, so unless you want to help me explain to him what the hell is going on . . . or maybe you want to explain it to both of us . . . What the hell, Say?" I gave her a little squeeze and set her away from me. She pushed the long, multicolored layers at the front of her hair back and smiled up at me.

I noticed she had on a sweater that looked really soft and kind of fuzzy in a bright coral color. She also had on teal pants that looked like they were painted on. It was a riot of color and it all looked really good on her, especially with the dreamy little smile toying with her now puffy lips.

"I took Hyde to your sister's house an hour ago, and Poppy is with Salem and Rowdy for the rest of the weekend."

I leaned back against the door. "Why? What's going on, Sayer?"

She reached out a hand and waited patiently until I put my much larger and rougher one in it.

"I want to show you the surprise I've been working on. Come with me."

I was hesitant and curious in equal measure. I'd been dying to know what she was up to, but that kiss had thrown me off stride. I jerked to a stop as soon as we entered the living room.

Gone were the sterile walls with no life or color. In their place was a pretty mossy green that was covered with bright and lively artwork. The ugly couch was gone as well and replaced with an oversize sectional that looked inviting and perfect for curling up on. It didn't look like the dentist's office anymore. It looked like a home. It looked comfortable. It looked loved.

I didn't say anything as she took me into her office, which was now a pale lilac. I looked at her and then at the space and then back at her again. "Is that a *Buffy the Vampire Slayer* poster behind your desk?" I couldn't keep the humor and stunned shock out of my voice.

She laughed and pulled me toward the kitchen. "Team Spike forever."

The kitchen hadn't changed much; there was still the poppy-colored wall, but on the big blank wall there were black vinyl decals of giant poppies that gave the room more movement and warmth. She had been busy. Every room was a different color and decorated in a haphazard way. There was no order. There was no rhyme or reason to any of it and I could tell she loved it. She had gone out and found things she liked, things that spoke to her, and made the space her own.

One of the bigger spare rooms was painted in train conductor stripes and the door was covered in a million handprints. All small and going every which way. Obviously that had been my son's contribution to the project. It was sweet and I wanted to ask her if she made room for my boy not only in her home but in her heart as well.

The last stop on the tour was her bedroom. Finally, I found the source of the blue paint that had been all over Hyde and in her hair a few weeks ago. The room had been transformed from a tranquil oasis to a Caribbean villa. It was the ocean and so much more. It was her eyes and her heart all tangled up and put on the walls.

"Blue is your favorite and you're my favorite, so I wanted them in the same place." I turned around to look at her, not sure what to say. She shifted on her feet and reached into her pocket and pulled out something. When she opened her hand I noticed it was a house key. I jerked my eyes back to hers and blew out a deep breath.

"Sayer . . ."

She stepped closer and grabbed my hand and put the key in it before curling my fingers around the metal object. I held it so tightly that the teeth bit painfully into my skin.

"You made this house, Zeb. You're everywhere in it. I feel you in every room. You belong here just as much as I do." She stepped closer to me and put a hand in the center of my chest. "You were the first man I ever kissed, do you know that?"

I grunted. "You were engaged, Sayer."

She curled around my waist and leaned her head under my chin. I wanted to hold her, but my head was still spinning. "I know, but he kissed me. I never kissed him. I wanted to kiss

you, Zeb. I wanted to have sex with you. I wanted to love you.
I wanted to be with you just for me, not for anyone else. Not
because it was right or wrong but because it felt inevitable. It felt
important and right. I wanted to be with you because I felt it . . .
still feel it . . . everywhere."

I slid the key she gave me into my pocket and put a finger
under her chin in a way that made her tilt her head back so she
had to look at me.

"What are you telling me?" I could see what she was trying
to say on the walls and in her liquid gaze, but I still needed the
words. I needed to know she had saved herself, that she was
where she needed to be, or at least getting close. I needed to hear
her tell me her truth before I could believe it.

"I'm telling you that I choose color, I choose happiness, I
choose to be all the things I am, and I won't feel bad about any
of them. I choose to be better than my parents were and not to
let them define me. I choose me and what I want. I choose to
be brave and risk my heart. I choose love, Zeb, so that means I
choose you and Hyde. I'm never going to be totally comfortable
with all the space you take up and how much you make me feel,
but I want you here, so you don't have to push against the door
anymore. I'm giving you the key to it. Being uncomfortable is a
good thing. It makes me human even after all my father did to
make me nothing."

She hugged me where she was holding on to me and I finally
lifted an arm to squeeze her back.

Her voice was quiet when she told me, "The walls are gone.
The ground is leveled. You can build whatever you want. I'm a
blank slate." She had found a way to speak to me that I couldn't
ignore. Her words were a balm to all the wounds her actions

had inflicted. She had told me I could make her mine, we could finally construct our future, together.

I swore softly and bent so I could put my cheek on the top of her head. "I love you, Sayer, and my kid loves you. If you do this, let us in, give us the key, then you have to be prepared for us to stay. I'm not letting Hyde love anyone else that might leave him, at least not if I can help it."

"I'm not going to leave, Zeb. Whatever we build we do it together, and it's forever."

"Did you reach the shore?" I slid a hand under the heavy fall of her hair and gripped the back of her neck. She tilted her face up so I could put my lips on hers.

It was a sweet kiss, a soft kiss. It was a kiss of homecoming, a kiss of settling in, and a kiss of breaking ground on something lasting and unbreakable. It was a kiss that sealed our fate, sealed us together, and forged something strong and resilient that would last no matter what came at us. It was a kiss that unified us, wound us together, and spoke to how we would fight for each other, for our family, and for this beautiful, brilliant thing we chose that lived between us.

"The shore is in sight and I'll keep kicking, but I reached you, and that was what I have been swimming toward since we met."

"I've got you, Say."

"I know you do, Zeb." She slid her fingers through the buttons on my shirt and pressed her lower half against mine. "Can we kiss and make up now?"

I growled low in my throat and walked her backward toward the bed. "Don't you have something you want me to fix before we get naked?"

She rolled her eyes and started pulling at my shirt. "Yeah, I need you to fix this endless and constant ache I have between my legs. It hurts all the time and only you have the proper tool to fix it."

I tossed my head back and laughed at her. "So really, you want to fuck and make up?"

She nodded vigorously, which surprised a laugh out of me as she hit the bed with the back of her knees and went down on her back, pulling me with her. She was wrestling my shirt off my shoulders and kissing the side of my neck. It felt like her hands and her mouth were all over me, and when I tried to tell her to slow down so I could fully savor having her back in my arms, she pouted at me in such a cute way I just had to kiss her, which led to lots of tangled tongues and my dick screaming at me to be set free.

I wanted to take my time. She wanted to take me.

She wiggled until I let her up and she crawled over me so that she could pull my shirt open. The buttons popped off and clattered on the floor, which made her laugh. I leaned up enough that I could pull it off and helped her get my T-shirt off over my head. She paused for a second and used her finger to lightly trace over my lips.

"I really missed you, Zeb."

I grunted as she scooted down and started to work on my belt and the zipper my cock was trying to push its way through. "Good thing, because I really missed you, too."

My very eager and ready dick jumped into her palm as soon as she had my pants open.

She snickered at me. "Obviously." Her face sobered up as she curled her fingers around my dick and rubbed her thumb around the throbbing tip. "You are the only thing I have ever wanted for real, Zeb, and that is the truth."

What a fine truth it happened to be. Her eyes sparkled up at me and then my dick was in her mouth and I forgot how to think. Forgot how to breathe. Forgot all the nights spent alone and wanting her because all I could feel was her pressed against me and her quick tongue rolling around and around. The time without her was insignificant and meaningless compared to the time with her.

I buried my hands in her hair and felt my eyes roll back in my head when one of her hands snaked between my legs and gently started to fondle my tightly drawn-up sac. She didn't let up when I told her to take it easy. She acted like she was on a mission to get me off, and while I appreciated the enthusiasm, it had been too long since I had been inside of her and there was no way we weren't finishing this beautiful reunion joined together and at the same time.

I growled at her and used my hold on her hair to pull her off my dick that was now shiny with saliva and harder than I think it had ever been. I started tugging at her brightly colored top and ordered her to peel out of those tight-ass pants. She pouted as she did it, but she complied with my demands. I took a second to appreciate her navy-blue bra and her barely-there panties before stripping her out of them. All I wanted on her skin was my hands and my mouth.

"Don't pout. You can have my dick in your mouth whenever you want, but right now I need to be inside you. It's how we said good-bye, it's how we're going to reunite. In fact, it might be how we communicate everything from here on out."

She laughed at that, but it faded into a groan as I kissed her and backed her into the bed again. This time when she fell backward her arms were around my neck, I had a knee between her spread legs, and when I landed on her I also landed inside her. I sank all the way in, deep, endless, and as far inside of her as I could go. Our hips pressed together. Her breasts rubbed against my chest, her nipples poked at me, and her eyes got a little misty.

I was more than happy to drown in her as her body welcomed me back and held on tight like it never wanted me to leave again. I was perfectly happy with that. I lifted up on an arm and clasped the side of her face with one hand. I bent down so I could kiss the very tip of her nose.

"I love you, Sayer."

Her arms wrapped around me and she curled one of her long legs up around her my waist. "I love you, too, Zeb." Her pale eyebrows lifted up and she smiled at me. "Now that the making-up part is done, can we move on to the fucking? Please?"

I chuckled and started to move with her. Every time I pressed inside of her, every time she lifted up to meet my thrust, I knew this was the only choice either of us could have ever made.

EPILOGUE

Eight months later

I was on top of Zeb and he was buried deep inside of me as I rode him like I was trying to break him.

He had one hand on my hip, another around my bouncing breast as he played with my nipple to the point that it hurt and burned a little. I was panting like I had run a marathon and my hands were curling into the ink on his chest as I felt my orgasm looming hot and blinding behind my eyes. It was so close. I was so close. All it would take was the slightest brush of his work-roughened fingertip on my clit to send me over and I wasn't above begging him to make it happen.

"Zeb . . . touch me." I pleaded with him in a hushed tone and continued to rock on him frantically. If he wouldn't get on board I had no problem taking care of it myself. I glared down at him so he would get with the program and then sighed when his hand skipped along the smooth skin of my hip and headed for where I needed him.

He skimmed his light touch along my slippery folds and teased me as he told me to bend down and give him a kiss. I grumbled a little through my groan of satisfaction as he finally made contact. It was right there and it felt so good. He always made it feel so good.

My lips were just about to land on his, about to swallow up his moan as my body clamped down on him—hard—ready to break apart in the release only he could deliver when suddenly we both froze and scrambled apart like the other person had skin made of fire. Tiny footsteps and the bedroom door creaking open had us sharing a frustrated and bemused look as Hyde was suddenly at his father's side of the bed.

"I had a bad dream."

I pulled the comforter up to my chin and hoped that the light coming from the hallway wasn't enough for him to make out the fact that Zeb and I were both flushed and sweaty.

"Did you really? Or do you just not want to sleep in your own room? We talked about this, little man."

Even though I had handed Zeb the key to my house months ago, we had both agreed it would be best to wait awhile to uproot and move Hyde again so soon. As a result, it had been eight months of us bouncing around from my house to his condo and trying to get the little boy used to the idea of living here full-time. He and Zeb had been officially moved in for two weeks, and at least three nights out of the week Hyde wanted to sleep in bed between us. Zeb typically gave in, but I doubted that would be the case tonight. Adjusting an active sex life around an inquisitive five-year-old had proven interesting for both of us. Needless to say, the shower saw a lot of action and I had become extremely proficient at getting off while we were both still mostly dressed.

"My room is far." His room was a level below the master suit and he had spent plenty of nights in it while Zeb and I were waiting to cohabitate. My personal opinion was that he missed having Poppy just down the hall. She had moved into her own apartment the week before the boys made my home their home.

"It's not that far, Hyde."

"Can I sleep with you guys tonight?" He was whiny and it was late, but Zeb still had a hard-on and his eyes were still blistering black with want.

"Not tonight, bud. You have to get comfortable in your room. It's yours for the long haul. Remember how much work you and Sayer put into making it special just for you?"

He tried to peek over the bed at me, but I was hiding under the covers and behind Zeb's much bigger frame.

"Yeah. I remember." He stuck his little lip out in an adorable pout and I almost laughed at the way Zeb groaned. He shoved his hands through his hair, which was tangled and wild from my hands.

"How about I come in and read you a story? I'll hang out with you until you fall back asleep."

I could see the little boy considering it and finally he nodded. "Okay. Sayer, you wanna come hear a story?"

I snorted and tried to cover it with a cough. "Thanks, kiddo, but I'm gonna pass tonight. You go with your dad and I'll see you in the morning."

His eyebrows dipped over his tiny nose. "I do like my room. Promise."

"I know you do, Hyde. Sometimes this old house makes noises and it can be hard to sleep. It's fine."

Zeb asked me to toss him the jeans I pulled off him a little while ago. He got himself situated and leaned over me so he could press his mouth to mine. The scrape of his beard across my face never got old. I loved how it felt now just as much as I loved it the first time I kissed him. I put my fingers on the new tattoo on the side of his neck that had a man holding a monster-like mask over half of his face. Dr. Jekyll and his Hyde forever imprinted for the world to see. It was Zeb's take on fatherly pride and I loved how him it was. It wasn't Hyde's name, but it was a more literal translation that the little boy would understand when he was older.

"I'll be back."

I giggled a little and snuggled farther into the covers. "I'll be here." I wasn't going anywhere no matter how many earth-shattering orgasms might be interrupted.

I watched my shirtless, tattooed, ripped, gigantic, and now sexually frustrated man handle his son like he was glass as he guided him out of the room, and thought about how foolish I had been to be scared of all the space he took up. With him being everywhere, there was no room for any of the bad things to fit anymore. Every day he made me feel like I was worthy of him, and that he was worthy of me and we were both worthy of this life and all the great things in it. I might not have earned it all just yet, but I wasn't scared of spending the rest of my life working toward it.

And it was work. There were still times I wanted to slip into old habits, to shut down and freeze everyone out because I was overwhelmed with the amount of feeling and love that existed in my every day. I fought against it and I fought hard. My boys and I deserved better.

Talking about things helped as well. When Poppy first moved out she had started going to a therapist to talk about her abuse and her past. The one-on-one sessions hadn't really helped but she found a women's group of abuse survivors, and hearing other women tell their stories, seeing some that had had it far worse than she had, made all the difference in helping her make strides toward living an independent life again. Watching her be so brave helped me be brave and it helped name the horrific emotional abuse that I had survived at my father's hands.

Once it had a title, once the demon had a name, I had an easier time talking to Zeb about it, and even discussing the past with Rowdy. I was a survivor, too, now that I was no longer floating.

I shifted under the covers and sucked in a breath as my still puckered nipples rubbed against the fabric. The lights were off, the door was shut, and I still had the sluggish thrum of desire in my blood. There was an orgasm hovering on the horizon and I figured there was nothing wrong with chasing it down on my own while Zeb was busy. I would just owe him one later. Like that was any kind of chore.

I let my legs drift open and skimmed my hand over my tummy and into the cleft that was still swollen and damp from where Zeb had been working at it. The first brush of my own fingers made me shudder. It wouldn't take very long at all to get there because my man was extremely good at what he did and I was already primed. I sighed into the darkness as I started to rub slow, agonizing circles around my straining clit. It felt good, but not nearly as good as when Zeb's rough fingers did it.

I shrieked in surprise when the comforter was yanked off of me and blinked up at Zeb where he stood at the end of the bed staring down at me with a lecherous look on his face.

"Don't stop on my account. You know how much I like to watch you get yourself off." He kicked out of his jeans as I stiffened up.

"Hyde?"

"Is out like a light. I didn't even get halfway into the book. He's settling. He just needs some time." A smile flashed in his beard. "If you aren't going to finish for me, then I'm going to do it for you."

I shouted his name as he caught my ankle and pulled me toward the end of the bed across the sinfully expensive sheets. Before I could protest he had my legs spread wide and his face buried between my quivering thighs. His tongue was on my clit and his facial hair was brushing enticingly against my inner thighs. I couldn't breathe.

That orgasm that I had to chase down on my own was back to being right front and center and he worked me over with his mouth and his fingers. I shattered on a deep moan and spilled all across his tongue as he refused to let up on me. He pulled away so he could kiss my belly button and then crawled up and over me so that he could seat himself inside my satiated body.

I wanted to tell him that after that orgasm there was nothing left for me to give him, but like always, I found more because it was him and he was worth everything.

I curled my legs around him and he knelt between my legs and started to work into me with slow shallow thrusts. We watched each other intently as he built the pleasure back up, as he worked the desire like it was a living thing until I was writhing under him again and my body was begging his for release.

He stretched out over me so he could move fast and hard, and before I knew it we were coming together and holding on to each other while we waited for the world to stop spinning.

His face was buried in the side of my neck as I stroked my palms over his painted and toned shoulders.

"Hyde asked me if you would mind if he started calling you his mom."

The words were soft and maybe the most important ones I had ever heard. They were so much more powerful than the ones my father had spewed.

I cleared my throat and hugged his massive frame with my entire body. "What did you tell him?"

He laughed softly in my ear and moved his chin so that his beard tickled my neck.

"I bet him a hundred bucks that when he asked you it would make you cry." I wasn't the only one who knew how to hedge a bet so that the adorable five-year-old would walk away with some cash.

I tunneled my fingers into his hair and held him as close as I could. "You're gonna owe him a hundred bucks."

"I figured as much. Hey, Say?"

"Hey, Zeb?" I rubbed my cheek against his and snuggled farther into him. I wanted to stay under him, connected to him like this forever.

"My kid wants you to be his mom, and if there are any more kids in the future I want them to be with you, so you should probably marry me."

I stiffened under him and took a handful of his hair so I could jerk his head up and force him to look at me.

"Did you just tell me to marry you?"

"Uh . . . yeah. I mean I did just get you off twice in a spectacular fashion, so I figured it would make it harder to say no." His eyes twinkled at me and he leaned forward and put his mouth on mine. "I gave you the house. You've had Hyde's heart and mine since the very beginning. You know we'll make beautiful babies and that you'll be the best mom in the world. Let me give you a ring, Sayer. I'll make sure it's classic and colorful. I'll make sure it's strong and beautiful. I'll find a ring that glows from the inside like you do." He wiggled his dark eyebrows up and down at me. "And when I find it I'll get on a knee and ask you the right way, but say yes, Sayer. You can be all the other wonderful things you already are, but you can add mom and wife to the list."

I blinked up at him and, of course, there was only one answer to choose. "Yes, Zeb, I'll marry you. And I don't need you to get on one knee because this way is perfect for me."

This was the way the man I chose to spend forever with asked me to be his.

Nothing could be better than that.

AUTHOR'S NOTE

I know from past experience that it's risky to write a heroine who isn't all warm and fuzzy, a heroine afraid to love when the hero is RIGHT THERE and so amazing and offering everything, but, my friends, it has to be done! Not just because I so strongly feel *all* types of women deserve a voice in my books, but because there are women out there who need to know they are not alone. There is nothing wrong with not being the warm and fuzzy sort. ☺ Frankly I am not often the warm and fuzzy sort.

Sayer is so important, her past and the woman she forces herself to be is a startling reminder that abuse can take so many more forms than physical and all abuse leaves its mark and its impact on those who suffer from it.

Writing Sayer for me was an immensely personal endeavor because there was a time in my life when I watched someone I cared a lot about change into a different person in a shockingly short amount of time at the hands of a skilled emotional abuser. I had no clue how to stop it or how to help, so I also understand Zeb's frustration with the situation on a deep level. (The person I knew worked very hard to heal, and made great strides, but the change, the struggle, was too much and we are no longer in touch even though she won her battle much like Sayer does in this story.)

I watched this person completely shut down, disappear, and become so remote it was like she was trapped inside herself with no hope of getting out. It killed me to see the suffering, and it hurt even more when the things she was going through were brushed off because no one could *see* the cause of that change.

All forms of abuse are horrific and terrible, but patience, love, and understanding go a long way toward helping a survivor heal.

I'm not an expert or an advocate, but I am someone who cares a lot about people . . . all people. So I'll leave these numbers here, and if you know someone who could use them or if you can use them yourself, please do:

National Child Abuse Hotline: 1-800-422-4453

National Domestic Violence Hotline: 1-800-799-7233

National Sexual Assault Hotline: 1-800-656-HOPE (4673)

If you are looking for a place to start: thehotline.org

SAYER AND ZEB'S PLAYLIST

This playlist is a little bluesy, a little twangy, a little rough, and a whole lot stripped down. Kind of like Sayer and Zeb when they start to fall in love. The entire list is composed of singer/songwriters, artists who take music down to the core of what it is and then build it up into something amazing. It's so very beautiful to me and every single song has a story to tell.

(Minus "Pour Some Sugar on Me" . . . but come on! That song is great regardless of whether it was arena metal or not!)

Shovels & Rope: "Bridge on Fire"/"Pinned"

Dawes: "Waiting for Your Call"

Heartless Bastards: "Could Be So Happy"

Ha Ha Tonka: "The Past Has Arms"/"Lessons"

Whiskeytown: "Excuse Me While I Break My Own Heart Tonight"

The Damn Quails: "Through the Fire"

The Black Lilies: "Cruel"

Turnpike Troubadours: "Diamonds & Gasoline"

The Dirty River Boys: "Looking for the Heart You Took from Me"

The Head and the Heart: "Shake"

Lincoln Durham: "Beautifully Sewn, Violently Torn"

Cory Branan: "All the Rivers in Colorado"

Folk Soul Revival: "Bent"

Chris Knight: "The Hammer Going Down"

Delta Rae: "Scared"/"If I Loved You"

The Lone Bellow: "Green Eyes and a Heart of Gold"/"Cold As It Is"

Jason Isbell: "24 Frames"/"I Follow Rivers"

Amanda Shires: "Hearts Are Breaking"

Def Leppard: "Pour Some Sugar on Me"

ACKNOWLEDGMENTS

I want to extend a special thank-you to Carla Dragon and Jessica Schwartz. They are both members of my private group on Facebook and they won the chance to have their names in *Built*. Carla popped up as Sayer's paralegal and Jessica got to name Auntie Echo . . . whom I liked a lot more than I thought I was going to, so maybe we'll see more of her around. Be quiet, brain, you already have enough stories filling you up! 0_o Anyway, thanks for being part of the Crowd, ladies, and I hope it was fun seeing your names in print.

I adore my readers, and being able to make them a part of my process in even this little way is pretty cool. If you are interested in joining the group, feel free to go to:

https://www.facebook.com/groups/crownoverscrowd/

I do a lot of giveaways and we have a pretty good time. It's really a place where I can connect one-on-one with readers and it is always all about the love. Believe it or not, there are safe places on the Internet. ☺

I usually wax on endlessly in my acknowledgments because I really do have a lot of love to give and a lot of people who push me and force me to be better, but I'm gonna attempt to keep things short and sweet this go-round. I have SO MANY books to write. A good problem to have, am I right?!

All my readers: Thank you for being you. Thank you for being honest and willing to take a risk. Thank you for letting me do my thing even if you wish my thing was something else. You are the best in the land and I really do owe you everything.

To the blogger nation: Thank you for being badass. Thank you for loving books. Thanks for keeping shit real. Thanks for working so hard often with little reward. Thank you for being invested and interested. Thank you for being on the front lines; sometimes it gets bloody and brutal there, but you never give up the fight . . . neither will I.

My professional team. Amanda, Jessie, Elle, Molly (the whole Harper crew) . . . all you kick-ass chicks in NYC who do what you do like no other, thanks. Thanks for putting up with me and believing in what I do . . . even if it never is quite the status quo. Your support and faith is humbling in a business that often feels like it can eat you up and spit you out. At the end of the day I never doubt really amazing things will happen when we put our heads together. Kelly Simmon, thanks for answering the Bat Signal whenever it lights up and being all the kinds of awesome you are. Thanks for being clever and quick and thanks for being my friend. Stacey Donaghy, thanks for being you . . . which is an awful lot like being me! Seriously, thank you for just getting it . . . whatever it may be at the time.

My inner circle, what would I do without you guys? Melissa Shank . . . you are everything and then some more things . . . you always have been amazing and I feel so lucky I get to walk this road with you every single day (yes, I named Zeb's mom after you), Ali, Debbie, Denise, Heather, Megan, Vilma, Jen Mc and Stacey (are you ready for my sweet dance moves?), thanks for simply getting me and getting what I do. Thanks for your honesty and time . . . I know how valuable it is. It may have all started out business but it feels so far removed from that now and I can honestly say you ladies are some of the real, true rewards that have ended up crossing my path along this journey. I love all your faces and want to smother you in so much love. You make me better and there aren't enough words to thank you for that.

Thanks to the people who have crossed my path and make me happy every single day just by being them and by loving books the same way I do: Renee, Christine, Pamela, Stephanie, Damaris, Melissa (Jersey), Matt, Becky, Pam, Courtney, LJ, and Carolyn . . . this is for you. Please just stay awesome and full of all the great things this industry needs.

To all the authors who are so disgustingly talented and so inordinately gracious with their time and gifts, thank you for being my inspirations and my friends. You are all brilliant and who you are as people as well as storytellers is unparalleled. This huge thanks and virtual hug goes out to Jen Armentrout, Jenn Foor, Jenn Cooksey, Jen McLaughlin, Tiffany King, Cora Carmack, Emma Hart, Renee Carlino, Nyrae Dawn, Kristy Bromberg, Aleatha Romig, Tammara Webber, Megan Erickson, Jamie Shaw, Katie McGary, Penelope Douglas, Nicole Chase, Kristen Proby, Amy Jackson, Rebecca Shea, Laurelin Page, Ek Blair, Adrian Leigh, SC Stephens, Molly McAdams, Crystal Perkins, Kimberly Knight, Tijan, Karina Halle, Christina Lauren, Chelsea M. Cameron, Sophie Jordan, Daisy Prescott, Michelle Valentine, Felicia Lynn, Harper Sloan, Monica Murphy, Erin McCarthy, Liliana Hart, Laura Kaye, Heather Self, and Kathleen Tucker. Seriously, I admire every author on this list, and what they add to this business and to my writerly life. If you are looking for a solid book to read, I promise one of theirs won't disappoint.

I can never thank my mom and dad enough for all the things they have done for me or for the enormous amount of support they have shown since this writing gig took off. They are just the best of the best and no kid is luckier than me. Thanks, Mom and Dad, for being all the things . . . ALWAYS.

As always, I love to give my buddy Mike Maley a shout-out because he's an awesome dude and he spends a lot of time taking care of things for me when I'm not around to do it. You're the best, Mike, and I don't know what I would do without you . . . at all!

Last but not least, thanks to my furry little entourage for being my heart. Woof!

If you would like to contact me, there are a bazillion places you can do so!

https://www.facebook.com/jay.crownover
https://www.facebook.com/AuthorJayCrownover?ref=hl
@jaycrownover
www.jaycrownover.com
http://jaycrownover.blogspot.com/
https://www.goodreads.com/Crownover
http://www.donaghyliterary.com/jay-crownover.html
http://www.avonromance.com/author/jay-crownover

Thank you for everything.

Love & Ink
Jay

IT TAKES A BRAVE MAN TO WEATHER
THE STORM WHEN HE'S *CHARGED* WITH
BEING BOTH LOVER AND LAWYER TO
A PINK-HAIRED HURRICANE . . .